LEGION OF SHADOWS

LEGION OF SHADOWS

DAUGHTER OF ERABEL ~ BOOK FOUR

KRISTIN WARD

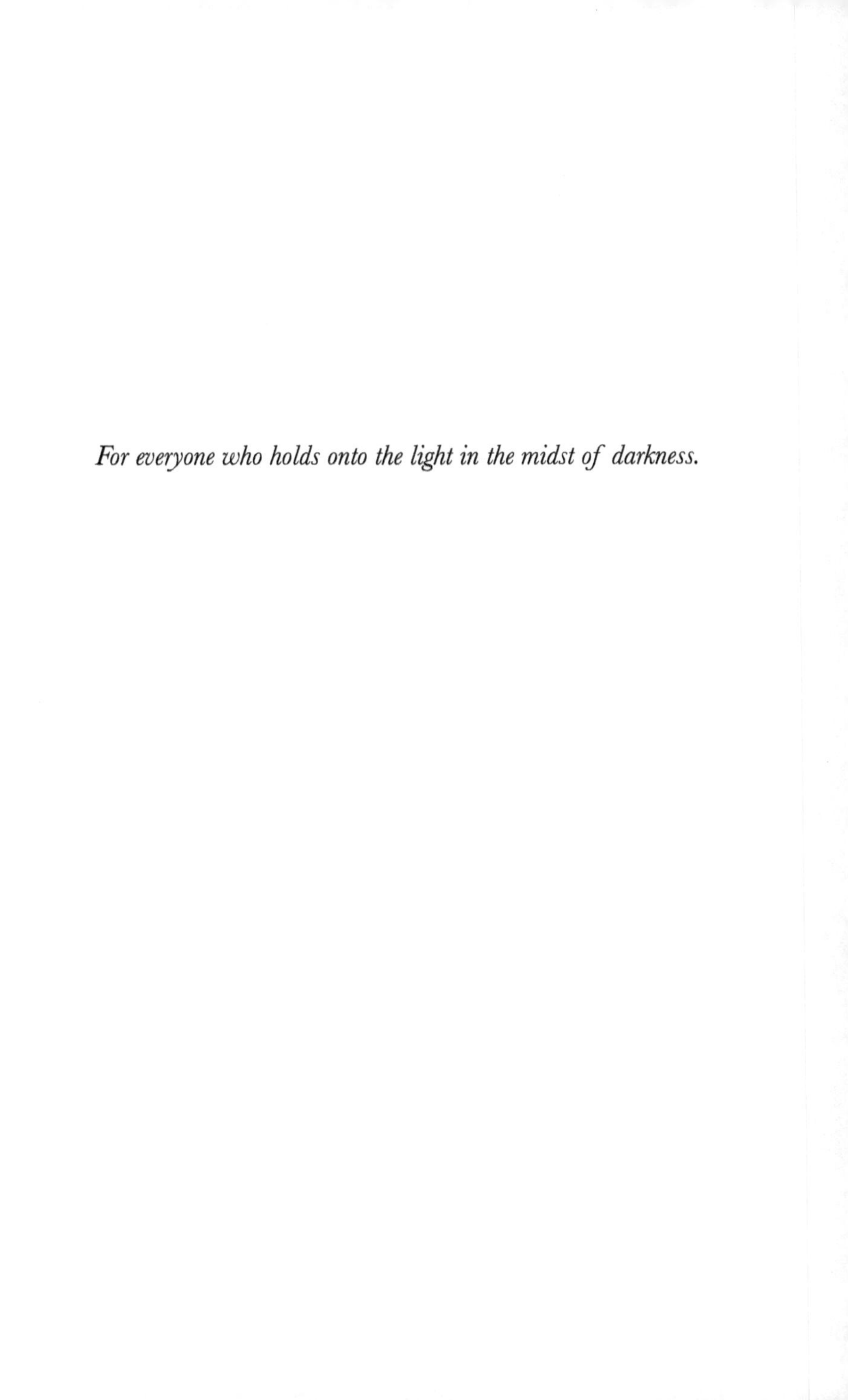

For everyone who holds onto the light in the midst of darkness.

PROLOGUE

Dothur, the sole surviving son of Carmun, slashed at the bars of his iron prison, made weak by the power of Crom Cruach, and watched them snap like brittle twigs. The clawed tip of each wing gouged the sheer stone walls of the pit as he dragged himself to the surface. Emerging from the gloom, he planted his taloned feet on the edge of the black hole and fanned his leathery wings, stretching his ashen body to its full height. With eyes glowing in the moon's light, he arched his neck and roared. The wind snatched his voice and carried it across the land into dark crevices where shadowy creatures bided their time—growing hungry for blood. The age of men, elves, and all things soft and beautiful was over.

The pale demon beckoned them. Rallying his forces.

And they answered, a legion of darkness swarming to its master.

CHAPTER ONE

Fiadh and her entourage crossed into the Felraine Vale on their way to Oadsera. Flanked by Krulan, a dozen Aos Sí, and one man, they arrived at the border of the elven land and stopped, allowing themselves to be seen by the sentries who hid among the thick trees. Sliding off Meera's back, Fiadh stroked her muzzle, smiling when the unicorn nickered softly. The others dismounted, leaping from their bareback mounts with practiced ease. All but Gideon, whose horse bore the trappings of mankind with saddle and reins. Aridius stood at Gideon's side, withers twitching. He held the reins and said something too low for her to hear. The gelding's ears rotated, and he blew with a head bob.

Krulan, leader of the Cù-Sìth that protected Erabel's queen, bumped Fiadh's shoulder, drawing her attention away from Gideon. She walked a few paces toward the border and paused, holding her arms loosely at her sides. The wards protecting Oadsera thrummed with energy, similar to those surrounding Erabel but different enough that she sensed a pale echo of Danu's strength within them as though the Great Mother had retreated, leaving only a piece of herself behind. Fiadh lifted her chin, strengthened by the presence of the Cù-Sìth at her side, her eyes sweeping a landscape layered in mist.

Fear and superstition had kept Oadsera safe for decades. That and the tactical advantage of the vale's steep and rocky climbs where granite and shale jutted from the earth like jagged teeth. A layer of low clouds hung over the landscape, concealing Oadsera. More than one army had tried to breach the elven stronghold, and all had failed.

Despite standing on the edge of a realm ruled by Aos Sí, the air smelled different than her home of Erabel. It was tinged with the scent of the human settlements that surrounded the deep valley. Though each was miles away, the smell carried on the wind: livestock, mills, dense habitation, and the stink of desecrated earth. Dasha, perched on a low-hung branch nearby, sneezed with a throaty croak, his grumbling echoing her thoughts. She resisted the urge to wrinkle her nose, aware of those who watched her every move from the cover of trees.

There are many eyes on you, Krulan's voice whispered in her mind.

Aye. I feel them.

Some will not appreciate a human among us.

She frowned. *I'm not here to pander to their prejudice. I'm here to carve out a better future.*

Krulan rumbled in agreement and rubbed her shoulder, his coarse fur brushing against the sleeve of her gown.

Kaelari had insisted she change into attire that befitted her crown. It was a lovely dress, deep green, with silver threads of embroidery on the bodice in patterns of vines and leaves. But it felt stiff. Or maybe it was her body that felt stiff in it. She smothered the urge to tug at the fabric where it hugged her waist, inhaling deeply to center herself.

Minutes passed, and she shifted her feet, trying to maintain what she hoped was a regal bearing. Then, at an imperceptible cue, branches shifted, slowly revealing Aos Sí. One by one, elves appeared, emerging from the undergrowth while keeping behind the wards that protected the largest remaining elven stronghold and her grandfather's seat of power before his death. Fiadh lifted her chin as Kaelari separated herself from the entourage and announced the arrival of the queen.

Shrewd eyes assessed the group, landing for a few protracted moments on Gideon before settling on Fiadh. She held her head high, meeting every stare. At a motion from the leader of the small fighting force, they let down the wards protecting their realm.

Separating himself from the Oadsera scouts, a tall, lithely muscular elf came forward and dipped his head to Fiadh. "Welcome. I am Ellisar, chief advisor to Saria, ruler of Oadsera." His sharp blue eyes flicked to Gideon and grew cold. The emotion was fleeting, quickly replaced by the etiquette of his station as he returned his attention to Fiadh. "You honor us, my queen."

"Thank you, Ellisar." It felt as though she should say more, but her mind went blank. This was all too new. Too practiced. Courtly life was an enigma. It was a dance whose steps she'd never been taught.

Lowering his chin, the chief advisor motioned for her to walk with him. His scouts formed two lines on either side of the entourage, guiding them to the seat of Oadsera.

Unlike Erabel, the lands surrounding the stronghold felt tamed, as though the trees and undergrowth had been groomed over thousands of years to form natural archways and paths that led to multiple destinations. Ellisar kept up a steady stream of conversation, providing insight into the realm. She listened, both to the words and the underlying emotions tangled within them. Threads of distrust wove themselves into the benign chatter. She'd expected as much.

The deeper they traveled into Oadsera, the more signs of inhabitants she saw. Small homes tucked into copses of trees, thin plots of tilled land. But of the residents them-selves, she saw nothing.

Ellisar, noting the small frown on her face as she saw yet another empty hut, said, "My people await your arrival at the keep."

Fiadh's brows rose, and she nodded, suddenly nervous. "How many live here?"

He cocked his head and thought for a moment. "Nearly four thousand, I should think."

The number was both daunting and tragic. Before the Great War, there must have been ten times as many. To think a paltry few thousand was all that was left of the greatest concentration of Aos Sí made her heart twist. If she couldn't convince her people of the wisdom of unification, those numbers would never swell to what they once were. Hatred and war between men and elves would ensure that.

A hum of many voices carried on the breeze as they drew closer to the keep. Vegetation thinned, allowing for more open spaces and dwellings. Above, Dasha swooped low, surveying the outskirts of the stronghold and passing the images he saw to Fiadh. She swallowed and straightened her shoulders as they rounded a curve. A sea of people greeted her. All eyes swung to the entourage, and a resounding cheer echoed through Oadsera. Relief eased the stiffness in her bearing, and a smile played on her lips. She was terrified and exhilarated.

Aos Sí lined the path on both sides, some standing and others squatting on low branches in the trees bordering their route. Whoops and cheers filled the air as Fiadh smiled and waved. Within minutes, she started to sweat, her face heating with the unaccustomed attention. A flank of elves darted forward to lead Meara and the horses to a meadow where they would be fed, watered and rubbed down. The unicorn snorted, her ears and eyes shifting as though she was looking for someone, then falling flat, her head dropping as she followed an elf dully away from the mass of bodies. Some of Oadsera's residents tossed flower petals onto the path ahead of her, pinks, yellows, and purples covering the hard-packed dirt in a carpet of color.

But it wasn't all celebration. As the group wound their way toward the keep, Fiadh caught black looks aimed at Gideon. It would take time, and they had little to spare.

The seat of Oadsera was a magnificent structure of white stone and spiraling towers. It rose up above the trees, a monolith of strength. Unlike Erabel, it was pristine. Time's relentless hand hadn't dulled the edifice. Vines didn't crawl up the walls nor wrap themselves around the spires. It was a castle to rival any in the human world.

Ellisar took her arm in a gentle grip, propelling her forward as they reached the base of the steps leading up to the keep. Standing in front of the yawning double doors stood Oadsera's ruler. Saria wore a gown of pale blue that fanned out from her waist like a lily. At her sides sat two Cù-Sìth, their yellow eyes fixed on Krulan.

With Ellisar gently guiding her up the steps, Fiadh reached the wide platform at the top of the stairs and stopped, easing her arm from his grasp. Saria gazed at her for a moment, crystalline blue eyes missing nothing as a small smile played at the corners of her mouth.

Hair so dark it was black fell forward as she dipped her head to Fiadh. "All of Oadsera welcomes Erabel's queen." Her voice was rich, and the words laced with power. Stepping forward, Saria took Fiadh's hands. They were not the soft hands Fiadh expected to feel, though she shouldn't have assumed Saria would live the pampered life of a courtier. Instead of softness, they were calloused and strong. This was a ruler who stood at her people's sides, not behind them.

"You have your mother's eyes," Saria said quietly. "She would be proud to see her daughter stand before her people."

The mention of Threa made her eyes prick. Fiadh nodded and whispered a thank you. Saria squeezed her hands and tugged her around to face the throng, coming to stand at the queen's side. A hush fell over the crowd.

With a voice that carried across the expanse of land in front of the keep, Saria said, "Long ago, Threa, daughter of Rygeil, hid her precious children among our enemies. The son was returned to us, but the daughter remained hidden, unknown by all except the greatest seers. Dark days followed. They cast a pall over our realm, and many lost hope. Now, that hope is rekindled. The Daughter of Erabel stands before you. Our queen has come home."

The crowd erupted, cheers mixing with the howls of Cù-Sìth. Saria held Fiadh's hand and lifted it into the air, their fingers intertwined, unifying the two realms. When the cheering subsided, Saria stepped back, leaving Fiadh at the forefront to address the elves.

I don't know what to say, she told Krulan. It was all she could do to still her body and fix a smile on her face when what she wanted to do was slink away.

Tell them the truth.

She gave an imperceptible nod and took a deep breath. "Until recently, I didn't know you existed. I lived a simple life with a human mother." She paused, memories of Riona's gentle hands flooding her mind. Her voice was thick when she added, "I was loved." Fiadh let the words hang in the air for a moment.

"She was all I ever wished to be before I understood my place in this world. I wouldn't trade those years for anything. Threa was the mother of my birth. Riona was the mother of my heart. I'm a woman of two worlds. It is with that perspective that I stand before you today." Faces bearing a mix of emotions stared at her. Her eyes swept the crowd, landing on Gideon, who stood at Kaelari's side. To the residents of Oadsera, he was the embodiment of their downfall. They had every right to hate him. Every individual who watched and listened to her words had been touched by death and loss at the hands of his race. But they could not afford to live in the grief and anger of past wrongs. They must let go of those ghosts. She saw the subtle nod of Gideon's head and fixed her eyes on the crowd.

"We can't remain in the shadows, hidden in sacred places that none but ourselves can enter. Like mankind, we're part of this world. The events of the Great War severed our people from it. My grandfather, Rygeil, sought to take back what was ours, but he did so with vengeance. I know many of you believe his vision was the rightful path. I ask you this: Is killing the path to peace? When our people were slaughtered, did you bend the knee to mankind and accept that you were beaten?" Her eyes swept down as she tried to slow her pace and breathing, fingers curling then loosening. Lifting her chin, she said, "Violence is not the path Danu would have us take. Would you forsake our Great Mother for retribution? My brothers and sisters, I hope you'll join me on the road to a better future. I hope I can prove myself and earn your trust. We will reclaim our place. Not as superior to those who are different. But as equal."

Silence immediately followed, broken by a low din as Oadsera's people considered her words. Saria returned to her side and stood shoulder to shoulder. It was a powerful message.

"You have delivered your vision," she said softly to Fiadh. "Now, you must see it come to fruition."

"If we're to have a future, it must."

Saria nodded slowly. She knew there would be talk among Oadsera's people with many voices of resistance. But she admired the young queen. Fiadh was truly of both worlds.

As a senior advisor of Rygeil's court, Saria had watched the king grow bitter and power-hungry. Shortly after the Great War, he'd dismissed her when she'd fought his desire to dabble in dark arts to increase his power and avenge their people. It pained her to recall how far her king had fallen while she'd been powerless to stop it.

The arrival of Rygeil's granddaughter was like the cyclical rhythm of the world. The ebb and flow of loss and abundance. Things had come full circle, but the nature of the former king's granddaughter was vastly different. It was not an easy road that Fiadh laid before their people. Hatred was a strong emotion that fed on itself and was blind to reason. Both men and Aos Sí felt it, and they had long memories. Forging an alliance would be nigh unto impossible. But she said nothing of those thoughts to the queen. Likely, Fiadh knew the hurdles she would face. It was pointless to drive them home.

Dispersing all but the realm's highest-ranking members, Fiadh and her entourage were ushered into the keep. A full staff lined the walls leading into the great hall, each bowing low as Saria led Fiadh to the throne. Like the one in Erabel, it was made of stone and just as cold, though larger and more ornate. Set on a dais overlooking the enormous space, it had all the formality of what she imagined the throne of Taigon embodied. King Stephan Laoghaire no doubt ruled Crethia from his seat of power. Faith had no designs to sit on the cold stone and doll out orders. But courtly ceremony dictated she climb the steps to the throne and face the crowd filing into the room.

Fiadh sat, body rigid, and looked at the sea of faces watching her every move. Murmurs drifted to silence as Saria entered the great hall and slowly walked between lines of onlookers toward the steps of the dais, holding a velvet pillow where the crown her grandfather had worn during his reign sat. Blood drained from Fiadh's face as it dawned on her that his crown would sit atop her head. How could she wear a symbol tainted with his treachery?

Heart pounding, she gave Krulan, who sat at her right, a sidelong glance. *I can't wear that.*

Aye. You can.

It was his, Krulan. Think about what he did.

Rygeil's actions did not leach into the gold like poison, young one. Be calm. The ceremony is important to your people. A large yellow eye rolled toward her. *Show them the queen you are.*

Saria reached the base of the dais, and Fiadh fixed her eyes on her, clenching her hands in her lap.

Relax, Krulan told her. *It will be over soon, and then you can gorge yourself and forget about the lump of metal on your head.*

Promise?

I can smell cakes fresh from the oven.

You better be telling the truth. He knew she often smuggled sweets from the kitchen in Erabel.

Pay attention, or I'll eat them all.

You hate cake!

I'll make an exception.

Fine. She unclenched her hands and tilted her chin up a few degrees, pasting a serene expression on her face. *Better?*

It'll do.

Oadsera's ruler stood in front of the throne and handed Ellisar the pillow. Taking the crown in two hands, she slowly turned to the crowd and lifted it high above her head. Blood thundered in Fiadh's ears, muffling the sound of Saria's voice as the realm's leader addressed the assemblage. This was really happening. She would be crowned. The sole queen of the Aos Sí.

Turning, Saria smiled at Fiadh and came forward, placing the crown on her head before stepping aside. Cheers echoed through the hall, intermixed with a few hisses of dissent. Krulan growled, a white fang flashing in his muzzle as his sharp eyes found those who protested. She shushed him and stood slowly, the weight of her crown both real and intangible.

Unprepared to speak to a crowd again, especially to a smaller audience with a larger mix of dissenters, Fiadh fumbled through a short speech. Despite her discomfiture, they applauded and broke ranks to mingle as tables and benches were dragged from the walls, followed by food and drink.

Krulan rose and sniffed her crown. *It suits you.*

Thanks. She wanted to yank it off.

I can see your hand itching to remove it, Krulan warned. *Stop fiddling. Let the people see you wear the mantle proudly. I would mark their reactions and know their allegiance.*

If I have to keep this on, then you can't snarl at anyone who balks at seeing me in it.

He huffed loudly. *Very well.*

Saria presented the newly anointed queen and her retinue with a feast and music. Fiadh sat at a high table with Saria, Ellisar, and a few others in official positions. As they ate a sumptuous meal, Fiadh kept tabs on her people, her eyes flitting to Gideon more than she'd like. He was so out of place sitting amongst the elves, though his former life trained him well to deal with the social discomfort. Looking at him, no one would know he was anything but secure in his surroundings. He made it look so easy.

Ellisar noted the direction of Fiadh's gaze. "I was surprised to see you traveling with our enemy."

Fiadh turned to him. "Gideon is not my enemy. Neither is his entire race."

"You didn't see what his race did to our people. If you had, you would think twice about flaunting him before us."

"I know what Rygeil did to humans—what he did to elves who stood against him. Should I judge our entire race by my grandfather's actions?"

He gave her a thoughtful look. "A solid point."

"I have no illusions about the challenges I face. I'm asking you to look beyond your hatred. There's no future for us or them if we continue to fight each other."

Ellisar sat back in his chair and glanced at Saria, who sat on Fiadh's opposite side.

Oadsera's leader said, "Now you understand why I am sending you to Erabel."

"Ellisar is returning with me?" Fiadh asked.

"He and a contingent of warriors will join you. I would send our seer, Dyvre as well, but he is visiting a small settlement near Malver Gorge." A look passed between Saria and Ellisar at the mention of that place, but she quickly added, "I'd send craftsmen, healers, and others with you as well if you'd like. I know your realm has many needs to rebuild."

Fiadh thought about the risks of adding more elves to their entourage. On their passage to Oadsera, they'd had to take circuitous routes to avoid well-traveled roads and populated areas. It would be harder to remain undetected with more people. But she couldn't deny the strain on those who were trying to rebuild Erabel with too few hands aiding their efforts. "I would appreciate that."

"It is settled, then. I will inform those who are chosen in the morning. For now, let us rejoice in your arrival."

Two days later, Saria bid the party farewell, speaking privately to Ellisar before he joined the group. It would do her people good to see so many of their own accompanying Fiadh and her entourage, especially those who'd passed the human warrior unfriendly looks. The chief advisor would be an asset to the queen as she established her court. In time, others would flock to her of their own accord.

From the platform outside the keep, Saria studied Fiadh and marveled at her bearing as the young queen mounted her unicorn. She was born to lead, though Saria sensed the queen's acceptance of that fact was rooted in rocky ground. It would take time. Threa would be proud of her daughter, and Saria was proud to stand with her.

CHAPTER TWO

Fiadh strolled along the border of Erabel, fingers trailing the filmy substance of the barrier that protected her sacred kingdom. She could feel Danu's power flowing through it, the gentle vibrations of the Great Mother passing through her skin to mix with her own unique hum of energy. Beyond the shield was the greater world, one that held much uncertainty, but it was a calmer place. The drums of war had ceased their relentless beating. Since returning from Oadsera, something fresh was in the wind. She liked to think it was hope.

Meara snorted nearby, snuffling through grasses and fruit-bearing bushes. Fiadh smiled at her, watching the unicorn's black coat shifting in the shadows of the trees. But the happy curve of her lips turned into a grimace as Kaelari rounded a bend in the thin trail she'd taken to reach the remote spot.

"There you are! I've been searching for an hour." The elf gave her a critical look, eyes traveling from Fiadh's worn boots laced halfway up her calves to the forest-green tunic and leggings that weren't quite dark enough to hide the dirt that stained them. By contrast, Kaelari looked practically regal. Her dark skin and vibrant blue eyes a perfect balance with the rich, earthy brown fabric embroidered with cerulean threads along the tight-fitting neckline and cuffs.

Krulan passed a look to Fiadh, who fidgeted, hands self-consciously picking at a crust of food on her sleeve from the morning's breakfast.

Fiadh caught his look and folded her arms in a huff. "Don't judge me, Krulan." Dasha, landing at her feet, snapped his wings and clacked his beak at the Cù-Sìth. Krulan lunged at the raven, who squawked and flew onto the branch of a tree, where he plucked a nut and lobbed it.

You deserved that, Fiadh told the Cù-Sìth when it struck his head with a satisfying thump.

Fiadh picked up the Cù-Sìth's thoughts as he groused. *The bird is lucky I don't like picking feathers out of my teeth.* Glaring at the raven, Krulan harrumphed and shook his body, debris floating in the air around him.

"Fiadh," Kaelari said, sighing, "You can't keep running off and avoiding your duties."

She raised a brow. "I was under the assumption that a ruler could do as they please."

Rolling her eyes, Kaelari shook her head and put her hands on her hips. "I have no idea where you came up with that notion. As queen, your actions are scrutinized, and right now, those actions say you have little interest in seeing to the well-being of your people."

Fiadh made a face and muttered.

"You must come with me now. Another envoy arrived, and it's your responsibility to greet them and reestablish our alliance."

She sighed and picked up a fallen twig, swatting it against a large rock jutting from the ground. "You're asking me to play the part of a queen, but I don't know how to rule!" She tossed the broken fragment to the ground and looked at Kaelari. "And, even if I did, who's to say I'd want to?"

"Fiadh, some things in life do not happen by choice. This is one of them."

Krulan let out a low rumble.

"Easy for you to say!" Fiadh snapped, glaring at the Cù-Sìth.

"I assume Krulan agrees with me."

Fiadh sniffed and lifted her chin. "You both share a similar opinion, but that doesn't mean I need to agree with it."

"Agree or not, the fact remains that you must accompany me now."

"Fine, but don't be surprised if I do something wrong and embarrass everyone." Trudging behind Kaelari's swiftly retreating form, she added, "You know, I'm too young to be in charge of *anything*, let alone an entire kingdom. I don't know what you all expect of me."

"I expect you to watch and learn," Kaelari tossed back to her as she led the way. "You are the heiress of Erabel. Whether you will it or not, this realm is yours. You would do well to pour your energies into becoming who you were destined to be rather than fighting it like a child."

Fiadh stuck out her tongue.

"And don't think I don't know what you're doing behind my back."

"Sorry," she mumbled.

Krulan bumped her shoulder. *You cannot fight who you are.*

I don't know who I am. You all want me to step into the role of queen like I've been preparing for it my whole life, but I haven't. I can't.

You can because you must.

Fiadh eyed him critically. *You're being entirely too optimistic. What's really bothering you?*

Her step faltered, and she sucked in a breath, considering his question. *That I'll do something wrong, something like before. I… I let the darkness in, Krulan. What if that happens again?*

Did you think you were infallible? Even the best of us fall now and then. What matters is we get up and start again.

Why do you have to be so positive? I'd prefer it if you'd let me wallow in self-pity, she grumbled, eyeing Krulan and wondering if his cheery outlook had anything to do with the dusky Cù-Sìth, Nym, who'd become part of his pack following the battle with Rygeil, her grandfather and the corrupt former ruler of Oadsera, the largest remaining elven stronghold.

He gave a wolfy chuckle. *You prefer me to be surly?*

She shoved him, laughing when her efforts resulted in little more than a twitch of his muscles. *I know you're right. I'm just scared.*

Aye, but you are not alone.

She nodded and squared her shoulders as they neared the keep. *Will you be at my side?*

Always.

There were over two dozen elves milling around the great hall when Fiadh walked in. She nodded at Ellisar, who'd nudged his way into a lead advisory position since arriving with Fiadh from Oadsera. She took her place on the ornate throne, watching Ellisar position himself to her left. It was made of stone and, while beautiful with its complex etchings, was cold and hard. Dasha didn't seem to mind the hard surface as he perched behind her. She wiggled in an attempt to get comfortable and looked toward Arel, one of Kaelari's most gifted fighters. At her nod, he stepped into an adjoining hallway and returned a moment later, leading a female envoy of the man-wolves, the Faoladh, into the room.

The Faoladh had smoky fur covering her body and slunk toward Fiadh, her posture a perpetual crouch. It was a bit off-putting, but Fiadh masked her emotions.

Arel, taking his duty much too seriously for Fiadh's taste, came to the foot of the dais and announced, "Sibaen, envoy of the Faoladh of Mactíre."

"Welcome to Erabel, Sibaen of Mactíre," Fiadh said, feeling foolish uttering such formalities.

The Faoladh's yellow-ringed eyes darted from Fiadh to those surrounding her, not in fear but rather as an innate predatory habit. She nodded at Krulan, who sat to the right of the queen. When her eyes landed on Fiadh, Sibaen said, "I send you greetings from King Ulfran. The Faoladh celebrate the return of the queen of Erabel and pledge our alliance."

"Thank you. I'm grateful to count on you as allies." She glanced at Kaelari, who simply raised her brow. Feeling like she ought to say something else, Fiadh blurted, "Your people are exceptional fighters."

Sibaen acknowledged her words with a short nod.

"May I ask how you knew we were under attack?" Fiadh asked, referring to their aid when King Stephen's army invaded Dorcha Wood immediately following Rygeil's attack. In the aftermath of the battle, the Faoladh had disappeared as quickly as they'd come. They couldn't abide the confines of the keep and its grounds.

She flashed a smile, revealing the sharp points of her teeth. "We smelled it on the wind."

Fiadh's eyes widened briefly. "Oh. That… that's a beneficial gift."

"Aye." She studied Fiadh, cocking her head in a distinctly canine way, ears pricked and rotating forward. "Our elders warned us of impending war in these lands, and we remained watchful for many years. When the scent of battle carried on the wind, we were ready and will be again."

Fiadh shifted uncomfortably at the suggestion of more fighting. "I hope our battles are over."

Sibaen shrugged.

"You're welcome to remain in Erabel for as long as you'd like," Fiadh offered, wishing to end the awkward conversation.

"I cannot stay, but I will return after I deliver news of our renewed alliance to my king."

"You will?"

"King Ulfran has given me to you as a symbol of our alliance."

"What?" Fiadh darted a glance at Kaelari, who averted her eyes.

"It is common among my people to offer a tribute for a term of service. Over the years, many who've dwelled within my realm were given by their rulers as alliances were made. I am honored."

"Um… that's very kind. I'm happy to have you with us, but—"

Kaelari quietly cleared her throat.

Fiadh fidgeted for a moment. "I'm sure we'll benefit from your skill." She looked at Kaelari, who gave a subtle nod. "I'm sorry to say I have no one to offer in return."

"You are young, and your kingdom far from its former glory. In the future, perhaps you will send one of your own." With that, she bowed and left the hall, slinking through the milling throngs of Aos Sí.

Fiadh sagged against the back of the hard, cold throne. "I sounded like a fool," she mumbled.

Kaelari chuckled. "Aye."

"Thanks." Fiadh gave her a look.

"But you'll learn."

Looking at her through slitted eyes, she said, "You could've warned me they'd offer up one of their own!"

"I had forgotten that tradition."

Fiadh made a face. "That's convenient."

Shaking her head, Kaelari announced, "It is time to train."

Folding her arms across her chest, Fiadh pursed her lips. "I don't feel like training with you right now."

"Would you rather work on queenly etiquette?"

Grimacing, Fiadh rose. "You're brutal. Remind me again why I have to work with weapons when I have no intention of wielding them."

Looking vexed, Kaelari put her hands on her hips and said, "As I've told you before, the focus and skill of mastering a weapon is much the same as what you use when practicing spellcraft. You are strengthening your mind and body. And, who knows, maybe one day your training will save your life."

"Fine. But we're working with bow and arrow."

Kaelari bowed with a smirk, and Fiadh reached over to swat her but missed, losing her footing at the edge of the dais. Gideon's laughter erupted as she staggered and righted herself. Finding him leaning against the wall, she huffed and stormed from the hall, leaving him behind and waving off Ellisar, who stopped her to have a word. She pilfered a tart from the kitchen, devouring it with angry chewing before heading to the armory for her bow and quiver.

Stepping into the expanse of the training arena made her heart catch, and she stepped closer to Krulan as he kept pace with her, the brush of his fur against her arm easing the ache in her chest. This was where Veren had molded her into a fighter who could stand on her ground when faced with an enemy. He had helped her find herself. It hurt to know she would never feel his strong embrace, never again to hear him whisper words of love in her ear. Their love was like a shooting star streaking across the velvety blackness of the night sky, illuminating the darkness in a brilliant flash before fading from sight as though it had never been. But it had been. Despite her efforts to protect herself and keep him out, he'd carved a place in her heart, and that piece of her would always be his.

Krulan bumped her shoulder, nudging her gently into the field. Gripping the bow, she looked up and yelled to Kaelari, who was just entering the field. "How about moving targets?"

The elf dipped her head and grabbed a basket of woven discs. At Fiadh's nod, Kaelari began tossing them into the air. By the time the basket was empty, she'd struck a third of them and stood proudly as Krulan complimented her skill.

Your aim has improved, he said from his vantage point a few paces away.

Thank you. She fingered the ornate knotwork that covered the shaft of the bow, thinking of its larger twin that had been Veren's. His weapon had been secreted away in her room after he'd died. She didn't have the heart to put it in the hands of another.

Do you think she's right?

Who?

Sibaen. She said her people will be ready as though she expects more bloodshed.

I have not the sight to know such things, but her kind have always come during times of war. It is as though war is in their blood.

Fiadh nodded and looked at Kaelari who was picking up the last of the discs. *Will it ever end?*

He grumbled but said nothing.

I'm tired of fighting, Krulan.

I know.

Gideon walked onto the field, bow in hand. After

speaking briefly with Kaelari, he made his way to her. "Would you like to work on improving your aim?"

She nodded and followed his movements as he came up behind her. His breath tickled her neck when he reached around and said, "When Kaelari releases the first disc, aim but do not release the arrow. Follow it as though you are going to fire." Reaching around, he wrapped his fingers around hers and lifted the bow, giving a quick nod to Kaelari. "Watch it move through the air and track its movement like this." The point of the arrow followed the disc through the air and as it fell to the ground. His chest pressed against her back, and her palms grew sweaty. "You are teaching your body patience. Instead of focusing on hitting the target, focus on tracking the target, following its movement. Again."

Fiadh squinted her eyes and grit her teeth, feeling the movement of his muscles, the soft huff of his breath in her ear as they worked in unison.

After the fourth disc had fallen to the ground, he stepped back, trailing the tips of his fingers along hers as he gave the weapon over. "Now, you try."

She bit her lip and jerked her head at Kaelari. The elf tossed another disc into the air, and Fiadh sighted, keeping the tip of the arrow on the center of the target. When it landed on the grass, she craned her neck to look at Gideon. "Like that?"

"Relax your shoulders," he told her, pressing down on them. "Imagine you're watching Dasha soar through the air. There is no tension as you watch his flight."

Taking a deep breath, Fiadh began again, tracking disc

after disc. In time, she felt a subtle shift in her body, an ease with the task of aiming and tracking.

"Very good!" Gideon announced after the last of the discs fell to the earth, and Kaelari trotted over to pick them up. "Do you feel a difference?"

She fingered the bow. "I suppose."

He snorted and shook his head, stretching his back with a twist of his body.

"How did you learn?"

He gave a pained smile. "My father taught my brother and I himself rather than placing us under the tutelage of one of his men. Doran and I spent countless hours practicing the same skills over and over until our father grunted his approval." He chuckled and shook his head. "There were many times I wanted to walk off the field and never return. But what he taught me saved my life many times over." Gideon's voice pitched low as he added, "It means a great deal to share what I know with you."

"Thank you." She looked away, feeling at odds with herself, and watched Kaelari pick up the last of the targets and drop them into the basket before striding off the field. Others lingered in pockets, chatting with each other, while some trained with swords or worked with the elements. So much had changed in only a few months. She dipped her head and played with the fletching on an arrow, feeling Gideon watch her. Her feelings for him remained a tangled mess. It was Veren's arms she craved, his words she longed to hear. But he was gone, and in his place stood a man who'd come into her life like a battering ram. She felt like glass around him, afraid he'd be the rock that shattered her.

"Fiadh," he whispered. "Can we start again? As friends?"

Her heart twisted, and her throat closed as a lump crawled up it. Part of her wanted to turn to him, let his arms wrap around her as she knew they would. But she couldn't do that. She wouldn't. It felt like a betrayal to seek comfort in another when Veren had been gone for only a few weeks. And yet, wasn't it wrong to wall herself off from him? To deny the offer of friendship?

Looking into his face, she saw shadows and knew they mirrored her own. Grief. Regret. Longing. They'd shared tender moments once, and she'd be a liar if she denied reliving them from time to time. But so much had gone terribly wrong. And now? She was at a crossroads. Her path, the one she wanted to walk for her people, called to her, begging her to accept his offer and begin again. "Aye," she said, her voice little more than a breath.

Gideon dipped his head. "Will you walk with me?"

Propping her bow on a short wall surrounding the perimeter of the field, she fell into step with him, darting glances at his profile, trying to gauge his thoughts and motives. He seemed at peace. As though he wanted nothing more than her company. When minutes passed with no words, she relaxed and let the warmth of the sun fill the cold places in her body.

CHAPTER THREE

asha stood on Fiadh's chest a few mornings later, his head cocked to the side, one violet eye staring down at her. She jerked awake and made a strangled noise, pressing her head into her pallet and going cross-eyed as he inched closer.

"What are you doing?"

He clacked his beak and peered at her with his other eye. She craned her neck to look around him and glanced out the window, noting the lateness of the hour. Sleep had been fitful again, and her body felt heavy. Dreams of Rygeil and Calum boring into her mind or Veren taking his last breath haunted her, and she woke every night gasping and clutching her chest. Yawning, Fiadh nudged the raven away from her face and gave a wobbly smile when he grumbled and stepped back.

"I know you're worried about me," she told him, stroking her hand down his back to the tips of his tail feathers.

The raven gurgled and bobbed his head.

"I miss him," she whispered.

Dasha crept toward her and lowered his head, pressing it against her chin with a series of tiny croaks.

"I love you, too."

His feathers puffed and flattened.

A knock sounded on the door. "Fiadh? Are you well?" Gideon asked.

She grimaced. He'd take one look at her and know something was wrong. "I'll join you in a moment," she called out.

The raven flew to the floor and eyed her as she rolled to her side and got up. From beyond the door, she heard Gideon move about, but there was no sound of retreating feet. Dressing quickly in a dark green gown embroidered with gold thread in patterns of ravens flying—a gift from Oadsera—she watched as Dasha paced and pecked the floor impatiently. Smoothing a hand down her dress, she shook off the vestiges of sleep and bad dreams.

Schooling her features, Fiadh opened the door and found Gideon resting against the wall with his arms folded against his dark tunic, sword hanging from the belt resting low on his hips. He frowned as he looked at her face. "You look tired," he said.

Her shoulders slumped. "You know, that's just a polite way to say I look terrible."

He smirked. "You said it, not me."

Fiadh scowled and stalked past him, picking up her pace when he fell into step with her. It was a pointless effort as his legs were longer than hers and easily ate up the distance. "You're annoyingly clingy," she grumbled.

"As a courtier, I must attend my queen."

"This queen would prefer you attend somewhere else."

"Ah, but what fun would that be?" He deliberately brushed his arm against hers, and she nudged him off balance. "That's not queenly behavior," he scolded.

She slowed her pace and arched a brow at him. "I could order you bound and gagged for pestering me like a mother hen. But I am a forgiving queen."

He dipped his head and put his hand on his heart. "Your loyal servant acknowledges your magnanimous nature."

Fiadh snorted and shook her head.

"It worked, didn't it?"

Looking up at him as they continued, she asked, "What's working?"

"Annoying you." A look of confusion crossed her face. He motioned in her general direction. "You don't look nearly as awful as you did when you left your chamber."

She sputtered. "You really know how to woo the ladies, don't you?"

He chuckled and tucked her hand in his elbow, not letting go as he hauled her toward the great hall. Before they entered, he pulled away and bowed his head, earning him a roll of her eyes. Straightening her shoulders, Fiadh entered the space and made her way to a large table where remnants from the morning meal sat beneath a white cloth. Lifting an edge, she spied a roll and crock of jam. Grabbing a helping of each, she sat with a dozen elves who lingered in the hall, discussing simple things like home and family. They dipped their heads to her, and she smiled, asking them to continue as she listened. Many of those present had come from Oadsera, and she knew they were but the first who would join and pledge themselves to her.

Gideon plopped down next to her, and she was surprised to see the others include him in their conversation. Who would've thought men and elves could sit at a table as friends? It gave her hope. Riani and Faraen, who'd pledged themselves to Fiadh following Rygeil's attack, chatted amicably with Gideon. He'd been training with them almost daily and she wondered if there would come a time when the lines that separated these vastly different people blurred, becoming nothing more than remnants of an awful past.

Brushing the crumbs off her hands when she'd finished her food, she bid everyone a good day and left the hall, Krulan joining her when she stepped outside. The two walked through the trees, stopping when Gideon jogged after them and announced, "I'm visiting Quinn today. Did you want to join me?"

She'd grown quite fond of the young soldier as she'd accompanied Gideon on furtive visits, but it was a risk to speak to him, and she worried for his safety should Lord Darragh find out. Broaching the idea of inviting Quinn and others to join her people in Erabel hadn't gone over well when she'd spoken to Kaelari. In fact, the elf had been appalled at the suggestion and had stalked off muttering.

Fiadh glanced at Krulan. *It's dangerous,* he grumbled.

Aye.

But you're going despite that.

She smirked. *Am I that predictable?*

Apparently. He huffed and disappeared into the woods.

"I take his leaving to mean you'll join me?" Gideon asked, looking toward the swaying branches of the bush Krulan had passed.

"It's a perfect excuse to avoid my duties."

He guffawed and shook his head. "You know, Kaelari is likely to expel me from Erabel if she thinks I'm a bad influence."

"Thinks you are?" Fiadh said, raising her brow. "She *knows* you are. I lay the blame solely at your feet."

"Then I suppose we should make the best of our time together before I'm forced to leave."

"I suppose we should," she said.

He watched her sail past him, green eyes flashing and black hair swinging, and marveled at how much she'd changed. An easiness had grown between them, one that reminded him of happier days when he and his brother, Doran, had jested with each other. It made him feel younger, as though the years of battle fell away from his shoulders like an old skin. At times, he wondered if it was Fiadh who did that. If the magic flowing through her veins spoke to him in some way, calming his warrior's heart.

"Aren't you coming?" she asked, hands on her hips. Dasha swooped by, cawing at him, and flew to his mistress, landing on her shoulder with a snap of his wings.

Smiling, he trotted to her side, and they made their way to a hidden waterfall among the craggy hills of Dorcha

Wood. It was a spot Fiadh had shown him shortly after the battle when he'd told her that he wanted to meet with Quinn far from prying eyes. They trudged up the steep path to the remote spot, animals of every kind showing themselves to her ready hands. A wildcat sidled up to him, sniffing at his clothes and eyeing him in the way beasts are wont to do. He watched it warily, frowning when Fiadh turned to look at him and giggled at his anxious expression. Flashing its teeth, the cat bounded away from him to curl around Fiadh's legs as she stroked its tawny pelt and crooned at him.

"He mocks me," Gideon grumbled as the animal looked at him and chuffed.

"Aye, he does." The wildcat purred, winding its body around Fiadh once more, eyes flicking to Gideon.

"His pelt would make a nice rug." As though it understood, the cat hissed, ears laid back.

"I'm not listening to you," Fiadh sang out, patting the animal on the rump and picking up her pace.

He chuckled and caught up with her, pleased when the wildcat grew tired of the trek and melted into the forest. The trees thinned as they climbed to the summit. Fiadh stopped and took deep breaths, easing the stitch on her side. Panting, Gideon joined her, and they stood shoulder-to-shoulder, looking out over Dorcha Wood. Old body aches pulled his mouth down and he rubbed his thigh, easing the throbbing muscles that never healed right. Along the east and north lay patches of burned trees like wounds marring the lushness. He felt pangs of regret when his eyes fell on them, remembering his part in that destruction. Surprisingly, Fiadh let go of her grudges, her initial looks of accusation since he'd joined her in Erabel fading over time. It was as though, upon entering her sacred realm, his past deeds were forgiven. Not forgotten. But forgiven nonetheless.

"Someday, I want to bring Aishling here."

Fiadh smiled. Gideon often spoke of his foundling. She wondered what the child would think of her realm and the people in it. Would she be frightened? Would she blame them for the death of her family? No matter how the girl felt, Aishling would be welcome. "I would like that," Fiadh said softly.

On the horizon, a hawk soared, its wings outstretched in the wind that carried it. It banked to the south, and Gideon tracked its movements, grimacing when Felmore came into view. The castle and grounds looked like a squat toad in the distance. He knew that within those walls, Lord Darragh plotted, his eyes fixed on Erabel. On retribution. Turning away from the ugly edifice, he nudged Fiadh. "Let's go. Quinn may be awaiting us."

She nodded and followed him around a jut of granite into a dark crevice. Scrabbling along the rough surface, they made their way through the rock, pausing in the sunlight when it opened up to a small waterfall that cascaded down moss-covered rocks and into a crystal blue pool of water. A young soldier sat on the banks of the water, hand swirling in the currents, unaware that they watched him. The red hair on his head and chin was in need of a trim, though his disheveled appearance perfectly matched his youthful character. Resting at his side with his leather chest armor was the sword Gideon had commissioned from the blacksmith.

The isolated location was needlessly far from Felmore, but Fiadh had shared it with Gideon, knowing that the fresh water and seclusion could hide and sustain the soldier should he be hunted by Darragh's men. It eased her mind to know Quinn had a refuge should he need it.

"Contemplating a swim?" Gideon asked sardonically.

Quinn bounded to his feet and spun around, face growing red at having been caught unaware. "Apologies, my lord. I didn't hear you."

Gideon shushed him and strode toward the young soldier, clasping his wrist with a hearty greeting. "It is good to see you."

The soldier, shy around Fiadh, stammered a hello. It amused Gideon to see his young charge so enamored, though he couldn't blame him. There was an ethereal beauty and sweetness to Fiadh. She was like the sun, drawing people toward her.

Finding a comfortable spot, they engaged in small talk for a few minutes before Gideon asked, "What news?"

"Lord Darragh sent runners to the king requesting more soldiers."

"Is he planning another attack?"

"He claims they are for defense in case..." Quinn glanced at Fiadh, face reddening when she smiled sadly at him. "Your men will not fight for him should he attempt another assault."

"Oh?" Gideon said, pleased.

"They are loyal to you and no other. Though Donal has

taken charge of us, and we pretend loyalty, we have one true commander. They await your call and will come when you need them. As will I."

"Thank you, Quinn. I am pleased to hear it."

"There's more," the young man said. "There's been talk of a witch."

Fiadh's eyes grew round.

"Not of you, my lady!" Quinn said. "An evil witch. Someone close to Lord Darragh. Some say she left the castle, others that she lives there still. After what happened in Dorcha Wood, there are many who wonder if it was she who summoned the beasts that chased Darragh's men from the forest."

"Hm. I too heard of this witch. I may have glimpsed her once."

"She is real?"

Gideon shrugged. "I don't know. It could've been an old hag I saw. Nothing more."

"They say Darragh was in a rage after the battle and rumor spread that it was brought on by the witch leaving his service."

"If the Lord of Felmore had dealings with an evil being such as that, he deserves whatever suffering her leaving wrought," Gideon said darkly.

"Aye. It may please you to know that many of the men who came when he raised his banners left to protect their own lands." He darted a look at Fiadh. "They fear an attack by the Aos Sí."

She frowned but said nothing.

"Their fear is groundless," Gideon said firmly, "but I

would rather they believe the elves will come for them. It keeps them from targeting Erabel."

"I count these as good tidings," Fiadh said. "If Lord Darragh is weakened, perhaps others will not fight for him."

Quinn looked toward Fiadh but couldn't meet her eyes, managing only darting glances. "I hope so, my lady."

"I've told you to call me Fiadh. My lady sounds so stuffy." She reached over and pat the soldier's hand, noting a flush of red creep up his neck. "You do me a great service coming here and sharing news. You risk much." Fiadh said the last with a whisper.

"I would do more should Lord Gideon command. It is an honor to serve you both."

"And I thank you for it, but I don't want you or others taking chances that could lead to discovery. Darragh is a ruthless man. If he found out…" she trailed off, shaking her head.

"I'm sure Quinn is cautious." Gideon gave the soldier a stern look and was rewarded with a quick nod.

"I'd feel better if he had a way of contacting us should things go badly," Fiadh said.

Gideon turned to her. "What did you have in mind?"

She let out a shrill whistle, and a hawk swooped down from a towering tree, landing at her feet and ignoring Dasha's grumbling croaks. Leaning over, she crooned at the bird, sweeping a finger down his breast. The hawk gave a catlike mew, beak parting as it stared at the elf. Fiadh reached out her arm, grimacing as its taloned feet tore tiny holes in the sleeve of her gown. Kaelari would give her another lecture on decorum if she saw it. Standing as the bird balanced, tail feathers dipping and raising with every movement, she took a few steps toward Quinn.

"This is Crea. If you find yourself in danger, call to her and we will find you. Hold out your arm so she can know your face."

Quinn looked uneasy but did her bidding, arm shaking as Crea's sharp talons gripped it. The hawk opened and closed her beak, cocking her head this way and that. Stretching her wings to reveal black edging along her flight feathers in contrast with her brown plumage, she flapped, making the soldier flinch though he held his limb steady.

"Whistle," Fiadh instructed. "The way I did."

Making his lips into a small oval, Quinn tried, frustration creasing his brow when all that came out was a gush of air. Licking his lips, he tried again, letting out a stuttering whistle. Gideon chuckled, earning a kick to his shin as Fiadh glowered at him. The soldier took a deep breath, eyes caught in Crea's sharp stare, and managed a high note that hung in the air for a moment. Relieved, he beamed at Fiadh.

"Well done." She took the hawk from Quinn and spoke softly to it. Unaware of how the men watched the exchange —the way the bird's feathers puffed with each whisper, eliciting involuntary smiles as though her words were meant for them. With a final stroke, she raised her arm and sent Crea into the sky. Dasha looked on, hissing, and swept onto her shoulder as soon as the raptor was out of sight.

"All I did was rub his feathers!' Fiadh said out loud as the raven clicked his beak irritably at her. The men chuckled as Dasha opened and closed his beak, feathers ruffled.

Fiadh sighed and crooned at him, holding out her hand in invitation and smiling when the bird bumped her fingers. When the raven was appeased, she looked at Quinn and said, "Crea knows your whistle now. Should you need me, you need only send out the call."

CHAPTER FOUR

Gideon strode onto the field, nodding at Arel, who lounged on the stone wall watching Kaelari and Fiadh train. "How about some friendly competition?" Gideon called out.

Krulan huffed and stretched out on the ground with a loud groan.

Fiadh waited for Gideon and fidgeted with her bow. "I've only had a few days to practice what you taught me."

"Then this will be a test of my teaching."

She smiled and shook her head. "You could be the greatest teacher in existence, and I'd still fail miserably."

"True enough, though I'd wager in a few weeks, with more lessons," he added with a wink, "you will be my equal."

Rolling her eyes, she drawled, "When pigs fly."

"Do they?" he asked wide-eyed. "You never know in this place."

"Ha ha." She shook her head and shoved him.

"How about for every disc you strike, I must hit it before it touches the ground?"

"That doesn't sound fair to you."

He chuckled. "Then it'll be easier for you to win."

With a nod, she nocked an arrow and gave Kaelari a signal.

Fiadh missed the first five discs.

"Your shoulders are too tight," he said and walked behind her, pressing his fingers into her rigid muscles. "I can feel the tension. Remember what I told you. Relax. Aim. Breathe."

She filled her lungs and nodded at Kaelari. A disc flew into the air as she raised her bow and sighted along the arrow, following it. Keeping her body still, she released and resisted the urge to jerk her head to see if she hit the target. Instead, she breathed deeply and listened to Gideon as he let fly. She saw his arrow strike the center of the target, lodging itself in the woven disc next to hers and pinning it to the ground.

Grinning, she turned to him. "How was that?"

"Perfect."

His words held more than praise as he gazed at her, and she maintained the moment of contact, not looking away until Kaelari's voice interrupted them. "You've got six more to go, and I'm getting hungry."

They took up their stances and continued. Fiadh struck two more, then missed another. Grumbling, she readied her arrow and mashed her lips as Kaelari tossed another target. It sailed through the air, and Fiadh followed it, pausing when something above the tree line caught her eye.

Lowering her bow and releasing the tension on the sinew, she asked, "What's that?"

Gideon squinted, and Kaelari shifted to get a better look. The shape grew larger and more defined. It was a snowy owl. The bird descended towards her, and Dasha let out a garbled caw as he tracked its flight. On silent wings, the owl angled its body, extending its talons to her outstretched arm and landing gently on the thick padding of her tunic. The owl pinned her with violet eyes and gave a pitiful hoot.

She glanced at Dasha sideways, then stroked the owl's breast and whispered nonsensical words. Gideon hovered next to her as Kaelari and others surrounded them.

"I've seen this bird before," Arel said. All eyes turned to him. "She belongs to Zaeleria."

Fiadh ran her hand down the bird's back and looked into its eyes. The most powerful seer of her people must have had an important message to send the owl far from her side. A barrage of memories flooded her mind. She saw her image reflected on the surface of the water. Gideon was there. And Veren. The scene abruptly shifted, and she saw the water stir, revealing pale eyes in a monstrous face.

From the owl's memory, she heard the creature speak. "You should not have looked this way, Zaeleria."

Pain erupted in Fiadh's mind. Her knees buckled, and Gideon lunged for her, catching her before she fell as the owl launched into the air.

"What is this?" he shouted, glaring at the owl.

Kaelari pressed her fingers to Fiadh's temple and closed her eyes, chanting softly.

Fiadh's lashes fluttered open. Gideon cradled her and brushed the hair out of her face. "Fiadh?"

She twisted in his arms, and he set her down, hand hovering behind her back. Looking at the concerned faces surrounding her, she swallowed hard and cleared her throat. "Zaeleria saw something, and it… it attacked her."

Kaelari cupped her face in her hands. "What did she see?"

"Dothur."

Gasps erupted, followed by rapid conversations among those gathered. Fiadh straightened, eyes flitting from one face to another. Walking toward the tree where the owl perched, she held out her arm again, soothing the creature when it came to her. She spoke softly to the bird, sensing Gideon standing so close she could feel the heat of his body.

"Is it injured?"

Fiadh shook her head.

Gideon studied the owl and reached toward it, hand pausing when the bird clacked its beak.

"It's all right. She won't bite you."

He tenderly ran his fingers down the bird's chest. The owl turned her head, eyes blinking slowly. "I can feel her emotions."

Fiadh's lips parted. "You can?"

"Aye. She grieves."

Loud voices drew Fiadh's attention, and she turned to see the elves leaving the field, hands gesticulating wildly, punctuated by sharp words of warning. Keeping her arm steady for the owl, she followed them, Gideon at her side.

No one could say whether or not Zaeleria lived, though Ellisar sent a raven to Oadsera requesting their seer come to Erabel. Fiadh paced the hall, head swimming with the knowledge the owl had passed to her. The feeling was amplified by the voices that peppered the air in a confusing collection of sounds as fear spread through those gathered. Covering her ears to block the noise, Fiadh fled the hall and went to the courtyard. It had grown dark, the long hours of the afternoon having bled into the evening while everyone debated what the message from Zaeleria's owl meant.

Meara joined her, nuzzling her hair with horsey lips. Fiadh patted her distractedly and walked through the space, seeing nothing. Krulan stood on the perimeter, his intense stare following her every movement, the look mirrored by Dasha, who hopped onto a bench cocking his head to keep one eye pinned on her form. Arel lingered nearby, always watching, the weight of his scrutiny heavy when compounded by the others. There was always someone watching. For a moment, she longed for her former life when she could run through Dorcha Wood. But those carefree days were gone, replaced with a heavy crown.

It didn't take long for Gideon to find her. "Who's Dothur?" he asked when he'd reached her side.

Fiadh stopped and looked at him. "He's something evil and powerful. Something I thought was killed long ago."

Gideon said nothing. Just let her talk as she shared the little she knew of the creature.

"Even Kaelari thought he'd been killed," she said, her

face stricken. "How could she not have known? What am I supposed to do now?"

He looked down, absently digging the toe of his boot in the dirt. "I wish I knew. If I had any army at my disposal, I'd hunt him down, but hearing how powerful he is, I'd be sending my men to death." Gideon paused and watched her for a few moments. "What do you think Zaeleria's message means for your people?"

"If Dothur's alive and... free..." She made a strangled sound. "I don't know. Nothing good."

He came closer, though not close enough to touch her, sensing she'd pull away if he did. "How can I help?"

"There's nothing you can do."

Gideon nodded. "The offer stands."

Their eyes met, and Fiadh said softly, "Thank you. Truly."

Dasha, picking up on her disquiet, tried to prod her into play. She shooed him away, but he remained close, dogging her steps with his awkward gait as she meandered through the courtyard. Gideon watched from a bench, glancing at Krulan now and then as the Cù-Sìth marked his mistress' movements from his spot on the ground. Eventually, she tired and sat next to Gideon, feet scuffing the dirt. He said nothing, waiting her out.

"Why is peace so hard to come by?"

His mouth turned down. "Because each of us longs for more than what we're given."

Fiadh looked up at him.

"We tend to think of lords and kings as those who covet. But even the simple farmer wishes for more." He paused and turned to her. "You're no different. Neither am I."

"You're right." She sighed. "But what I want… what I wish for is an end to the fighting. Isn't that what's best for everyone?"

"That depends on how peace is attained. Fighting could cease with the worst kind of ruler installed to keep it. So, an end to fighting is not really what you're working toward."

"I suppose not."

Kaelari's voice calling out to her interrupted their conversation, and Fiadh's shoulders sagged. "And so it begins again."

"You should go," he told her.

Krulan rose and nudged her between her shoulder blades, prodding Fiadh to return to the keep where Kaelari waited impatiently. She gave Gideon a last look and left.

Reentering the hall was like walking into a newly constructed war room. Tables had been moved, and a map laid out and held down at the corners with rocks. Those standing around it talked fiercely of strategy and battle. Fiadh glanced at the map, seeing every realm, both Aos Sí and human. All were threatened if Dothur chose to unleash his power. Flicking her eyes to each face, she clenched her jaw and accepted that times of peace were not to be had. Not yet.

Stepping to the edge of the table, she said, "I need your counsel."

Talking stopped as all eyes swung to her. Ellisar shifted his position to move closer. Other elves who'd traveled with him from Oadsera shifted behind him. The message was clear.

Fiadh ignored the subtle power play and said, "I don't know much about the evil Zaeleria warned us of. What do you advise?"

Piercing blue eyes found hers as Ellisar answered her question. "As you may or may not know, Dothur is a son of Carmun." He cursed the demoness and spat on the floor. "It was said he'd be driven into the sea by Kaelari and a band of fighters, not trapped in an iron prison by our most powerful seer. It appears that was a lie." He gave a cold glare to Kaelari, who stiffened, anger flaring.

"I don't recall you volunteering to help us hunt him down, Ellisar," she snapped. "My warriors and I tracked the monster and drove him into the sea. The last *we* saw of him, he'd been snatched in the jaws of a beast and dragged beneath the surface to his death. Zaeleria said nothing of his survival or imprisonment."

"A convenient omission."

Arel planted his hands on the table. "Are you calling us liars?"

The question was said softly, but there was an edge to it that alarmed Fiadh. She held up her hand. "Cease! It benefits no one to argue about the past. What can we do *now*?"

Ellisar held Arel's stare for a moment longer, then turned to Fiadh. "We could send scouts to hunt him down before he becomes too strong."

Fiadh pursed her lips. "If he was strong enough to escape whatever prison he'd been confined to, would our scouts have a chance?"

Kaelari folded her arms across her chest and responded before Ellisar could open his mouth. "If Dothur escaped a prison of Zaeleria's making, he's too strong already. Sending our warriors is a death sentence."

"What do you suggest?" Fiadh asked.

Gideon had slipped into the hall and stood beyond the circle of Aos Sí. Some looked at him with wary acceptance, and many more with open disdain. Lifting his chin, he watched and listened.

"We must await a seer who can communicate with Zaeleria… if she lives," Arel suggested.

"Aye. I hope your raven returns soon with news," Kaelari said to Ellisar before addressing the gathering. "In the meantime, we should reinforce our barriers and ready ourselves for attack."

Fiadh's jaw clenched. Hadn't there been enough bloodshed? It felt like the fighting had ended only yesterday, though weeks had passed since the fires stopped burning. Sighing, she swept her eyes through the group. "I'll start on the barriers, and we'll post scouts along our borders." A chorus of agreement moved through the group. "If Dothur has his eyes fixed on Erabel, we need to stand together. Fighting amongst ourselves will do nothing but weaken us."

Ellisar lifted his chin.

"We're stronger as one," she added quietly, then turned and left the hall, Krulan at her side.

You did well, he said.

Did I? She glanced at him and shook her head. *We aren't one people, not even now after so much has happened.*

Change takes time.

We may not have time.

He gave a deep rumble in his chest and turned toward the sound of someone jogging toward them. Ellisar dipped his head and asked, "May I have a word?"

"Of course."

Krulan sat, ears rotating forward as the advisor flicked his eyes to the Cù-Sìth before fixing them on Fiadh.

"Erabel is small," he began. "Without a robust fighting force, you are vulnerable. An alliance with Oadsera would provide the strength you need to face what is coming."

"An alliance? I thought we had one." Fiadh's eyes narrowed when she saw him shrug. "What exactly are you suggesting?"

Ellisar clasped his hands behind his back. "Marriage."

"Excuse me?"

"If we wed, you would have the soldiers you'd need to protect Erabel."

She raised a brow. "Are you saying that as queen, those forces are not already mine?"

Drawing on years of politics, Ellisar said, "Your rule is tenuous as long as you remain behind Erabel's wards. You may have been crowned in the seat of Oadsera, but you haven't led them, bled with them. They do not know you. And with your affinity for humans, they do not trust you. Oadsera's people know me. Marriage would signify a unification of our realms in their eyes." He took her hand. The callouses from years of practicing the art of warfare softly abraded her skin where he rubbed his thumbs in slow circles. "It isn't fair that you are put in such a position when so young and new to the crown. If we had time, I would woo you. Do not make a decision now. Consider my offer. Together, we could wield a force powerful enough to destroy Dothur."

Fiadh stood mutely as Ellisar bowed and walked away. Marriage? She looked at Krulan. *Was he serious?*

Aye.

Do you think he's right? She couldn't believe she was even asking. It's not like she'd actually consider his offer.

I think his people do not know you.

Of course, they don't know me! She folded her arms and stared at the window where Dasha sat on the ledge, carefree and preening. *I can't think about this now.*

Then don't.

She mashed her lips. *As if I didn't have enough to worry about, now I have to deal with Ellisar's advances.*

I thought you weren't going to think about it.

You're not helpful.

Krulan barked laughter. *Ellisar is not altruistic. Marriage would advance his position. He would be king.*

Good point.

But that doesn't mean his idea is meritless.

You should've stopped with the previous comment.

Gideon came into view. "You showed true leadership today," he said.

"I don't feel like a leader," she said despondently.

"A good leader strengthens her people, brings them together."

"A leader brings her people together," she repeated. "Maybe Ellisar was right."

"Right about what?"

Fiadh tilted her head to look at him. "He suggested we marry to unify our realms."

Gideon stiffened. "I see. Did you accept?"

"No, but I didn't decline either."

"I see." Gideon noted the strain in her features. He wanted to reach for her face, to run his fingers across her brow and erase the worry he saw there. Instead, he kept his hands at his sides. "You don't need a man by your side to lead. I hope you know that."

Fiadh smiled at him. "Thank you." She motioned to Krulan, who stretched, claws scraping the stone, then went to her side. "I need to walk, and the barriers need reinforcing," she told Gideon.

"May I join you?"

She nodded. The three of them left the hall while Dasha flew ahead. Gideon darted glances at her, finally saying, "I could learn from you. Should I ever return to Belfirth, knowing how to lead would benefit me."

The mention of his home sent a pang through her heart. It could've been her home, too, had things gone differently. But, too much had happened. Those days were old wounds that still had a sting.

He looked at her, pain in his eyes. "Or, perhaps, I will never return. Only ghosts live there now."

Fiadh wanted to reach for him, to give him a soothing touch, a healer's touch, but she clenched her hand and said, "You have your own path to walk. Maybe it will lead you there someday."

They made their way to the closest border in silence. Stopping a few paces from the barrier, Gideon watched

Fiadh walk to it and hold her hands to the invisible sheath that protected her realm. It still amazed him to know it was there, had been there for hundreds, maybe thousands, of years. If only the kingdoms of his people had such protections, Belfirth could have survived the attack. His people would still live.

Fiadh felt Danu's energy as she raised her arms. Beyond the barrier stretched Dorcha Wood, filled with a myriad of life that would bend to her will should she call upon it. As she considered that, she frowned, wishing the protections of Erabel could go beyond that sacred place and encompass the forest of her childhood. There had to be a way. Closing her eyes and opening her mind, she poured her energy into the barrier, feeling it mix with that of the Great Mother. Power throbbed at their joining, and as it did, she attempted to push it, gasping when she felt it stretch and expand. Sweat beaded her brow, and she hunched her shoulders, forcing the barricade outward. Arms trembling, she gritted her teeth and gave a final infusion of energy and magic before dropping her hands and bending over, panting.

Gideon came to her and hesitantly put his hand on her shoulder. "Are you all right?"

She nodded her head. "Just weary. I wanted to see if I could expand our protections into Dorcha Wood."

He raised a brow and looked toward the forest, though he could see nothing. "Did it work?"

"Sort of," she said, smiling weakly. In reality, the barrier only flexed a few yards into the forest, its magic resisting her efforts.

Her head pounded dully. She was doing this wrong. She

felt it. There was so much power in the earth, not only Danu's but something else too. It fluttered in her mind's eye like the flickering of shadows. If she could harness that power, if she knew how, Fiadh was certain she could protect the forest and everything in it.

CHAPTER FIVE

Raised voices echoed through the hall when Fiadh entered it the following day. Lifting a hand for quiet, she waited until all eyes were on her, then made her way to the dais. Only the sound of bodies shifting could be heard as she sat and cleared her throat.

"Quarreling and panic will get us nowhere." Fiadh's gaze swept the assembly. "We must assume Dothur will target Erabel."

Mutters of agreement raced through the gathering.

"While our borders might repel his power, the rest of Dorcha Wood remains at risk. I would like to extend our protections beyond Erabel and rally our people and allies. There is power in numbers, as we've seen in the armies of men, and we'll have a better chance of defeating Dothur if we unify our strength."

Ellisar cocked an eyebrow. "Forming a symbolic alliance with Oadsera would speed the process."

"That is a discussion for another time, Ellisar," Fiadh said irritably.

"As you wish. May I clarify what you're suggesting?" He waited for her approval and continued. "You suggest expanding the barrier beyond Erabel. But such a move would weaken our greatest defense and leave the seat of your kingdom vulnerable. It is a risk."

Elves from Oadsera murmured their agreement. Fiadh leaned back on the cold throne and laced her hands in her lap. "Protecting the forest that shields Erabel is a necessary risk. Rygeil and Darragh's attacks taught us that. If Dorcha Wood is destroyed, Danu will grow weak. With her, so will all of our people. At that point, what's to stop an invading army from assailing our barriers and bringing them down?"

His jaw flexed as he glanced at Gideon, who stood beyond the loose ring of Aos Sí. "The realms of men remain a threat, but their weapons of war cannot bring down the forest. Dothur is another matter. If we stretch our protections too thin, he will carve through them like a scythe. Had you more experience in the ways of war, you would see the folly of your suggestion."

"That's a fair point," she agreed. "I have much to learn, but I know enough to understand that abandoning Dorcha Wood is not the path to victory."

Ellisar studied her in silence for a moment, his face darkening before he accused, "You want to shield men in the forest, don't you?"

Grumbling from the elves surrounding Ellisar ensued. Fiadh raised her voice to be heard above the din. "And what if I do? Are they not part of this world?"

Saria's chief advisor stiffened. "Are you insinuating mankind deserves our protection after all they've done to our people?"

"Are you saying all must pay for the wrongs of a few?"

His nostrils flared. "Humans are an evil race. If you were more experienced, you would know this."

"It sounds as though you're implying our people are without fault. I would remind you of the evils my grandfather, your former king, committed before his death."

Ellisar glanced at the assemblage, noting how Fiadh's words hit their mark on many faces, even some of his own people. His role as chief advisor to Oadsera's ruler gave him broad powers, but this was not Oadsera, and Fiadh was his queen. Defying her publicly would set her against him, and his desire for marriage would be lost. Schooling his features, he dipped his chin. "You are right to remind me of our dark past."

She knew he wasn't genuinely capitulating, but, for now, he backed off, and she appreciated the gesture. "We will speak more of this. For now, know that I intend to expand our protections."

Murmurs filled the hall as bodies shifted. Fiadh swept her eyes across every face, stopping when she found Kaelari. They stared at each other, the connection breaking when Arel stepped to her side and leaned in close.

"A raven from Oadsera has returned," he whispered.

She nodded and rose, the action drawing everyone's attention. "I will protect Dorcha Wood. The work of extending those barriers would be easier with your aid."

A few nods met her announcement, but a greater

number of doubt and fear overshadowed them. Motioning for Kaelari and Ellisar, they left the hall.

Krulan kept pace with her. *A raven from Oadsera arrived,* she told him.

Pray it has good tidings.

She grimaced and ducked into the solar. Dasha swept into the room before the door closed, landing on her shoulder. She stroked his breast, then turned to Arel.

"What did you learn from the raven?"

"Dyvre will arrive in two days. He brings a small contingent of fighters who wish to pledge themselves to you."

Fiadh glanced at Ellisar. "Who's Dyvre?"

"He is a powerful seer, though not as strong as Zaelaria," he said. "However, if anyone could locate her, it would be him."

Nodding, Fiadh paced in front of a large window. A few panes were missing, one with a spiderweb of cracks extending from a small chip in its center. She paused and studied the translucent glass, imagining the trees beyond the filmy pane. It was a barrier in itself—a thin wall insulating her from the forest beyond it, so much like the protections surrounding Erabel. And like those, it was easy to see those barriers through a glass-like pane, never looking beyond them and considering the lives that dwell there. She knew that her people had to see the world differently to survive. They mustn't insulate themselves from it.

Her eyes flicked to an open frame where the glass had been. Everything was so much clearer. "I will extend our barriers," she said to herself.

"Fiadh." Kaelari went to her side. "You gain the support of the council. To rule means to compromise."

She turned slowly. "Are you suggesting I sacrifice the lives beyond Erabel for the sake of those who cower within its borders?"

Anger flared in Kaelari's face. "Do not make accusations of cowardice! Lives were lost defending this place, defending *you*. Don't take those deaths lightly."

She shook her head. "I don't make light of them. But I can't live in a bubble of safety while the forest that shields our kingdom is unprotected, and those beyond it at the mercy of a creature who has none." Kaelari opened her mouth, but Fiadh cut her off with a slash of her hand. "You've told me that I must rule. That I need to fulfill my destiny. What if *this* is my destiny? What if I can protect all of Dorcha Wood and those who seek shelter within her borders? Isn't it worth trying?"

"It's more complicated than that," Ellisar said, having listened to their conversation.

"It doesn't have to be!" she shouted at him. "You talk of bringing our realms together to become formidable enough to stop Dothur, but that alliance means nothing if we lose everything beyond our borders."

Kaelari's eyes narrowed as she stared at Ellisar. "What's she talking about?"

The advisor met her stare. "Marriage. A show of unification between Erabel and the most powerful Aos Sí realm."

"Don't mask your ambitions with talk of an alliance," Kaelari said. "You seek the throne."

"I seek to protect our people from annihilation!"

"Enough," Fiadh said quietly. "There will be no talk of marriage."

"Are you rejecting my proposal?"

"No. I just can't think about it now." Sighing, Fiadh strode to a musty chair in a dark corner of the room. Puffs of dust drifted from the cushion as she sat. "Tell me how to sway the council."

Kaelari glared at Ellisar and then turned to Fiadh. "I'm not saying expanding our protections isn't worth trying. It is," Kaelari said, "but if you stand against the majority of those who are here to give you counsel, you'll sow dissent. And we can't afford that."

"I won't abandon the home of my youth."

She looked sharply at Fiadh, the corners of her mouth pulling down.

"Your advice is valued," she said to Ellisar and Kaelari, "and I will heed it so long as it doesn't contradict what I know is right. For now, I'll work on building my strength and appealing to our people. I won't flaunt my attempts to extend our barriers, but I won't stop either."

Ellisar shifted his feet and crossed his arms. "Fiadh, there is only so much energy in the barrier. The smaller the area it's protecting, the more impenetrable it becomes. The larger, the easier it will be to break. You know this. The more you extend it, the weaker it becomes."

Fiadh studied him. "Then we'll have to find a way to make it more powerful."

Kaelari sighed from her spot against the window. "Did anyone ever tell you that you're irritatingly stubborn?"

"Frequently."

Ellisar stepped forward and bowed his head. "I will follow your lead and do my part to sway your opponents."

"Thank you."

They watched him leave. When the door closed, Kaelari turned to Fiadh and stared at her from hooded eyes.

"What?"

"Wasn't it only days ago that you complained you're too young to be a leader? Yet here you are taking charge."

Fiadh smiled. "Oh, that hasn't changed. I'm too young and inexperienced, but no one around here seems to care. Well, maybe Ellisar does."

"He's just too hung up on his role as Saria's chief advisor. It gives him a big head, not that he needed more of an ego." Kaelari rose and walked to the door, pausing before she opened it. "It's true that you have much to learn. It appears I do as well."

Queen Fiadh, Krulan said when the elf left.

She snorted and plopped into the newly vacated chair, waving her hand before her face and coughing when dust billowed out of it. *It may be a short reign if I keep angering everyone.*

We shall see.

Minutes passed as Fiadh considered how she wanted to proceed. It may be a fool's pursuit to try to encompass the whole of Dorcha Wood within the powerful barrier, but she had to try. Erabel couldn't hold all of her people should they come under attack from Dothur and need sanctuary. And, though she'd never utter it before the council, there may be men, women, and children who seek protection from that evil being. Could she send them away to die? Fiadh looked out the window again, seeing the contrast between the sections that shrouded the world beyond and those that revealed it.

Snarls of hunger interrupted her thoughts, eliciting a wolfy chuckle from Krulan when the sound drifted to his keen ears.

Come on, Krulan, she said, standing and brushing off her clothes. *Let's find something to fill our bellies.*

He rose and grumbled. *I will not be eating one of those repulsive oatcakes again. They taste like dirt.*

How do you know what dirt tastes like?

He snarled and nipped at her playfully.

She laughed and jumped away from his sharp fangs. *Very well. No oatcakes for you. I will give Dasha your share,* she said with a wink. *I have a mind to sneak into the larder for sweets, too, and then leave the grounds unseen. You could hunt in Dorcha Wood while I eat my disgusting breakfast.*

The great hall had cleared somewhat as she skirted the perimeter and ducked into the kitchen with Krulan on her heels. While those in attendance marked her passing, they said nothing, though she felt their stares itching between her shoulders. Dasha met them outside, and the trio headed to the eastern border of Erabel.

Finding a mossy patch of ground, Fiadh settled against a fallen log and broke off a small chunk of one of the oatcakes she'd pilfered, handing it to Dasha, who pecked off bits as she devoured the rest. Krulan eyed her food with distaste, then launched into Dorcha Wood. She tried not to think about what poor creatures he hunted. Death was a reality. It was the cycle of life, and she held no ill will for the lives he took to sustain his.

She felt Gideon's presence before he came into view. "You keep showing up like this, and I'm going to wonder if I'm a lodestone rather than a queen."

He paused, his mouth curving up with a smirk. "Are you a shapeshifting lodestone? Is that one of those elven magic things?"

"Damn. You figured out more of our secrets."

Gideon tapped his temple. "Humans are smarter than elves."

She snorted. "You wish."

"I do. I'll have to live with my tiny brain and enormous envy. May I join you?" he asked.

Tearing off the end of her second oatcake, she nodded and held it out to him. He smiled and opened his satchel, revealing three of the cakes, two pieces of fruit, and a jug of watered wine. Scooting over, she patted the ground, and they sat silently for a few minutes, concentrating on their meal.

Gideon handed her the jug, and as Fiadh reached for it, his fingers stroked hers. She froze for a moment, startled by the warmth of his skin and the memories that came with it. Her arm twitched, and she snatched the flask from him, making a face when it sloshed over the rim. Taking a long pull, she let the liquid run down her throat, focusing on the tangy and sweet taste instead of the sensations buzzing in her stomach.

"Things are weighing on your mind," he said quietly. "Care to share?"

"Am I that easy to read?"

He shrugged, letting his eyes drift to a pair of tiny beings —gruagach—who'd left the sanctuary of their hazel grove to forage, stuffing provisions in miniature satchels slung across their human-like bodies. Feeling his scrutiny, they paused what they were doing and gazed at him with dark, beady eyes. Disconcerted by the intensity of their stare, he looked away. "Sometimes it feels as though this is all a dream. This place." He turned toward Fiadh. "You."

"I know. I feel it, too."

He leaned back against the fallen trunk and said, "Tell me what's on your mind."

Fiadh released a puff of air and fiddled with her hands. "Besides Ellisar proposing?"

He made a face. "As if you'd even consider marrying such an arrogant ass."

"I might," she said, her stoic expression shifting to a smirk. "Being queen isn't what I thought it would be."

"What had you expected?"

"Well," she considered for a moment, eyes lighting, "I guess I thought I could just give a command, and you all would hop to it."

"I don't hop."

"That's unfortunate." She leaned back on her hands. "My people are reluctant to protect anyone but our own. I don't imagine yours are any different."

He shook his head, tearing off another hunk of his oatcake.

"They wish to strengthen our barriers to withstand an attack by Dothur while leaving everything beyond our borders vulnerable. I can't agree with that. If Dothur sets Erabel in his sights, what's to stop him from targeting other realms?"

"You mean realms beyond those of the Aos Sí, don't you?"

She nodded.

Gideon frowned. "What you're proposing has never been done, and I can understand your people's reluctance. There's a dark history between men and elves—wrongs done on both sides. They fear for their future."

"I fear for all our futures. If we remain at war with each other—divided—Dothur could use it to gain an edge. We have to be united, Gideon. There's no other way, and my people won't see it."

"Try to view it from their perspective. You're asking them to harbor the enemy. How did you expect them to react?"

Grumbling, Fiadh picked at her dress, pulling at a thread that had come loose and winding it around her finger. "I don't know what I expected. But their prejudice isn't going to stop me. I know what's right. I won't abandon the world outside this realm for the sake of my people." She gave him a sidelong glance. "Besides, they no longer balk at you being here."

He chuckled. "True enough. Though Ellisar isn't too keen on me attending council gatherings."

"He is pretty obvious about that."

Krulan broke through the trees just then, Nym at his side. She'd become a fixture in Erabel, having forgone her allegiance to Rygeil during the attack on Erabel. Fiadh studied the female Cù-Sìth, letting her eyes travel over her pelt's green and grey hues. Nym could never replace Rivya. The loss of Krulan's mate was a hole that could not be filled, but the female eased his pain, and for that, Fiadh was grateful.

I see you have company, Krulan said.

I see you do, too.

He flicked his eyes to Nym. *Aye.*

She nodded.

Krulan stepped in front of her and lowered his head. She came to her knees and pressed her forehead against his, twining her arms around his neck. She breathed in his musky odor, the scent having become so familiar it felt like home. She felt his grief and shared her own, clinging to his strength. *I love you,* she told him.

And I, you. He pulled away and gave her a quick lick on her cheek. *Come, young one. You must train if you are to see your plans to fruition.*

Gideon helped her to her feet, his hand lingering in hers before she broke the connection. Packing up the remains of their meal, they made their way to the keep, and though it was Krulan at her side, she felt Gideon's presence as though he, too, walked with her. At that moment, she acknowledged that, somehow, he was part of the future she wished to forge.

CHAPTER SIX

*L*ord Darragh sat brooding in Haegna's cell, the light of a single candle flickering against the walls. Dark eyes set in a narrow face cast about the room, thin lips twisting in a grimace. He hadn't bothered to change his tunic in days, and a sour stench emanated from him, blending with the dank aura of the dungeon. *How had it come to this?* he thought.

All of his mother's possessions were untouched, just as he'd found them when he'd discovered her stiff corpse and that of her servant, Emer. Even the blood stains remained on the floor and walls, evidence of their violent end. Who had killed them was a mystery. For all he knew, one of his own men had come across the women and slain them for sport or in defense, though the wound on his mother's arm spoke of something more sinister.

It mattered little how they died. Haegna was dead, and he was alone.

Thousands of the king's men had been slain when

they'd attacked Rygeil's army, but there were plenty more where they came from, and his fighting force had suffered little in comparison, having been held back until the elf king's fighters had begun to retreat. But even his minor losses stung. Fleeing the battle as creatures from childhood nightmares poured out of the forest only to return to find his mother murdered had sent Darragh into a rage. Even after all this time, the great hall still bore the signs of it.

It galled him to have been thwarted by Rygeil's spawn. The soldiers from the north and west who had come when he'd raised his banners had left after the battle. He'd promised them victory and given them defeat. They did not stay to hear what new promises the Lord of Felmore made. Now, failure hung over Felmore like a fog.

Slumping in the chair, Darragh considered his options. The situation was dire. There was no denying it. The elves would be back, and this time, they would bring more of their kind. The remaining soldiers from the garrison wouldn't be enough to defeat the invaders. He'd sent another missive to the king following the siege, warning him of the threat the elves posed to the entire kingdom.

What he'd gotten in return was the message that the Western Fold was on its own until the spring when another legion of the king's soldiers could safely cross the Icy Plains. Crumpling the communication in his fist, he held the parchment over the candle and watched it fold in on itself and blacken before tossing it into the cold hearth.

Sighing loudly, he made to rise but paused and cocked his head, listening to a soft whisper that filled the room. Darting a glance about the chamber, fear raced down his spine, causing his skin to pebble. A tingling sensation crawled along the base of his skull as his eyes drifted toward Haegna's scrying bowl. The dark liquid remained still and fathomless under his scrutiny, but his body lurched toward it, drawn to its power. With a fixed stare, he studied the blackness, seeing nothing, not even his reflection. But, as he watched, it came again. A sound like the rasping breath of a demon scratching its way out of the dark pool.

"Darragh," it crooned with a voice that curled around his skull.

Gasping, he staggered back, terror flooding his muscles, screaming at him to flee. But his feet held, anchored to the floor.

"Darragh, my son."

His eyes widened, his mouth hanging open.

"Come, my son. Come closer that I may gaze upon the face of my beloved."

Darragh's legs shook as he crept to the small table and gripped the edge. "Mother?"

The voice purred. "Aye, my son. I am here."

"But, you were killed. I saw your corpse!"

Laughter made the smooth surface vibrate. "Did you think death could keep me from you?"

His legs felt weak, and he reached back, fumbling for the stool. Sitting with a thump, he rested his elbows next to the scrying bowl. "How?"

"I could teach you," the voice promised. "There is much I tried to share, and you refused to learn... out of fear." The last was said in a voice dripping with disdain.

His lip curled. "Cheating death is not a power you

spoke of."

"There is much you were not willing to hear."

"I am willing now. Speak, woman," he hissed. "Or do you simply dangle your powers before me?"

A rumble of laughter spilled from the surface, making his hair stand on end. "Very well, my son. Come closer."

Darragh leaned forward until his face hung above the scrying bowl, the puff of his breath marring the calm surface. Beneath the blackness, something stirred. A shadowy figure grew, becoming more distinct. Words followed the image as it became more defined, taking on the appearance of a hag before shifting, becoming the face of a grotesquely malformed man.

The muscles in Darragh's neck grew rigid, and his jaw clenched. He tried to pull away as Crom Cruach filled the surface, but his body was no longer his own. Awful power radiated from the liquid. He gaped, helpless, as words— powerful and horrible—slipped from Crom Cruach's lips, traveling through space and time and into the cell. Behind the old god, a hideous winged monster materialized, pale eyes boring into Darragh's as a scream of fear crawled up his throat before it was caught behind his teeth. Nefarious will snaked through the dank air and encompassed Darragh's mind, clutching it in a ruthless grip and then stabbing into him. Blood trickled from his nostrils as his body shook.

What had been Haegna's son skittered away from the invasion like a spider, hiding in an untouched corner of his subconscious as Crom Cruach took over, becoming Lord of the Western Fold.

CHAPTER SEVEN

Dyvre, Oadsera's most renowned seer, arrived a few days later on the back of a unicorn, flanked by elves from that realm who'd asked to join her budding court. As the group crossed into Erabel, Meara emerged from the trees and whinnied, trotting forward to nuzzle the seer's mount with bobs of her head and soft nickers. Fiadh, with Krulan and Kaelari at her sides, joined the gathering, her mouth curving in a smile as she watched Meara's joyful exuberance. She studied the dark pelt of the unicorn Maera rested her head against, noting the massive horn with its translucent tip before landing on Dyvre, who perched atop the unicorn regarding her. He had a striking face, angular and pale beneath the fine white strands of his waist-length hair. Piercing violet eyes studied her with curiosity. Her chest ached as she held his gaze. His face was so like Veren's— deceptively youthful if one didn't look into his eyes and see the decades of experience that lingered there. Others flanked him, their bodies shifting as they greeted friends and kin.

He slid off the unicorn in a graceful swirl of limbs and fabric, the deep green of his leggings peeking out from between two long slits in the full-length tunic. Reaching for her, they clasped wrists, his long fingers encircling her arm. They were warm. She looked down at their joined flesh, eyes welling as his mind whispered to hers. Fiadh looked into his face and was lost, caught in a gaze so deep and pure she let go of herself and drifted with him. She listened to him tell her of the love he felt flowing through her body—mixed with the grief. He soothed her aching heart as he told her that Veren saw her still. Loved her still.

When he released his hold, she reached for him, wanting more of the solace in his mind. Dyvre smiled softly and murmured, "We will have time, my child. For now, show me your kingdom."

She blinked slowly and lowered her arm. "I—" Fiadh cleared her throat, "I welcome you to Erabel." Backing away, she swung her arm to indicate the path they would take and fell into step with the seer. Behind them, Meara whinnied happily. Fiadh smiled and craned her neck to see the two unicorns resting their heads on each other's backs.

"She missed her son," Dyvre said.

Fiadh's eyes widened. "That's her son?" She studied the creature, noting his black coat and long mane, so like Meara's. His horn was more massive, thicker at the base, with darker hues before tapering to the glassy tip.

"Arion is the last of her foals. She will have no others."

"Why not?"

Dyvre cocked his head and looked down at her. "Like most of her kind, Meara's mate was killed in the Great War. They have but one mate in life."

Fiadh looked stricken. Meara hadn't shared that tragic history with her.

"Do not feel pity for her. She is content, especially now that Arion is with her. When I return to Oadsera, I believe he will remain here." He stared wistfully at the unicorns. "There are so few of them left."

They walked in silence, Fiadh sneaking glances at the seer and listening to the chatter of the elves who followed in their wake. Dyvre had a serene expression, and she wondered how he could appear so calm when he'd been summoned as a result of dire news. Gideon awaited the party outside the keep. He stood awkwardly as they approached, body twitching, though he fixed a cool mask on his face. His eyes flashed to Fiadh's, and she gave him a small smile.

The seer slowed his pace as they neared the man, stopping when he was a few steps from Gideon. "I am glad to see that you found your way."

Gideon glanced at Fiadh, brow furrowing.

Dyvre gave a knowing look. "Aye, it is as you guess. I have been watching the path you've taken and am pleased to see it has led you here."

The Aos Sí who'd been listening to the exchange showed an array of reactions to the seer's words, with some eyeing Gideon critically and others with curiosity. Gideon met every glare with his own before turning to Fiadh. She lifted her chin, mouth curving in a small smile.

"Without Fiadh's leadership, I would not be here," he said.

The seer studied him, weighing his words. "I believe you would have found your way to our people regardless of our queen—though she is certainly the catalyst of many things." Gideon fidgeted under the elf's scrutiny. "Your part in this has only begun, young one."

Dyvre dipped his head, and Gideon mirrored the action, stepping aside as the assemblage passed, his gaze following Fiadh and catching her sidelong glance. Inside, Ellisar greeted the seer. More elves gathered shortly after, and the din grew as greetings passed from one to the other. Leading Dyvre from the crush of Aos Sí, Fiadh, and Ellisar traveled to the oak—Danu's embodiment—Gideon trailing behind them. As they walked, Fiadh asked the seer about Zaelaria's warning. He shared what he knew of Dothur, adding little more to what she'd already heard.

When they reached the open space where the oak sat like a tower, Dyvre stopped and turned to her. "Your grand-father did much to hasten the release of Dothur. He aligned himself with an evil being, and I fear the two have formed an alliance."

"Crom Cruach," she whispered.

Kaelari, who'd followed close behind with Arel, scowled at the mention of his name.

"Why Crom didn't attempt to capture or kill you when he escaped into Dorcha Wood remains a mystery," the seer said. "Even with the power you took from the Merrow, you were no match for him. We must assume he had a reason for letting you live."

Fiadh's face reddened. "I'm ashamed of what I did."

He patted her hand. "You need not be. Each step you have taken has led you to this place. To this moment. I have seen what you desire." He paused and craned his neck to look at Gideon. "Without your missteps, you would not know the future you seek to shape."

She swung her eyes to Gideon's. He stared at her, and she saw her own turmoil in his gaze. "I don't know what I seek, Dyvre," she said, breaking contact with Gideon. "I just know things can't go on the way they have. We can't keep fighting each other."

"You are wise for one so young. Have faith in yourself as your people do." The seer walked to the oak and pressed his hands to the bark. He greeted the Great Mother, closing his eyes as Danu filled his mind. Using his sight and power from the goddess, he untethered himself from his body and went beyond the borders of Erabel. His spirit traveled north, deep into the Scarlet Mountains.

Fiadh watched, marveling at the way his body glowed subtly. It was as though Danu wrapped herself around him like a diaphanous blanket. After many minutes, the seer rocked back on his heels, bid the Great Mother goodbye, and stepped away from the oak. As he turned toward her, his eyes showed with such brilliance she gaped.

Do I look like that when I commune with Danu? she asked Krulan, who stood at her side.

Aye.

She wrinkled her nose.

Krulan chuckled, the sound radiating through her. *You begin to see what we have always seen.*

Her eyes widened, clouding over as she considered his words. *I think you're biased.*

He huffed. *You have never seen yourself as you truly are. One day that will change.*

Fiadh made a face and turned to Dyvre. "Is Zaelaria… does she… does she live?"

He nodded, and she sagged with relief.

"Zaeleria is weak but lives. The Great Mother tells me she struggles to make her way to Erabel. With a map, I will show you the route Zaeleria takes."

Kaelari murmured a prayer of thanks under her breath, then looked to Fiadh. "You could send a contingent of fighters to intercept her and aid her journey here."

"Aye. I would like to do that. Perhaps you and Ellisar can find volunteers."

The elves nodded and strode away. Gideon watched their departure and cleared his throat. "I couldn't help over-hearing your good tidings but wonder if your people will be at risk traveling beyond these borders."

"Ah," Dyvre said. "That is a sound plan."

Fiadh looked confused. "What's a sound plan?"

"The young lord wishes to accompany your fighters lest they encounter bands of men. He thinks he could sway them from attacking your people."

Gideon looked uncomfortable, having had his thoughts plucked from his mind with such ease. Fiadh's face softened as she looked at the man who'd come barging into her life like a wild boar. To think he was willing to escort her people. "Gideon?" she whispered.

"Dyvre is correct. I would like to help, my queen."

Her eyes went wide at his use of the title. Shifting into a courtly role, she said, "I accept your aid gladly." Fiadh dipped her head, trying not to smirk.

He bowed low, the formality tugging a smile from her mouth. "I will inform Kaelari and pack for the journey."

She watched him leave, realizing there was a part of her that ached to see him go.

"Your affection for him is not misplaced," the seer said quietly.

Fiadh glanced shyly at him. "Ours is a troubled history."

"Even in the most turbulent times, we find bravery," he said, cupping her cheek. "And love."

She looked away. "I don't know what the future holds for Gideon and me. Do you?"

"My gift doesn't allow me to see such things."

Nodding, Fiadh smoothed a hand down her dress. "Come, I imagine you'd appreciate a meal and then a quiet place to rest."

The seer followed her as she showed him to the solar. When he was settled, she fetched a trencher with vegetable stew and brought it to him, sitting with Krulan at her feet as he ate and discussed the changes he'd seen in Oadsera since Rygeil's death. Pain over the loss of her brother, Calum, and grandfather tainted her enjoyment of his tidings. She didn't miss the subtle warnings of those who resented her ascendance to the throne and the death of their king. Much work needed to be done if her people were to be united. Ellisar's proposal flared in her mind, and she struggled to block it out. How could she bind herself to someone she didn't love? Veren had come from Oadsera. If he'd asked for her hand… her heart twisted. No. There had to be another way.

Gideon and Kaelari eventually joined them. The elven warrior shot Gideon a look and said, "He wishes to accompany my fighters when they seek Zaeleria, and I have accepted his offer. They will leave at dawn."

Fiadh studied Gideon. He met her gaze, a wealth of emotion in his stare. Perhaps he saw this gesture as a form of atonement. It made her wonder what sacrifices *she* should make for her mistakes. Whatever his reasons, his willingness to put his life at risk for people he'd been raised to hate and fear was humbling.

A group of elves and one man gathered at the base of the keep's steps as pink hues of dawn lit the sky. Fiadh swept her eyes over each of them, stopping when she reached Arel. An arm's length from him stood Lura, whose sharp eyes missed nothing. Both had large satchels slung across their backs, along with bows and quivers of arrows. They wore tunics and leggings that were brown, better for blending into the dried grasses of a wintery landscape. "May the Great Mother guide and protect you," she murmured.

He bowed. "I will send a raven when we have found her."

She acknowledged his promise and flicked her eyes to Gideon. He stepped forward, knelt, and lifted his sword so it lay across both hands. "I serve you now, my queen. You and your people have my sword."

Fiadh's face softened. "Gideon," she whispered.

He looked up at her, his heart in his eyes. "I will protect them with my life. You'll look after Quinn while I'm gone?"

She nodded, eyes welling.

He turned to Krulan. "You'll keep her safe?"

The Cù-Sìth lifted his massive head and gave an irritated growl. *Arrogant whelp.*

Be nice, Fiadh scolded.

Krulan huffed and looked away.

Gideon nodded and sheathed his sword. Leaning down, he picked up a satchel and swung it over his shoulder, pausing when Fiadh reached for him. He took her hand, tracing the pale skin over her knuckles, then pressed his lips to her fingers. His kiss was like a brand, burning through her skin. She looked at her hand as he let go, still feeling the softness of his mouth, remembering the feel of his lips on hers. It was a lifetime ago. When she looked up, he had joined the others. Fiadh raised her arm in farewell, holding it aloft until they disappeared, catching him glance back at her before he rounded the corner, swallowed by the forest.

CHAPTER EIGHT

Gideon and ten Aos Sí warriors emerged from Dorcha Wood under a mist of Fiadh's making. The cover wouldn't last long, only to the cluster of trees beyond an open meadow. But it kept their movements concealed from any scouts Lord Darragh may have sent to mark their movements. Once the group was well beyond the border of Dorcha Wood, they increased their pace. Keeping to tree lines when they could, the band traversed the greater world, heading north toward the Scarlet Mountains. The elves kept a quick pace, their energy seemingly inexhaustible, and Gideon fell behind, his old leg injury making his muscles seize. Arel noticed and called for a break.

Nodding thanks, Gideon limped to a large boulder and sat down with a sigh. Thoughts of Aridius filled his mind—what he wouldn't give for the comfort of his mount. But the elves had insisted they go on foot. It made them easier to hide and harder to track. They'd made good progress, having traveled three and a half leagues—a grueling distance riddled with hills and valleys. Resting his arms on his knees, Gideon looked at the elves through hooded eyes. They appeared unfazed by the rigor of travel, as though the Great Mother gave them strength in addition to the magic running through their veins. If he were a jealous man, he'd resent it. But he only watched them in wonder. Their chatter was no different than the talk of any group of warriors. They boasted and joked like he had hundreds of times. As Gideon watched the elves, he saw what Fiadh must have seen: people. Different but the same.

He wished his brother, Doran, were here to see him sitting among the enemy. Doran had always been strangely fascinated by stories of the Aos Sí, and Gideon wondered, in hindsight, if his brother would have been able to forge peace with Rygeil had their father not ordered them to go into battle. He shook his head, a sad smile playing about his lips.

As he rubbed his hand over his black breeches to massage his leg, a noise drifted on the wind. Gideon cocked his head and listened. Standing slowly, he turned toward it, mouth parting slightly as he realized it was the cry of a child. The elves quieted, each rising, their ears trained to the source of the wailing.

Arel stepped close to Gideon. "What do you think it is?"

"A child," he replied. Frowning, he glanced at the elves. "It could be marauders who came upon a homestead. It is not unheard of in remote stretches such as this."

Lura came to Gideon's side. "Are these bands usually large in number?"

He pursed his lips. "I've rarely seen more than a dozen at a time, but they'll be well-armed regardless."

She cocked her eyebrow and lifted her bow. "Then we'll have to surprise them."

Gideon grinned and drew his sword. Leaving their supplies, the group followed the sound of crying over a rocky hill and into a small valley in which sat a remote village surrounded by fallow fields. Remnants of a forest bordered the community, and they kept to the trees, listening to cries that grew faint. Holding up his hand, Arel called a halt to their progress and flicked his wrist to the right and left. Aos Sí fanned out while Gideon remained at his side. Minutes passed as the two hid in a thicket while the others darted among the undergrowth. A high warbling drifted through the air, and Arel jerked his head at Gideon. He followed, marveling at the silence of the elf's footfalls along the leaf-littered ground. They reached Lura, where she crouched behind the wide base of a pine tree. Her brown leggings and dark green tunic blended so well in the landscape that she looked at through she was birthed from the forest itself.

Swinging her crystalline blue eyes at them, she whispered, "There, just beyond that tree." She raised her arm and pointed to the solitary tree in the dormant field.

Gideon squinted, zeroing in on a large lump next to which was a small child. The distance from the village was considerable, though it was well within the fields that would ripen with crops come summer. As he watched, the child tilted his head back and let out a pitiful cry, coming to his knees and shoving at the prone form on the ground. Why had no one from the town come to his aid? Rising, he moved toward the edge of trees and studied the community.

People moved about, but even from his distant view, he could see that many of them were dragging something in their wake. Unease washed over his body, causing the hair on the back of his neck to stand on end.

He swung his gaze to Arel, who'd silently joined him. "Can you see what they carry?" he asked the elf.

"Their dead."

Gideon frowned. It was as he thought. But who would attack such a remote village? And why? Even Rygeil's forces had avoided such places, preserving his fighting force for more important targets. "We should return the child to his people and offer aid."

Arel slowly turned to him with a cold stare in his violet eyes. "Why should we help them? They'll slay us where we stand."

The others had joined them and now formed a loose ring around the two. Gideon glanced at every face, seeing Arel's words reflected in each of them. "You're right. They would kill you if given the chance." Grumbles of agreement met his remark, but he held up a hand to quiet the elves. "Why did you kneel before your queen? Was it to follow the old ways or to walk a new path?"

Eyes flashed as they muttered, their bodies shifting. Lura pinned him with a stare and said, "What are you really asking?"

Arel cut Gideon off before he could reply. "He's saying that when we knelt at Fiadh's feet, we gave fealty to a ruler who wants to unify our people—all people. She asked you to let go of the old ways. Old hatred. To create a new world. If you don't believe in her vision, you had best find someone else to serve." His words were met with cold stares, but the elf lifted his chin and continued, "It is not an easy path your queen asks you to walk, but it is the right one. And it begins here."

Lura was the first to bow her head and step to Arel's side. The others followed, their eyes flicking to the village—fear and distrust reflected in them.

"Let me act as envoy to your people when we reach the village," Gideon instructed. "At the very least, it may keep them from attacking."

They nodded and followed Gideon as he made his way to the child who'd gone silent and lay in an exhausted heap at his dead mother's side. He wore a soiled bedgown, the hem showing evidence of a nighttime flee into the fields. The boy's hair was matted with dirt, and what Gideon could see of his face showed smudges of blood and grime. Fixing his gaze on the corpse, his heart twisted. Like the child, the woman wore nothing but her bedgown, though it could hardly be called that as it lay in shreds atop her mutilated body. His stomach heaved when he noted bite marks among the deep furrows in her skin. She'd been clawed to death and… gnawed upon. One brown eye stared blankly from beneath lanky strands of red hair.

"What could've done this?" Gideon whispered. Kneeling, he reached over and closed her eyes, saying a prayer to the Great Mother. Twisting his head, he looked up at Arel.

The elf's mouth was pulled in a grimace. "I've heard stories of an ancient monster that devoured the flesh of its victims, but that creature was said to live in lakes and rivers. I saw none near the village."

Lura gripped her bow, her knuckles going white. "This place is cursed if such a thing has visited it. We should leave."

Gideon stood up and faced her. "You may do as you wish, but I will see the boy to whatever family remains." He bent down and picked up the boy, watching the child's head droop over his arm. Gideon shifted his burden and began walking toward the village.

The boy's body hung limply in his arms, head gently bouncing against his chest with every step. When they were halfway across the field, his lids fluttered open, and he looked at Gideon, eyes welling. "Mama won't wake up."

"She's with the Great Mother now," Gideon told him.

A fat tear rolled down the child's cheek, making a track through the dirt and blood caked on his skin. With a shaky breath, he clutched Gideon's tunic and craned his neck to see the figures at Gideon's sides. The elves glanced at him but said nothing as though waiting for the boy to squeal with fright. But he said nothing, only looked at them curiously before shifting his head toward the tiny hamlet. Body tensing, he wiggled, struggling to free himself from Gideon's arms.

"It's all right," Gideon said, gripping him tightly.

"There's monsters!" he cried.

His wailing reminded him of little Aishling. As he held the boy and hushed him with soothing words, he couldn't help but think of his foundling. Was she well? It had been weeks since he'd gotten word. With those thoughts came an aching emptiness. He missed her.

A bell rang as the group neared the community. People

rushed about, some screaming in fear, others grabbing pitchforks and hammers. A dozen men gathered outside the town's mill, makeshift weapons in their hands.

Gideon looked at the elves. "Stay here. Let me talk to them first."

Arel gave a curt nod.

With the child tucked against his chest, Gideon aimed for the men who stood nervously, eyes darting from him to the elven warriors waiting a short distance away. One man, a burly individual with the biceps of a blacksmith, broke away from the group and met Gideon. He reached for the child, setting him on the ground and sending him off with a gentle swat to his backside. "We don't take kindly to strangers. Especially those who consort with elves." He spat on the ground and glared at Arel and the others. "If you've come to finish us off, we won't be going down without a fight."

Holding up his hands, Gideon said, "We have no wish to harm you or your people. The cry of the child drew us to your village."

The man eyed him. "I know what that kind does to our people. We heard what happened in the east," he snarled, pointing a large hammer toward the Aos Sí. "You best be off. We want nothing to do with elven scum… nor people who travel with them."

Gideon bent his leg and put his hands on his hips. "I understand your hatred. It's true that I spent my life feeling the same way. But they are not the monsters we've made them out to be. Their old king was overthrown and slain, and in his place, they had a queen who sought peace with mankind. They've come to help. As have I. Your people need aid. Will you allow us into your village?"

Lifting his chin, the man studied the elves. "All I can say is that it wasn't their kind that came in the night. I can't say nothing more than that." He paused as the men behind him muttered. "My name's Malcolm. Give me leave to talk to my men, and we'll see if we'll give welcome to you and your… friends."

"Thank you, Malcolm." Gideon dipped his head and watched the man walk away. He could hear nothing of what was said, only saw angry gestures and wary glares. Other villagers gathered between wattle and daub structures. Their eyes were haunted as they took in Gideon and the elves. Many of the women wore linen aprons stained with blood, while the men bore signs of grave digging—their worn tunics and trousers coated in dirt. The child he'd rescued sat in the arms of an elderly woman, perhaps his grandmother, his thumb stuck in his mouth. Beyond the milling crowd were bodies lying in a neat row, each of them bearing signs of a vicious attack.

Malcolm moved away from the group of men and strode to Gideon. "If what you claim is true—that you wish to help us—I invite you and your fellow travelers into our village and ask that you slay the creatures that have hunted us these three nights past."

Gideon bent his head and whistled to the elves. They loped over, their vibrant eyes flicking from person to person, and formed a half-circle around Gideon. "Malcolm and the people of his village," he said to the Aos Sí, "have given us leave to enter their hamlet on the condition that we slay the beasts that attacked their people."

Arel stepped to Gideon's side and looked at Malcolm. "We accept your terms."

The man's shoulders lost some of their tension, though he remained guarded.

"What fell thing happened here?" Arel asked.

"They came three nights ago. I never saw how many. From the screams of the dying, I'd say it were hundreds, but I know that's not right. We thought they were horses." He swallowed hard. "My good wife had a fondness for horses. But they weren't no horses. They were monsters."

CHAPTER NINE

rel, Lura, and Gideon stared down at the mangled corpse of a farmer. Crouching, Lura studied the partially eaten flesh and deep gashes across the man's torso and limbs. "My mother told me stories of the Kelpie," she said. "Terrible stories. But I've never heard of an attack like this. They're solitary creatures, luring their victims onto their backs and hieing them into the depths of their lakes and rivers to devour them. This—" She waved her hand over wounds and rose slowly, sweeping her gaze to the other figures that lay in neat rows. "No single Kelpie did this."

"Are you certain it was Kelpie?" Gideon asked mouth turned down as he glanced at a distant river, then at the small form of a child.

Lura pursed her lips. "Not certain, but from what the townsfolk described…" She shook her head. "It could be something else. But what? And why attack this village in such numbers?"

"Could Dothur have done this?" Gideon asked, turning to Arel.

The elf frowned. "He could've lain waste to this village with little effort, but it would be pointless to do so. These people are no threat to him or his power."

"Malcolm said the first arrived three nights past, though none in the village saw it, not even the wife of the poor soul who'd been taken when he'd gone outside to investigate his agitated oxen." Gideon paused and looked toward a small winding river that cut through the valley. "They didn't find his body, only muddy hoof prints leading toward Sruth Beag."

Lura studied the slow-moving river in the distance. "If a Kelpie lives in those waters, I would think they'd have known before now."

"They say Sruth Beag has never been home to a single Kelpie—much less in the numbers they saw here. Until now."

"That makes no sense," the elf said, shaking her head. "Kelpie are territorial. Once they claim a body of water as their own, they never leave it."

Gideon crossed his arms. "Should the Kelpie return tonight, we'll be ready."

"Will they fight alongside us?" Arel asked, glancing toward the villagers who gathered in small groups mourning the dead.

Nodding, Gideon swept his eyes over the elves who had formed a loose circle around them. A handful avoided his gaze, muttering. Arel shot them a look, then focused on

Gideon. "You're so sure they trust us? What makes you think want us to stand and fight with them?"

Lifting his chin, he said, "Because no one else will."

"And if they decide to attack us?" an elf from Oadsera challenged, his violet eyes flashing.

Lura took three huge strides toward him, shoving him back. "You are rank with fear, Gael. Perhaps you should stay behind and let the real fighters do their work."

Gael's lip curled, and he lunged at Lura, stopping when a dagger appeared in her hand, the tip pressed to the underside of his chin.

"Enough!" Arel yelled. "Save your anger for the creatures who plague this place!"

Gael held Lura's stare for a moment longer, finally shrugging and backing away. "We'll see who screams in fear when those monsters return."

"Aye. We will." Lura tucked her dagger into her belt and spun on her heel, stalking away.

Gideon watched her go, then leveled Gael with a hard look. "I hope you know whose side you're on."

The elf's mouth turned down.

"Your queen does not abide traitors. And neither do I."

"I am no traitor," he hissed.

"Prove it." Gideon turned and walked away.

The bodies of the fallen were shrouded and placed in a large pit in the village cemetery. There were too many to bury in single graves, and daylight would only last so long.

Better to get the dead in the ground lest predators smell the rotting flesh and come to feast in the night.

Sir Philip Wode, the country knight who'd been gifted the land for service to the crown, was one of the first killed when the creatures invaded the community. He'd lived in the small manor in the heart of the hamlet. Now the townsfolk were leaderless and scared. Malcolm, the blacksmith, took up the mantle of the fallen knight and spent the long hours of the afternoon with Gideon and Arel, shoring up what little defenses they could and discussing strategy. It was with a wary acceptance that the blacksmith took Arel's suggestions. His hatred for elves—though he'd never met one until that day—made him guarded.

Most of the villagers kept away from the Aos Sí, giving them cold stares and muttering about attacks in the east they'd gotten word of months ago. Many wondered if their aid was a plot to lure them into complacency, then slaughter them and move on to the next village. A group of four young men—barely a scrap of beard between them—swaggered by the elves brandishing scythes and bows. Gideon watched from the sagging roof of the tanner's cottage as they paused within earshot and hurled curses at the elven warriors.

He leaned against the stone and mud wall. "Have you got the skills to back those insults?"

The four men spun around, their gangly forms tensing as they met his gaze. One stepped forward, the leader of the ragtag group. "I wager I could best you!"

Gideon cocked a brow and stepped away from the structure. Walking slowly, he came into the afternoon light, his shadow stretching to where the young men stood. All but the leader shifted uncomfortably, darting glances at one another as they watched Gideon approach.

When he was an arm's length away, Gideon slowly drew his sword from its sheath, letting the blade rub against the leather with a drawn-out sound. "Here I am, little man." He opened his arms, the haft of his blade clutched in his fist. "Prove your mettle."

The leader swallowed hard, his eyes tracking the glint of Gideon's sword. "I'd rather spend my energy killing an elf," he blustered.

"Oh, aye?" Arel asked, having silently come upon the group. The three young men watching the exchange yelped, bumping into each other rather than getting too close to the Aos Sí fighter.

Chuckling, Gideon looked at the elf and said, "Perhaps you should teach them a lesson in humility."

Arel grinned and whipped his blade through the air. It spun in a mesmerizing blur as he launched himself at the men, disarming them in moments as they fumbled with their weapons. With the tip of his blade, he approached the leader, causing the man to back away, hands out in surrender. The elf prodded the air menacingly, never touching his skin as he herded the man backward.

Sweat beaded the leader's forehead as his progress abruptly stopped when he hit Gideon's chest. His legs trembled, and he fell to his knees, whispering, "Mercy."

Arel looked down at him, violet eyes flashing mischievously. "Mercy? Would you show my people mercy?"

The young man gulped. "Aye," he rasped, his face pleading.

Spinning his blade away from the man and into its sheath, Arel extended his arm. The leader looked at it as if it were a snake, then tentatively reached forward. They clasped wrists, and Arel hauled him to his feet.

The elf looked down at the man from his greater height, his striking face softening. "I am not your enemy."

Looking abashed, the young man nodded. "And I am not yours."

Gideon slapped the man on his back. "Now, if you truly wish to help your people and hone your skill, I am happy to show you a few moves that may save your life should your village again come under attack."

The man nodded, eyes darting from Arel to Gideon. Licking his lips, he said, "I'm Thaeren."

Glancing at Arel, Gideon gave a quick nod. Together, they rounded up the youths and took them to a small field. There, the warriors taught the young men to wield their crude weapons as instruments of war. By the time the four men cried peace, they were soaked in sweat, limbs trembling. But beneath that fatigue was a new-found sense of respect. The villagers who'd gathered to watch slapped the men on the back with murmurs of approval. A few separated themselves and approached Gideon and Arel, giving them sincere, though cautious, thanks. It was a start.

Come nightfall, Lura and Gael took posts on the highest points of the village—on the rooftops of the manor and smithy. Tucked in a deep crevice of the thatched roofs, they were invisible. Gideon, Arel, and the others hid in shadowy corners of the hamlet, each taking up a spot that would allow for an ambush should the creatures enter the town. Malcolm kept the farmers and the group of young men Gideon and Arel had trained hidden in a stable and armed with everything from swords to scythes. They would join the Aos Sí when and if the fighting began.

Back pressed to a wattle and daub wall, Gideon listened to a mother soothe her children, singing them to sleep with a lullaby he recalled from his brother's cradle days. Soft murmurs were eventually followed by snores.

Scanning the village, he caught the flash of eyes reflecting moonlight as Aos Sí met his gaze. Cold crept into his bones, and he spent many minutes watching his breath cloud before his lips. Winter was waning, but frost still coated the land each morning like a crystalline blanket. Tugging the hood of his cloak tighter about his head, he tucked his hands under his arms and closed his eyes, listening to the subtle shifts of the elves and the gentle song of the distant river.

It was well past midnight when a warble drifted into the air. Gideon stiffened and pulled his cloak off his head, looking toward the roof of the smithy. Gael, pale hand flashing under the light of the moon, motioned toward the fields east of the village. Gripping his sword, Gideon ducked into the shadows and strained his ears, listening for the sound of footfalls.

A lone rider approached, though to call him a rider was to believe that such a thing could fit within the natural realm. He was an affront to the senses. Headless, he sat atop a horse as black as the night save for the animal's eyes that glowed like coals from a fire. Clutched under the rider's arm was a severed head—pale like dough with saggy, rotting flesh. Sunk into the skull were eyes—twin balls of flame—that scanned the village with sickening intensity. They entered the center of the hamlet slowly, each hoof striking the ground with a soft thump. A foul stench, like fetid meat, came to him on the breeze, making his stomach churn. Gideon flexed his fingers along the haft of his sword, readying himself to attack, when the rider abruptly dropped the reins and raised his arm, swinging it forward with a jerk. From the darkness behind him emerged a dozen Kelpie.

Their forms resembled horses, though to look at them for more than a few moments shattered that illusion. With manes woven from the slimy leaves of plants from the depths of lakes or rivers and dripping with dank waters, they fanned out, sniffing the air and chuffing. They were walking nightmares led by a figure so frightening Gideon was forced to look away from its headless form lest he be caught in the gaze of those horrible eyes. Movement in the shadows indicated the Aos Sí were readying themselves. Gideon waited for a signal from Lura or Gael. His muscles tensed as he focused on the creatures that were stalking toward houses in search of victims. Watching their movements, it was clear that this was no random attack. Somehow, the headless rider had summoned the Kelpie and was using them to wipe out the entire village, one individual at a time. It made no sense. Why this village?

An eerie shriek rent the air, followed by a cacophony of wailing so like the horrible cries of the sluagh that he looked up, sure he would see them streaking across the sky. The Kelpie bolted toward the houses, rearing and thrashing their sodden hooves. Lura and Gael gave a series of shrill whistles, and Gideon leaped from the darkness, sword raised. With whoops and battle cries, the Aos Sí sprang from their hiding places. Malcolm burst through the stable, leading a group of men who swallowed their fear and charged.

The rider drew a sword so dark it blended with the night and cut through one man, then another. Farmers and craftsmen fled, only to be chased down by the headless phantom. Red eyes spilled terrible light on the fleeing men, illuminating their forms as they ran. Gideon snarled and gave chase, legs pumping on the hard-packed earth. He was no match for the speed of the demon horse, but he didn't need to catch the creature, only come within range. With a roar, he swung his sword, hurling it at the headless rider's back. It spun through the air, blade winking in the moonlight before it stabbed into the rider's form, impaling him. The creature yanked on the reins and came to a stop. Twisting his hand, he turned his mount and faced Gideon. From the severed head came a wet cackle as its eyes lit like kindling in a fire. All around him, Gideon heard the sounds of flesh meeting arrow and sword severing limb. Squeals of pain and yelps of fright filled the village. He dared not turn his attention away from the dark figure that slowly approached to see if the elves were beating the Kelpie back or dying beneath their slashing hooves and dagger-like teeth.

Gideon held his ground, accepting that he may be looking at the face of his death. He pulled a wickedly sharp dagger from his belt and spread his legs in a fighting stance. "Come on, you bastard!"

The skull grinned, revealing rows of rotted teeth. Dropping the reins, the rider reached up and ran a finger along the tip of the sword protruding from his chest. "Do you think your paltry weapons can kill me?" A wet clicking sound spilled from the skull's swollen lips. "I am not for you to kill." Pressing his palm against the tip of the blade, the rider pushed the metal back into his chest, pushing the sword out of his body one inch at a time until the weight of it ripped it from his flesh to fall useless on the ground. "Kill this army, and I will but raise another. Run along now, little lord. Tell your mistress we are coming… and there are none who can stop us."

Digging his heels into the horse, the rider bolted through the town, knocking over Kelpie, who watched their master abandon the fight. Aos Sí chased them down, slicing through equine backs and spilling their rank insides onto the earth. In minutes, it was over. A pall of silence fell over the town as Gideon stood, arms hanging limply at his sides, and stared into the darkness that embraced the rider and Kelpie like a mother.

CHAPTER TEN

Fiadh hobbled to her bed, sinking onto the pallet with a weary sigh. Between Dyvre and Kaelari, her mind and body were little more than a bag of bones and useless gray matter. Both had spent the last two days pushing her to her limits. Kaelari, always the perfectionist, wouldn't permit her to move on to a new skill until she'd mastered the one she'd been tasked with. And Riani—a formidable fighter in her own right—had joined her tutelage, increasing the intensity of each lesson.

Other Aos Sí found it amusing to watch their queen flail about and grumble at her lack of improvement. Even Sibaen, given to the people of Erabel as a symbol of her alliance with the Faoladh, often lounged in the shade observing the training, tongue lolling with a throaty laugh when Fiadh lost her patience. She did her best to ignore the attention, especially from Ellisar, who frequently lingered nearby. Though she couldn't always contain her temper and muttered vulgarities, she'd picked up from Gideon. Her mother, Riona, would've been appalled at her behavior. Young women, especially ones who find themselves in a seat of leadership, should not behave so poorly. But Fiadh's patience only lasted so long, and the ache in her heart couldn't be filled with hours of shooting arrows at targets, swinging her delicate blade, or calling on the elements to create wind and shift the earth. She had no intention of using weapons against mankind, but Riani and Kaelari—like Gideon—would hear none of that, convinced that the training of her body also trained her mind.

She could almost withstand the grueling hours in the arena with little complaint if not for the knowledge that once she left the field, Oadsera's seer would be waiting. Dyvre was convinced that Fiadh had abilities that rivaled his own and sought to draw them out.

In the quiet of the solar, he motioned for her to sit on the floor across from him. They faced each other, palms pressed together as though in prayer. He invaded her mind, peeling back layers of living to plumb the well of her magic. When he touched the core of it, she shrieked, body falling backward, head striking the stone floor. She lay there, stunned, staring at the wooden beams along the ceiling as he rose slowly and crouched above her. His perfect face, those striking violet eyes. He looked down at her with a crooked smile so like Veren's that a sob crawled up her throat, shaking her chest as it ripped free.

His face softened as she rolled to her side, clutching her ribs as though to keep herself from falling to pieces. "You grieve, and I am sorry for it," he said softly. "To you, I am his face upon the water."

She nodded and sat up slowly, wiping her eyes.

"In time, the hurt will dull."

Fiadh hung her head. "I know."

"Come," he reached out and hauled her up. "Let us see if we can use the energy within your sorrow for a different purpose."

Sighing, Fiadh rubbed her hands across her face and followed him as he led her to his bedchamber. Sitting on a small table was a shallow bowl made of onyx and filled with water. Dyvre told her to sit on the stool opposite it and stood behind her, hands resting on her shoulders. "There are only a handful of seers left, most having died in the Great War, or shortly after. It is a gift. And a curse."

She craned her neck to look up at him. "I'm not a seer, Dyvre."

He gave her a small smile. "How do you know?"

Her brow wrinkled, mouth turning down. "I... wouldn't I have felt... something?"

Dyvre shrugged. "Perhaps. But would you have known what it was had you felt it? Danu gave you many gifts. Let us see if this is one of them." He ran his hands down her arms and lifted them, gently placing each limb on either side of the bowl. "Lean forward and look into the water."

She did, spending many moments staring at her reflection. Darting her eyes to his where he leaned over her shoulder, she caught his gaze, then returned her attention back to the surface. Her breath sent tiny ripples along the thin skin of the water, and she followed them, watching as they hit the edge of the bowl and bounced back. It was mesmerizing. The subtle bands of water stretched back and forth from one side to the other. Cocking her head, she squinted, staring at the center of the bowl where soundless ripples clashed and parted. Her eyes widened as the space between the tiny current flickered with something that was not a reflection, something from within.

The room fell away from her consciousness. Dyvre's face disappeared until there was nothing but the point at which she stared. From outside herself, she heard the seer whispering. "Fix your mind on Zaerleria. Follow the tenor of her name, and you will find her."

She took a deep breath and conjured an image in her mind of the powerful elf. It was one she'd seen when Danu had shown her the past. The moment her mother, Threa, weak and heartbroken, had slipped into a dreamless sleep. Somehow, Zaeleria had known, had come, encasing Threa in a protective shell where she slumbered for decades. Until Riona crossed her path. Focusing on the memory of the seer, her violet eyes and knowing face, Fiadh stared into the water, willing herself to find the one she sought.

Minutes passed. Head pounding with the effort, she sighed, body sagging, and craned her neck to look at Dyvre. "I can't do it."

"You're trying too hard. Let the power of sight flow through you."

She made a frustrated noise. "I don't understand what you mean. I'm not like you."

He chuckled softly. "Aye, there is truth in that." Placing his hands on either side of her head, he angled her face to the scrying bowl. "You are not like me, child, for you are infinitely stronger."

"I—"

"Hush, now. Listen to my words. Listen, not with your ears but with your mind. With your well of power."

Fiadh wanted to shake her head, but his fingers held her in their gentle grip. Placing her arms on the table on either side of the bowl, she took a deep breath, letting it out slowly as Dyvre's voice filled the room. His words slipped through her skull, circling about her mind where she struggled to make sense of them. It was a strange language, melodious and intricate—vowels flowing into one another like a song. It was both familiar and foreign. The chanting continued, and she struggled to focus on it, her thoughts dulled as though muffled by the words themselves. Fiadh's eyes shifted to the pool of water, Dyvre's voice fading, having led her to some place she couldn't see but felt. Like a fish on a hook, she felt a subtle tugging, not in her mind, but in her core, where it bloomed. Her well of power opened like the petals of a flower—blood-red and pulsing.

Dyvre let go and stepped back, though she felt his presence behind her. Something shifted in the water as she stared into it: Zaeleria, tucked into the dark recess of a rocky ledge, stared back at Fiadh, a tired smile playing about her lips.

Fiadh fought the urge to reach out to her and kept her body still, instead sending thoughts to the Aos Sí seer, asking her where she was and how to find her. Cocking her head, Zaeleria tapped at Fiadh's mind, prodding her to use their connection like a tether and extend her sight to encompass the land in which the seer hid. Brows wrinkling, Fiadh tried to do as she was bid, slowly pulling her focus away from

Zaeleria to look at the elf's surroundings. Craggy rocks tucked in the folds of a mountain met her eyes. Fiadh's sight flickered like a candle near an open window. Sensing she was about to lose the connection, she zeroed in on Zaelaria, seeing the seer's weary gaze before their link was severed.

She was about to look away from the dark water when another image bubbled to the surface. Fiadh's mouth parted as Gideon's face filled her vision. His beard had grown out, much like it had been when she'd found him outside Dorcha Wood—bloodied and lost. The image she saw in the bowl was haggard. His full mouth turned down as he studied something she couldn't see. As though she called to him, he turned to her. Gasping, Fiadh leaned away from the bowl but kept her eyes on Gideon's face as he spoke. "We're too late. They're all dead."

Her chest constricted as the image grew in scope, revealing the smoldering remains of a village and the bodies of those who'd lived there scattered in tangled heaps. A soft mewl broke the silence in the room as Fiadh's eyes scanned the tragic scene upon the water's surface. The small currents flowed into each other, shattering the images only to conjure a new, darker picture. Hands curling into fists on either side of the scrying bowl, she watched as creatures flew through the sky, ran on the ground, and swam through rivers and lakes, led by a winged monster. A demon. Her heart beat wildly, blood pounding in her head, as the sinister being flapped his pale leathery wings, scanning the ground below. She felt the moment he sensed her presence and knew, from one ragged heartbeat to the next, that this was no glimpse into the future. This was now.

Dothur turned his head, pinning her to the stool under his fetid stare. She wanted to look away, to sever the connection and curl under a bench where he couldn't find her. But she sat, body rigid, fingernails digging into her palms. His cold, alien face shifted, black lips curling into a grotesque smile of pointed teeth. "I see you," he hissed, the words erupting from the dark surface of the water and crashing into her with such force her body flew back, smacking into Dyvre, who stood stunned.

The scrying bowl trembled, then cracked, splitting in two and spilling water onto the table and floor. Fiadh stared at the broken pieces. They were a warning.

CHAPTER ELEVEN

The people of Felmore stood in the town square furtively watching Lord Darragh as he strolled among them, arms loosely clasped behind his back, burly soldiers at his sides. Darragh's gaze slid from one person to another, assessing, choosing, casting aside. With a flick of his wrist, boys were pulled from the arms of their mothers, old men from their wives, and herded like sheep to a group of grim soldiers. Farmers and craftsmen. Apprentices and masters. The lord of the land took them all. And to those who looked closely, who truly knew their lord, what they saw in his face wasn't human. Something truly wicked surveyed the world from his eyes.

But woe to the villager who stared too long at the lord, for when those eyes fell on an onlooker, their mind froze, and they became little more than a puppet until they were broken and cast aside like a child's plaything. So, Felmore's folk bit their tongues, muffled their cries behind hands pressed to their mouths, and watched as men young and old were conscripted for service in Darragh's army.

Crom Cruach surveyed the townsfolk through Lord Darragh's eyes, his body far from Felmore, deep in Malver Gorge. He served his master, Dothur, though it rankled to be bound to another as he'd been bound in Rygeil's service. But the demon was strong. Too strong to overthrow.

Dothur would soon travel to the Lloathren Mountains. A well of dark power lived in the heart of those peaks, and he would suckle from it, regaining his former strength. Until then, Dothur took command of the sinister creatures who flocked to their master, ready to do his bidding. Carmun's son used magic to breed demon stock from his minions, giving rise to rabid soldiers whose lust for blood matched his own. He molded his army and unleashed them in contingents, each led by one both loyal and powerful. They would feed on the fear and blood of mankind, growing stronger. Insatiable. Feeding until their inherent darkness built to a crescendo. And when they were an unstoppable force, when Dothur had drained the well of dark power, and Darragh's part was complete, they would turn their eyes on the elves and slaughter them.

But that time had yet to come. Crom bided his time, burrowing into Darragh's mind like a bloated tick. Through the weak lord, he lived among the children of men, and even if that visceral experience was born of possession, it was a heady thing, and Crom Cruach relished it.

The demon squatting inside Darragh sniffed the air, licking his lips. Their fear and suffering was a sweet scent, their choked cries an aphrodisiac. *How easy it would be to crush them all*, he thought, batting away the true Darragh's fumbling as the man sought to regain control. *Save your strength, my lord. I'll let you go when the time is ripe and not a moment before.*

The sound of Lord Darragh sniggering sent chills down the spines of those who heard, causing some to look away and others to make signs of protection amidst muttered prayers to the goddess.

"My lord," Donal said quietly. "If you take all the men, there will be none to fill their roles."

Darragh smirked. "Oh, aye?"

"The village will suffer, my lord."

He studied the group of men and boys who'd been selected. "Well, we wouldn't want that, would we?"

"Nay, my lord. The castle depends on the village folk for its survival."

"Does it now?" Darragh cocked an eyebrow and looked at Donal. Whatever the commander saw had him glance away. "So be it, Donal. You may choose those who can remain."

Donal bowed and strode to the group of villagers, singling out those whose place in Felmore was necessary. If he had his way, they'd all go back to the arms of spouses and mothers, but he knew he couldn't thwart his lord—if his lord was still in that being who walked in Darragh's body. Whatever had transpired a sennight ago had changed the Lord of Felmore, made him into something… other. Even now, Donal couldn't hold his gaze, afraid that what he saw lurking there would come for him as he'd seen happen to others who balked at ever more sinister commands.

Soldiers had begun talking in their barracks. There were whispers of witchery, and, more than once, he'd seen men slip into the darkness, abandoning their service and the castle for parts unknown. He didn't blame them and had even considered doing the same. The only thing that kept him from leaving was the hope that Lord Darragh, the true Lord Darragh, would return and set things right.

When those selected had been thinned to a mere thirty, Donal returned to Darragh, who stood staring into the distance, eyes fixed on Dorcha Wood. He followed the lord's gaze but saw nothing more than an expanse of trees. Clearing his throat, he said, "My lord, the men are ready." Darragh slowly turned to face him, and as their gazes met, Donal saw a shadow flit across his lord's eyes, casting a dark hue over the sclera. Swallowing hard, the commander motioned to the waiting men. "Your orders, my lord?"

"Outfit the men with short swords."

"And the boys?"

Darragh considered, an ugly smile crawling across his mouth. "Sling targets upon their backs and let my archers test their skill with arrows on something that moves."

"My lord," Donal gasped. "I won't endanger our men."

"No?"

Donal shook his head.

Darragh folded his arms. "Hm. Perhaps you're right. We could put one on your back instead."

The commander's lips mashed together, and his eyes grew cold. "That won't be necessary."

"Are you sure?"

"I'll have the men outfitted."

"See that you do."

Not waiting for his commands to be doled out, the Lord of Felmore returned to his keep. Ignoring servants who bustled about, he strode through the great hall and into the dungeon, where he walked into Haegna's old cell. Placing a torch in a sconce, he pulled out the stool and sat before the scrying bowl. He preferred the dark. The dank stone walls surrounding the cell blocked out the incessant chatter of the minds above. Gripping the edges of the table, he closed his eyes and started to chant. Words laced with dark magic fell from his lips, dancing across the black liquid in ripples. Flinging his head back, the muscles of his neck stood rigid, veins throbbing, as Crom Cruach erupted from Darragh's body, hovering in the air for a moment before diving into the water. Darragh went limp, flopping to the ground face-first with a meaty thud. A thin line of blood trailed from his nostril and onto the floor, where it pooled.

Oily blond hair clung to his skull, sticking to pallid skin covered in a thin layer of sweat. Gasping, Darragh came to, cracking open his eyes to survey his surroundings. Wincing, he brought shaky fingers to the corner of his mouth and wiped away a trail of drool, pausing when he noticed smears of blood. Swiping the back of his hand under his nose, he blinked, grimacing at the grime-covered stone beneath his cheek. Rolling onto his side with a groan, Darragh tried to make sense of where he was—when he was—head pounding viciously as he struggled to recall the last clear memory, realizing he'd been in this very cell, seated at his mother's vile scrying bowl. *How long have I been out?* he

wondered, irked that he'd been so weak as to lose consciousness, to begin with.

With a grunt of effort, he sat up and clutched his head.
As the fuzziness left his mind, he realized he wore a different
tunic and leggings than what he'd recalled. Rubbing his
hand along the woolen fabric covering his thigh, Darragh
flipped through vague images in his mind. They were
yellowed and dull, grainy, as though he were looking
through the thin film of a water bladder against the light. As
if he'd watched the world around him as though separate
from it. Frowning, he slowly raised his head and stared at the
bowl sitting on the table.

"He wakes," a voice whispered from the water. "Come
closer, my lord. I have something to tell you." Darragh's eyes
went round, and he braced his hands on the floor, scooting
his body backward. A loud sigh emanated from the bowl.
"Fear does not become you. Do you think I am bound by
this witch's tool? That I cannot hurt you with a *Word*?"

The scrying bowl trembled, and Darragh watched in
awestruck fear as the dark water rose from its center like a
spike, curling at the tip to point at him. Like a finger, it
waved him over, the motion accompanied by a raspy voice.
"I grow tired of your whimpers."

Darragh clamped his mouth shut.

"Rise, Lord of Felmore, and see the face of the god who
will shape your destiny." Crom Cruach waited for a
moment, sensing Darragh's reluctance. "Rise!" he yelled,
the force of his command creating a tiny wave along the
surface of the scrying bowl.

As though he were little more than a marionette,

Darragh got to his feet and took a few stilted steps toward the water. Looking at the dark liquid, he saw a grotesque creature—face covered in fleshy lumps of skin.

The demon smiled, revealing a set of rotted teeth. "While I've enjoyed my sojourn in your body, I grew weary of your puling form."

The man paled. That thing was in my head? *Inside* me?

The demon laughed, the sound bouncing against the stone of Haegna's cell. "Oh, aye! And a grand time I had! You shall see evidence of it when you leave this cell. Until then, listen to what I have to say."

Darragh narrowed his eyes and mashed his lips.

"Your anger is amusing, but do not forget that you are naught but a pawn for me to wield. Should I wish it, I could force you to remove the dagger from your belt," he taunted, weaving a spell into his words and watching with glee as the Lord of Felmore removed the blade and raised it to his neck, "and open your own throat."

The metal pricked Darragh's skin, drawing a tiny bead of blood. Arm shaking as he fought against the demon, he stared into the liquid and rasped. "Enough."

Lifting his chin with a triumphant gesture, Crom Cruach released him. The dagger fell to the floor with a clang, and Darragh stared at it as though it were a venomous snake.

"I have left you a gift, Lord Darragh, which you will wear lest you wish me to visit my wrath upon you and your men. The medallion you wear is more than a trinket. It is power. My power. And I have bestowed it on you so that you may fulfill your destiny as ruler."

Reaching into his tunic, Darragh drew out the medallion, letting it dangle on its leather thong. It was a crude circle bearing a series of foreign markings at the center of which was an eye. He stared at it, unnerved by the sensation of it staring back. The disc thumped against his chest as he let go.

"My eye is upon you, Lord Baoill. Pray what I see is rooted in *my* will… not yours."

He clenched his hands into tight fists and ground his teeth until they ached. But in the end, Lord Darragh dipped his head to the old god, as Crom Cruach knew he would.

"A wise decision. Due to your—" the demon paused, smirking, "absence. You may be unaware of what has transpired in realms you call allies or enemies. A war is coming, though I imagine it is one even your grandfather, Magnar, would have cowered to witness. Make no mistake. The kingdoms of men and elves will fall, and those who are obedient… those who curry favor in deeds and actions shall find themselves rulers in a new era. I see you sitting upon a throne."

"What must I do?" Darragh asked, his wariness evaporating as opportunity dangled its sweet lure.

"For now, you will do nothing. Listen to those who come with wild tales of beasts and blood but offer no support. Tell them to seek counsel with King Stephan. Assure them you are doing the same."

"The king does naught for the Western Fold! He would see us fall under elven rule!" Darragh spat.

Crom Cruach sniggered. "He is weak and weak men… well, they are easily dealt with." A cruel smile tugged at Darragh's lips. The demon knew how to ply Felmore's lord, and he did so deftly. "Admire the changes I've wrought for your people. Feast upon their obedience. But know that when I command you, you will submit, or I will carve my way through your mind until you're nothing more than a meat sack." Crom Cruach's image faded to a shadow in the scrying bowl, slowly disappearing with a whisper. "Soon, we will go to Taigon, where you will fulfill your destiny."

CHAPTER TWELVE

Gideon and Arel took two Aos Sí warriors and resumed their route to intercept Zaeleria. The others remained behind to aid the small hamlet should the Kelpie and demon rider—a Dullahan, the elves called it—return. It was a tenuous alliance against a greater threat, but having seen what came in the night, the elves were keen for a fight. Already, plans were being laid, traps to ensure none escaped another attack.

Before leaving, Gideon watched Malcolm offer mugs of ale to the Aos Sí, who stood in a loose circle strategizing. The blacksmith was quickly welcomed into the discussion, the action prompting others to join. Soon, the group was comprised of an equal number of men and elves—a sight Gideon never thought he'd see in his lifetime. It was as though Fiadh's vision of the future was slowly coming to fruition.

Before heading north, Arel had them follow the tracks of the Kelpie and Dullahan. At first sight, they looked like prints of a herd of small horses, though on closer inspection, one could see the cloven tracks of Kelpie as each false hoof split into three toes capped in sharp nails. Crouching to inspect them more closely, Gideon wondered if those nails could cleave a man. He ran a finger in the deep groove of one of the prints, noting how it cut through hard-packed soil, even splitting rock into shards. What kind of beasts were these? His grandmother had told him stories in his youth, but he could remember little more than tales about children dragged into the water and never to be seen again. The elves had a deeper knowledge, Arel having regaled him with the dark history of a creature whose violence was matched by its appetite. Shapeshifters, Kelpie had long preyed on mankind, often taking the forms of pure white horses. Should someone find themselves astride their back, they'd be unable to free themselves, their limbs twined in water plants and stuck to the Kelpie's skin. Once drowned, Kelpies ate their victims at their leisure.

But what came to the village surpassed even Aos Sí knowledge of the creatures. They were not known to hunt in packs nor travel too far from their lakes and rivers. It appeared the Dullahan commanded them, and, of that demon, the elves knew little. One had not been seen in centuries, and the stories were forgotten.

"Do you believe the Dullahan commanded them?" Gideon asked, shifting his body to look at Arel.

"No. There are too many. I'd wager that Dothur is behind these attacks. Perhaps the Dullahan is one of his commanders."

"Can it be killed?"

"I don't know."

The shores of Sruth Beag offered no clues about where they came from and in whose command. Among the mud and rocks, they saw nothing more than tracks leading into the water. Even the hooves of the Dullahan's mount appeared to lead there. When Gideon asked Arel about it, the elf shrugged. "Mayhap it lives in the deep with the Kelpie."

Gideon made a face, unconvinced. The surface of the lake was smooth, glasslike, and so dark it looked like a black pit. As he stared at it, the hair on the back of his neck stood on end as though something looked back at him from the darkness. Taking a step away from the water's edge, he nudged Arel. "Unless you're planning on entering those waters, I suggest we move on."

Arel's striking face remained fixed on the dark water for a moment before he gave a curt nod. "Aye. Let's go."

They journeyed into the evening, not stopping until the sun began its descent. All the while, Gideon kept to himself, struggling to rein in his thoughts and keep his eyes from drifting east toward Aishling. But the hours wore him down, a crick forming in his neck from turning his head too often.

Arel interrupted his lonely musings. "What ails you?"

Gideon caught his violet stare. Glancing to the east, he said, "I worry about my foundling. Should creatures like we saw be on the move, she could be at risk. Though, I admit she lives on a remote homestead, making it less likely." He sighed. "All the same, I worry about her. She'd be safer in Erabel."

"You think this was not a solitary attack?"

He pursed his lips. "I don't know. It doesn't feel random. It's almost as if it's a test, like a training."

The elf wrinkled his brows.

"What I mean is," Gideon explained, "perhaps Dothur is testing his army on small towns. You know, honing their skills as he prepares for an attack on your people."

Arel's mouth pulled down. "If what you suggest is true, that could align with the idea of the Dullahan in the role of commander."

"We should consider stopping at other villages as we head north. See if they've come under attack."

Nodding, Arel picked up the pace, the other two elves easily matching his stride. Gideon mustered his strength and broke into a jog, keeping to the rear of the group rather than exhausting his body too soon by trying to remain at their sides. They often stopped, though it was obvious it was for his benefit.

In the late afternoon, Arel sent Elraen to investigate the surrounding area for signs of human habitation. The elf, an unusually tall and aloof fighter who often scouted ahead of the group and came back to report his findings, loped through the landscape with little sound of his passing and was soon out of sight. The trio continued without him for a span of time, stopping when he returned, emerging from a cluster of trees. Gideon stood, favoring his bad leg as it throbbed. Knee bent to relieve the strain, he resisted the urge to rub his muscles and listened as Elraen delivered his findings.

"I found naught but the remains of a remote farmstead," he told Arel.

Arel's brows creased with a frown. "Remains? What did you see?"

Elraen's mouth turned down. "Only claw marks and blood."

Gideon gripped his sword and stared in the direction Elraen had come. "Are you sure nothing lived?"

"Aye."

"What about the surrounding area? Was there a body of water nearby?" Arel asked.

Shaking his head, Elraen spat on the ground. "It wasn't Kelpie. There was a stink, like rotting flesh, hanging in the air. Whatever slaughtered the family was something I've never come across."

Gideon's jaw tightened. "I don't like this. Whatever is attacking these settlements… it feels coordinated."

"Perhaps Zaeleria has knowledge of it," Arel offered. "We must press on."

Loosening his grip on the hilt, Gideon rolled his neck and nodded. "Aye. Let's go." But uneasiness washed over him as he followed the elves, eyes flicking from shadow to shadow, wondering if something watched their progress. If it bided its time, waiting for a moment to strike. With those misgivings came thoughts of Aishling and an urgency to finish this task and fetch her. Conjuring a memory of her face, Gideon wondered if she'd welcome the sight of him. The sound of her cries as he'd left her with Owen and Marion, the middle-aged couple who'd taken the child when he'd gone to Felmore, still haunted his dreams. Would she turn her back on him for leaving her? Would she come willingly? He shook his head. It mattered not if she wanted to go to Erabel. He'd take her there regardless. She'd be safe, and so would the couple who took her in. He hadn't been able to save his brother and parents, but he could ensure Aishling was protected—that she had a future.

By nightfall, Gideon's legs felt like jelly, and he collapsed beneath the bowers of an ancient pine that easily stood two hundred feet above the ground with branches spanning thirty feet. Leaning against the trunk, Gideon dug into his satchel and pulled out a loaf of bread and a wedge of cheese, offering some to the Aos Sí. Arel took a portion and walked to a small creek. Setting aside his meal, he dipped his hands into the water, cupping the liquid in his palms and raising them toward the sky while muttering a prayer to Danu.

Gideon had seen the ritual each evening and knew the elf was communicating with the Great Mother while using that link to reach for Zaeleria. A stiff wind bit through his tunic, and he pulled his cloak tighter, tugging the hood over his head so that only his eyes peered from beneath it. The water must be near freezing this far north, but Arel didn't seem to notice, so intent on whatever connection he felt. The whisper of his voice came to an end, and Gideon watched him drink what was left in his palms, the sweep of his fingers in a gesture of worship following the act.

Arel rose slowly, leaning over to fetch his food, then joined the others. "She's not far, just over that ridge." All eyes followed his hand, and Gideon's shoulders sagged as he noted the distance. It would be a steep climb when they reached the mountainside.

"Gideon," the elf said, "if you feel you cannot make the journey…"

He grimaced. "It's that obvious?"

The elf chuckled.

"You could've traveled twice the distance today, couldn't you?"

Arel shrugged. "Not twice the distance."

Gideon snorted. "Three times, then."

The Aos Sí laughed, their eyes bright as they ribbed each other and boasted of how far they could run in a day. Gideon watched the exchange, feeling like an old man among the young, yet knowing they had walked the earth far longer than he.

Seshka, a sprightly elf who'd readily volunteered for the mission, flashed him a smile from beneath her cloak, her white teeth a striking contrast to her lustrous, dark skin. "Oh, I think Gideon was holding back. Not wishing us to feel inferior."

He barked a laugh and puffed his chest. "I wouldn't want to exhaust you all should I go at my normal pace."

She grinned and tore off a hunk of bread, chewing thoughtfully as conversation circled the concern over Gideon's ability to continue the journey.

When small talk drifted to silence, Arel eyed Gideon's leg, watching the man knead his thigh. He felt the elf's stare and paused the motion of his hand, curling his fingers. Sighing, he looked at the elf. "I appreciate your concern, but I'd like to continue. I—" He hung his head for a moment, then looked up. "I need to see this through."

Arel nodded and slapped him on the back. "Then you shall." He smirked and added, "And we will go slowly to ensure you do."

"Your patience for this feeble human is commendable. Truly," he said with a sardonic smile.

They lay side by side that night—three Aos Sí and one man—using each other's warmth against the bitter wind. At one point, Gideon woke, thinking he heard the soft pad of footsteps, the rustle of branches bending with someone's passing, but when he cracked open his eyes, nothing was there. The moon shone through the branches of the trees as shadows danced in the dimness, each feeling like a living thing. The sensation of being watched lingered, and Gideon swept his eyes about the darkness, fighting exhaustion and, eventually, losing the battle. As his eyes drifted closed again, he could've sworn he heard the murmur of voices.

As dawn spread across the frosty landscape, Arel nudged Gideon awake. Squinting, he looked up at the elf, groaning as he rolled to his side and got to his knees. "You're much too spry for this early in the morning," he grumbled, staggering to his feet and bending over to grab his blanket and roll it up.

"I do it to annoy you." Arel handed him an oatcake. "It's good to see it's working."

Gideon chewed slowly, holding the elf's humorous stare.

"Are you sure the Great War wasn't started because the Aos Sí are so irritating?"

He chuckled. "Our historians forgot to include that bit. Though I believe it's your kind that is most vexing."

With a grin, Gideon popped the last of his food in his mouth and brushed off his hands, taking the water skin from Seshka's outstretched hand. He noted the Aos Sí were already packed and ready for the journey. Their efficiency put his former army to shame. As he washed his breakfast down with a couple of swigs of water, he recalled the strange sounds and feelings he'd heard the night before. Clearing his throat, he asked, "Did any of you hear or see something come into our camp last night?"

Seshka looked at Arel, who nodded. "A couple of Urisk have been following us since we left Sruth Beag," she told him. "They're rather reclusive and stealthy. I'm surprised you sensed them."

"Urisk?"

"Hm. How to explain?" Arel said. "To your eyes, they would appear to be goat-people. They rarely leave their territory, but when you appeared among us, they grew curious."

"You've known they were following us all this time?"

Arel nodded.

"And why didn't you tell me?"

The elf shrugged. "I didn't want to alarm you. They have no ill intent. Their early history is much like ours. They once lived among mankind but were driven out of their lands and hunted. Those who remained went into hiding.

But the Urisk hold no hatred for your people. They wish to return to the old ways when they lived among you."

"Huh." He put his hands on his hips. "I thought I knew so much of the world. Yet, with each passing day, I realize I knew very little." Gideon's eyes swept the camp, delving into the shadows under the trees, wondering if the goat people were there, watching. "They need not hide. I don't wish them harm."

Arel gave him a faint smile. "I have said as much. For now, they remain hidden. In time, they may reveal themselves."

Nodding, Gideon sat on a rock and laced his boots, readying himself for a grueling trek to the jagged mountain range Arel had indicated. He felt like a burden. If not for the promise he'd made to Fiadh, he'd abandon this quest and fetch Aishling. But he had to see this through. What Fiadh was trying to accomplish was bigger than him. Slinging his satchel across his back, he set off with the Aos Sí, quickly falling to the end of their group. Despite the many stops and slowed pace, Gideon struggled to keep up as the steepness of the land took its toll. They passed no more villages, the terrain too rocky and steep to sustain farming.

When they reached the base of the mountain two days later, beyond which Zaeleria hid in waiting, he craned his neck, studying the angle of the climb, legs trembling at the thought of scaling it. The camp was made beneath an outcropping of rock that blocked the group from the rain that had turned into hail the day before. They sat around a weak fire, faces obscured under hoods, though Gideon wondered if the elves were as affected by the cold and damp. While he hunched beneath his cloak, arms tucked around his chest to keep warm, they chatted amicably, hands and teeth flashing against the dark fabric as they gesticulated and smiled.

As the evening wore on, he caught glimpses of movement beyond the flickering flames and tried to focus on them, wanting to see the elusive Urisk Arel had told him about. But if they were there, none showed themselves, and he was left wondering what kind of people they were. Sleep came fitfully on the hard ground, wind and hail howling around the mountain. Under his sodden cloak, Gideon felt the cold in his bones, reminding him of a time he and Doran had been caught in a winter storm with their father while on a hunting trip. They'd lost one of their men that night. He'd wandered from their camp at some point before dawn and not returned, having gotten lost in the blinding snow and frozen to death. It was a harsh lesson on the dangers of foul weather but one he'd never forgotten. Pulling his hood so far over only the tip of his nose was visible, he forced his mind to quiet and waited for the dawn.

By late afternoon the next day, Gideon knew he'd reached a breaking point. Rain pellets had turned to snow as they climbed, making the journey up the side of the mountain slippery and treacherous. Swaying with pain and fatigue, he stumbled to a mound of rock and slumped, hands dangling from his knees. Seshka elbowed Arel, who stopped the group and leaped over boulders like a mountain goat as he came to Gideon.

He looked up at the elf through weary eyes, mouth pulling down with strain. "I'm done."

Arel pursed his lips. "Aye. I've watched you push yourself too hard."

He shook his head, lip curling his disgust. "I'm no better than a cripple!"

A look passed between Arel and Elraen. After a curt nod, Elraen crouched in front of Gideon. "If you allow it, I can look at your leg."

Gideon looked up at Arel. "He has healing ways. It is one of the reasons he was chosen to accompany us."

"You can heal me?" Gideon said, looking back at the male on the ground before him.

Elraen glanced at Gideon's thigh. "I promise nothing, but I may be able to mend the muscle."

"Why didn't you offer this before? My leg's been killing me!"

The elf chuckled. "I didn't think you'd accept."

"Wrong assumption. Have at it, my friend. You certainly can't make it any worse." As Gideon leaned back and stretched out his leg, he caught a look that passed between the three Aos Sí. "What?"

"You called me friend," Elraen said quietly.

"Aye, I did."

The elf smiled and kneeled on the ground, turning his hands, palms up. Gideon listened to the murmur of his voice, the lilting cadence of his words as he prayed to Danu, flakes of snow falling silently all around them. It was surreal.

To be here. With people he'd been told were little more than murdering beasts. As his chanting ended, Elraen leaned forward and swept his hands over Gideon's limb before pressing them to his thigh. Closing his eyes, he cocked his head and kneaded the flesh, feeling beyond the leather leggings and layer of skin. Brow creasing, he said, "The wound is not old, but it healed oddly."

"Can you mend it?" Gideon asked, tracking the elf's movements.

"I would need to tear the muscle and bring it back together." He sat back and looked up at Gideon. "It will be painful and would be tender."

He nodded. "I don't mind the pain. Will I be able to continue the journey?"

Elraen eyed his leg. "Aye. Though you'll likely be even slower than you already are," he said with a smirk, adding, "That is, until it heals fully."

Gideon shook his head and grinned. "I'll be sure to temper my speed when I'm fully restored so you can continue to feel superior."

The healer laughed and got to work. As Elraen's hands moved over Gideon's old injury, the elf chanted, and he could've sworn that for a moment, he heard the soft response of a female voice. It was indeed painful as the elf tore apart the badly mended muscle. Gritting his teeth, Gideon stared at the horizon, seeing the world before him through flecks of snow. At one point, his thigh felt as though it burst into flame, and he looked down, shocked to see nothing more than Elraen's hand pressed to his leg. The heat lessened, growing warm, tingling with pins and needles, until it felt no different than his other limb, save for the subtle warmth of Elraen's hands.

Standing, the healer reached down and took Gideon's arms in a firm grip, hauling him to his feet. Gingerly putting his full weight on his leg, he tested his muscles, feeling them stretch and flex. Rubbing his hand along his thigh, he marveled at the relief he felt even through the raw soreness. Taking a few steps, he pinned Elraen with a look of wonder. "I could've used your talent on the battlefield! You know, I've got a few other old wounds." Giving the elf a friendly pat on his shoulder, Gideon said, "Thank you."

Elraen nodded and flashed a smile. "You're welcome… my friend."

CHAPTER THIRTEEN

Perched atop Meara and with Kaelari at her side, Fiadh rode toward the southern border of Dorcha Wood, a place she avoided for the bad memories it held. Krulan growled softly as they neared the edge of the forest, tugging on the edge of Fiadh's tunic when he deemed she'd gone far enough. She slid off the unicorn's back and studied the trees. Gone was the life that had once bloomed within them, replaced with rot. Gnarled trunks, covered in thick layers of slimy moss and blackened lichen, spread outward from Felmore. Along the ground lay a carpet of fungi and the putrid remains of dead animals and rotting plant life.

Sibaen, tribute from the man-wolves, froze and sniffed the air, body hunched in a feral crouch. She sneezed and rubbed her snout, eyes flicking to Fiadh, the coarse hair on her back bristling. "You must return to Erabel." She reached for Fiadh, the sharp points of black claws elongating from the tips of her fingers.

"What happened here?" Fiadh asked Kaelari, holding a hand toward Sibaen, who snarled softly, trying to pull her away from the unnatural decay. Meara snorted and pawed the ground, the whites of her eyes showing.

"I don't know. One of my scouts came across it while patrolling Dorcha Wood." She crouched and traced the blood-red edge of a mushroom, rubbing her fingers together, smearing residue that attached itself to her skin like a parasite. Wiping her hands on her leggings, Kaelari surveyed the trees. "From the decay, I'd say it started months ago, but I know that's wrong. As impossible as it seems, it's much newer than that. Days, maybe." Frowning, she spun slowly on her heel, studying a healthy expanse of the forest that led to Erabel and beyond, adding, "And it's spreading."

Fiadh got to her knees and pressed her palms to the ground, cocking her head with a grimace as she made contact with the sickness that rooted itself in the earth. Digging her fingers into the rotted soil, she felt a warm pulse of malice-filled energy radiating up her fingers. Krulan bared his teeth, sensing what she felt and uneasy at its meaning. Gritting her teeth, Fiadh delved deeper, reaching for Danu, wondering if she'd been cut off from this part of the forest. Or worse. If she were succumbing to whatever infected it. Minutes passed as she reached for the Great Mother. But the goddess was gone from this place, as though she'd been chased from it like a child runs from an incoming tide.

Slowly pulling her fingers from the soil, Fiadh was about to release her connection when she felt an awareness tap at her mind. She threw up impenetrable mental walls, shielding herself, as a sinister consciousness prowled through her skull, seeking entry. It was a familiar invasion. One she'd felt as her kingdom was attacked. Crom Cruach.

Snarling, Fiadh lashed out at the old god, pummeling his oily will with magic born of Danu. She cast spells to repel his advance, needle-like daggers of thought, rebuffing him, smiling grimly as he retreated. When she let go of her connection, she sat back on her heels and looked at where her hands had pressed to the ground. A patch of healthy soil in a loose circle sat surrounded by the rot of Crom Cruach's toxic evil. And within it, a tiny green shoot rose from the ground in defiance of the darkness surrounding it. She stroked the budding leaf and murmured a spell she hoped would shield it from the encroaching rot.

"What did you feel?" Kaelari asked after Fiadh whispered a prayer to the Great Mother.

"Crom Cruach."

The elf hissed and drew her sword, vibrant blue eyes darting from tree to tree as Sibaen released a menacing growl, teeth flashing between her lips. The sound was echoed by Krulan, who stalked around Fiadh in a tight circle.

"He's returned. If he ever left." Fiadh rose and brushed her hands on her tunic, following the Cù-Sìth's progress as he paced, hackles raised. She looked out at Felmore through a break in the decaying tree line. The heads of Rivya and her pups were gone, though the wall still bore stains of old blood below where the stakes had been erected. Her heart burned with anger, and she felt her well of magic swell in response. With it came memories of what she'd done in the name of wrath. Glaring at the castle, Fiadh breathed deeply through her nose, tempering her emotions, each inhalation diminishing her fierceness until all that was left were embers.

If the demon aligned with Darragh, they needed to fortify and extend their barriers. Now, more than ever, they must shield Dorcha Wood lest they find the demon's evil at their borders. The council would agree, or she would rally those who supported her and do what she must in defiance of their decision.

Closing her eyes, she focused her mind and reached out. *Dasha, come to me.*

The raven acknowledged her thought and left the safety of Erabel, flying on swift wings through the forest to her outstretched arm. He clacked his beak, and she stroked his breast. *I need your eyes and wings, my friend. Search Dorcha Wood and show me how far the rot extends into the forest.*

Dasha butted her fingers and launched into the air, flying low through thick branches, then up and above the canopy. Fiadh opened her mind and flew with him, in him, seeing the decaying forest as he swooped in and out of the tree line. The ground was black and sickly grey. Fingers of rot reached into the healthy landscape, causing leaves to wilt and curl as though they could escape the smothering toxic moss's relentless approach. On and on it went, feeding off the forest like a parasite. Nearly the entire southern border of Dorcha Wood was overcome.

With a soft flurry of wings, Dasha returned to Fiadh, landing on her arm and racing to her shoulder, where he plucked at her hair. "Ssh," she crooned, fingering the feathers along his beak. He gurgled, violet eyes wild.

"Return to Erabel." He nipped at her ear with his beak. "Dasha. Please."

Tilting his head to stare at her with his left eye, he poured his fear and worry into her mind. She took it, whispering to him before finally kissing his beak and commanding him to go. Unable to refuse, the raven took to the air, looking back at her with pleading before disappearing into the trees.

You should return with him, Krulan told her.

And leave Dorcha Wood to rot? I can't do that, Krulan. I won't.

He grumbled, flashing his teeth.

"Kaelari," Fiadh said, turning to the elf. "We need to keep a close watch on this." She scanned the ragged line of growth that separated the decay from the rest of the woods.

"I will assign a watch. Perhaps Krulan's pack can assist."

The Cù-Sìth rumbled in agreement.

"There has to be something we can do to slow it down," Fiadh muttered, resting her hands on her hips.

Sibaen's husky voice interrupted her thoughts. "You should leave and consult the seer." Fiadh looked at her. "Even my people know of the knowledge and power they wield."

"I will speak with him, but I'm not leaving just yet."

The Faoladh dipped her head and stepped back, toe claws digging into the soil, making deep ruts. Fiadh stared at the disturbed earth, at the tiny web of roots now exposed to the light. Bending down, she touched the tendrils, feeling the life that throbbed in them. Speaking more to herself than the audience that watched her, she said, "We'll create a wall shielding the remainder of the Dorcha Wood from this encroaching threat."

"A wall?" Kaelari asked.

"Aye." Moving to an untouched patch of earth a few feet from the edge of Crom Cruach's poison, Fiadh raised her arms and began to chant, weaving spells to call the roots of plants, commanding them to sprout. Pulling them from deep within the ground and imbuing them with spells of protection. Woody shoots erupted from the dirt, writhing like worms, folding in on themselves and reaching upward, creating a living bulwark. Tiny buds grew along the thick tendrils, splitting open to reveal pale green vines that wrapped around the limbs until all that was visible was a mass of greenery. Lowering her arms, Fiadh studied the growth, pressing her palm to the thickest part to feel the magic flowing through it and test its strength. It was no larger than the width of her extended arms and shoulder height.

Kaelari's mouth pulled down as she walked around it, Sibaen at her heels sniffing the small barrier. "The demon's evil will swallow it whole and continue to advance. You cannot believe it would stop its progress."

Fiadh shrugged. "It might slow it down."

Kaelari folded her arms, face pinched.

"What harm is it to try?" Fiadh asked, pinning the elf with a look. "Aren't the lives within Dorcha Wood worth saving?"

"I thought you wished to extend Erabel's protections into the forest. Now, you wish to build walls like those of men. It is not our way."

Gripping a woody vine, Fiadh tugged, feeling the structure, seeing it for what it was. Aye, it may keep the rot from spreading and shelter those within it. For a time. But it would also keep others out. Quinn and others like him would be barred from entering, from seeking sanctuary. She realized that at its heart, it was a reflection of Felmore, making her stomach churn. Sighing, she held her hands above the bulwark. Vines twitched and shifted, moving toward the earth, where they spread out in a knotted carpet. When the last greenery settled into place, Fiadh hung her head. "I need to do something. If Crom Cruach's evil spreads, Erabel's barrier won't matter."

"Let's not borrow worry," Kaelari told her, pulling her away. "Sibaen is right. You should go back to Erabel and speak with Dyvre. He may know how to combat this." She added with a sweep of her arm.

Grim faces met them as they crossed into Erabel. Fiadh scanned the group gathered in the great hall and nodded at Riani. She came forward and dipped her head, a braid of dark hair slipping over her shoulder to hang above the earthy green of her tunic. "Ravens, sent from Oadsera, have arrived along with a hawk sent by one of Arel's contingent. Ellisar opened the missives they bore and shared the news with the council."

Fiadh cocked an eyebrow. "Did he?"

"He said news from the east couldn't wait."

Riani stepped aside as Fiadh scanned the room, eyes

falling on Ellisar. She stalked toward him, Krulan and Sibaen at her sides. Kaelari followed, scowling at those who met their queen's sharp gaze, watching them grimace and look away. When she'd ascended her throne, Kaelari and Riani stationing themselves on either side, Fiadh stared at Ellisar until he came to her, bowing deeply. He remained, head down until she cleared her throat and said, "Rise and explain why it is you felt compelled to read and share information meant for me."

"You were not here."

She sat back and laced her fingers. "I see. Whom do you serve, Ellisar?"

"You, my queen."

"I'm relieved to hear it. For a moment, it appeared as though you thought yourself king." Or a husband, she thought blackly.

He met her challenging stare. "I would never presume such a thing, though I would welcome the opportunity to rule at your side."

She gave him a sour look. "Your actions only serve to harden my refusal."

"Forgive me. In my haste, I did not think."

"Nay. You did not." She leaned forward. "I may be young, Ellisar, but do not mistake my youth for weakness."

"My queen." He got to his knees and pressed his head to the base of her throne.

Fiadh watched him silently for a few moments. She leaned back against the cold stone and said, "You may rise and report."

Ellisar stood, balling his hands into fists. "Oadsera sent

word of attacks along their borders and in surrounding human settlements. Arel also sent word of an attack on a village they passed."

"What kind of attacks?"

"Information from Oadsera was sparse." He frowned. "They don't know its origins."

"And Arel's missive?"

"He claims they came across a village attacked by an army of Kelpie. He says a Dullahan led the creatures."

Kaelari gasped while Riani spat on the ground, issuing a vile oath. Craning her neck to glance at the two females, Fiadh asked, "What are these creatures?"

They darted a look at each other, Kaelari lifting her chin to Riani, who moved around to stand in front of Fiadh. "Legends tell of Kelpie, shape-shifting creatures who live in lakes and rivers. It is said they lure their victims onto their backs and drown them, eating the corpses at their leisure. But..." she paused, taking in the faces in the hall, "I have never heard of them banding together. The stories I'd been told cast them as solitary creatures. If Arel fought against an army of them—" She shook her head.

"And the Dullahan?"

Ellisar cleared his throat. "They are demons. Some say they are headless. Others that they pour fire from their eyes. I've heard tales of Dullahan riding atop carriages made of skulls while other stories have them astride a black horse with glowing eyes. But each of the tales held one common thread: they kill all who cross their path."

Fiadh bit the inside of her cheek. "What do you think this means?" Her mind conjured the image of the broken scrying bowl, the feel of Dothur's power holding her pinned —the warning in his pale gaze.

"Only one could raise such an army," Dyvre announced, separating himself from the Aos Sí who filled the hall. "Dothur had an affinity with such creatures. He is behind this. You feel the truth of it."

She nodded slowly. "Aye. I felt the awful weight of his mind. The violence in it." Taking a deep breath, she marked each face in the room and said, "We will fortify our kingdom and extend our barriers. Already, Dorcha Wood is threatened. I felt the presence of Crom Cruach's evil. It is spreading from Felmore, leaching the forest of its purity and leaving behind a rotted wasteland." A chorus of gasps followed that pronouncement. She swept her gaze through the gathering. "If we do not take steps to protect it and shelter those seeking refuge, it will spell our doom."

asha flew to Fiadh's side as she sat at a large table in the center of the hall with a map spread out before her, discussing where to put their efforts as they fortified their protections. Landing on the rough wood, he went to her, talons tapping, and let out a series of raspy croaks. She focused on him, opening her mind to the images he passed to her.

Turning to Krulan, who'd come to stand at her back, she whispered her thanks to the raven and looked the Cù-Sìth in the face. *Quinn is in Dorcha Wood with others. Something is wrong.*

He turned his massive head toward Vaymir, his second. *Set up a patrol and alert me if you see anything amiss.*

Vaymir rumbled in agreement and bolted from the room, the edges of the map fluttering in his wake.

Fiadh watched Vaymir leave, and Nym arrive. Her sleek body sidled up to Krulan's. He nuzzled her face lovingly, and her heart caught. He'd once shown Rivya, his mate, such endearments. It was good to see him healing, but with that joy came an ocean of sorrow.

Is Nym joining us? Fiadh asked.

She is not. I need her strength and skill guarding our kingdom. He said the last to both of them, and Fiadh watched the Cù-Sìth nudge Krulan and lope through the doorway to join Vaymir.

Krulan stared at the empty space momentarily, then turned, pinning her with a hard, yellow stare. *You will not be hasty and make decisions without thinking them through when meeting with Quinn.*

She gave him a crooked smile. *Krulan, are you suggesting I'm rash?*

He curled his lip and flashed his teeth.

Fiadh chuckled and excused herself from the others who watched the exchange without knowing its meaning. Ellisar watched her closely and she met his gaze, turning away when he shifted his attention to one of the elves across the table. As she left the hall with Krulan, Fiadh heard feet padding after her and turned to find Sibaen. "You need not join me, Sibaen. This is a private matter."

"King Ulfran commanded me to act as your guard when he sent me to you. I cannot do so if I leave your side."

Fiadh made a face. "Well, that's very nice, but Krulan will protect me."

Sibaen sneezed and scratched her neck. "Then you will be doubly protected with me at your side."

Do not try to sway her, Krulan told her. *The Faoladh do not make light of their oaths. She will follow us whether you will it or not.*

"Fine. But I want no interference."

"As you will, my queen." Sibaen bowed, though her wiry body made it look more like a crouch.

"It's too bad you obey only when it suits your will and not mine."

"If you'll forgive me, I have walked this earth longer than you and know more of the greater world than your youth has afforded you."

Fiadh raised a brow and swatted Krulan as he let out a shrill bark. "For a queen, I seem to have many people telling me what to do."

The Faoladh shrugged. "A wise queen seeks the advice of others."

"I suppose that's true." She sighed and marched through the courtyard, her irritation diminishing with every step as she thought about what it could mean that Quinn had come to the hidden shelter. She jogged through Erabel and crossed into Dorcha Wood, Krulan, and Sibaen at her sides while Dasha flew overhead.

She wondered if Quinn's actions were somehow connected to Crom Cruach's evil staining the forest. Perhaps the demon and Darragh had formed an alliance. Together, they could have easily ferreted out Gideon's spies. If that were the case, they would need sanctuary in Erabel. While Fiadh would give it, she didn't look forward to the reactions of her counsel, especially if Ellisar led them. He wasn't all bad. His experience was needed, as were his connections with Oadsera. But he was grasping, and she didn't like feeling trapped in a net of his making.

If there were other dissenters, it wouldn't take much to incite a revolt with Ellisar leading the charge. His hatred of mankind tainted his view of the world, and she worried there was too little time to alter his perception before Dothur was at their borders. It would take more than elven might to combat such a force. She needed him on her side, but that didn't mean in her bed.

Hushed voices met her ears as Fiadh tucked her body into the crevice, hands gripping the rough stone as she climbed over rock and plant life. Krulan, too large to fit comfortably, grumbled, snarling softly to himself as tufts of fur clung to the gritty surface along jutting points he struggled to maneuver around. Sibaen was silent, the only sound that of her claws scraping against the rock and making Fiadh cringe at the shrill sound.

Fiadh hung back for a moment, tucked into the shadows of the crevice, and scanned the area around the gentle waterfall. There were six men, all young, sitting or resting on their heels. Each carried a small satchel and short sword—their only possessions. Quinn was perched on a jut of granite, hands moving as he spoke. She couldn't make out the words over the noise of the rushing water but she noted the five young men surrounding him nod.

She emerged slowly, a thin shaft of sunlight illuminating her form. There was a collective gasp when Krulan and Sibaen followed. Her eyes flicked to the hands of those soldiers who gripped the hilts of the swords and stared, wide-eyed, at the Faoladh and Cù-Sìth. Quinn fidgeted for a moment and cleared his throat, nervously looking away from Krulan and Sibaen and fixing his gaze on Fiadh.

Licking his lips, he stood and bowed. "My lady."

She tilted her head and smiled softly. "Please rise, Quinn."

He gave a jerky nod and motioned for his friends to stand and release their weapons. Fear washed over their faces as Krulan came to Fiadh's side, his size and girth dwarfing her. She put a hand on his shoulder. *Stop scowling. They're afraid of you.*

They should be.

Be nice. They are here for aid.

Sibaen slinked to Fiadh's other side, her body slouched with one arm bent at her chest, black claws twitching. The soldiers moved closer to one another while Quinn made a visible effort to remain still.

"It's all right, Quinn. Sibaen and Krulan are here to protect me, nothing more."

Quinn fixed his face and put back his shoulders. "My lady, you and Lord Gideon told me I could seek you out should things go badly in Felmore. We are here to beg for sanctuary."

"And you have it." The relief he and the others felt was palpable. Fiadh smiled and said, "Now, tell me what's happening in Felmore." She moved closer to the group of wary men, lips twitching as they clumsily dipped their heads or attempted to bow. Motioning for them to sit, she perched on a fallen log and turned to Quinn, Krulan settling at her side while Sibaen stood at her back, unnaturally still.

Swallowing hard and averting his eyes from the Faoladh's sharp gaze, Quinn began. "A sennight past, Lord Darragh… started to change."

"How so?"

Quinn looked to his comrades, then spread his hands. "It's hard to explain without seeing it. He has always been a harsh lord but of late... he's different. It's like before his harshness at least served some purpose folk could understand. He wanted to make Felmore strong, wanted to raise armies, and increase his power. Maybe we didn't like it, but we at least understood it. But now..."

Fiadh didn't say anything, but Darragh and cruelty were hardly new. Keeping her thoughts to herself, she listened as Quinn and the others spoke of the actions their lord had taken and the way in which he did it. Of villagers of all ages requisitioned to his army—even children. Of those who'd gone missing. It was cruelty for the sake of cruelty.

When he finished, he lifted his hands and said, "We couldn't serve a lord like that any longer. He commanded us to cull men and boys from nearby villages—peasants and farmers who'd never held a sword." Quinn shook his head. "We've seen enough and want no part of it."

If you take them in, it will sow division among your people, Krulan warned with a growl.

So be it. I can't leave them here. I won't. She thought of Gideon. Of the promise she'd made to him to keep Quinn and the others safe if she could. Ellisar and those of his ilk would either support her decision or leave. The choice was theirs but she refused to let their animosity for innocent people mar her actions.

Never, in all of Aos Sí history, had the children of men been invited into Erabel. Not until Gideon. It was a bold move and a strong statement she was about to make. But it was necessary. Many of her people saw themselves as separate, the past clouding hope for the future. Between what Darragh was doing on his lands and the threat of Dothur, they couldn't afford to isolate themselves. It would be their downfall.

"I give you leave to enter Erabel but warn you that many of my people will resent your presence just as they resented Gideon's."

The men shuffled their feet, one of them speaking up, "Do you think it's wise to anger them?"

"I think they need a little nudge," she told him. "They have spent decades nursing their hatred and must put it aside now and see it for the petty thing it is."

It is not petty, Krulan protested.

She ignored him and continued. "Show them who you are and what you stand for. The rest will come with time."

Quinn got down on one knee, pulling his sword from his scabbard. Sibaen let out a soft snarl but made no move toward the young man. Dipping his head to rest on the pommel, he pledged himself to Fiadh. The others followed suit. The magnitude of their actions did not escape her.

"I have never seen the like," Sibaen whispered in a thready voice. "You are truly as the prophecies said."

Fiadh glanced at her, then stepped forward and placed her hand on Quinn's bent head before moving to the others. They rose, a couple blushing as they feasted on her beauty. She was too beautiful. Too perfect. Like a goddess among men.

Krulan led the party through Dorcha Wood, Sibaen bringing up the rear—though the men were clearly discomfited by her presence at their backs. As they made their way through the forest, Fiadh considered her plan to extend the barrier protecting her realm. It felt more urgent now. Others would come, and Erabel wasn't big enough for all. It was time to band together and protect as much of the woods as possible, thereby providing safety for those would may seek it.

Holding her palms to the invisible shield around her kingdom, Fiadh did what had never been done before. She let them in. With unease, the group of soldiers passed into Erabel, bewildered by what greeted them as they made their way toward the keep. Creatures of all types watched their progress, most curious though some fled in fear and others glared as they passed. *It will take time*, Fiadh thought. The men were silent as they approached the keep, though she heard a gasp from one as it came into view.

Kaelari was the first to greet them, a scowl on her face. "You leave on a secret errand and return with this rabble?"

"I'm making friends, Kaelari. What have you done today?"

She snorted. "Friends? You do realize the uproar this will cause. Your people could turn on you. If Ellisar leaves, he'll ensure Oadsera offers no aid."

"I understand the risks."

Kaelari eyed the men and shook her head. "Regardless of the outcome of this meeting, I stand with you."

"Thank you."

A pall of silence engulfed the great hall as the group

entered the keep. Fiadh lifted her chin and strode to the dais, indicating where the soldiers should stand.

Ellisar, true to form, glared at the men and then swung his head to his queen. "What is the meaning of this?"

"These men begged sanctuary, and I gave it." She schooled her features, looking bored. "Is there a problem?"

He tensed and flicked his gaze to others who stared at the young men with disdain. "A problem? Aye. There's a problem. Bringing our enemy into our realm is a problem."

She cocked her head. "Is Gideon your enemy, Ellisar?"

His lip curled. "Gideon is one man, and he has proven himself. I think we've all been accommodating with regard to him. But this," he said, waving his hand at Quinn and the others, "is reckless. These men threaten our existence. They could be spies for Lord Darragh!"

Quinn stiffened, flinching when Sibaen put a restraining hand on his arm. Ellisar marked the exchange and snarled. "You see? Already he goes for his weapon. How do you know you can trust them?"

Fiadh leaned forward, pinning him with a cold expression. "Do not forget I am your queen. My word is law. These men are under our protection and more will join should I will it."

"A queen is only as powerful as the people who follow her," Ellisar said.

"Is that a threat?" Fiadh asked. Krulan stood at her side growling, the fur on his shoulders spiking.

"I would never threaten you. But, as an advisor, I must warn you that your people do not see mankind kind worthy of saving." He glanced at the elves fanning out at his sides, those who were more loyal to Oadsera than Fiadh. "Our resources would be better spent on our people."

"I won't argue about whose needs are greater, Ellisar. All of us face many threats. Division among our people is the path to failure. You could be a unifying voice if you choose. I leave that to you. For now, you must decide whether to keep your place among us or seek out another."

His face revealed nothing as he considered her words. He could leave Erabel and return to Oadsera, resuming his role as Saria's advisor. Perhaps she'd eventually establish herself as queen. He had power there and soldiers at his command. But he had to acknowledge the history and significance of Erabel. It was sacred to the Aos Sí. Abandoning it—abandoning Fiadh—was a betrayal. The Great Mother had chosen Fiadh to lead the Aos Sí. He should not question her wisdom.

The men Fiadh had brought into the hall shifted uncomfortably, and he looked over at them. Really looked. What he saw were young men, a couple barely past boyhood. Begrudgingly, he admitted they were not the enemy. Gideon, whom he had grown to trust to an extent, must have seen something in these men to warrant their request for sanctuary. Maybe he needed to look beyond the past, the old hatred, and see things with new eyes.

"Countless of our people died at the hands of men," he said to Fiadh. "I will not pretend to care about their fate, but I understand the path you seek, though I may not agree with it." He went to his knee and bowed deeply. "I am your loyal servant."

She swept her eyes across the room, noting the others

who'd voiced dissent. They, too, bent the knee. "Rise, Ellis-ar." He stood in one smooth motion, facing her. "I do not expect nor want blind followers. You are not sheep. As you've pointed out, I am young, and I need and respect your counsel."

He bowed and stepped aside.

Fiadh released a quiet breath, and Krulan's ear twitched. *You are a wise leader. Young. Impetuous. But wise.*

She made a face. *For a moment, I thought you were going to rip his throat out.*

Never without your permission.

Well, that's heartening, she told him, shaking her head.

You will need to watch him and those swayed by his words.

He speaks for many. I will not maintain their loyalty if I ignore their views and silence their voices. Casting him out is not the way to forge a future.

As I said, you are a wise leader.

CHAPTER FIFTEEN

Zaeleria hobbled out of the mouth of the cave she'd taken refuge in as three Aos Sí and one man made their final descent. Holding up a hand, she called out to them, clasping wrists as each of them greeted her. When it was Gideon's turn, she held onto him and gazed deeply into his eyes. Her straight waist-length white hair and violet irises contrasted with the dusky tone of her skin as she studied him. He was lost in her, as though his mind was gently pried open. Its secrets spilled into her waiting hands as she saw more than he'd knowingly give. It lasted only a few moments, but in that time, he relived so much it felt like hours. When she let go, he felt off balance, eyes clinging to hers. Their vibrant hue shone with inner light.

"I can see why she likes you," she said, lips curving into a sly smile. "But your part in all of this has only begun. Your loyalty is yet to be tested."

He looked flustered, unsure what to say.

Zaeleria reached up and cupped his cheek. "Fear not. You are a good man."

"I haven't always been," he whispered, lost in her face as though they were the only two beings on the side of the mountain.

"We all lose our way from time to time. You have found the path back to the light, and she will help you remain on it. If you let her."

He nodded, feeling off-balance as she broke their connection and turned to the elves. "I will need your aid, Elraen."

The healer dipped his head and stepped forward, gently taking her hands in his. Seshka placed her bedroll on a rocky outcropping and motioned for the seer to sit. Every eye watched Zaeleria's progress as she leaned on Elraen and made her way to the blanket. No injury was evident, but it was clear her strength was failing. Stepping aside, Gideon watched Seshka and Arel stand on either side of the seer, hands raised in supplication. Elraen stood between Zaeleria's legs and pressed his palms to her head. As one, all four Aos Sí started to sing, the words strange and lyrical. They called to him, tugging at his memories of Fiadh. He closed his eyes and pictured her, recalling her laying on a pallet in her small hut, hand cupped under her cheek, mouth parted in peaceful slumber. Fiadh walked through Dorcha Wood with animals at her sides, crooning at them as they stared blissfully at her. The shattered innocence when he'd lashed out at her, trying to cut her out of his life rather than accept who she was. Every memory, the bitter and the sweet, spun through his mind in time with the melody the elves sang. As their voices quieted, slowly drifting to silence, one final image floated through his mind: Fiadh sitting in Erabel as he placed a crown of flowers on her head.

Gideon's eyes were bright as the Aos Sí formed a ring around Zaeleria, hands joined, praying to Danu. She sat in the center, head bowed, lips moving though he couldn't make out the words. When they released their hands, Zaeleria turned her head toward him and smiled as though she'd seen every moment his mind had conjured. He had no cause to doubt that she had and didn't question the rightness of sharing those memories with her.

Rising slowly, Zaeleria took a deep breath, giving thanks to the Great Mother. She looked stronger, though still wan. It would take more than what he'd witnessed to heal her. She needed Dyvre. She needed the power of Erabel.

They slept in the cave that night and left at first light the next morning. As the group summited, Gideon stood on the peak and surveyed the land spreading out before him. It was the realm of men. And, yet, it was also the realm of elves and so many other peoples—though each of them had been forced into hiding, becoming nothing more than legend or nightmare. Shame coursed through his veins. He'd been no better than his ancestors. But he could be better. He wanted to be. Not only for Fiadh but for Aishling and the genera-tions who would follow.

"Your heart is a deep pool," Zaeleria said, coming to his side.

"Aye. I suppose it is." He looked down at her. "There's darkness and light in me. I know you've seen it."

"You speak of the duality that is reflected in each of us.

You cannot have light without darkness." She pressed a palm to his chest. "You must accept the past. It is unchangeable. What you can shape is the future."

With a pat, she left him, her place quickly taken by Arel. "She sees a lot."

"I guess that's why you all call her a seer," Gideon said with a sardonic grin.

The elf chuckled.

Gideon tracked Zaeleria's progress as she chatted with Seshka and Elraen. "Can she see the future?"

Arel pursed his lips. "She catches glimpses of what could be, but the future is not set."

"Why does she live outside of your realms?"

Sighing, the elf said, "After the Great War, many survivors took refuge in Oadsera. But for each one who did, another found a peaceful existence elsewhere. Zaeleria had seen too much, and felt too much. I've often wondered if the grief of losing so many of our people would've killed her had she stayed."

"I'm sorry."

"For what?"

"For what my people did to yours," he said softly.

Arel put his hand on Gideon's shoulder. "I'm sorry too, brother."

Trekking down the mountain was a new kind of hell on Gideon's still-healing leg, but the group made it to the base where four Urisk waited. They stood in the open, and he did his best not to stare. Two males and two females. Each had pale eyes and the horizontal pupils of a goat set in their human faces, matching their lower halves of wooly legs and small hooves. The males sported impressive horns protruding from their skulls, curving around in a spiral just above their rather ordinary ears. Whereas the females' were short, jutting delicately from their regal heads. Gideon tried, unsuccessfully, to avert his eyes from the bare-breasted chests of the females who wore bows and quivers across their chests, accentuating their femininity. Arel chuckled at Gideon's expression, causing him to flush and mutter.

The leader stepped forward, a richly embroidered loin cloth swaying softly at her waist. She kissed Zaeleria's cheeks, then raised her hands, palms up. "The Great Mother blesses us with your return."

"It is good to see you, Corene." She motioned to Gideon, knowing the Urisk would be uneasy without a formal introduction. "Meet Gideon. He is a friend of our queen. The others, you know."

Corene leaned forward and kissed Gideon's cheeks in greeting. She smelled of pine and freshly turned earth. It was wholly appealing. He mumbled a greeting, feeling like a fresh-faced youth. Corene smiled and rejoined the other Urisk. "We have been tracking Arel since he left the human encampment."

"Aye. He told me. I thank you for watching over them." Zaeleria moved to a fallen log and sat. "I assume you are here for other reasons."

A pained expression crossed Corene's face. "Many

human settlements have been attacked. We have not intervened, but it grieves us to see such willful slaughter."

Zaeleria frowned. "Dothur is free."

The Urisk gasped in unison, their bodies twitching as though about to flee. Corene held out a hand to calm them, but the two males moved closer as though they wished to herd the females to safety. With wickedly sharp spears drawn, they were formidable.

"Have your people seen what attacked the villages?" Arel asked.

"Our scouts reported seeing strange creatures. They've gone after those who are defenseless. If Dothur is behind this…" Corene's strange eyes swept the group. "As of yet, my people are not under his eye. But I fear that will not remain so."

Gideon cleared his throat. "Perhaps you should seek safety in Erabel."

The leader of the Urisk stared at him, her porcelain-like face still. "You would speak for the queen?" It was asked with amusement.

He caught Zaeleria's beam of approval and said, "Fiadh wishes to unite us. All of us. I am confident she would give you sanctuary should you seek it."

Corene turned to the seer. "Does he speak the truth?"

"Aye. Our queen walks a new path for our people."

The Urisk's face beamed approval. "Erabel has always been a haven should we need it." She looked at Gideon meaningfully. "It is good to hear that shelter is now offered to *all* peoples."

Arel slapped Gideon on the back. "Doling out invitations now, are we?"

He elbowed the elf and watched as Corene drifted away to speak with her warriors. It was decided the Urisk would travel with them to the village where the rest of their party remained aiding its inhabitants. They made camp a short distance away, aiming to speed up their journey before the attacks increased or threatened Corene's people.

Sitting beside the fire, Gideon looked to the east. He needed to fetch Aishling. She and her adopted family weren't safe. They'd be lambs for the slaughter should a band of Duthor's monsters descend on their land. He caught Zaeleria watching him and sensed she'd plucked his thoughts from his head.

She confirmed his suspicion when she said, "Your foundling is safe."

"For how long?"

"Long enough for you to collect her and bring her to Erabel."

Gideon nodded and rubbed his chest, trying to ease the worry that sat there like a rock. He should leave the group and head east.

As the odd collection sat around a small fire that night, Zaeleria shared the vision of Dothur she'd seen in her scrying bowl. "It was a warning," she looked away for a moment, adding quietly, "and a punishment."

The elves said nothing, not asking her to elaborate, and Gideon followed their lead, though he wondered what she meant. What had Zaeleria done to earn the wrath of such a being?

A few days later, Lura greeted the party at the edge of the north field on the outskirts of a tiny hamlet. She went to Zaeleria first, genuflecting for the powerful seer before speaking briefly to the Urisk, who left moments later to prepare their people for their journey to Erabel. Turning to Arel, she launched into a recounting of events since the party had left to locate Zaeleria.

The Dullahan had returned, leading Kelpie in a coordinated assault. But the creatures took little interest in the men fighting alongside the Aos Sí. Instead, the demon who commanded them focused their efforts on the elves, testing their skill and assessing their numbers. They retreated as quickly as they arrived, leaving none of their wounded behind. After that, every soul in the village watched and waited, but after two nights of nothing, the people grew complacent. Despite warnings from the Aos Sí, they returned to their routines, less vigilant in the daylight hours. That was when the creatures struck. Of the Dullahan, the elves saw nothing, but his presence was felt, and his scent—death and decay—thick in the air.

The Kelpie targeted a small group of women and children who'd gone to a stream to collect traps they'd placed in the water for small crustaceans. Though an elf had gone with them, he was quickly overrun and whistled for aid as the creatures came at him from all sides. By the time Lura and the others arrived, one of the women had been taken and a child injured. But it was a diversion. The greater strike came as the Aos Sí aided their comrade. It was too late when they realized the ruse.

Lura hung her head after she finished the recounting. "I failed you."

Arel placed a hand on her shoulder. "Do not blame yourself."

"I should've known," she said, mouth pulling down. "By the time we returned to the village, a dozen men had been gutted and hung from the tanner's roof along with a message."

"Let me see the missive," Zaeleria said.

The female grimaced. "I don't have it."

"Where is it?"

A look of disgust passed over Lura's face. "Carved into the blacksmith's chest."

Gideon curled his hands into fists. "Malcolm is dead?"

"Aye. He and many others."

Zaeleria touched his shoulder, the contact cooling the anger running through his veins. "What was the message?"

Lura gritted her teeth. "The age of men and Aos Sí is over."

CHAPTER SIXTEEN

ozens of Aos Sí fanned out along the border of Erabel, awaiting Fiadh's command. Dasha flew from branch to branch, cawing, ready to take flight should his mistress need his keen sight. At her signal, the elves raised their arms. Low chanting filled the air, spinning on the breeze before sinking into the invisible bulwark protecting Erabel. Fiadh closed her eyes, feeling Dyvre at her side, and pushed outward, forcing the barrier to expand. Sensing it flex beneath her will, she pictured Dorcha Wood in her mind, imagining the ragged border of the forest.

Her power grew, fed by Danu, whose essence churned under her feet. Without conscious thought, she linked her will to those of the Aos Sí at her sides, showing them how to mold Erabel's protections. Dyvre's mouth lifted at the corner as he felt the power flowing from his queen. She was indeed the daughter of Danu, blessed with a well of magic so deep he'd never seen the like. Like fireflies, the consciousness of every elf lit up in Fiadh's mind. She felt them all and directed them toward Dorcha Wood, pushing them to their limits until one then another flinched, their magic exhausted. Fiadh soothed their minds, gently severing each connection with a neat snip until all but Ellisar remained. His power was strong. Together, they anchored the barrier to the earth, sheltering a huge swath of the forest under a protective bubble.

Lowering her arms, Fiadh whispered a prayer to the Great Mother, feeling her loving caress throughout her body. As Danu retreated into the womb of Erabel, Fiadh cocked her head, sensing a stirring in the earth. Getting to her knees, she pressed her palms to the ground, worry flaring as Dothur's name floated through her mind. She closed her eyes and listened, feeling Dyvre lower himself at her side while Krulan stood at her back, hackles bristling.

She tentatively reached through rock and dirt, brows raising when she felt a flow of water—an underground river carving itself through the mantle. Fiadh opened her mind, trying to get a sense of it, its depth and path, but all she felt was a cavernous abyss weaving itself through granite and limestone. Frowning, she dipped her mind into the water itself and sucked in a breath.

Something responded to her intrusion—slippery and massive. It marked her presence, then plunged into the river, into the darkness, leaving only a faint impression of its ancient power.

Fiadh sat back on her heels and turned to Dyvre. "Did you feel that?"

"I sensed... something."

Looking at the moss and dirt as though she could see

beyond it, Fiadh mulled over what it could mean. What it could be. If the Great Mother had felt it, she'd given no indication or any alarm at its presence. Her people gathered as she stared at the ground, talking softly as they furtively watched her. Krulan gave a low snarl, causing those who'd come closer to back away.

What's wrong? he asked.

I don't know. I felt something.

He growled and dug a paw in the dirt, creating a deep rut. *Was it the demon?*

She shook her head. *I don't know what it was. But it felt… familiar.* Craning her neck, she looked up at the Cù-Sìth, who towered over her. Their gazes locked, and a memory floated through Krulan's mind of her staggering from the woods, clutching her stomach as Felmore's forces invaded the forest. She latched onto it—her wan face, the way her eyes had darted toward the thick copse of trees she'd left.

Fiadh blanched as memories exploded behind her eyes. Of the Merrow. Of stolen magic and terrible legends. She'd gotten sick, just as Krulan had recalled, heaving up a wormy black mass that had turned its slick black head at her with awful awareness before diving into the earth like it had never been. They'd had a name for it—Ithraen, the Merrow queen, had sought a way to birth it into the world. And Aelrah, Ithraen's oracle, had planted the seed within her where it grew, blossoming with the combined magic she'd stolen from Eradar mixed with her own. A ruler of Merrow legend. A conqueror, if Ithraen's stories were true. Fiadh stared at the ground in horror.

Oilliphéist.

Fiadh sequestered herself in the solar with Kaelari, Dyvre, Krulan, and, because she would not leave her side, Sibaen. She paced as she recalled events in Abadon, the Merrow Kingdom, and the subsequent sickness that had overcome her as she fought Lord Darragh's soldiers in Dorcha Wood. Krulan was angry upon hearing Fiadh had hidden such startling news and scraped the floor with his claws in agitation.

Dyvre's reaction was unexpected. Rather than expressing the fear and concern others showed, he sat quietly, a placid look on his face. Ceasing her constant pacing, Fiadh stood in front of him. "You've nothing to say?"

He leaned back in his chair and laced his long, pale fingers. "I've heard tales of Oilliphéist. The Merrow believe that Caoránach, the mother of the Oilliphéist, is the true ruler of the world. While I know little of their legends, one says Caoránach embodies the power of rebirth. To their thinking, perhaps this means she will consume the world and remake it with the Merrow as her servants. They would become rulers over all peoples in Caoránach's name."

Kaelari mumbled a foul oath and spun away from Dyvre. He watched her with a sly smile.

"Do you believe their stories?" Fiadh asked.

He pressed his fingers together and rested them against his lips before dropping his hands to his lap. "To discount their legends would be arrogant and foolish."

Fiadh made an exasperated sound. "That doesn't help."

Dyvre smiled serenely. "We fear what we don't understand, child. In this case, a creature our people know little of, if anything at all. Rather than see this as a portent of evil to some, I ask you this," he paused and leaned forward, "did it feel sinister? Did it seek to harm you?"

Frowning, she thought about the moment of contact as she'd reached through the dark waters of the underground river and connected with the Oilliphéist. It had sensed her, even pausing as though it sought her out. But was there malice in its actions? Her brow furrowed. The only emotion she was certain of was curiosity. While not ready to relegate such a creature as innocuous, she admitted that it hadn't felt dangerous. There had been no intent, wicked or virtuous, as she'd delved into its watery realm. It simply was. Unlike the rot encompassing portions of Dorcha Wood, the Oilliphéist was present yet separate. An unknown entity.

"What do you suggest we do?" she asked.

"Do?" Dyvre's eyes crinkled for a moment, making him look the centuries-old that he was. "What *can* you do? Invade its world? Attack it? For what purpose?"

Her lips thinned. "It's foolhardy to do nothing, isn't it? The Merrow believed the Oilliphéist was the true ruler of the world. They wanted to see it reborn, and I have a hard time believing its birth would be to our benefit."

Dyvre sighed. "I imagine Ithraen wishes many things for her people, and perhaps she sees the old legends as a way of fulfilling them. But until this creature proves nefarious, I suggest we leave it well enough alone. After all, what more can we do?"

"I don't know." She paced away, glancing at Kaelari,

who was suspiciously quiet. "Don't you have anything to say?"

She cocked her head at Fiadh. "I wouldn't know how to guard against such a creature. Besides, until today, you had forgotten its existence, only stumbling upon it by chance. And, yet, it has lived beneath your kingdom undetected. Let's focus our effort on securing Erabel's borders and protecting Dorcha Wood."

Fiadh faced Krulan and Sibaen. "Do you both agree?"

The Faoladh rose from a crouch and sneezed. "My people are not diggers. Finding and killing an enemy who burrows in the earth feels risky. Kaelari is right. You should fortify your protections here rather than hunt something that may not pose a threat."

You cannot fight such a creature, young one. Best to leave it alone, Krulan told her.

"Very well." Fiadh sat and tugged at her tunic. "We'll continue building up our barriers, but I am not so certain the Oilliphéist means no harm. I'd feel better if I knew its intentions."

"If you are comfortable, reach out to it as you did today," Dyvre suggested before offering a warning. "But be mindful of intruding in its territory."

Fiadh begged for solitude as the conversation waned. Krulan was the last to leave the solar, turning to look at her at the threshold of the door. "I'm all right." He nodded and left, tail swishing behind him.

She let out a long-suffering breath and walked to the window, pressing her palm to a pane of glass. If Gideon were there, she'd have asked him to stay, but he was far away, too far for Dasha to fly. It was strange how he'd made his way back into her heart, carved out a little space that was his. Part of her resented it. The other part... she shook her head. Closing her eyes, she reached out to the Great Mother, feeling Danu's embrace. She asked the goddess to keep Gideon and the rest of the party safe, knowing she could not grant such a request. Rather than offering a promise, the Great Mother flooded her mind with a sense of peace, muffling her worry. With a whisper, Danu receded, but Fiadh knew she wasn't far. Gideon would return, Zaeleria with him, and they would face the looming threats that circled their lives like vultures.

CHAPTER SEVENTEEN

Gideon's party returned days later as the sky shifted from blue to orange with the setting of the sun. Fiadh greeted them as they crossed Erabel's border, their impending arrival having been reported by one of the scouts monitoring Dorcha Wood. Dyvre went to Zaeleria, bowing low as the female leaned on Arel's arm, her strength waning after the arduous journey.

"My friend," she murmured, reaching for him. He clasped her hand and rose, locking eyes with the powerful seer. Through their connection, Dyvre saw and felt Zaeleria's memories of the moment Dothur sensed her eye on him. The awful weight of the demon's will as he flayed the seer's mind. Dyvre staggered back, eyes widening. It would've killed him had he been the one to fall under Dothur's eye.

Zaeleria nodded slowly, releasing his hand, and turned to Fiadh. "My queen." She dipped her head. "The Great Mother bless you."

Fiadh moved away from Gideon's side and faced the seer. "Erabel welcomes you." Stepping closer, she peered into Zaeleria's face, seeing more than her striking visage. Galaxies swirled in her eyes, knowledge so vast, she felt untethered, and within the knowledge, she saw and felt her birth mother, Threa.

With a gentle smile, the seer reached up and pressed the tip of her finger to Fiadh's temple. Tiny zaps lit up her mind as the seer entered it. Fiadh blinked, lips parting. There, in a wealth of memories, was Threa and in front of her—Riona. Eyes welling, Fiadh saw them kneeling face to face. Human and Aos Sí. It was the moment Threa gave the woman the only thing she could, her most precious possession: her children.

A tear slid down Fiadh's cheek as the image faded. "Thank you," she whispered.

Trailing her finger down the side of Fiadh's face, Zaeleria said, "I see them in you. They are with you still."

Lowering her head, she took a deep breath, letting the seer's words sink into her. When she raised her head, Zaeleria gave a knowing look and followed Fiadh to the keep. Gideon fell into place at her side, passing a look of gratitude to Krulan, who huffed.

As if I would be unable to keep you safe. Humans think they are the masters of the world, and we are just beasts in it, Krulan grumbled.

Ah, Krulan. I do love your grumbles.

He flashed a wickedly long canine at her, and she chuckled, laying a hand on his shoulder as Gideon snagged her attention.

"It is good to see you again," he said, voice pitched low.

"And you."

They walked silently for a time, Dasha swooping amongst the trees, cawing at Gideon, who smiled at the raven. Listening to the idle chatter of the elves as they caught up with one another allowed her to sift through her feelings for the man who walked at her side. That she was glad to see him was clear. Giving him a sidelong glance, she noticed he still had a bit of a limp. It was the leg Riona had stitched. That realization caused a slight pang in her heart, but within that was the knowledge that her mother would be happy with her chosen path. There was solace in that.

Turning her head as they picked their way through the undergrowth, Fiadh said, "You'll be happy to know that Quinn and a few of your men have been granted sanctuary." Gideon almost stumbled, a flash of fear crossing his face. "Not to worry. They are well and eagerly await your guidance." She shook her head and gave a breathy laugh. "I think they're afraid of us, though Quinn does his best to mask it."

"I can't fault them for that. You're a scary lot!"

She elbowed him, their banter easing the tightness in her chest.

"Thank you," he said quietly. "It means a great deal to me that you welcomed them here."

She lifted her chin. "You were the first; they will not be the last."

"Our queen is wise," Zaeleria said as she trailed behind.

Dyvre tilted his head in deference. "Aye, that she is. We need her wisdom in these times."

Fiadh blushed, embarrassed by the praise. "We received Arel's missive about the attack on the village."

Gideon's mouth turned down. "I'm afraid the attacks continued when we split up. Lura can tell you more. I fear this is only beginning." Clenching her hands into fists, her eyes darted toward the south, where Felmore sat like a blister on the earth. "Is that why Quinn sought refuge here? Because of attacks?" he asked as they neared the keep.

"As far as I know, Felmore hasn't seen any of the creatures you've encountered. He came for a different reason." Gideon raised an eyebrow, waiting for her to continue. "I felt the presence of Crom Cruach. He's returned, if he ever left, and poisons Dorcha Wood with his malice. Quinn said Lord Darragh isn't the same. He's changed. I would wager the demon is the cause."

Gideon's fingers twitched, reaching for the hilt of his sword. He balled them into fists. "I assume he's in league with Dothur."

"You are correct," Zaeleria said, slipping her hand around Gideon's arm. He bent it, taking her weight, and slowed his pace. "It is Crom Cruach, and the mages Dothur rallied in the Great War that set him free. Rygeil doomed us all when he released the old god. His power helped weaken the iron I'd imbued with old magic to imprison him. And now, Dothur seeks vengeance for the death of his mother and brothers. He wishes to fulfill Carmun's vision and remake this world."

Lura cleared her throat. "One of his minions, a Dullahan, left us a warning. It was carved into the body of a villager." Every face turned toward the elf. "The age of men and Aos Sí is over."

The powerful seer pursed her lips. "Had I been strong enough, I would've killed him all those years ago. But his power far surpasses my own."

"How can we fight against a creature that strong?" Gideon asked.

Zaeleria looked at Fiadh, into her. "We can't do it alone."

Ellisar's eyes narrowed as Fiadh laid out her plans to the council. "You wish to ally us with the children of men?"

She met his stare. "I do. Do I have your support?"

He folded his arms and dropped his head. "You do, but I must caution you of the risks of such a venture." Ellisar met her eyes. "Mankind is fickle. They swear loyalty to one another only to betray each other for power, status, or riches. How do you know they won't betray *you*?"

"I don't."

Ellisar looked at Zaeleria and Dyvre, who sat a short distance away. "Do you sanction such a move?"

Zaeleria rose slowly, each movement like the petals of a flower unfurling. When she came to her full height, she strolled toward Ellisar, stopping when she was mere inches away. "You are afraid," she murmured.

His nostrils flared.

"That is good. We all feel fear. It is a necessary emotion.

It reminds us of the fragility of life. But fear is not all you feel."

Ellisar looked away.

"Hate blinds you. Because of it, you cannot accept the path your queen commands. Do not fool yourself into thinking you can bide your time in Erabel or Oadsera and remain unscathed. Carmun's spawn is coming, and those who stand alone will fall beneath his talons as he carves his way through our world. Fiadh has shown you the way. It is up to you," she paused and looked at every face in the room, "to follow it."

Zaelaria eased back into her chair, every eye on her as she folded her hands in her lap. "It is time to let go of the past. If we don't, there will be no future."

CHAPTER EIGHTEEN

*L*ord Darragh woke gasping and clutched his chest. The medallion around his neck burned, singeing his skin to a purpled welt. Jerking the covers off, he sat up and grabbed the disc, feeling it pulse sickeningly. His palm grew warm, then hot, and he yelped, dropping the offending object where it bounced against his sternum, causing his heart to squeeze painfully. Swinging his legs over the side of the bed, he fumbled for the candle and staggered to the fire, poking a thin reed into the coals to light the wick. The yellow glow filled the space around his trembling body, creating sinister shadows beyond its light that danced upon the walls like wraiths.

Slipping his thumb beneath the leather cord, he held the medallion away from his chest, angling the candle to see it, expecting the strange metal to glow orange with heat. But it looked no different. Dull. Unremarkable. He traced a finger along its edge and hissed, yanking it back and curling the appendage into his fist. Narrowing his eyes, he made to lift the necklace from around his neck, stopping when a needle-like pain ripped through his skull.

Darragh stood rigid, teeth clenched so tightly that three of his molars cracked. Neck muscles throbbing, he clenched the leather cording, arm shaking as he fought against a will far more powerful than his. His eyes bugged as Crom Cruach's voice thundered through his mind.

"You dare!"

His back arched painfully, bladder letting go in a gush as the demon brought him to his knees. Darragh's body crashed to the cold stone floor as, one by one, the fingers holding the medallion upright opened, stretching unnaturally until each digit on his right hand popped, dislocated, and useless. He shrieked, thrashing against magic that kept him immobile.

"Shall I continue?" Crom Cruach whispered through Darragh's mind.

The lord of Felmore watched in agony as his left hand uncurled, fingers splayed as an unseen force methodically bent them backward. Through gritted teeth, he begged the old god, his squeals bouncing off the walls. The moment the demon released him, he sagged to the floor, curling into a ball atop the slick mess of his urine.

"Know your master, Lord Darragh. Should you refuse my call and seek to release yourself from my power, I will show you just how merciful I have been."

Darragh clutched his right hand to his chest, hate blooming so fiercely he could do nothing but nod.

"Good. Rise, Lord of Felmore, and go to your sweet mother's cell. It is time for you to prepare for a journey."

Kicking the castle's healer awake, Darragh ordered her up and stalked to the kitchen, where the feeble light from a fire illuminated the room. She scurried in, wiping sleep from her eyes, and rushed to pull a stool out before the hearth. After a quick inspection, during which she bit the inside of her cheek to keep from asking about the source of the injuries, the healer gave Darragh a wooden spoon instructing him to bite down on it as she reset his fingers. His jaw and teeth ached as he clamped down on wood that tasted of the cook's sweat.

It took only a few minutes, but when it was over, a sheen of perspiration covered Darragh's pale face. The woman was silent as she watched the lord drop his wooden spoon and spit on the floor. When he stood, she fidgeted, bunching the coarse fabric of her shabby dress in her hands.

"Speak," he said harshly.

She fixed her gaze on the floor. "There will be some swelling. If you need anything for the pain, I can make you a draught."

He studied his hand, tentatively flexing it, scowling at the flares of pain that radiated from each appendage. "I will find you should I need aid." Darragh turned and stalked from the room, ducking through the narrow door to the dungeon.

Rubbing his chest with his good hand to ease the ache where the medallion rested against his skin, he grabbed a torch and descended into the depths. Rank misery met his nostrils, and he smiled, recalling the music of tormented souls who'd been consigned to the darkness never again to see the light. Seizing on the violence and bloodlust, the memories stirred. He strode through the dank passageways, each step stronger, more determined.

His mind was fixed by the time he'd reached Haegna's cell. Let the old god use him as he saw fit. He would embrace it and reap the rewards. The door squealed as he shoved it open, echoing through the corridors like the screams of ghosts. Placing the torch in a sconce, he stared at the scrying bowl, nostrils flaring when the black surface undulated.

Crom Cruach's raspy voice traveled through the gentle ripples in sinister whispers too garbled for him to discern. He stepped toward the table and paused, listening to another voice intermingled with the old god's muttering. It was deep and powerful, causing the hair on the back of his neck to stand on end. Without conscious thought, Darragh walked to the table, his body pulled like a puppet on a string. Knees banging into the stool, he swayed in front of the scrying bowl, eyes wide and fixed on the dark water. Shadowy images danced on the surface in time with two voices speaking a language he'd never heard but could somehow understand. The words cut into his skull, making his ears throb and his head pound. He wanted to block the sound, but his arms were dead weights at his sides. Useless.

Two faces emerged, clarifying, becoming more hideous than the murky things they'd been. Pale eyes in a monstrous corpse-like face with pointed ears and thick black lips filled the bowl, the hint of massive wings extending beyond its obscured form. It overshadowed Crom Cruach, casting the old god aside. This was the true master. Crom was nothing more than a tool.

The creature gazed balefully at him, its mind like beetles in his brain. Darragh sank to the stool, unable to look away from the monster that sapped his will even as it transferred awful power into his body. He grew rigid, arms locking, fingers clamping onto the table's edge. A surge of warmth rushed through him, followed by the sensation of tiny needles running through his veins.

"A sip of my power for your journey," the creature said, its voice thrumming through his skull. As Darragh sat immobile, the image faded, replaced with the twisted form of Crom Cruach.

The old god smiled, rotted teeth winking between his bloated lips. "In the morning, you will go to Taigon and seek an audience with the king."

Felmore's lord blinked, mouth parted.

"You will tell King Stephan of a growing threat from the Aos Sí. Rygeil's heir has claimed her birthright and fixed her eyes on taking the Western Fold. You need his counsel and more men to raise an army against the coming elven horde."

Darragh stared vacantly as Crom Cruach continued, meting out commands he could not resist, each one filled with such power he could do nothing but feel them sink into his mind like barbed hooks. When he was released, his mind swam with the lingering effects of the spells, and he toppled over, striking his head on the stone with a crack.

Hours later, Darragh awoke on the hard floor, wiping away a line of drool hanging from his lower lip. His head felt heavy, and he struggled to rise, coming to his knees and using the stool as leverage like an old man. Legs shaking, he stood and looked around the room, gaze falling on the scrying bowl that sat on the table, innocuous. His eyes skittered away from the black surface, and he staggered to the wall, bracing his hands on the cool stone. Hanging his head, he forced his mind to be quiet, trying to remember how he'd come to be on the floor. The last thing he recalled was staring at the liquid, seeing images, and hearing strange words. Running a hand through his oily, blond hair, he muttered to the emptiness, imaging Haegna's teasing voice mocking his weakness.

Pushing away from the wall, Felmore's lord grabbed the torch and left the cell, slamming the door behind him. The clang echoed through the passageway as he straightened his tunic and went through the winding corridors to the stairwell. As he put his foot on the bottom step, a sharp pain stabbed his skull. He dropped the torch and grabbed his head, face twisting. When it was over, all expression was gone. He was blank. Empty.

Lord Darragh Baoill, the grandson of Magnar, the elf-slayer, shrank from the dark power that took over, hiding in the recesses of his mind like a scared child. The medallion slung around his neck glowed as Crom Cruach's spell burst from the sigil, surrounding him in a cocoon of vile will. With rigid movements, he made his way to the great hall and sat on the dais, hands dangling from the arms of his chair. Servants avoided him as they scurried about the castle, keeping their faces averted lest they feel his foul gaze, sensing something was wrong with the castle's lord. It was as though a dark haze hovered over him. One of the kitchen help swore she could see it as she peered from an alcove.

In the kitchen, maids whispered behind cupped hands, growing silent as Donal strode in. He gave the youngest woman a passing glance, focusing on the head of the kitchen staff. "Where is your lord?"

She lifted her grizzled head and pointed to the great hall. "On the dais, sir."

Donal's heavy tread sounded through the hall as he came toward Darragh. There was only a flicker in his lord's eyes as he cleared his throat and waited to be given leave to speak. When a minute passed, the commander said, "Six more men have gone missing, my lord."

Darragh's eyes slowly came to life, shifting to Donal's face. "When?"

"Their absence was reported today, though it is believed they disappeared a few days ago. They were Gideon's men. Shall I send a contingent to search Dorcha Wood?"

A sly smile tugged the corners of Darragh's mouth. "No need. An envoy from Lord Burleigh's holding on the coast of the Stygian Sea arrives today. On the morrow, we leave for Taigon. When I return, I will have reinforcements who will hunt them down and any who shield them."

Dipping his head, Donal said, "I will gather the men and prepare for our departure."

"Rueben will remain at Felmore," Darragh said, indicating the man who would take his commander's place one day. "I need a man I can trust to oversee my lands."

"Very good. I will inform him."

Dismissing his commander, Darragh absently rubbed his

chest where the sigil burned into the skin beneath his tunic. His skull crawled with the presence of Dothur and Crom Cruach. But the demon had not wholly consumed him. Not yet. Whatever spell that monstrous, winged creature had imparted made him into a marionette. A toy for the old god. He wished he could disappear as he'd done before, but Crom Cruach enjoyed his torments, relishing the feel of Darragh squirming under the weight of his will.

CHAPTER NINETEEN

Ravens were sent to Oadsera and other known remote settlements Aos Sí had fled to following the Great War. Aos Sí were warned of the looming threat and offered sanctuary in Erabel. Word of attacks was requested along with aid for any willing to travel. Throughout Erabel, they fortified and extended barriers with the assistance of the seers. However, Zaeleria's magic grew weak before the work was finished, leaving the bulk of the effort in Fiadh and Dyvre's hands. With Ellisar aiding them, they managed to push the protections further into Dorcha Wood, but much of the forest was exposed, and Fiadh had to face the realization they didn't have the power to shield it all. They needed help. She could only hope other powerful Aos Sí would respond to her request for aid.

But with every raven that returned carrying news, the atmosphere in Erabel became grimmer. Attacks were occurring across the landscape. Entire towns were razed. Oadsera sat in the center of an area experiencing much of the violence, and its inhabitants worried they would soon be under siege. Ellisar considered leaving Erabel to defend his homeland, even going so far as to ask Faidh's permission. When he received it, he realized the folly of leaving his queen and resumed his advisory position.

Word came that a remote elven settlement, blessedly unscathed, would arrive soon. Rooms were readied, and open sections of land around the keep were prepared if they ran out of space. Fiadh doubled the number of scouts patrolling Dorcha Wood.

As she sat in the great hall, breaking her fast, Gideon found her. Behind him stood Quinn and other young soldiers, both human and elf. The men had aided in the preparations and formed bonds of friendship with some of Fiadh's people.

The queen smiled at them, offering a place at the table. They sat, two of the men blushing when she looked their way. They seemed so young, though she was sure they must be her age, maybe a year or two older. Life had aged her.

"Good morning," she said.

Gideon's eyes crinkled. "And to you. I wanted to ask leave to fetch my young ward and bring her to Erabel."

Fiadh looked confused, eyes flashing to Quinn.

"Do you recall me telling you about Aishling?"

Her lips parted, and she smiled. "Yes. I remember."

"With news of attacks throughout the kingdom, I worry for her safety. May I have permission to bring her here with the couple who took her in?"

She put her hand on his. "Of course."

"Thank you. I… I've missed her these many months."

"Go to her, Gideon. She and her new family are most welcome."

Her eyes widened as he reached forward and took her hand, bending it gently and kissing her small knuckles. The sensation of his lips on her skin sent flutters through her body, where they pooled in her stomach. He looked up at her, and she held her breath at the emotions laid bare in his face. For a moment, she wanted to reach for him, cup his cheek, and feel the rough texture of the stumble peppering his jawline. Instead, she curled her fingers and held herself rigid, but she couldn't stop her eyes from feasting as they remained tethered to his for a few protracted moments. Quinn, shifting on the bench next to him, broke their connection.

Gideon let go of her hand, fingers trailing hers, electrifying her skin. He rose slowly and glanced at his men. "We leave in an hour." They nodded and left the hall to make preparations. Turning back to her, he said, "I'm taking Aridius but we'll have to a few more steal horses from Felmore before we head east."

She frowned. "That's too dangerous. I believe Darragh is in league with Crom Cruach. Felmore's lands will be watched."

"No need to worry. They'll never know we're there." She looked confused. "Didn't I tell you that Aridius made a few friends? One whinny, and they'll come running."

"I hope you're right. It seems like a big risk."

"I can't go on foot, and it wouldn't be wise to travel alone. If it makes you feel better, perhaps one of your people can join us until we get the horses and then report back to you."

Fiadh rolled her eyes. "You have an answer for everything, don't you?"

He grinned and loped out of the great hall. Sibaen, who'd been lingering nearby as she always did, came forward. "I'll go, my lady."

Surprise flashed across Fiadh's face. She knew little of the Faoladh's history with mankind and wondered at the female's willingness to see that Gideon and his men were safe. "Are you sure?"

Sibaen glanced at the door where Gideon had just left. "He is a good man. Like you, my people don't believe the children of men are born evil. There is hope for them. I'll make sure he and the others are safe."

Fiadh glanced at her dark, sharp claws, imagining the damage they could do to flesh. Aye, she was formidable. "Thank you, Sibaen. I would appreciate that."

The Faoladh turned on her heel and slunk toward the door, pausing for a moment and looking back. "You like him. I think… I think this is a good thing."

Before Fiadh could respond, Sibaen bolted after Gideon. The queen stared at the open doorway for a few minutes, feeling Krulan's presence as he came to her side. *Who could've imagined such a gathering of peoples?*

I have never seen the like, he told her. *It is an auspicious beginning.*

CHAPTER TWENTY

The seven men crested a hill and looked at the valley before them. A small farm with a field and little pasture sat in the folds of land. Gideon sighed, relief pouring through his body, easing the fatigue of days of hard riding.

Quinn nudged his mount to stand next to him, Aridius nickering softly. "It looks untouched."

"Aye." He smiled wearily. "Let's finish this journey and return home." Once the words were out of his mouth, he realized how strange they were. Home. Erabel. Stronghold of the Aos Sí. His father would be incensed. Doran in awe. He shook his head.

"My lord? Is something wrong?" Quinn asked.

"Just musing at the strangeness of my life."

"I know what you mean. Who could've imagined an alliance with our enemy?"

"They're not our enemy. They never were," Gideon said, digging his heels into his mount's sides.

They rode into the valley, calling out a greeting to alert Owen of their arrival. The middle-aged man came from the barn extending from the tiny cottage. Shading his eyes, he watched the rider's approach, calling out to his wife when he recognized the Lord of Belfirth.

"Milord! Welcome, welcome!" He lumbered to the horse, noting the makeshift bridle and lack of saddle. His eyes flicked to the other men and their mounts, all missing tack. "Were you robbed, milord?"

Gideon looked surprised for a moment, then realized why he'd asked. "Nay, we are traveling light."

Owen looked nonplussed but said nothing as Gideon swung down from Aridius' back, his men doing the same. He stretched his legs, bracing a hand on his mount until the numbness in his backside disappeared, then took a step toward the farmer. As he extended a hand in greeting, the cottage door burst open, and a flurry of skirts and blond hair raced toward him. He went to his knees and flung out his arms, nearly losing his balance as Aishling leaped into his embrace.

"Gideon!" she cried.

The sound of his name on her lips made his eyes well. He ducked his head in her hair, breathing in her sweet scent. "I thought you might have forgotten me," he whispered against her hair.

She pulled back, huge blue eyes full of laughter. "Never! Did you come to see me make my letters?"

He laughed and kissed her cheek. "Of course I did. I had to see for myself that you were the one writing me such wonderful messages."

She wriggled out of his arms, and he struggled not to reach for her again. *Daughter,* his heart sang, and he knew it to be true. Gideon watched her scamper to Aridius, her little hand reaching up to stroke the gelding's velvety muzzle. The horse stretched his long neck, snuffling her palm and eliciting giggles. Turning her head toward him, she squealed, "He remembers me!"

Gideon smiled. "Aye, that he does. I'm sure he's hoping you have a carrot or two."

Aishling waved at the soldiers standing beside their mounts and darted into the cottage, yelling for Owen's wife, Marion. Gideon took the opportunity to introduce his men and ask if the farmer had seen or heard anything unusual, face tightening when the man recounted a story he'd heard from a tinker who'd passed through not long ago.

Marion came out a few minutes later, her presence stopping their conversation. One hand clutched the child's, and the other held a bundle of carrots with leafy stalks. Handing the vegetable to the girl, Marion went to Owen's side and greeted the young lord.

He reached out, cupping her hand in his. "It is good to see you, Marion." He turned his attention to Aishling as she extended a carrot to his horse, crooning to him when he took the food between his blunted teeth. "She looks well. You both have my sincere appreciation."

Owen nodded, and Marion took his arm, worry marring the wrinkles in her face. She elbowed her husband, and he cleared his throat. "We have yet to speak of the reason for your coming, but my wife and I hoped we could keep the child as our own."

Pain flashed across Gideon's face at the thought of losing his young ward to the couple, though he knew they would provide a good life for her. Still, it didn't sit right. "I am indebted to you for your care of Aishling, but I have not come to discuss a permanent place in your home. Owen," he caught the man's stare, "you mentioned the tinker had seen the remains of a village he'd visited regularly. I'm afraid these are not isolated occurrences. Hamlets are being attacked across the kingdom."

Marion's face paled, and she gripped her husband's arm tighter, eyes flicking to the child. Owen patted her hand and asked, "What are you saying, milord?"

"You're not safe here. I've come to fetch Aishling and take her to a place where she'll be protected. I would like you both to join us."

"Where is this place?"

"In the Western Fold," he said vaguely.

The farmer turned to his wife, who looked stricken. "You would have us abandon our home?" he asked, returning his attention to Gideon.

"I would have you save yourselves. The attacks we've seen and heard of are carried out by creatures you cannot hope to fight or outrun. If they come across your farmstead, you'll be slaughtered. I can't leave Aishling to that fate. I won't."

"Why would they come here?" Marion asked. "We live leagues away from the nearest village and have little to steal."

Gideon scuffed the ground with his feet and put his

hands on his hips. "They don't come to steal, good woman. They come to kill."

She gasped and said to Owen, "Perhaps we should leave."

The man frowned. "We did not pay for our freedom and carve out a life here only to abandon it."

"Owen," Gideon said, trying to be patient, "this isn't about losing your farm. If you stay, these creatures will find you, and they will cut you and your good wife down. There is no reasoning with them."

He crossed his arms and jutted his chin. "We are too remote for them to bother. Our home isn't on a normal route, and we see only a handful of passersby each year. We've worked too hard and too long to walk away."

"I understand what you're saying, but I had hoped you'd make a different decision. We will stay the night. During that time, please consider what I've told you. In the morning, I will leave with Aishling. My hope is that you join me."

"Where would we go?" Marion whispered.

Gideon looked at her and said, "To an elven stronghold."

Owen gasped and sputtered. "You would take us to the hands of the enemy? Those beasts will slit our throats and laugh whilst they do it!"

Quinn stepped forward. "They are not evil, and they are not our enemy. Their new queen took us in," he said, indicating the young soldiers behind him. "If she hadn't, we would likely be hanging from a castle wall."

The farmer slashed his hand through the air. "My wife

and I will not beg for refuge with the enemy. We are not traitors."

"Owen," Gideon said, "I, too, had the same doubts, the same hatred, but I have learned that these people are not the monsters history had painted them to be. If you come with us, you will be made welcome, and you will be safe from the horde of creatures that are going from town to town, killing every man, woman, and child. Please, I beg you, reconsider." Marion gave a short nod, but Owen remained indignant. "Discuss this with your good wife. We leave in the morning."

The next day, Gideon and his men waited outside the cottage while Marion gathered Aishling's things. Owen stood a short distance away, face hardened as he listened to his wife quietly sobbing, though his eyes often traveled to Aishling, where she stood at Gideon's side clutching his hand. He leaned down, told the child to go to Quinn, and then walked to the farmer.

"Please reconsider."

"This is our home, milord. I will not leave it. If we're to die, it's the Great Mother's will."

Gideon sighed and reached into his tunic, pulling out a crudely drawn map on a strip of hide. Handing it to Owen, he said, "If you change your mind, follow this map to Dorcha Wood. Scouts patrol the forest and will send word to me of your arrival. They will not harm you."

The man folded the map and tucked it into his homespun tunic. "Thank you, milord."

Marion came through the doorway, a cloth bundle against her chest. Her eyes were red and aching as she looked at Aishling. Running to Owen, she said, "Perhaps Lord Gideon is right. We should go and look after Aishling."

"We will not be leaving."

A sob lodged in the woman's throat. Wiping away her tears, she slowly walked to Gideon and looked up at him. What he saw made his heart twist. He knew her agony. He'd felt it the day he'd rode away, leaving Aishling behind. He gently took the bundle from her and said, "I will keep her safe. She will grow up in a place of magic with a race of people who will protect her with their lives." Marion nodded, her throat too tight to speak. Gideon took one of her hands. "I have given your husband a map. Should you hear or see any hint of danger, you must convince him to flee."

She gave a watery thanks and went to the child, picking her up and cradling her. Gideon didn't listen to Marion's words but could hear Aishling pleading with her to go with them, not understanding when the woman refused. Owen was next, plucking the girl from his wife and holding her in a fatherly embrace."You be a good girl, now."

"I will," she said, picking at a loose thread on the neckline of his tunic.

The farmer kissed her cheek and set her down, slinging his arm around his wife and tucking her close. He looked at Gideon with watery eyes and said, "You take good care of our girl."

Gideon clasped wrists with the man. "You have my word. If you change your mind, there will always be a place for you in Dorcha Wood."

Owen dipped his head and stepped away, hugging his wife, who stood sobbing, eyes glued to the child as Gideon mounted his horse, Aishling cradled against his chest. He bid them farewell, the child waving enthusiastically, too eager for an adventure to understand she was leaving the couple. As they rode away, Gideon craned his neck and looked back, hoping he'd see them again and praying to the Great Mother to keep them safe.

CHAPTER TWENTY-ONE

*L*ord Darragh Baoill led a contingent of men through the gates of Felmore. To the villagers who witnessed their departure, a palpable sense of relief followed as the party rode through the muddy grounds and into the greater world. Rumors of dark magic circulated through Felmore's people, many pointing to the strange rot that grew in the forbidden forest, others to the coldness that had taken over their lord. Words like witch and sorceress fell from the lips of some, while others imagined something darker lurking in the halls of the castle.

As the riders kicked their horses into a trot, those who'd heard of their destination whispered, making wagers on whether King Stephan would once again send reinforcements. Most believed he'd leave Felmore's people on their own. Too many of the king's soldiers had been lost under the onslaught of Aos Sí, who'd come to Dorcha Wood.

The men riding with Darragh took surreptitious looks at

him, none wishing for his foul gaze to fall upon them. Fear and unease cast a pall over the party, for their lord was not himself—he hadn't been for some time. Those brave enough to speak claimed they saw something else skulking in the lord of Felmore's eyes, something dark.

The party camped in the folds of a small valley alongside a narrow river. Talk was sparse among the soldiers, the mood reflecting Darragh's odd behavior. Donal kept an eye on Felmore's lord, watching him pace as darkness fell, his form looking more sinister and predatory in the fire's flickering light. As men tucked themselves in the folds of coarse blankets in small groups close to the warmth of the flames, Darragh slowed his feet, becoming stealthy. From hooded eyes, Donal watched his lord move closer to the banks of the river until he stood just beyond the lapping water.

From his vantage point, he saw Darragh crouch at the water's edge, pressing a hand on the surface. Fragments of words came to him on the chill breeze, but he was too far away for Donal to make them out. Not wishing to draw attention to himself, he slowly rolled away from the soldiers, getting to his feet in the shadows. Creeping toward Darragh, he froze when he heard the lord's voice and a watery reply. Squinting, Donal ducked behind a boulder and strained his ears, tilting his head to catch the words floating through the air.

It was a language he'd never heard. Curling his hands

over the rim of the rock, he stretched his neck and peered at the lord of Felmore, eyes going round when he saw whom he was speaking to. At first glance, it looked like a horse, its head equine in shape, but all similarity ended as Donal saw the pointed teeth flashing in its muzzle, the slick mass making up its mane. A vile chuckle slipped from Darragh's lips as the lord slowly spun on his feet and scanned the soldiers sleeping nearby. Turning back to the creature, he muttered something and pointed to a sleeping form far from the other men.

Donal gripped the rock, nails scraping against the stone, and watched a monster emerge from the water like a nightmare. Darragh stood facing it, saying something as he craned his neck to look at the creature. A rumble and flash of teeth was the reply. It stood on four legs like a horse, then rose onto two like a man, its equine head fixing on the man Darragh had indicated. The commander shifted and drew his sword, the whisper of metal loud in his ears, making him cringe. He stepped away from his hiding spot and gripped the hilt, eyes fixed on the monster that slunk toward the sleeping man.

One moment, he was padding toward the soldier on silent feet, and the next, his body was rigid, the tendons of his neck standing out as his muscles locked painfully. Arm trembling, he watched Darragh come toward him, his eyes glowing in the dark like an animal's. Clicking his tongue, Felmore's lord circled his commander. When he spoke, it was someone else's voice, low and powerful. "You are too observant for your own good, commander."

Donal's panicked gaze flicked from Darragh to the man prone on the ground. A shout of warning caught in his throat, lodged behind clenched teeth as the creature bent over the soldier, fetid water dripping onto the man's face. As the commander watched in horror, the monster snatched the man from the ground with inhuman strength, snapping his neck with a vicious twist and slinging the corpse over its shoulder. Thick lines of drool fell from its mouth as it loped to the water and dove in with a small splash, taking the body of the man with it.

"The Kelpie will feast," Darragh said, staring at the river's surface. Turning to Donal, he stretched out a hand and traced a scar on the commander's neck, a battle wound that would've killed him had the blade gone any further into his throat. "I could feed you to the beast, too. They are never satiated, you see. But such a thing would arouse suspicion."

Darragh cocked his head and gripped Donal's chin, forcing the man to stare at him. Swirls of something dark and inhuman flickered in his eyes. He wanted to pull away and raise the alarm, but his body was immobile.

Placing a finger on the commander's temple, Darragh muttered a spell. The magic pierced the man's skull, digging into his mind with sickening power. He started to move on legs that were not his own, each step in time with Darragh. The two returned to the camp, stopping when they reached Donal's bedroll.

"I have half a mind to let you remember what you've seen only so I can toy with you. But that could prove problematic, so I will let you forget." Darragh's lips moved quickly with a spell, pausing as he smiled cruelly at the commander. "Before I strip away what you've seen, perhaps you'd like to know to whom you're speaking?" He waited momentarily, laughing softly as he read Donal's thoughts. "No, I am not Haegna's spirit, though I wonder if Darragh knew you'd known of the witch's existence all these years. She fought hard in the end, but she was no match for me and her blood…" He licked his lips. "Her blood tasted divine. No, I am not that witch. I am ancient. Eternal. Death and suffering. Your people once kneeled at my feet and slit the throats of newborn babes in my honor. And you will again." He leaned in close, lips almost touching Donal's ear. "I am Crom Cruach."

The commander's jaw clenched, a scream building in his chest. Slanting his eyes at the face hovering next to him, a small whimper escaped from behind his teeth before he collapsed on his pallet, unconscious, mind wiped of all he'd seen and heard.

In the morning, a search party fanned out, looking for a soldier who'd gone missing. Donal, the stain of nightmares from a restless night lingering in his head, led the group, reporting back to Darragh when nothing but tracks were found. "The men found nothing new, my lord. Without footprints to mark his departure, I would suggest an animal took him. We can continue searching, but I feel all we would find is a body."

Darragh frowned. "We have no time to search for a corpse. Tell the men to break camp."

Donal dipped his head and strode toward the cluster of soldiers. Their voices stopped as he neared. Folding his hands behind his back, the commander marked each face, noting the fear in them. "I think we all agree that there is no hope of finding Cody alive." Feet shuffled as the men muttered. "We must press on, but I will post a watch each night. I will take the first. Nolan," he said, turning toward a man with grey along his hairline and a thick beard covering his face, "you will assign a rotation of two-hour shifts."

"Aye, sir."

Scanning the soldiers, Donal lifted his chin. "This is not the first time we have seen one of our own fall, and it will not be the last. Rumor and speculation do none of us any good. It lowers morale and makes for carelessness. We go to Taigon. For most of you, this will be your only chance to visit the seat of the king. I expect to arrive with each of you in attendance. Nolan, see that they do."

The second in command nodded. "You heard the commander. Break camp. We leave immediately."

Grim lines marred the soldiers' faces as they hastily rolled up blankets and aided the cook in packing up supplies. Talk was limited and hushed, each man wary of calling Donal's attention to their misgivings. He would report to Darragh.

In the distance, Darragh poured over a map, motioning for Donal to join him as they discussed the best route and whether to circumvent the Icy Plains—the most direct way to Taigon. Some of that land had likely thawed, but the bulk of it would be riddled with huge swaths of treacherous ice. The fastest way around that stretch was southwest, through the Misty Bog and the Wandering Mountains.

Donal rubbed his chin. "If we take the route through the Icy Plains and lose any of the horses to broken legs from trekking through slabs of ice, our journey will be slowed considerably. Going through the Misty Bogs and Wandering Mountains," he said tracing his finger along the map, "poses its dangers, but I believe it is our safest route."

Darragh's mouth pulled down. "It will take days to cross those."

"Aye, but snow cats are known to stalk the Icy Plains this time of year. With the loss of Cody, the men will be wary of traveling through those hunting grounds."

Folding his arms, Darragh eyed the map, darting a glance to the soldiers who busied themselves readying for departure. If another man went missing, they would talk, which could prove dangerous. Not to him but to them should he have to show them who their true master was. A few extra days wouldn't matter and would potentially allow him time to meet with another of Dothur's army as they would pass by fiefdoms and remote villages along the way. Perhaps he would come across a Dullahan. "Very well. Have you established a night watch?"

"Aye, my lord. Nolan will assign two-hour shifts. You will not lose another man to one of the beasts that roam this area."

"Good." Darragh strode away, a smile playing on his lips. *Humans are so pliable,* Crom Cruach thought as he infused the medallion around Darragh's neck with more dark magic, causing the man he held prisoner to shrink from his control, hiding in the recesses of his brain. The old god whispered, "Not yet, Lord of Felmore. You still have a part to play. You're mine until your task is finished."

The real Darragh squirmed inside, his sanity fracturing as the poison of Crom's control slowly devoured his mind.

CHAPTER TWENTY-TWO

rel met Gideon and his men at the edge of Dorcha Wood. The elf raised a brow when he noted the child sitting in the man's lap and craned his neck to look beyond the group. "The man and woman didn't come?"

Gideon shook his head. "They would not leave their home, though I gave them a map and told them to come should they need to."

The elf nodded and looked at the young girl. She watched him curiously, her large blue eyes fixing on the pointed tips of his ears. Her mouth parted as excitement flooded her face, followed quickly by a flash of brutal memories. Aishling whimpered and tried to burrow into Gideon's chest. He patted her back and murmured, "It's all right, Aishling. He means no harm."

"He killed people," she sobbed, covering her head with her arms.

He pried her hands away and titled her chin up. "This is Arel." Her eyes flicked to the elf, growing misty, before settling on Gideon. "He is my friend. Do you remember me telling you about my new friends?"

Her little hands twisted in her woolen dress. She nodded and darted a look at the elf. He smiled and dipped his head. Casting a glance at Gideon, her face wobbled.

He cupped her cheek. "Do you think I would let someone hurt you?" She shook her head. "The people I told you about are good. They are not the ones who came to Belfirth."

Understanding washed over the elf. He blinked slowly and then came forward, ignoring how the child cringed away from him. "I welcome you to Dorcha Wood. My people look forward to meeting you."

Aishling looked from Arel to Gideon, straightening when the man patted her reassuringly. "Hello."

Arel smiled, his face lighting so beautifully it disarmed the child. "What is your name?"

"Aishling," she whispered.

"Aishling, I am Arel." He reached out and took her hand, clasping her wrist gently. She bit her lip and curled her tiny fingers in response, a hesitant smile tugging at her mouth. "I wonder if you'd like to meet a unicorn."

Her eyes grew wide, and she sat up straight, eliciting a chuckle from Gideon. "Is that a yes?"

She twisted around to look at him. "Aye."

Gideon smiled. "Then I think you ought to go with Arel," he said, jerking his head toward the elf.

She scooted forward, hesitating momentarily before reaching for the Aos Sí warrior, who took her in his arms and set her on the ground. Hand in hand, they walked a few paces, Aishling stopping once to glance at Gideon, who waved her on. Into the forest they traveled, the soldiers filing in at a slow walk. When they went a few hundred feet, the elf stopped and gave a shrill whistle, tilting his head to look down at the child. "Listen."

She nodded and pinched her lips between her teeth. In the distance came the sound of hooves padding on the ground through the undergrowth. Aishling squeezed Arel's hand as the noise grew louder, mouth dropping open when Arion, Meara's son, broke through the trees. The unicorn bobbed his head, nickering softly, and reached the elf's outstretched hand.

Arel murmured to the animal and cast a glance at the girl. Arion snorted and bent his neck, lowering his head to snuffle at her hair. Aishling gripped the warrior's hand tightly, letting go as a giggle escaped. She turned her head. "Look, Gideon! A unicorn!"

He smiled. "Aye, that is Arion."

She gazed into the unicorn's face that hung at eye level, hand reaching toward the massive horn, fingers tracing its ridges before petting his jaw and muzzle. Arion lipped her hand, and she squealed, rubbing her palm against his velvety nose. "Hello, Arion." The unicorn nickered and nudged her when she stopped rubbing his face.

"I think he likes you," Gideon said.

"I like him too."

Arel put his hand on Arion's shoulder and said something in a language Gideon couldn't understand. The unicorn bobbed his head and looked at the elf, a silent message passing between the two. Turning his large body,

Arion walked a few paces and stopped at Gideon, ears rotating forward. "Hello, my friend," he said, reaching over to rub the skin around the base of his horn.

The unicorn sighed. Gideon, a horse-lover since birth, had gravitated to Meara's son when he'd arrived with Dyvre. Though a different species than a horse, Arion reciprocated the attention and even began to mingle with Aridius and the other mounts as they grazed.

"I hope your mother's mistress hasn't gotten into any mischief while I've been away," he murmured, leaning back as Aridius started to paw the ground.

Arion tossed his head and let out a breathy snort. Gideon laughed. "Well, I suppose that answers that question." He looked at Arel. "Is she well?"

"Aye. But word arrived from a small Aos Sí settlement," he paused and glanced at Aishling, who was poking a stick at a giant mushroom. "They were attacked."

Gideon frowned. "Let's move on. I'd like to hear what she plans to do with this news."

The elf scooped up Aishling and swung her onto Arion's back. She clutched his long, black mane and crooned at him as Arel walked at her side, leading the party to Erabel.

At the barrier, Arel stopped and warbled like a songbird, the sound carrying through the quiet. A similar call sounded moments later, and Kaelari jogged into view. She nodded a greeting and raised her arms, palms lifted to the sky, her position matching Arel's on the opposite side. Chanting in unison, they opened the gates to Erabel. She stood aside and watched the party pass through, raising a brow and giving a small smile when Aishling waved shyly. "Fiadh will be happy to hear you've returned," she said to Gideon. "Was her new family not able to come?"

"They didn't wish to leave their home, though I told them they're welcome to join us if they change their minds."

Kaelari looked surprised. "Did you not explain the danger?"

"I did. They would not be swayed."

She mumbled about arrogant humans and loped into the trees to alert her queen of their arrival. As the party progressed, Gideon took Aishling from Arion's back and put her on his lap, pointing out the various creatures poking their heads out and monitoring their passing. The child was especially taken with the Gruagach, whose beady gaze followed them. "Little people!" she cried, clapping her hands. "Mama told Keiran and me stories about them. I thought she was fooling, but they're real!" Aishling practically fell off the horse, trying to look at a female Gruagach holding a tiny baby in her arms. Gideon tightened his hold and hoisted her more firmly onto his lap, eyes pricking when her heard her whisper to her dead brother as though his spirit lingered nearby, "Keiran look… little people just like Mama said."

Fiadh rushed out to greet them as they entered the courtyard just outside the keep. Gideon slid off Aridius, Aishling in his arms, as she slowed and walked to him. Nodding to Quinn and the others, Fiadh fixed her eyes on the young girl, crouching low to look her in the face.

"Hello, Aishling. I'm Fiadh."

The child popped a knuckle in her mouth and mumbled a response.

Gideon pulled her finger away with a laugh and said, "Let's try that again without your finger."

Aishling's singsong voice repeated her greeting, and Fiadh reached out, running a hand over her head. She'd never been around children but had surreptitiously watched them scamper about in Felmore throughout her childhood. It was clear from how Gideon looked at the girl that he felt a solid connection to her. It was a father's look.

"It's good to finally meet you, Aishling. Would you like to come inside and meet more of my friends?" Fiadh rose and extended an arm, wrapping her fingers around the child's soft hand as they entered the keep.

Wreaths of smiles lit the faces of the Aos Sí gathered, many offering welcomes followed by soft looks when the child responded. As they circled the room and made introductions, Fiadh wondered about the children of the Aos Sí. None had arrived, and though she'd heard from Veren that many had been born, the elves who'd joined her in Erabel never mentioned their progeny.

When they came to the Faoladh, Fiadh tensed, expecting the girl to shriek, but Aishling cocked her head and said, "Mama didn't tell Keiran and me stories about your people."

Sibaen grinned, sharp teeth winking in her dark muzzle. "Then I will have to tell them to you."

"Promise?"

The Faoladh dipped her head. "Aye."

Aishling was led through the rest of the hall, stopping before Krulan. He stood towering above the girl, his greenish coat shifting with the twitch of his muscles.

It has been many years since a child has graced these halls, he told Fiadh.

Then it is past time.

Krulan slowly lowered his body to the stone floor to look Aishling in the eye. They stared at each other for many moments until the girl stretched out her hands and ran them along the thick fur around the Cù-Sìth's head. He rumbled low in his chest, almost purring. It was a sound he would use should he ever have pups.

The child looked from him to Gideon, smiling broadly. "I like this place."

Gideon laughed. "I'm glad to hear it."

With a final look at Krulan, she clutched Gideon's hand, and they followed Fiadh as she was led to a bedroom where she could rest after her long journey.

"But I'm not tired," she whined as she looked at the bed. "I want to see the little people again."

"You can see them after you've had a nap," Gideon said, plopping her on the raised pallet and slipping off her shoes.

Just then, Dasha swept through the open door and landed on Fiadh's shoulder. Gideon grumbled and shook his head, knowing the raven's presence would further the child's fight to stay awake. Aishling perked up and stared at the bird. He bobbed his head and croaked, swooping to the ground and walking toward her. She hopped off the bed and sat on the floor, holding out her hand. Gideon sighed and straightened, leaning against the wall next to Fiadh rather than fighting the girl's curiosity. She'd tire soon enough.

Aishling crooned to the raven, and he puffed his feathers, gurgling softly. Cocking his head, he stared at her with one of his violet-tinted eyes opening and closing his beak slowly with a breathy sound. Dasha glanced up at Fiadh, then at the child, and in that moment, she realized Aishling reminded him of Threa. He'd met her birth mother when she was young. The raven went to Aishling's hand, burrowing his head into her fingers, feathers pulsing with happiness.

"I think he may have chosen a new favorite," she said quietly to Gideon.

"Aye. It looks that way."

They left Aishling and Dasha. The child's small voice, peppered with throaty croaks, followed them down the corridor. Before entering the great hall, Gideon clasped her hand and said, "I tried to get the farmer and his wife to come, but Owen refused to leave their home. I left them a map and bid them join us if things become dangerous."

Fiadh looked down at their entwined fingers, feeling a pang of regret as he unlaced them and looked up at him. "I fear the hatred between our peoples runs too deep."

They stared at each other in the quiet alcove. There were so many things each wanted to say to the other, but their painful past stopped them. Whistling from beyond the keep had them turning to the sound. Fiadh strode through the great hall and outside, stopping next to Krulan and Kaelari.

"What is it?"

"Riders from the north."

A line of Aos Sí burst from the trees atop a collection of horses and two unicorns. They kicked up dirt and leaves as they came to a halt, swinging from their mounts in graceful leaps, their feet making hardly any noise as they hit the ground. Fiadh's scouts, having jogged aside the group as they passed into Erabel, led the newcomers to the foot of the steps.

Bowing low, a female with auburn hair and reddish skin came forward, lowering her violet eyes and dropping to a knee at Fiadh's feet. "My queen, I bring news from Tangry Forest."

"Please rise." The elf stood in one fluid movement and lifted her face to the queen. "I welcome you to Erabel…"

"Elred," the female offered.

Fiadh smiled. "Elred. You and your people are most welcome. Please come inside, and we'll discuss the news you bring us."

Elred dipped her head and motioned for the warriors who traveled with her to follow. Krulan walked with Fiadh, his fur brushing her shoulder as they made their way to the large table where the council met. The elves from Tangry Forest joined her committee around the table. Ellisar chose a spot to Fiadh's left, and she lifted her chin to him before turning to Elred.

The female clasped her hands on the table, her face devoid of emotion aside from eyes that flashed as she spoke. "We received your raven and come to seek aid. The soldiers of Tangry Forest spent a sennight battling creatures most of us had never seen or heard of. We have taken many casualties, and our forces are dwindling. We are a small settlement, and I don't know how long we can hold out."

It was startling to hear of an elven community coming

under attack. Especially one hidden and far from Oadsera. Until that point, human villages and fiefdoms had borne the brunt of Dothur's armies. "I regret that I cannot send aid."

Elred's face hardened. "Our seer is dead, along with half my fighters. Without help, you doom us all."

"If I could send warriors, I would, but I have none to spare. Without reinforcements from Oadsera, the people you see here and without the hall are the sum of our fighters."

The female's shoulders sank. "I had hoped…" She shook her head. "Please forgive my anger."

Fiadh gave a pained look. "I'm sorry. The only thing I can offer is a refuge. You know of the strength of Erabel's borders. We have extended the barrier into Dorcha Wood. There is room for your people who are not fighters. We can keep them safe. As for you and your warriors, I ask that you join us in defending this realm."

Elred's eyes flicked to a male across the table. He nodded, and she swung her gaze back to Fiadh. "Thank you, my queen."

Zaeleria, who'd lingered in the shadows, stepped forward and called out, "What manner of creature attacks your people?"

She looked at the seer, eyes flicking to the varied faces, listening for the reply. "Mages."

CHAPTER TWENTY-THREE

arragh's men were a superstitious lot, Crom Cruach groused from inside the broken man he'd possessed. As the group neared the border of the Misty Bogs, they grew restless and short-tempered. The soldiers whispered of strange noises they heard in the wee hours of the morning and shadowy things they saw out of the corners of their eyes as they sat around fires at night. Donal did his best to quiet the men, sensing Lord Felmore's ire when they balked at night patrols or hunting in woods that became thinner and more remote the farther they traveled.

By the time the contingent reached the first watery stretch of the Misty Bogs, the soldiers' nerves were frayed. Before them stretched leagues of muddy waters laced with brown clumps of grasses and thin reeds. Few trees dotted the landscape, and those they saw were twisted things struggling to survive in a land of fetid pools. Donal commanded his men to make camp along a thin stretch of earth free of the bog's tangled vines and sodden moss.

Fires were lit, though the flames were blue and green from whatever soaked into the damp wood, the soldiers found, causing many to make signs to ward off evil as they sat close together. Mud rat stew was ladled out as the evening wore on, though appetites were scarce despite the grueling pace they'd kept that day. Horses snorted and pulled at their tethers beyond the light of the flames as though they, too, sensed a fell presence.

Darragh watched it all through the slit in his tent. Baleful eyes locked onto the men, his small dagger scraping against a whetstone. He was hungry, and their foul slop wouldn't slake his appetite. The demon had been anchored too long in Darragh's body, and it was taking its toll. Running a thumb along the blade's edge, he tested its sharpness, licking the blood off his finger with a long swipe of his tongue. Staring through the lord's eyes, Crom Cruach marked each soldier huddled around the fires, landing on one who separated from the group to relieve himself. Flicking his eyes to those nearby, he gave an ugly smile as they took no note of the man. Rising swiftly, he slunk from the tent, cloaking himself in darkness with a spell to follow the young soldier.

The demon found him behind a tall clump of grasses, tucking his manhood into his leggings. He never saw Darragh coming, never made a sound as the knife whispered across his neck. The real Darragh recoiled as the old god lapped up the spray of blood, words of power spinning through his mind to draw out the essence of the slain man. When he'd drunk his fill, he dragged the body to a deep pool, placed a heavy rock on the corpse's stomach, and pushed in it, watching it sink into the muddy water, all traces of its passage vanishing with a wave of his hand.

Sated, he cast his eyes to the sliver of the moon breaking through the thick clouds and raised his arms, feeling the life force of the soldier coursing through his veins. Power surged, leaching into the air around him, causing the wind to stir and race across the landscape. Darragh smiled and slowly turned his head as a shape melted from the darkness, taking the form of a headless rider.

The massive black steed stepped onto a slip of earth, its hooves squelching in the moist ground. Darragh clasped his hands behind his back and waited for the rider to approach. Tucked in the crook of its elbow was its fleshy skull, mouth slack, and eyes glowing a dull red. When the Dullahan was a few feet away, its mount stopped, stamping and tossing its head.

"Master," the rotted face rasped, blackened tongue lolling as though it would spill from its swollen lips onto the ground.

Crom Cruach preened within Darragh's body. To be called master after so many years of solitude in the pit of an elven prison was intoxicating. He lifted his chin. "What news?"

"We've begun the assaults on settlements in the north and east. The humans are easy prey and put up little fight, but some of the troops are unruly. The Sluagh do not see themselves beholden to anyone."

Darragh raised a brow. "Do they not? We shall have to remind them who is master."

"Troya, the leader of the Sluagh, resists," the Dullahan

said, flecks of foamy spit spraying from his bloated lips. "Her sisters look to her; she claims they will bow to no one. They were summoned by an Aos Sí female not long ago and have ridden the skies with no master since. We do not think they will be easy to control."

He considered the creature's words. The Sluagh were powerful fighters who cut through a line of men like stalks of wheat. He'd seen their brutality on a massive scale long ago—the Wild Hunt—led by Xodros before Balor slew the winged god in the war with the Fomorians. The Sluagh had scattered, lost, aimless, and without purpose when their leader was killed. Fiadh, that innocent pawn of Danu, had lured them from hiding, unleashing the winged wraiths upon the world. It filled him with sick pleasure to think the elven queen was the reason for such beautiful carnage.

"I will see if I can reason with Troya once this task is finished. In the meantime, let them spill what blood they may. The killings will foment fear, which we can use to our advantage."

The Dullahan's eyes glowed brighter, then dulled again. "As you wish."

"Have the Sluagh attacked Oadsera?"

"The dark lord forbids an attack on that holding, and, for now, they abide by his wishes. He awaits word when your work in Taigon is finished."

Darragh rubbed his hands, imagining the destruction of that vile realm when his plans fell into place. The Aos Sí would fall under the coming onslaught, and he would be there when the ash cleared from the skies to take his place at Dothur's side. Conqueror. King. God.

A thick fog covered the Misty Bogs as dawn chased away the stars. The men stirred, faces lined with exhaustion from too many sleepless nights, and ate quietly. Felmore's lord emerged after they broke their fast, buckling his long sword to his side. Soldiers watched him from hooded eyes, gauging his mood as their talk turned from dim noise to furtive whispers.

Donal strode to Darragh, a grim look on his face. "Another has gone missing. Your men are wary of traveling deeper into the bogs."

A sneer lifted the lord's lips, revealing his stained teeth. "They are no better than a pack of women." He stalked into the camp, kicking an empty kettle from his path until he stood among his soldiers. "Your commander tells me you refuse to go any farther."

From a small group, a grizzled soldier rose and cleared his throat. "We've lost eight men since we set out from Felmore, and naught has been done. Unless you can guarantee our safety, why should we continue?"

Darragh raised a brow. "How many of you agree with this man?"

The soldier glanced at the group he'd been seated with, nudging those closest who reluctantly stood, nodding. Sweeping his gaze through the other troops. Three more got to their feet, the others looking away. Darragh returned his attention to the hardened warrior and his comrades. "It appears less than half wish to turn tail and run."

Jaw ticking, the man glared at Darragh. "More would join us if they weren't afraid of retaliation."

Raising a brow, Felmore's lord glanced at Donal, whose face grew hard, then returned his attention to the soldier. "Is that right?" Stepping toward him, Darragh paced back and forth, hands tapping against each other as they hung loosely behind his back. "It sounds as though you mean to encourage a revolt among my men," he paused and stared at the man, face darkening as Crom Cruach's malice flared, "and I do not take kindly to threats."

Lips barely moving, Darragh murmured and bent his head to the side as a spell shot like an arrow into the soldier, dropping him as though an invisible spear sank into his flesh. His body thrashed on the ground, sending the soldiers around him springing back in horror. The demon inside Darragh knew he shouldn't be showing the men such power, that their suspicions would be proved correct, but they had begun to revolt, and he meant to end such inclinations. Better to fear him than think him too weak to stop them. He cocked his head and stared at the writhing man. Back arching, the soldier's face spasmed, neck extended until the bones snapped in a series of pops that chased his spine. Flopping spastically, the soldier gasped, pain pulling his mouth into a horrific grimace. With a subtle wave of his hand, Darragh crushed his rib cage, smiling as the soldier gurgled and grew limp. Silence fell upon the group like a crushing weight.

Darragh scanned every man through slitted eyes, jabbing at their minds and watching them flinch. "Does anyone else wish to abandon their lord?" Heads shook, though none met his gaze. "Good. Break camp. We leave in an hour." He turned to Donal, pointing to the dead man. "Get rid of that."

Darragh ducked into his tent, feeling furtive glances at his back. *Let them talk,* he thought. They would tell stories to King Stephan's men when they arrived in Taigon. Word would spread, as it always did. His mouth curved at the corners. Weak lords curry favor with strong ones and those they fear, he mused. In time, they would come to kneel at his feet.

Talk amongst the soldiers was muted as the group trekked through Misty Bogs. The words they spoke were muffled by a thick fog that swallowed them. Things, real or imagined, were seen in the peripheral, disappearing as the looker started, trying to discern what darted in and out of the reedy grasses and misshapen trees. Horses, having more sense than the men who rode them, tossed riders who hadn't the strength or skill to keep their seats and bolted for safety. Some didn't make it, their legs broken in sinkholes, shrieks filling the air though no one came to end their suffering.

On foot, some of the men grew careless, losing their footing, slipping into the fetid water, their limbs pulled under as though claws grabbed feet and legs. The screams were music to the being inside Darragh, though they ended too soon, rescue silencing the sweet sound or a head going under and never resurfacing.

By the time Darragh and his men traversed the last of

the bogs three days later, they'd lost two soldiers, and rumors were rampant. Those brave enough to whisper in tight clusters spoke of the evil lurking in their lord. Some believed the witch who'd inhabited Felmore Castle now lived within Darragh like a tumor. Others said he'd made a bargain with a demon in exchange for the power to battle the elven plague that was spreading across the kingdom. Many wished to leave, realizing they were nothing but pawns, sacrificial lambs for whatever dark magic Felmore's lord wielded. But it was just talk. After seeing what Lord Darragh could do to those who stood against him, none had the appetite to attempt a revolt.

Donal skirted the camp, listening to the men's talk, seeing evidence of relief in their smiles and banter, undoubtedly the result of leaving the foulness of Misty Bog. But even in their somewhat lighthearted conversation, he heard talk of witchcraft and revolt. Having seen what Darragh had done to one of his men, he couldn't blame them. Felmore had reeked of evil since Haegna's mind fractured when the young lord was only a babe—the years after that proved fertile ground for her dabbling in dark arts. Darragh's father, Lorcan, had tried to heal her mind, but he had no patience for her antics and eventually left her to her own devices. As expected, her eyes fell on her only son, whom she warped into what Donal saw before him today.

He found Darragh crouched next to a clear pool of water, washing blood splatter off his dagger. He had no desire to inquire about its origins. "My lord, we must replenish supplies before we cross the Wandering Mountains."

Nodding, he wiped the edge of the blade on the sleeve of his tunic and rose, facing his commander. "Lord Rawlf's land borders the mountains. We will gather what we need there."

"Very good, my lord."

Donal lingered, drawing his lord's eye. "What?"

"The men are restless. There is talk of leaving, though I don't believe any brave enough to act on it."

Turning toward the encampment, Darragh clasped his hands behind his back. "Perhaps they need a reminder of what happens to traitors." He stepped toward the nearest tent, pausing to stare at his arm when Donal grabbed it. Slowly raising his head, he looked at the commander with hooded eyes. "You try to stop me?" The question was asked calmly, but only a fool would fail to hear the threat.

Letting go, Donal flexed his jaw and said, "You will sow discord should you punish them."

"You suggest I do nothing?" he asked with a warning.

"I believe we should be vigilant. Let us wait and see if the dissension wanes now that we've left the dangers of Misty Bog."

Darragh studied his commander, head tilting as he watched the man temper his innate fear of what he saw in his lord's eyes. He'd been reckless to wield his magic in front of the soldiers, but each day, it grew more challenging to maintain a facade of humanity. Crom Cruach longed to split Darragh's skin, erupt from this pitiful meat sack, and lay waste to the puling men who followed him. They were weak. Cowardly. Even the man standing before him, struggling to maintain a veneer of authority, would be nothing more than a plaything should he attempt to pit his will against the demon. Still, Donal was right. There was no sense in foiling his plans just to slake his thirst for violence. Blood would flow soon enough. He must do better to appear as Darragh—shrewd and calculating, cold and cruel without the savagery the demon craved.

"I hold you responsible. Continue to watch and listen. Should the need arise, I will remind them whom they serve."

Donal dipped his head and left. Whatever fell thing had claimed Felmore's lord, pray the Great Mother protected them from it.

CHAPTER TWENTY-FOUR

Fiadh watched Riani work with Quinn and his comrades, teaching them how to fight as elves did, using the natural landscape to attack or defend. It felt as though the fighting would never end. She was tired. Not her body but her mind and spirit. Every swing of a blade or release of an arrow felt wrong. She sat in the shade, listening to the bark of Riani's commands, and thought about the past.

When Rygeil attacked Dorcha Wood, she'd drawn on powers that flowed in her veins like a river. The magic she'd wielded that day had felt good. She'd felt invincible. But, at one point, she'd lost control. Men died at her hands. Fathers. Sons.

Taking a life was wrong.

But the forces that now roamed the land like rabid wolves were not the children of men. They were dark beings, and if she backed down, who would pay the price of her refusal to spill the blood of such evil creatures?

She swept her eyes across the field, seeing Quinn chatting with Riani while his companions wandered off to mingle with a group of elves. Watching them felt like the calm before the storm. The tenuous bonds they were forming would be tested in the coming months.

Fiadh leaned back against the tree she sheltered under and closed her eyes. Branches swayed, and insects hummed. She breathed deeply, opening her mind to the living things surrounding her. Brow furrowing, she felt a thrumming vibration intermingled with the hum of life. Pressing her hands to the blades of grass at her sides, she chased after the sensation, gasping when it paused in reaction. She lowered herself to her knees and pressed her ear to the ground.

"What are you—" Riani started to ask as she strutted over.

Fiadh shook her head and listened with more than her ears as the Oilliphéist stilled beneath layers of the earth, tail lashing slowly in the black river snaking deep underground.

She reached toward it with her mind, sensing it snap its teeth as she tried to slip into its consciousness. There was such power coming from the creature. Ancient power. But within it was a piece of herself, a sliver she'd left behind when she'd inadvertently birthed it. It recognized the magic flowing in her blood and hummed, the sound carrying through rock and dirt, deep and low.

Riani heard it and stepped back, eyes darting to Ellisar, who'd watched the exchange from across the field and come running over. Other Aos Sí joined them, forming a circle around Fiadh as she stretched out her body fully on the ground. Fear was evident in every face as the queen whispered too softly for their elven ears to hear.

The words were meant for the Oilliphéist. She tapped at its mind again, and like a massive portcullis, it opened. Her eyes went round as she slipped into its thoughts. Dragon. Serpent. Ally. This was not the master of the world the Merrow had imagined. It wasn't a destroyer of enemies and ruler supreme. But it was powerful—kindred—as much a part of this world as other races. And it was female.

Zaeleria shut the solar door and looked at Dyvre. "She has grown strong."

The seer leaned back in his chair, hands resting on the ornate arms. "I have only begun to plumb the depths of her power."

Her pale blue gown swayed around her lithe body, like the fins of a fish, as she sat opposite him, tucking strands of white hair behind her pointed ears. "And the Oilliphéist?"

"Fiadh told me of it, and I have felt its presence from time to time, but it does not speak to me."

She considered that. It was an interesting twist to learn of the rebirth of the ancient creature. Her sight had been frustratingly vague when she'd tried to delve into the future —too much uncertainty. The only events she could clearly see were those of Fiadh's journey into the realms of men. But not all was clear, no matter how deeply she looked. It felt as though Dothur had dulled her power, shredded it when he'd spied her looking his way. Only the Great Mother could restore her, but she hesitated to reach out to Danu. The goddess' energies would be better spent on her chosen.

"It is an interesting development. One I had not foreseen," Zaeleria told him, folding her hands in her lap, fingers lacing in such a way that they wrinkled despite her Aos Sí blood, revealing the centuries she'd walked the earth. "I hear rumors of Crom Cruach. Kaelari tells me his foul presence reached Dorcha Wood, polluting it."

"Aye. The forest rots, though the young queen extends Erabel's protection and goes out daily to reinforce and heal the barrier. The latter has yet to prove successful. For now, the decay ceased encroaching on the wood, but I expect that respite will not last."

"You will take over those duties." He dipped his head. "I will train her in what little time remains. Let us hope it is enough." *And that I am up to it*, she thought, feeling an ache in her bones that had never been there before. Her time was running short. Pray the goddess she'd live to see the end of these dark days.

Fiadh slipped into an alcove in Erabel's keep. Completely smitten with Aishling, Dasha was nowhere to be seen as she made her way out a side door. Gideon spied her, and she gave him a short wave, picking up her pace as he turned his attention back to Quinn and the other men. Kaelari was occupied with the Aos Sí as they prepared for Dothur's inevitable assault, and Sibaen, usually lurking in the shadows wherever Fiadh went, had returned to her people to speak with Ulfran, king of the Faoladh, in Mactíre. It was a perfect opportunity to duck out unseen, but Krulan, being Krulan, didn't allow her to get more than ten feet into the forest before he appeared at her side like a shadow.

Krulan sidled up to her. *Where are you sneaking off to?*

I'm not sneaking.

He snorted, rolling a massive yellow eye, the soft thump of his paws keeping time with her feet.

I wanted to be alone, she complained.

Now you'll have company.

And I won't be alone. She walked quicker, sighing in defeat moments later when Krulan's head hovered above hers in her peripheral.

Where are we going?

She made a face and ignored him. He huffed and walked sedately next to her, saying nothing until his silence proved too irritating. *I'm going to see if I can speak with Eradar.*

Mention of the guardian of the Merrow, the male who'd imprisoned her to be a pawn of their queen, Ithraen, made his hackles rise. Krulan leaped in front of her, blocking her path so quickly that she bumped into the massive wall of his chest.

"What are you doing?" she yelled, rubbing tufts of fur off her nose and mouth.

You cannot see him.

I can do what I please, she told him, glaring.

He's dangerous. Have you forgotten his betrayal?

Of course not! She strode around him, squeaking when he snatched at the hood of her cloak, tearing the fabric. "Krulan!"

A strip of dark green wool dangled from his teeth. *I forbid you to go.*

You are not my keeper.

He spat out the fabric and butted her chest, pushing her backward. Her right leg swept back to keep her balance as she flung her hands out and gripped the thick fur around his neck. Glaring up at him with fistfuls of his scruff, she ground out, "Let me go."

Power resonated in each word, and she saw them take root, watching his muzzle go slack though he fought it. A low whimper slipped from his chest, so at odds with his bulky form that, for a moment, she regretted using her magic to force him to back off. But she needed to speak to Eradar if he would deign to speak with her after everything that had happened. Krulan's body shuddered, his hind feet sliding back.

She released her hold, dropping her arms. *I'm sorry, Krulan.* She looked up at him. *You have to understand. I need to speak to him.*

He growled and turned his head, sharp eyes piercing the trees and bushes as though he could see the hidden grove where the entrance to the Merrow's kingdom lay hidden behind a fortress of rock to keep Ithraen's people safe. He would never forget the terror he'd felt when his mistress went missing. The despair that he'd failed, that he'd never see her again. And then to lose his mate—Rivya—shortly after. And their unborn pups. They were wounds that would never heal. Krulan swung his head to the Aos Sí queen, seeing her jaw tick as she folded her arms across her chest. Hanging his head, he told her, *I will come with you.*

Fiadh's shoulders lost their tension. *Thank you. Believe me. I have no wish to be held captive again. I'll be careful.*

His teeth flashed with a gruff breath.

She shook her head and patted his shoulder. *Have you so little faith?*

Every gray hair on my pelt has your name on it.

Fiadh chuckled and trudged forward, picking her way past a jeboa bush, wishing one of the delicious fruit was ripe. She hadn't visited the pool of still waters since she'd escaped captivity in Ithraen's kingdom of Abadon. Breaking through a ring of trees surrounding the entrance to their realm, she paused, letting her eyes trail the jagged rocks and scraggly plants that dotted the wall surrounding the water. It had been her doing to hide Abadon from any who might breach Erabel's defenses. Keeping the Merrow safe was the least she could do after stealing Eradar's power and abusing it.

Krulan hung back as she walked around the wall protecting Abadon, watching every step she took. Pressing her hands to the stone, she closed her eyes and felt the rock beneath her fingertips, the gritty texture, the tiny specks of life. It started trembling, vibrations racing up her arms as a small fissure snaked down the side of the wall. Nearby, Krulan growled a warning, the sound muffled by rock grinding. Beads of sweat sprang from her pores. She hadn't honed this skill enough, having spent too much time perfecting other techniques. A large chunk of rock landed with a thunk next to her foot, barely missing her toes.

The Cù-Sìth snarled.

You try doing this and find out how hard it is! she grumbled at him.

When more pieces of the wall started breaking off, she jumped back and eyed the stone face, frowning when the wall shifted and grew silent with little more than a crack for her labors. Grumbling, she wiped her forehead and considered the minimal progress she'd made.

You should've asked someone more experienced to do this work.

Fiadh gave Krulan a sidelong glance. *I was being discreet.*

You mean reckless.

She muttered and returned to the stone, running her fingers along the crack. A small line crisscrossed the side of the jagged opening, and she followed it, tracing its path with her finger. Pressing her palm to the fissure, Fiadh focused her energy, closing her eyes and using her mind to see the tiny split in the rock. It took many minutes, but she finally sensed the fracture and sent a pulse of power into it. The wall groaned, and Krulan lunged for her, hauling her away and behind him, as the earth shook and a slab of rock the size of a large doorway teetered and then fell to the ground with a thunderous crash. Birds shot into the air, wings flapping in panic, as other creatures fled their burrows or feeding grounds. Fiadh reached for them, connecting with their consciousness instantaneously, soothing their fear and coaxing them to return to the safety of the forest. A Gruagach poked her head out from a clump of moss at the base of a hazel tree and gave Fiadh a stern look. The expression was so at odds with her delicate face and black eyes that Fiadh bit her lip to keep from smiling as she apologized.

Stroking Krulan's back, she stepped around the Cù-Sìth

and went to the opening, feeling him follow her steps and hover behind her as she knelt at the lip of the pool. Leaning forward, she gripped the edge and held her face above the water's surface.

"Eradar," she whispered, seeing ripples race along the water to the opposite edge.

Nothing answered, and she tried again, sitting back on her heels. Minutes passed, the pool remaining still and glass-like. Fiadh hung her head. "I need to speak with you. Please. Let me see you."

The water parted around Eradar's head as he broke the surface. Pale blue eyes fixed on her face, his expression unreadable through his stoic features.

Fiadh squirmed under his perusal, fisting her hands in her lap. "Thank you for seeing me."

He blinked, the only indication that he heard her.

"I wanted to see you, to ask about a legend Ithraen and the oracle, Aelrah, spoke of." Eradar lifted his chin and swam toward her, his movements slow and measured. She realized with a start that he was afraid of her. "I don't mean you or your people any harm, Eradar."

The Merrow paused and studied her. "Very well. What can I tell you."

She licked her lips, recalling the nightmarish experience she'd had when Aelrah overpowered her, slipping a piece of the Oilliphéist into her body. "Ithraen held me captive because she sought to use my power to bring forth a serpent-like creature from your legends."

"The Oilliphéist."

Fiadh nodded. "She spoke of it as though it were the

true ruler of the earth, and she wanted to return it to its rightful place of power."

Eradar's mouth curved up at the corner. "She has always been overdramatic."

She smiled. "Can you tell me about it?"

"I know only the legends my people have passed down through generations. Why do you wish to hear them?"

Fiadh ducked her head and looked at him through hooded eyes. "You do know that Aelrah… did something to me, right?"

"I know that she tried to perform the rights that would eventually bring forth Caoránach, queen of the Oilliphéist. But, as you know, you escaped before she'd finished her work."

"She left something behind," Fiadh whispered.

Eradar drifted closer, stopping when Krulan let out a warning growl. "What do you mean?"

"The Oilliphéist lives. It… grew inside of me after I stole your power. And, one day, it came out."

His mouth parted, eyes going wide. "What are you saying?"

"It lives. And I need to know what your legends say of its intentions."

He looked away, considering, brow furrowing as his lips moved in silent mutters. Turning to her, he said, "You saw it?"

She nodded. "And felt it. Connected with it."

Eradar swept a hand over his face and shook his head. "Nothing like this has ever happened in our histories. Our legends speak of the Oilliphéist as the ruler of all watery realms, but some interpret the stories to mean that she and her kind held sway over all peoples with Merrow as the highest ranking."

"Does it mean us harm?"

He shot her a look. "No. While Ithraen may believe such a creature would bring power to Merrow, that is not what the legends speak of. Our folklore says Caoránach and her children once ruled all of the waters in this world and brought about renewal in times of strife. They are not evil, nor are they wholly good. At least, that is what my mother told me in my youth."

Fiadh glanced at Krulan. *Do you think he's telling me the truth?*

The Cù-Sìth studied Eradar, meeting the male's steady gaze. *Aye. I believe he is.*

Turning her attention back to the Merrow, Fiadh said, "So, you believe the Oilliphéist poses no danger to my people?"

He shook his head. "I would guess it is content to be reborn and claim its watery kingdom. Unless something threatens its realm or survival, I imagine it would simply exist, unknown to all but those who sense it."

"Thank you for speaking to me. It eases my mind to hear that this creature doesn't seek us harm." She looked down at her lap. "There is something else I need to tell you."

He raised a brow, the motion causing a fine line to appear on his otherwise porcelain-like face.

"I assume you know of the events surrounding the death of Carmun." He nodded. "It was thought she and her sons were killed, but, as it turns out, one survived. He was imprisoned in a cell of iron after the Great War. With the help of Crom Cruach, he was freed."

Eradar leaped backward, water sloshing around him and creating a wave. He stared at her with wild eyes, tail lashing under the surface. "The son of Carmun is aligned with Crom Cruach?" he hissed, eyes narrowed.

"Dothur lives. He created an army, and the attacks have begun."

His mouth twisted as he looked at her with accusation. "How could you let this happen?"

She leaned back. "I? I didn't cause this!"

"One doesn't simply escape the confines of an iron prison. The old god was consigned to darkness long ago. How is it he was free to unleash the spawn of that evil witch?" She looked away momentarily, and he swam closer, silently moving through the water. "Tell me."

"Rygeil thought he could control him. He sought to wield him as a tool to… to capture me."

Eradar spat a curse, his face a mask of anger. "It appears you and he were not much different."

She recoiled, and Krulan jumped to his feet, hackles raised. The Merrow looked at him with a raised brow. *This was a fool's errand,* he told Fiadh. *His kind has no love for anyone but themselves.*

I have what I came for, she replied, slowly getting to her feet as though the weight of Eradar's words had substance.

"I'm sorry you think so little of me and my family. We're fallible. Apparently, you believe you're not." She turned her back and walked away, feeling Eradar's eyes boring into her back.

"Your grandfather has doomed us all!" With a splash, he dove into the water and sped toward the rocky outcropping that hid the entrance to Abadon. Ithraen must be told. The Oilliphéist is reborn, and with its rebirth, the greatest threat his people would ever know.

he Aos Sí queen studied Gideon as he parried with Quinn while the other men watched and commented to one another. These soldiers were her allies, but she needed more. Thousands more. Numbers. That's what could push back the tide of darkness converging on her world.

But even with vast armies, she would be called upon to wield her power as she'd done before, and if that failed, she would need skills with weaponry that Kaelari insisted she hone. The pommel of her blade grazed her bent elbow, and she looked down at it, seeing the etched metal above the leather wrappings on the hilt. The weapon sparked a memory, and she scanned the field, finding Riani. Striding across the trampled grass, she caught the female's attention and motioned for her to follow.

When they'd reached a shaded spot far from the others, Riani stood waiting with her hands behind her back. Violet eyes tracked Fiadh's slightest movements, though the smooth planes of her face showed nothing as she waited for her queen to speak.

"I wanted to talk with you about something." The female nodded. Fiadh cast her eyes downward, fingering the pommel of her blade, thumb tracing the whirls and grooves of the etchings. "My grandfather, Rygeil, had great power. Terrible power. You saw it." She lifted her gaze to the elf, watching Riani pale and look away.

"I saw many things I wish I could forget," she whispered.

"I need you to remember."

The female looked up sharply.

Pointing to the blade strapped to Riani's side, Fiadh said, "The swords of many of Rygeil's soldiers were infused with some kind of… toxin." Memories of Gideon's illness after he'd been struck by one of the poisoned blades flooded her mind. From what he'd told her when Rygeil's forces attacked him and his men, many were slowed or hindered by whatever permeated the metal, making for an easy victory over highly trained fighters. "How did he do it?"

Riani hesitated. "Using such a weapon would require hand-to-hand combat. You don't want to get close enough to a mage to use a sword."

"No. I don't. But mages aren't the only things at Dothur's command."

The female stared at Fiadh. "I don't know how he did it. They were not dipped in the oils of a weeping nettle or spiny creeper, as you might assume. It was… unnatural. Faraen's old blade held such magic when we attacked various human holdings, but he discarded the weapon, suspicious of the toll whatever was imbued in it was taking. It is good that he did so, as I believe it was Crom Cruach's hand in making that toxin."

Fiadh frowned. Had it been an herb with properties that would slow or stun an enemy, she would consider such a tactic, but not dark magic. Not something of that demon— whose power was, even now, rotting away sections of Dorcha Wood.

"You don't need weapons laced with dark magic." Fiadh looked at her and cocked her head as Riani continued. "Danu lives in your blood, my queen. That is magic enough to overpower a mage, even one as strong as Xander."

The elves of Tangry Forest had mentioned Xander's name, but none had seen the mage. The past and his betrayal caused them to suspect his part in the attack. If Dothur led the mages, their strength might have grown tenfold with the power of Carmun's son.

Zaeleria, as though she'd been summoned, drifted onto the field, Dyvre at her side. They looked like a king and queen, each beautiful beyond imagining with profound wisdom that only comes from ages of experience. The seers came to Fiadh, tilting their heads as Riani bowed and left.

"You should listen to her," Zaeleria said, making her wonder how the seer had known what they were discussing. "All the power you need is here." She touched Fiadh's forehead. "And here," she added, pressing her palm to the queen's heart. "Dyvre tells me you have been training under him while not working with the weapons of war."

She nodded, flicking her eyes to Dyvre, who looked at her with Veren's calm expression.

"You will be a student, and I the teacher. We will build on what you have learned." Zaeleria took her elbow and led her off the field, leaving Dyvre behind, and toward the burial grounds. Fiadh balked as they neared. "Fear not, young one. You must embrace your grief. It is part of you."

Her mouth wobbled as they stepped onto the loamy ground, feet sinking into the lush earth. White and purple flowers grew along the edges of every tomb. Fiadh's attention drifted to the mound of rock and mineral encasing Veren's body. The seer watched her young queen, feeling her sadness. Letting her elbow go, Zaeleria stood aside as Fiadh went to the tomb, laying her hands on the cool stone. She closed her eyes, sealing her mind, giving Fiadh privacy to whisper to her lost love. Having spied the pair leaving the field and following, Dasha gurgled softly, leaning forward from his perch on the limb of an oak tree to better look at the seer.

"Aye, she's well, my friend."

In the distance, Aishling's singsong voice rang out, and the raven turned toward it.

"Go on," Zaeleria said. "She calls you. I will look after your mistress."

With a flap of his wings, Dasha left the females, the seer marking his flight as he ducked beneath branches and into an alcove where the young girl waited. Fiadh wiped her eyes and went to Zaeleria, following the seer's gaze. "The young one reminds him of your mother, Threa."

Fiadh smiled. "Aye, he told me."

"It is a good thing that your soldier brought her here. The child and the other men under his command."

"Not everyone thinks so."

"They are bitter. So many were killed in the Great War, and they hold hatred in their hearts." Zaeleria positioned her body to face Fiadh and took her hands. "You see these grounds as a place of mourning. It is understandable. But while their bodies lie beneath the rock, their power lives in the earth, with Danu."

"What do you mean?"

"You come here to speak to him, do you not?" she said, lifting her head toward Veren's tomb.

Her throat closed on a lump of sorrow, and she nodded jerkily.

"Does he reply?"

Brow furrowing, Fiadh said, "Of course not. He's dead."

"The dead speak to us, young one. You must learn how to listen."

"I don't understand." Her eyes flashed to the tombs of Threa and Aeson.

"Our bodies are but shells. When we leave them, we return to the Great Mother. We become part of her—the magic in our blood returned to the one who gave it. She blessed you with her power, but you can reach out to the ones you've lost and call upon their magic, draw it into yourself." Zaeleria tugged on Fiadh's hands, pulling her to the ground where they sat facing one another, knee to knee. Grasping her wrists, the seer pressed the queen's hands flat on the ground and covered them with her own. "Reach for Danu."

Fiadh closed her eyes and sent out a tendril of thought to the goddess, feeling the warmth of Danu's connection.

"Now, feel the power flowing through you and find the magic of your mother and father within it."

Bending her elbows and leaning down so her face was a foot from the ground, Fiadh felt threads of magic flowing between her and the goddess. It was familiar. Safe.

"Call to Threa. She is there."

She channeled her energy into her connection with the Great Mother, feeling her body grow warm as their magic intertwined. Drawing upon a memory of Threa—a gift from Danu—Fiadh latched onto the tenor of her mother's voice, her essence, which had felt tangible when the goddess gave her entry into the past. Threa's face bloomed in her mind, growing dim until it was a fuzzy image, soft pink around the edges like a shadowy being. She heard Zaeleria's voice from outside herself telling her to open her mind and feel for the magic that had coursed through Threa's veins in life. Wrinkling her brow, Fiadh let down her mental shields and focused on the tendrils of power lingering in the essence of her mother. They snaked toward her, fingers of energy like the roots of trees. Tiny pinpricks erupted along her palms and fingers, radiating up her arms and neck before wrapping around her skull in a web of interconnected currents. Her flesh grew hot as pulses of power lit up her mind, growing in intensity until they receded, fusing with her magic, tightly knitting with the core of her power.

Threa—nothing more than a ghostly form—smiled, then drifted into the earth's womb, where Danu cradled her. Fiadh opened her eyes, noting Zaeleria's frank curiosity. Sitting back on her heels, she looked down at her fingers, rubbing them together in slow circles. Hovering her hand above the ground, she whispered, watching dead leaves and dirt rise and dance in the air. She shaped them, marveling at the ease with which they obeyed her command. Concentrating, Fiadh pulled particles of water from the air and combined them with the debris, creating a ball of mud which she flung outward, the mass smacking into a tree trunk.

Under Zaeleria's watchful eye, Fiadh repeated the process, her heart catching when she reached for her father, Aeson. His power was dull compared to Threa's, but when it fused with hers and her mother's, it grew in strength as though magic spoke to magic. Their union in life came full circle with their daughter.

Fiadh sat back on her heels, her entire body humming with energy.

"Your brother is there, too. And Veren," Zaeleria said quietly.

Giving a jerky nod, Fiadh leaned down again and tapped into that place of power and awareness. Her mind whispered Veren's name. She paused to listen, sensing the moment he answered. A dam broke inside Fiadh as he greeted her. She crumpled and pressed her head to the ground. His face and voice blotted out everything else.

Fiadh, his voice whispered through her mind.

I miss you.

I am here.

She dipped her chin, a lump clogging her throat. Fiadh embraced him as though he opened ethereal arms, feeling his love flow through her with so much power. The illusion of ghostly hands stroked her skin, grazing the tears that ran down her cheeks. He spoke to her, and she smiled, *I am with you. Always.*

Fiadh's heart whispered goodbye, aching as Veren slipped from her mind.

Somewhere in the darkness was Calum. She sensed her brother's awareness. Her twin. But she would not take from him. Not because she feared his power or resented what he'd done in life. Calum had earned her forgiveness before he'd drawn his last breath. No. She couldn't accept a gift of his magic because opening herself to him would be like feeling part of her restored. A piece of who she was that she'd lost so long ago, only for it to be ripped away once their connection inevitably severed. He was her other half. His loss was a ragged wound that would never heal.

So she spoke to him instead, feeling his warmth and welcome. He was with their mother and father now. Part of her family was whole. One day, she would join them.

CHAPTER TWENTY-SIX

The Wandering Mountains sat on land plagued by tremors and massive seismic shifts. Many an army had disappeared among the jagged peaks when the ground swelled and split, swallowing those caught in the treacherous landscape. Lord Darragh jerked on the reins of his mount, the bit biting into the horse's mouth and drawing blood. He sniffed the tangy scent and smiled. The company halted behind him, watching his every move with hooded eyes, many wishing the ground would open up and consume him.

Donal nudged his gelding to his lord's side and pulled out a map, tracing his finger along a thin valley that cut through the mountains like a river. "If we take Eidolon Pass, we could reach Taigon in less than a sennight, but it's risky. If the earth shakes, we'll be trapped between these ranges," he said, pointing to massive peaks bordering the pass.

Inside the husk of the lord of Felmore, Crom Cruach considered the suggestion, weighing the risks with the speed at which they'd reach the king. They'd lost time stopping at Lord Rawlf's holding for supplies, though he admitted the mood of his troops had improved following the brief respite. Still, he could sense the elven queen was preparing for her journey. Time was not something he could waste.

"We will take the pass."

"Aye, my lord." Donal dug his heels into his mount's sides and trotted to the men, commanding them to form a line.

The army entered the Eidolon Pass with Darragh at its head like a venomous snake. The wind whipped through the air in haunting wails as it blew through the pass, curving around the rock and ruffling the hair on the soldiers' necks like a woman's fingers. Horses snorted and balked, the whites of their eyes showing the deeper they traveled into the Wandering Mountains. Men darted glances across the surroundings, seeing shadowy things in crevices of rock or feeling the sour breath of death at their backs. The sun dipped below the sharp peaks of the mountains, dimming the pass so that more than one soldier made a sign of protection.

At the midday meal, talk was scarce, and appetites lean. While the men ate, Darragh climbed to an outcropping of rock and stood overlooking the soldiers, ears trained to their murmurs and the thoughts they didn't utter. High above, a dark shape emerged in his peripheral, hurtling above the craggy peak of a mountain. It flew through the air so quickly that he saw little more than leathery wings and spindly legs before disappearing behind a ridge. Turning toward the area of its descent, he cocked his head and reached out his senses, feeling the creature's slick mind. It waited for him, having been sent by Dothur—a Sluagh.

He flicked his eyes to the men milling around below. They were oblivious to the creature lying in wait, its arrival too swift for their dull eyes. Muttering a spell of concealment, he cloaked himself in shadow and climbed the face of the mountain, using magic to propel Darragh's weak human body forward at greater speeds. In minutes, he'd reached the summit and leaped down the other side until he came to a dark crevice where the Sluagh crouched nearly concealed between the rocks.

Clicking sounds, like that of the Carrion Beetle, met his ears as he stood at the mouth of the fissure. A skull-like face bobbed in the dimness, its eyes—black pools of hideous awareness—watching him. Inside Lord Felmore's body, Crom Cruach squatted, using the fleshy hull as a shield when he spoke. "I assume you've come with news."

Troya's raspy voice slithered through the dark crevice to his ears. "My master moves east and north with his armies. He will await your arrival at Oadsera."

Darragh nodded. "And our enemies?"

"The Aos Sí have yet to attack. They watch and wait behind their borders. Only one small band engaged with our forces. They were from Erabel."

He lifted a brow. Erabel? Hmm. Was the young queen sending contingents to surrounding areas? He would not have thought she'd risk losing any members of her paltry army. Not when her people had yet to come under attack. "Interesting." He leaned in to peer into the dimness. Troya's ghostly face looked back, her pale head hovering in the blackness, looking disembodied. "Tell your master I will leave this body once we've set things in motion in Taigon. Perhaps you and your sisters will fly me to Dothur," he added with a smirk.

Troya hissed. "Should we hoist you into our domain, be assured we will drop you from the sky and watch your body smash itself against the earth."

Darragh chuckled. "Then I will heed your warning and travel on foot, though the trek from Malver Gorge to Oadsera would be much quicker with your wings."

"I am no pack mule," she said, her breath wafting through the aperture with the scent of death.

He shrugged. "Our business is done here. I will lead the men through the pass, and when we reach Taigon, I will truly see the lord of Felmore's worth." He turned away, cloaking himself as he propelled his body over the lip of the ridge and down the opposite side, stopping when he came to the jut of rock overlooking the contingent of soldiers. Dispelling the magic shielding him from view, he stared down at the men, lip curling in distaste as he smelled their emotions seeping from their pores. They were not meant to rule. Their race was defined by petulance and fear. Once his work in Taigon was complete, those traits would come to the forefront and be their downfall.

On the second day, the ground trembled beneath the feet and hooves of Darragh's men as the group made their way through Eidolon Pass. They froze, eyes wide, scanning the ground and mountains on either side, wondering if the peaks would shift inward, crushing them. Darragh hugged his legs to his mount's sides, clenching so hard the horse's flanks twitched with discomfort as it snorted and tossed its head. A low rumbling reverberated through the earth beneath the men, and Darragh eyed the surface, searching for small fissures. Rocks broke free of the mountains pressing in on them, careening down the sides in clouds of dust. Donal's horse reared, forcing the commander to arch his body forward to keep his seat. Men yelped as tiny shards hit them or the legs of their mounts.

With a violent jerk, the ground heaved, throwing soldiers from their saddles and sending others staggering to their knees. Darragh leaped from his horse, waving his hand in the air to silence the shouts of alarm breaking out around him. Going to his knees, he planted his hands on the ground and drove his will through the mantle to the massive tectonic plates grinding against each other. Spells filled his mind, falling from his lips into the ground, where they sank into the sediment. With a cruel smile, he felt Danu—Mother of the Earth—flinch at his presence in her domain. The ground spasmed, buckling beneath him. Darragh ground his teeth and forced his will into the rock. Sweat beaded his brow, plastering his lank blond hair to his skull while blood trickled from his nose. Crom Cruach knew he was pushing Darragh's body too hard. The man's mind was brittle; if he wasn't careful, it could break, bursting like a bloated waterskin.

He felt Donal come to his side, felt the man's eyes drill into his back as thoughts swam through his head of what and who he saw bent over the earth. But the commander remained quiet, shying away from a truth he chose not to face. Minutes passed as the demon fought with the earth, soldiers panicking as they tried to calm their mounts or duck beneath juts of rock to escape the debris falling from the mountains.

Finally, Crom Cruach broke through one of the plates far below his hands, sending a crack along its edge where it butted against another massive slab. The ground shook as the fissure spread, easing the pressure and stilling the ground. He hung his head, heart hammering, and willed the body he controlled to return to its normal rhythm. Within the human husk, he felt Darragh squirm like a child, the feel of him recoiling, making the demon want to shred that speck of humanity to ribbons. But he had use for the Lord of Felmore and stayed his urges, staggering to his feet and facing his commander.

"Take command of your men and get them ready to continue," he said hoarsely. Donal nodded, mouth opening and closing briefly. Darragh studied him beneath heavy brows, reading the thoughts in the man's head. He could wipe his mind with a whisper but knew even that bit of magic would take a toll on this strained body. Straightening his shoulders, he barked an order to be ready in five minutes and walked to his horse, forcing the beast's head down when it balked. It took two attempts to find his seat, during which Donal came out of his stupor and gathered the men, reassuring them the threat was over for now.

Crom Cruach needed to replenish his strength—his hold on Darragh's body. He needed sacrifice and blood, but taking one of the men would further divide the company, and he couldn't risk rebellion this close to his goal. Hunching his shoulders, he resumed their travel through the pass, ignoring the whispers and looks of hatred or fear. Three days later, they reached the end of Eidolon Pass and found themselves on the outskirts of Taigon.

CHAPTER TWENTY-SEVEN

Fiadh sorted her clothes, stuffing those she'd take into a satchel. A few doors down, Gideon was doing the same. Krulan stretched, claws scraping the stone floor, watching her. Her body thrummed with power, the sensation becoming more familiar with each passing day since Zaeleria had guided her to the latent magic of her family and Veren that lingered within Danu. She stopped and flexed her fingers, feeling them ache with a need to release whatever was building inside of her.

Glancing at Krulan, she made a face. *Zaeleria could've warned me I'd feel like this.*

Perhaps she didn't know.

I doubt that. She laced her fingers and cracked her knuckles, sighing with pleasure when they popped.

He flashed his teeth at the noise. *That can't be healthy.*

Frowning, she shook her hands out and went back to packing. *I want to crawl out of my skin,* she told him, body twitching.

The Cù-Sìth raised a brow, yellow eyes sparkling with humor. *I don't think that would be a good idea.*

Fiadh huffed and gave him a scathing look. *It's nice to know what a sympathetic soul you are.*

He snorted and rested his head on his massive paws, listening to her muttering, ears flicking when a peal of laughter rang behind him.

In the hallway just beyond her door, Aishling played on the floor with Dasha, her giggle bouncing off the stone walls, so at odds with the maelstrom growing beyond Erabel's borders. Fiadh paused, tunic dangling from her fingers, and watched the girl, a soft smile playing on her lips, growing warmer when Gideon's baritone voice drifted to her.

"Is there a pixie in the halls of Erabel?" he joked, slinging his satchel to the ground and going to one knee, leather leggings stretching around his muscular thighs. He ruffled Aishling's hair, eliciting another fit of giggles. "Aye, you are a pixie."

"I'm not a pixie, Gideon!" she said, scrunching her face.

He reached over and tapped the sweetly upturned end of her nose. "Is this not the face of a pixie?" Dasha croaked and tapped the ground with his beak. "It seems the raven agrees with me, so it must be true!"

"That's not what he said!"

Gideon's brows shot up, and he spun on his heel, pinning Fiadh with a questioning look. She cocked her head and shrugged, not sure what to make of the girl's comment. Quickly folding the last item into her bag, she joined them in the hall, stepping over Krulan, who refused to move. Crouching down, she stroked the raven's breast, gazing deeply into his violet eye as he tilted his head to the side to look at her. She read his mind, feeling his wish to communicate with the child and his frustration that he couldn't. Fiadh pursed her lips, telling him she wished she could help, but Aishling lacked her bloodline. Dasha looked at the girl, then back at Fiadh, and in that look, she heard the raven's worry. Their time would be fleeting in his unnaturally long life. But there was nothing to be done about it. Fiadh told him to make every moment count. He pressed his head to Fiadh's hand as her fingers trailed his plumage.

Clicking his beak, he turned his attention back to the child, spreading his wings and walking in circles, much to her delight. Fiadh watched for a few moments, the image of the two of them blurring with memories of her mother, Threa, playing with the raven when she was young. She felt the weight of Gideon's stare and turned toward him. Their eyes met, and something arched between them, some connection, a flow of energy thrumming within her skin, reached for him. Her mouth parted slightly, eyes going round. He blinked, then shook his head, brow furrowing.

The moment passed as quickly as it came, but a thready tether remained.

Sibaen had returned from Mactíre with King Ulfran and a contingent of their best fighters, bearing news of sightings of Dothur's army. Sluagh and mages had been spotted attacking human settlements on the outskirts of their borders. The Faoladh army, under their king's orders, hadn't engaged, but some had ignored his command and slipped into the villages, saving who they could and killing a mage. Ulfran, fearing retaliation, sent the bulk of his people to their ancestral grounds deep in the Whispering Caverns along the Southern Sea to protect them. He brought the most skilled of his army to Erabel, Sibaen leading them.

The Aos Sí and Faoladh troops greeted each other like old friends with slaps on the back and jugs of mead. King Ulfran stood in front of Fiadh as she greeted the allies. Grizzled and scarred, his thick fur, once black, was mottled with silver. Across his well-padded chest, he wore an intricately woven sash with threads of gold held together by a large pin with a bust of a Faoladh carved into it. He winked at her as she averted her eyes from his lower half. Like all Faoladh, he wore nothing save the adornment on his torso, marking him as ruler. With his elongated muzzle curled into a smile that looked more frightening than friendly, he said, "Greetings, Queen Fiadh of Erabel."

She wiped her face of lingering unease and replied, "Welcome, King Ulfran. All of Erabel thanks you for joining us."

He smirked and stepped forward to take her elbow, leading her across the hall to a small table with two ornate chairs. "Enough of the formalities. I'd bend a knee, but these old bones would groan and pop so loudly I fear I'd need one of your people to help me rise again, and I'd never hear the end of it."

Fiadh chuckled and motioned for one of the elves to bring them food and drink. Ulfran sighed as he sank into the cushioned seat and accepted a mug of mead and a handful of blood berries.

"It's been ages since I set foot in these halls," he said casually, popping bulbous fruit into his mouth. "Though the last time was just as dire."

She dipped her head and fidgeted with a stray thread poking out of her dress. "Did you know my parents?"

"Not as well as I wished I had, but, aye. Enough to know their lives ended much too soon, and the world lost what would've been great leaders."

"Thank you," Fiadh said quietly.

"You remind me of her. Your mother." He looked at her, the yellow rings in his dark eyes glowing. "She, too, had a fondness for strays." Ulfran jerked his head toward Gideon, who lurked in a corner, far enough not to hear their conversation but close enough to keep an eye on her.

Fiadh laughed. "I'd be hard-pressed to say who the stray is between the two of us."

The Faoladh nodded. "My people have a long history with humans." He picked at one of his long, dark nails. "It is not without bloodshed, but I've always believed there are two sides to every conflict. My people are not innocent, and neither is theirs. But... I believe the world would be a darker place without mankind. And, so, we do not hunt them, though they'd be easy enough to catch." Ulfran gave a positively feral grin and folded his hands, the pads of his fingers scraping softly against each other in the quiet. "My daughter tells me you have similar feelings—minus the hunting, of course."

Her eyes rounded, darting across the room and landing on Sibaen, who stood with Riani and Kaelari. "Your daughter?"

"Aye. My pride and joy, that one. Though I admit the bulk of my gray is due solely to her antics as a cub."

"I didn't know." She turned back to the king. "How could you part with her? Give her as tribute."

"You believe I made that choice?" He wiped a hand over his mouth, muffling a laugh. "I could no more force Sibaen to be tribute than you could stop the sun from rising. She pleaded with me for nigh unto a sennight." He held his palms up, silver strands of fur around each digit glinting in the candlelight. "I could not refuse such heartfelt cajoling from my favorite daughter."

Sibaen headed toward her father's side as though she'd been summoned, her lithe body slinking through the crowd until she stood at his elbow. "Ah, here she is." He said, tilting his head to give her a wily look.

The Faoladh eyed him, the tip of a canine winking between her dark lips. "What are you about, old man?"

"I? Nothing! Simply regaling the young queen with stories of my favorite daughter."

Sibaen sighed. "I'm your only daughter."

He chuckled. "Aye. True enough. Great Mother protect me from daughters."

Fiadh let out a startled laugh, slapping her hand over her mouth. Never had she seen the usually stoic female so free with her words. It was like seeing Sibaen, the real

Sibaen, for the first time. The female shoved her father's arm off the chair and planted her backside on it. "Not to worry, my queen. I will keep this one in line."

"That's your mother's role, and she's not here," he groused.

Sibaen gave him a warning glance. "Shall I give her a full accounting?"

Ulfran huffed and grabbed his mug, downing the mead in a long pull. "I am king and your father. Show some respect."

She leaned over and licked his cheek. Fiadh smiled, their love for one another a tangible thing amid the hall. Ulfran returned the affection and patted his daughter's head, the action pulling a memory of her father doing that when she was small. Setting the mug down, Ulfran said, "Sibaen tells me you are to depart on a journey."

Fiadh settled into her chair, readying herself for an argument. "We can't defeat Dothur's army in isolation. I intend to broker an alliance with King Stephan and his vassals. Only united do we have a chance at a future."

Ulfran cocked his head and scratched his neck, the sound of his nails sliding along his skin like sand against a rock. "Agreed." It took an effort to keep her mouth closed at his response. She'd assumed he'd try to argue against an alliance as Ellisar had done.

His eyes crinkled at the corners. "You are surprised?"

"I… I assumed you would balk at an alliance with the children of men as many of my people have."

"Ah. But I see mankind's children are already among you." He eyed Gideon and Quinn, who'd sidled up to

Belfirth's lord. "Unlike the Aos Sí, my people do not have a history so fraught with hatred. In my great-grandfather's time, we lived side-by-side. I would see those days returned."

She sagged. "You have no idea how much it means to hear you say that." Fiadh looked up at him. "I was afraid you'd try to stop me."

He laughed. "I know better than to tangle with a determined female." Sibaen swatted at him. "It is a compliment I give, daughter! I swear it." The mischievous look on his face said otherwise, and Fiadh bit her lip to keep from giggling. "I assume my tribute shall join you on your travels."

Fiadh made a face and fidgeted. "I don't know if that would be a good idea."

"Oh?" He leaned back.

She glanced at Gideon, then turned her attention back to the Faoladh. "I'd fear for her safety." Sibaen sneezed. "Humans haven't seen Faoladh for a hundred years. They may attack out of fear."

"True enough. But they haven't seen the creatures Dothur is unleashing either." He gripped Sibaen's hand. "When mankind sees you and my daughter fighting against dark forces together, they will come to understand us as allies."

"You place great faith in their ability to see reason."

"Faith must begin somewhere," he countered.

"I can't argue with that. It's why I'm going. I just—" She looked at the female. "I don't want to lose a friend."

Sibaen's muzzle curved in a smile, fangs stark against her dusky fur. "Neither do I, which is why I will join you."

King Ulfran rose and extended a hand, gently pulling

Fiadh to her feet. "Then, it is settled. You leave on the morrow?" She nodded. "Good. For now, the scents of the kitchen are calling to me. My belly is empty, and my mouth lacks the sweetness of wine! Let us feast as we prepare for what the morning brings."

CHAPTER TWENTY-EIGHT

ishling clung to Gideon as he bade her goodbye the following morning. He held the child in his arms, promising he'd return soon.

"Will you bring me a present?" she asked wetly, leaning back and twisting her fingers in the neckline of his tunic.

"A present?"

She nodded.

"Aye. I will bring you a present. Is there something you're wishing for?"

She whispered in his ear, and he smiled, eyes wrinkling at the corners. Cupping his hand around his mouth, he softly replied, poking the tip of her nose with his finger before setting her down where Dasha was pacing. The raven plucked at Aishling's dress, lifting his head for her small hand as she ran it down his head and back. Nym, Krulan's new mate, came to stand at the girl's side—her guardian while Gideon was away. The warrior nodded at the Cù-Sìth and hefted his satchel onto the back of Ariduis' saddle before swinging onto his mount.

Fiadh knelt at Aishling's side, tucking strands of hair behind the girl's ear. "Will you take care of Dasha while I'm gone?"

The child looked at the raven, who parted his beak with a breathy croak. "Aye."

The queen looked at her stalwart friend and held out her arm. The raven hopped onto it and preened her hair. "I'll miss you, too," she whispered. "Look after her, all right?" He snapped his beak and pressed his head to hers, feathers puffing. She kissed him and set him down.

Meara stamped a hoof and bobbed her head, impatient to leave. Fiadh gave her a look and went to Krulan. *I don't suppose I can convince you to stay.*

Where you go, I go.

She shook her head. *I had to try.*

He huffed and turned from her to nuzzle Nym.

Fiadh made her rounds, bidding farewell to those who would remain behind defending Erabel and the elves who would travel work to rally her people and offer aid to human settlements while she and a small contingent went south to Taigon. King Ulfran waited patiently for his turn, resting his clawed hands on her shoulders when she came to stand before him. The look he gave was that of a father, and she realized, as she stared into his yellow gaze, that of all those she'd met, he was the first to naturally step into that role. Fiadh didn't question the right of it, didn't balk at the reality that she'd only known him for a day. He was a father. A leader. And right now, she needed both.

The weight of his hands pressed into her. "Our seers, like yours, prophesied your coming. They saw the path you would walk, and I am proud to walk it with you. Fear not for your people. I will keep them safe."

Her throat clogged. She knew her quest could be a fool's errand. She'd been called one enough times to accept that she was often rash and pigheaded. But that didn't change her course. It didn't change her will to fight for a better future. "Thank you. I'll bring your daughter back to you. I promise."

His eyes narrowed slightly. "You cannot make those promises, but know that I trust you with her life—whatever comes of your journey."

The truth of what he said was a rock in her chest. He was a pragmatist. Ulfran had seen enough in his lifetime to know some things were beyond his control, and he relinquished those to the Great Mother. She envied his ability to do so as she fought so hard against accepting those she'd lost and feared losing. Fiadh nodded and pulled away as he patted her back.

Swinging onto Meara's bare back with only a satchel slung across the deep green of the embroidered tunic extending mid-thigh over brown leggings—her weapons left behind as she sought peaceful alliances. She glanced at the small company that would enter hostile territory as they traveled to Taigon to seek an alliance with King Stephan. Gideon stared at her, waiting, his handsome face accented by the shadow of a beard, dark brown hair unbound and free of war braids. At his side stood Corene, the leader of the Urisk. She watched Fiadh with goat-like eyes on her placid face, her lower half adorned in a beautiful breech-cloth. The sinew of her bow rested between her small breasts. A quiver of arrows and an ornate saber were strapped to her sides. Though slight, her reedy body was powerful and fleet. She'd need no horse to keep pace with the group. Sibaen, on the other hand, was atop a restive mount who'd never had one of the Faoladh upon his back. The female looked positively giddy, tongue lolling out of her mouth like a dog as she perched on the horse in a squat, her furred hands gripping the reins. Fiadh smothered a giggle at the growl of excitement Sibaen shared when their eyes met.

Kaelari, Ellisar, and five other elves, including Faraen and Thallen, flanked them, nudging horses Aos Sí had brought or stolen aside as Fiadh lifted her heels into Meara's ribs. Never in Aos Sí history had there been such a collection of races bound together for a common cause. They followed their queen, Lura, and Seshka, at the rear, trusting her to lead them out of Erabel and into a dangerous world. She couldn't guarantee their safety, but Ulfran was right about that. But they went anyway, willing to lay down their lives for her. How had it come to this? How had she ascended a throne when she'd been nothing but a young woman flitting around her beloved forest a moment ago? She took a deep breath and raised her chin, relaxing her grip on the unicorn's mane. Danu had led her to this place and time, and she trusted the Great Mother.

The party left the courtyard outside the keep, snaking through the undergrowth toward the western border of Dorcha Wood. They would take a route around Felmore before heading south, traveling along the Crooked Gap—a hidden pass through the Wandering Mountains known only to the Aos Sí.

Arion, Meara's son, stood in the shadows watching the party leave, ears flicking and giving a soft nicker when his mother spied him. He whinnied, stepping from beneath the bough of an oak. A wealth of feeling passed between the two as they stood, faces resting aside each other. Fiadh's heart caught when Arion stepped backward, his soulful eyes finding hers, asking her to keep his dam safe. She promised to do all she could to protect Meara, and he dipped his head, returning to his sanctuary under the tree.

Leaving Erabel, they entered Dorcha Wood, trees bending toward Fiadh in welcome as forest creatures watched her progress through the dimness. The party was silent, save for the muffled sound of hooves on the leaf-covered ground. Gideon rode behind Fiadh. His eyes fixed on her regal form, the soft sway of her lengthy, black hair, and the curve of her hips as she kept her seat on the unicorn's back. That she'd asked him to join her filled him with emotions he struggled to accept, knowing he had no future with the ruler of the Aos Sí. Neither his people nor hers would welcome a union, should she even consider one after what he'd done to her. But he couldn't deny his feelings, only hide them, push them aside as much as he could, lest she see them in his face.

When they reached the border, Kaelari and Ellisar scouted ahead while the rest of the group waited within the line of trees. Fiadh stroked the low branch of an oak, feeling its ancient awareness. The life thriving within it. She clutched a web of leaves, head swimming as a horrible vision of Dorcha Wood swamped her mind. Rot, like the stretch of forest along Felmore's border, consuming every living thing. It was so real. She could smell the rankness, feel the mushy texture of the dying tree in the palm of her hand, where a moment ago, there was life. She knew Danu was showing her what would happen if Dothur succeeded. And beyond the forest? Her blank stare swept the landscape outside the woods, seeing towns in ruins, Aos Sí, and humans enslaved for labor or something much darker. Food for creatures whose appetites were never slaked.

"Fiadh." Gideon's voice cut through the dark images careening through her mind. "Fiadh," he said with more force.

She turned to the sound, her eyes slowly clearing. Around her form and Meara was a wall of wind in debris, obscuring Gideon and Aridius, though she could hear the worry in his voice. A perfect funnel, like a vortex, shielded both of their forms, making it impossible to see anything beyond a few feet. But it comprised more than matter from the air and earth. Something was woven within it, something she'd created without conscious thought. Much like the one protecting Erabel, a shield was embedded within the swirling mass, and she knew if someone tried to cross that barrier, it would be the last thing they did.

Fiadh focused on Gideon's voice, pulling her magic back into her body like winding a spool of thread. The air settled, dirt, leaves, and small rocks falling. She stared at Gideon, eyes flicking to the elves at his sides whose concern mirrored his own. "We can't fail," she whispered, head swinging to the break in the trees where Ellisar was reentering Dorcha

Wood. "If we do, everything," she motioned to the forest and land beyond it, "will be lost. Everything."

Gideon nodded. "Then we won't. We'll make them understand." She looked at him with haunted eyes, the vision slow to fade from her memory. He nudged Aridius forward, his leg brushing against hers. "King Stephan will hear you out, and if he won't act, we'll go from fiefdom to fiefdom and speak with every lord. We'll convince them of our shared threat. By now, they've heard of the attacks if they haven't already seen them firsthand. If the king won't ally himself with us, others will."

She held his gaze, seeing the determination in his face, hearing it in his voice. It gave her hope. Nodding, she glanced at Kaelari, who'd just rejoined their party. "What news?"

The female scanned each face before landing on Fiadh. "There was a scout on the northwest border of Felmore. Aside from him, I saw nothing."

"There *was* a scout?" she asked, frowning.

Kaelari gave her a wry look. "Fear not, my queen. I only gave him a tap on the head."

Slaughtering those she hoped to ally with was not a good look, and Fiadh was thankful her warrior took that knowledge to heart. "No doubt he'll be feeling that when he wakes."

"Aye, but he'll still have his head," Kaelari said, smirking and nudging Ellisar, who chuckled softly.

They left the sanctuary of Dorcha Wood, Ellisar taking the lead, followed by Fiadh, who was flanked by Kaelari and Gideon, with the others falling in behind. It felt like a lifetime ago that she'd left the forest for the first time. Giving Gideon a sidelong glance, she saw his body stiffen as the group entered an exposed swath of land. His blue eyes, bright against his dark hair and stubble, scanned their surroundings with a warrior's look. Leather armor creaked softly as his body shifted atop Aridius' back. Fiadh's eyes slid down his arm, noting the roped muscles and landing on his hand where it gripped the worn leather of the reins. Gideon's other hand twitched at his side, ready to wield the sword he wore strapped to his back. She hoped he wouldn't be forced to pull the weapon from its sheath, but a gnawing feeling churned in her gut, and she feared blood would be spilled before this journey ended.

Ellisar and two other Aos Sí scouted ahead, reporting back periodically as the party made their way through lands not traveled freely by the elves for a century. Fiadh sensed the unease of those around her, it mirrored her own, and she sought to allay their fears by starting up a conversation with Gideon, reminding them that not all saw her people as enemies. "Have you had many dealings with holdings in the Western Fold?"

He turned his head to her. "Belfirth was small with few ties to the crown. We were content to align ourselves with other lords in the east and leave the squabbling for power and alliance to those with greater strongholds. My father, Ross, visited Wareham, Haevington, and Felmore in his time but didn't consider the lords of those estates allies as they were too remote to be of aid should we call on them."

"He knew Lord Darragh?"

Gideon's face tightened. "Father knew Lorcan, having

spent time with Darragh's father when they were young knights stationed in Taigon. When Lorcan died, he paid his respects to the lord's widow and son, but something happened during his stay, though he never told me of it, and I always felt he distrusted the young lord of Felmore." His mouth turned down as he glanced at her and turned away. "I hope you know desperation drove me to Felmore when Belfirth was destroyed. I'd heard the stories. I knew Darragh's reputation, but——" His eyes looked haunted. "I was blinded by hate, wanting to punish anyone who wore the face of my enemy." Gideon looked at Fiadh, shame stamped across his features. "I wish I could change what I've done, who I became. But I can't, and I will bear the weight of my actions until death. I… I have nothing left to fight for, save you."

Fiadh's face softened. "You have much to fight for. Think of your ward, Aishling. I know you want her to grow up in a better world." She ached to touch him, the healer in her wanting to ease his pain. That was how it all started, this path she walked now. With a wounded man falling at her feet. Afraid of what it would mean to reach for him, she gripped Meara's mane and said, "You can't carry your guilt forever. You need to let it go. I've forgiven you. It's time you forgave yourself."

He clenched his jaw against the wave of emotions coursing through his body and nodded stiffly. "In time, I will. Until then, my strength, my sword… all of me… is yours."

CHAPTER TWENTY-NINE

Taigon was known as the Golden City, named for the brick—a yellowish clay with flecks of pyrite —forming the outer wall and every structure inside the sprawling town. It sat on a high point, rolling hills filled with farmsteads and tilled swaths of land surrounding it. At its heart was the citadel, a fortress with towering spires, from which King Stephan Laoghaire ruled all of Crethia.

Darragh eyed Taigon, mouth curving in a cruel smile as he pictured the orange glow of fire filling the sky and the screams of the dying echoing through the landscape. He cocked his head as he watched a farmer leading a pair of oxen, pulling a cart laden with sacks of grain, through the gates. Perhaps he should save the city, slaughter those who refused to bend the knee, and enslave the rest, accepting offerings of sacrifice from his throne. It would bear thinking on.

Donal halted the group, calling up one of Darragh's knights to bear Felmore's banner while the others closed ranks around their lord as they made a slow procession to the manned gate into the city. Men traversed the wall walk, eying the approaching party, bows at the ready should they sense a threat. At the massive wooden gates, Donal nudged his mount forward and announced Lord Darragh. The soldiers scanned the group and stood aside, allowing them to pass. Taigon was five times the size of Felmore. Everywhere was a hum of activity as vendors hawked their wares and residents did their business.

Darragh rode slowly through the narrow, crowded streets, his mount's hooves clomping on the hard-packed dirt. His nose twitched as they passed the outskirts of a less savory section of the city, the stink of unwashed bodies and human waste wafting through the air. Street urchins crowded around the men, their grimy hands extended as they begged for coin while others ducked in and out between the horses, their nimble fingers slipping into saddlebags for food or something they could trade.

A shout had Donal twisting in his saddle and barking an order to one of his men who held a scrawny youth by the neck of his soiled tunic. "Let him go."

"He's a thief!" the man snarled.

The commander eyed the child swinging in the soldier's meaty fist, vainly swatting at the man to let him go. "Can't you see he's starving? Put him down."

"Count yourself lucky, whelp. Next time you steal from me, I'll cut off your hands." The soldier dropped the boy, smiling as the youth landed with a wince, then rolled to his feet and bolted.

Darragh chuckled. "I would've liked to see Myles rid the

boy of his slippery fingers." Donal's jaw ticked. "Ah, well. Mayhap the little urchin will try again, and we'll have our entertainment."

The group wound their way to the keep, stopping when they reached the inner bailey where stable boys took their mounts and a pair of the king's knights greeted them. Darragh took the lead as the ornate doors to the castle opened wide. Sun spilled from stained glass windows, filling the great hall with colorful light. Clusters of lords and ladies filled the hall, the murmur of their conversation a constant din. The royal steward greeted the party before informing the king's herald of their arrival. With Donal at his side, Darragh meandered through the hall, accepting a mug of ale from a servant. His soldiers were undoubtedly glad to leave his presence as they took to the barracks.

He studied the men and women, quickly picking out the vipers from the lambs while mulling over which of them he could lure to his bed. A hush fell over the crowd as the king, led by the herald and a small group of royal advisors, entered the room. King Stephan was well past middle age, his once muscled frame gone to fat. Red splotches marred his face, his nose rosy and bulbous, the effect of too much wine. He motioned to his herald with a flick of his wrist, sitting back on his throne, bejeweled hands resting on the curved arms of the chair.

Darragh and Donal stepped forward and bowed low, awaiting the command to rise. It galled Crom Cruach to show fealty to that puling meat sack. He could flay the king open with a whispered spell, raise this entire city and all who dwelled in it if he were in his true form. Instead, he bided his time in the Felmore's Lord, paying homage to the man. With a nod to his herald, they were given leave to rise.

King Stephan drummed his fingers on the wooden frame of his throne, the digits swelling beyond the constraints of the rings adorning every finger, tapping with irritation at having been deprived of his nap. "What brings a lord of the Western Fold to my court?"

"I have news of Aos Sí who seek refuge in Dorcha Wood." The king raised a brow and motioned for Darragh to continue. "Their newly appointed queen commands her people to attack small settlements throughout the western reaches. They have their eyes fixed on Felmore and other strongholds."

An advisor leaned into the king's side, the sly-eyed man whispering in his ear before stepping back with a smirk. Stephan lifted a goblet of wine from a tray held by a young maidservant and took a long pull of the tart liquid, the folds of his throat working as he downed the contents. A dribble of red stained the corner of his mouth as he set down the glass and stared at Darragh. "I seem to recall you blathering about the threat of elves before. Didn't I already send you men?"

"Aye, you did, my lord, and we beat them back. But the threat remains. If you do not act, no one will be left to rule over all of Crethia."

The king's eyes narrowed. "I hear you say you beat them back, but, as I recall, less than a third of my men returned. I begin to wonder if your army stood aside as mine was led to slaughter."

It was a dangerous accusation. The hall grew silent, their

attention moving from Darragh to the king as they waited to see the outcome of such slander. Darragh clenched his jaw, the demon writhing inside of him, wanting to spill blood and struggling to stay that inclination. Clearing his throat, he said, "I assure you my men fought and died beside yours, my lord. And they will fight again, but I cannot hold back the tide of elven scum that threatens the entire Western Fold alone. I need more men to keep that elven witch at bay."

The king's advisor leaned in again, talking too softly for Darragh to hear, though the old god squatting inside him could read the man's thoughts as easily as words on parchment. Colm Gilroy, Duke of Winfell and Stephan's most trusted advisor urged the king to hear Darragh out privately. As the most prominent lord of the western reaches, he'd be an asset to his royal highness. Taigon's coffers were running low, and the nobility of Crethia would balk at additional taxes unless they were given something in return, something more than land and title. Security. Perhaps Darragh could be used as a tool of the crown.

Stephan tried to smother the smile creeping across his mouth as he returned his attention to Felmore's lord. "I would speak with you on this matter in private, Lord Baoill." Darragh nodded, bowing low as the king rose slowly from his throne with a loud fart. His gout was acting up again, and he had no patience for these country lords with their whining and pleas for aid. Looking sullenly at the crowd and Darragh's bent head, Stephan lumbered out of the hall, feet aching painfully with each step. He needed a pitcher of wine and a fresh, young maid to fondle before he'd meet with the lord of Felmore.

Darragh straightened once the king had passed by, watching the monarch lurch toward stone steps leading him to his private solar. Scanning the advisors' minds as they followed Stephan, he searched their memories, finding the information he needed and squirreling it away. With a curt nod to Donal, he found the steward and followed a male servant to quarters in the castle's east wing. His commander would sleep in the anteroom of the chamber, though Darragh assured him they'd return to Felmore as soon as he'd had a word with the king. Ordering a meal for them, Donal joined Darragh in his quarters, stoking the fire before pulling out a chair beside his lord.

"Do you think King Stephan will give us aid?"

Watching the flames in the fireplace, Darragh said, "The king is swayed by the Duke of Winfell, who sees my request as an opportunity to gain a stronger foothold in the Western Fold."

"Are you planning on speaking with the duke?"

Darragh's mouth curved at the corners, with stained teeth winking between thin lips. "I wouldn't worry about the duke. He hasn't the stomach for courtly intrigue."

Donal heard the implicit threat but said nothing, leaning back in his chair and enjoying the fire's warmth. Part of him wished the flames would leap from the grate and consume them both, ridding the world of whatever fell thing had taken over the lord of Felmore.

Darragh heard the commander's foul wish and whispered a spell, lips moving so swiftly Donal saw nothing but a twitch of his mouth. The fire grew, flames writhing in arcs of orange and blue, the tips reaching toward the two men like fingers. The commander glanced from Darragh to the fire, body stiffening as his lord stared at the fire with boredom. "My lord," he said, voice shaking as the fire grew with a muffled roar.

With a wave of his hand, the flames sputtered, crawling back into the grate, settling into a soothing flicker. "Is something amiss?" Darragh asked, not bothering to look at his commander.

"Nothing, my lord," Donal said, tasting the lie like ash on his tongue. The lord of Felmore was indeed gone, only the shell of the man remaining, a marionette for the thing inside of him to control. Rising, the commander dipped his head, saying, "I will see to a meal and have it brought to you." He strode out the door, shutting it tightly and wanting nothing more than to nail the wood to the frame and keep whatever lurked in that chamber locked away.

CHAPTER THIRTY

By the third day, Fiadh's backside felt like one giant bruise as the party made their way to the Crooked Gap in the Wandering Mountains. Meara appeared unfazed by the grueling pace, her steps light and irritatingly spry despite days of travel. She glanced at Gideon, mouth turning down as he looked tired but comfortable enough in his saddle, as though he'd been born to it. Even Sibaen's enthusiasm hadn't waned, evidenced each morning when she leaped onto her horse's back, tongue lolling. Fiadh shifted her weight, muscles spasming painfully.

Perhaps you should ask one of our company to massage it for you, Krulan told her drolly.

She glared at him and swung her foot, nearly losing her balance on Meara's back. Krulan gave a short bark, eyes dancing with amusement as he sidestepped her vain attempt.

Gideon turned in his saddle, mouth curving up as he

watched her clumsily regain her seat, thighs hugging the unicorn's sides though her grip was less than it had been when they'd started from Erabel. "Troubles?" he asked, smirking.

Fiadh lifted her chin and gripped Meara's mane, back smarting as she tried to straighten her body. Gideon chuckled and shook his head. "After my first campaign, I couldn't stand up straight for two days, often slinking into dark corners to rub my backside. When Doran spied me doing such, he took great delight in taunting me, often giving me a thwap on my rear as I passed and bolting before I could muster the energy to chase him."

She giggled. "I hope you had the pleasure of repaying him when he was older."

"Oh, aye." Gideon grinned. "Mercilessly." He reached into his saddlebag and pulled out a small container. Stretching out his arm, he handed it to her. "Rub it on your sore areas tonight. It'll help." Fiadh unscrewed the wooden lid and sniffed, nose wrinkling. "It works better than it smells. I promise."

"Thank you." She tucked it into the satchel slung across her back.

"Of course, if you'd like help rubbing that in, I'd be happy to assist."

Her mouth gaped, face reddening as she sputtered.

He laughed and kicked Aridius into a trot before she found her voice. Fiadh muttered, watching him slow his mount as he reached Faraen's side, her mouth tugging at the corners. She enjoyed his wit. It was like seeing a part of him that he'd lost for a while.

He cares for you. Krulan's yellow gaze fixed on Gideon.

I know.

He's a good man.

Fiadh raised a brow and turned to the Cù-Sìth. Krulan met her gaze, unflinching, massive paws digging into the soft dirt as he kept pace with Meara. *I know what it means for you to say it,* she told him.

They are not inherently evil. You've shown me that. He's shown me that.

Her eyes softened, understanding the depth of what he said, knowing the spirit of his mate, Rivya, and his unborn children still called to him for retribution. Before she could respond, whistling rent the air. Her eyes swung to a thick copse of trees where, moments later, Kaelari burst from their cover, body tucked low against her mount's back. She wheeled her horse to a stop, dirt and leaves swirling around the animal's hooves. Krulan growled, hackles rising, readying himself to attack.

"A village to the west is under attack," Kaelari said, swinging her gaze from face to face as her horse pranced in a tight circle.

All eyes turned to Fiadh. "Dothur's army?"

"Aye, though I didn't get too close as I was outnumbered. There is a large group of Kelpie, led by a mage, and something else. I don't know what they were, but I could see them feeding on the dead."

The effect her words had on every Aos Sí was palpable. Bodies stiffened. Teeth ground and nostrils flared. Each of them itched to go into battle to slaughter the wizard and his army. Mages had once been allies to the elves, but Carmun had corrupted them, played upon their innate desire for power, and they'd turned on the Aos Sí. Xander, the most powerful of his people, had ambushed Aeson, Fiadh's father, in the Great War. Killing him and making his wife a widow. Kaelari, Aeson's friend since childhood, thirsted for revenge, the urge not having dimmed over the decades since his death.

"We cannot leave the people of that village to be slaughtered," Fiadh said. Fists thumped against chests as her warriors showed allegiance. "Kaelari, I give you leave to plan an assault."

The female nodded and swung off her mount in a graceful leap, landing on the balls of her feet with a muffled thump. The other elves followed suit, joined by Sibaen, Gideon, Faraen, and Corene—the Urisk drawing a reed-thin, wickedly sharp spear from a sheath strung across her back. Fiadh slid from Meara, wincing as she landed, the impact reverberating throughout her aching body. Struggling not to limp, she joined the group, wedging between Krulan and Gideon. Kaelari crouched on the ground, using a stick to sketch a rudimentary map of their route and the village itself.

"It appeared the humans were being herded toward this field," she said, dragging the stick and circling the area. "But many were fighting, others fleeing into these woods. I assume there are women and children taking refuge in their homes."

"Have they begun to burn them out?" Gideon asked.

Kaelari frowned. "I saw smoke but no torches." She leaned back on her heels, her arm resting on her knee, stick dangling. "But the mage won't need them to light the town. And from what I could see, the creatures were… hungry."

Fiadh paled, her voice a whisper. "We have to help them."

The female nodded, giving curt commands. The elves sprang into action, readying themselves in minutes, as Kaelari led them through a patch of forest to the outskirts of the village.

They heard the screams and smelled the smoke before breaking through the trees. Tethering their mounts to low branches, they drew swords and bows, fanning out and slinking through the tall grasses to come at the small hamlet from multiple sides. A large manor house near the center of the village was in flames, sparks from the fire landing on nearby thatched roofs. The villagers, over a hundred, ran in every direction, some carrying children or dragging the injured, others so filled with terror they accidentally fled straight toward monstrous jaws.

Fiadh climbed onto Krulan's back, having commanded Meara to remain behind, ignoring the unicorn's stamps of anger as she left her in the protection of the woods. Krulan ran low, Fiadh pressing her body tightly against him, face peering between his ears. In the distance, she caught a glimpse of Sibaen, her feral movements winking in and out of sight. Gideon had gone with Ellisar, the two of them looping around to where the bulk of the attack was being carried out.

Fisting her hands in Krulan's thick pelt, Fiadh hitched up her legs, reaching into him with her mind to see what he saw—a talent she'd honed with Dasha. The Cù-Sìth's mind stuttered momentarily at her invasion, then opened.

That's a neat trick, he told her. *Hold on.*

She tensed, muscles aching as he lunged into a sprint. The smell of blood and death hit her in the face like a battering ram, causing her body to flinch. She gripped his fur tighter and gritted her teeth.

Now! Krulan commanded.

Fiadh sprang from his back, tucking her body and rolling when she hit the ground before jumping up just beyond the village's perimeter. Flinging out her arms, she called to the elements, power surging through her blood like a living thing. Wind ripped through the air as invisible currents of electricity gathered around her hands, the hum of energy tingling along her palms as the particles clustered into tight masses, flickering as her fingers twitched. She searched the chaos unfolding before her, her mouth falling open as her eyes fell on a creature from a child's nightmare. At first glance, it was a horse, but its form shifted, muzzle parting to reveal dark, pointed teeth grinding down on torn flesh. In its webbed hands, it held a struggling man, his body twisting to escape the creature's grasp, one arm dangling in a bloody, pulpy mass. Kelpie. This is what Gideon and Ellisar had spoken of. And darting in and out among the Kelpie were grey-skinned monsters who loped on all fours or stood on two legs, clawed hands grabbing and tearing, blunted teeth biting and chewing. They were like nothing her most terrifying nightmare could conjure—twisted beings created for one purpose: slaughter.

Krulan snarled, the sound jolting her out of her paralyzing horror. Particles of electricity coalesced before her hands as the wind swirled around her, awaiting her command. Drawing on her power, she molded the elements, shaping them into a dagger of lightning and flinging it at the creature. It ripped through the Kelpie's neck, nearly severing its head. It brayed grotesquely, arms going slack as it swayed and hit the ground. The man scuttled away, whimpering as he clutched his mutilated limb.

The battle exploded in front of Fiadh's eyes as the creatures shrieked, realizing they were under attack. Above the din, she heard a booming voice and swept the village, searching out the source. Krulan nudged her. *To the east!*

She shifted her body and flung out her arms, wrapping herself and the Cù-Sìth in a protective shell as a wall of fire roared toward them. Through the flames, she made out a dark form clad in a hooded robe. Mage. Fire ballooned around her, bouncing off the barrier she'd thrown up. The heat caused sweat to pool on her skin, drops trailing down her face, between her breasts, and along her spine. Gritting her teeth, Fiadh pulled water particles from the air and doused the flames, hearing them sizzle against the shimmering shell of power. Lip curling, she whipped her hands through the air in a series of motions, lips moving as she murmured a spell and sent it toward the dark figure.

Grim pleasure filled her face as the mage stumbled back. She released the shield around their bodies and funneled all her power into her attack. Krulan rushed forward as Fiadh continued her assault, dousing flames dripping from the wizard's fingers, pelting him with wind and shards of ice she pulled from the darkening sky. Her attention was so fixed she didn't see the Kelpie slinking toward her. With a meaty whack, the creature rammed into her, sending her flying to the ground. Fiadh yelped, the sound reaching Krulan. He dug his paws into the earth and spun, muzzle peeling back in a vicious roar. Rolling, she got to her knees and thrust out her arms, but the Kelpie was on her, webbed claws yanking her by the hair toward its gaping maw. Fetid breath washed over her face as it hauled her up, feet dangling.

With one hand clawing at the creature's fingers, she dug into her waist and pulled out a hidden dagger; one Gideon had given her before they left Erabel. With a flick of her wrist, she spun it in her hand and thrust upward, feeling the tip slide through the slick skin of the Kelpie's neck until it hit the base of its skull. It dropped her with a throaty gurgle and clutched its throat, falling to its knees. Krulan was on it, ripping its head from its body with a brutal twist.

War cries from Kaelari and the others rent the air. She climbed onto Krulan's back, hands coated in the Kelpie's greenish blood. "Find the mage!"

His body sprang into motion, swerving through villagers —men, women, and squalling children—who ran past the pair, their faces masks of shock and horror. The mage cast a spell to cloak himself and lend his body speed, outrunning the Cù-Sìth. Krulan's body undulated beneath her as she leaned into him, spilling some of her energy into his form. His muscles drank it, soaking it in as they coiled and released. He shot forward like an arrow, yellow eyes fixed on his prey. The mage, sensing them closing in, launched into the air, body spinning with unnatural ease and landing on the balls of his feet atop the roof of the smithy's hut. He crouched low, pale hands with long, black nails digging into the weathered thatch. The black hood of his cloak fell back as he tipped his head and shouted at the sky.

A horrible wailing cut through the sounds of battle. Villagers covered their ears and fell to the ground while the Aos Sí flinched, crystalline eyes scanning the horizon for what they knew was coming. Sluagh swept through the storm clouds like wraiths, shrieks following in their wake. Krulan slammed his paws into the ground, back twitching as he craned his neck.

Fiadh sat up, keeping one hand firmly latched onto a thick tuft of fur. She reached out her senses toward the incoming Sluagh, mind fixing on the leader, the tenor of her thoughts all too familiar. Above them, the mage roared triumphantly as the monstrous creatures dove toward the tiny hamlet.

"Troya!" Fiadh shouted.

The leader of the Sluagh banked toward her voice, the black pools of her eyes finding Fiadh in the melee. Troya landed on the roof of the smithy, batting away the mage who tried to sidle up to her. "The queen of the Aos Sí has come to witness the power of my sisters," she said, her voice like the hum of a thousand beetles.

The mage hissed, trying to regain control, and she spat at him, a thick glob of black mucous spraying across his face. He squealed and clutched his eyes, losing his balance and tumbling from the roof where Ellisar found him and buried his sword in the wizard's chest. Troya flapped her pale, leathery wings, tucking them close to her body before scuttling to the edge of the hut to look down at Fiadh, skull-like face bobbing. "Do not think to command the Sluagh, young one. We are the Hunt and answer to none but ourselves."

Fiadh slid off the Cù-Sìth's back and stood her ground, clenching and unclenching her hands, her fingers sticky with the blood of the Kelpie and strands of Krulan's fur. "I have no wish to command you and your sisters."

The slash of Troya's mouth flashed open, revealing needle-like teeth coated in black saliva. "A wise decision. Though I wonder why you are here if not to try and stop us."

Above, the other Sluagh wheeled and dipped in the air, appearing and disappearing among the dark clouds. Without the mage, the Kelpie scattered only to be cut down by Fiadh's forces. Troya, aware but unmoved by the slaughter, kept her dead eyes on the queen. Lifting her chin, Fiadh said, "You claim to be under no one's rule, yet you align yourselves with Dothur. Is he not your master now?"

Troya hissed and edged closer to the ledge. Krulan growled, teeth snapping, and put himself between Fiadh and the Sluagh. "I have no master!"

Fiadh cocked her head. "Did you not come when the mage called you?" It was a dangerous game Fiadh played, goading the Sluagh. But Troya had yet to send her sisters after the frightened villagers. Perhaps she could buy them time as they played cat and mouse.

A line of drool slipped from Troya's blackened lips. "Baiting me is unwise. Speak while you still have a tongue to do so."

"You are the Hunt," Fiadh said, watching the leader of

the Sluagh dip her head in acknowledgment. "If Dothur sees his vision to fruition, none will be left to fulfill your purpose."

The Sluagh blinked.

"What will you do, then?" Fiadh paused, watching Troya digest that taste of the future. "You would cease to be the Hunt."

"You suggest my sisters and I become your... *allies*?" There was a warning in her query, in her jaw clicking as she awaited Fiadh's reply.

"I wouldn't presume to suggest such an alliance. You are free to do as you wish. I'm simply pointing out the detriment of going to war with mankind on behalf of a creature who seeks to rid the world of them."

Troya tapped the thatch roof with the toe claw of one of her spindly legs. In the distance, frantic braying signaled the slaughter of Kelpie, who were unable to outrun the elves. Muffled cries and groans of dying villagers pounded in Fiadh's head as she waited for the Sluagh to either fight or leave. Kaelari, wiping her blade on a scrap of cloth she found, strode toward Fiadh, sharp eyes fixed on the creature atop the roof. Fiadh held out a hand to stop her progress, keeping her face fixed on the leader of the winged battalion.

Bending the knee of each spiderish leg, Troya leaned forward. "I make no decision today, but you have given me much to think about. My sisters and I leave you to these puling humans who would sooner gut you than stand at your sides in a fight. Choose who you will as your ally, young queen. I leave you to it." She leaped into the air, wings stretching to the full length, and flapped into the sky, the only sound that of the ghostly wailing of her passing.

Fiadh's shoulders sagged as Kaelari jogged to her side and slapped her on the back. "You've become quite the diplomat for someone who complains so much about the role of queen."

Staring at her empty, gore-slicked hands, she said, "I bought us time, nothing more." Fiadh wiped the grime on her leggings and scanned the destruction, wincing when her eyes skipped over the remains of the fallen. "Did we lose anyone?" she asked, gaze fixed on the sightless stare of a dead woman a few feet away.

"Thallen is wounded, but it's not serious." Fiadh raised her brows, and Kaelari explained. "She was bitten. Elraen is working on her now." She jerked her head toward an empty paddock where the female lay on her back, the healer's hands hovering above her form while Faraen stood opposite, palms lifted to the sky as he chanted.

Gideon joined them a moment later, sweat and blood splatter covering his face. Fiadh swept her eyes over his body, looking for injuries, relieved when she saw none. Sheathing his sword, Gideon asked, "What did you say to get the Sluagh to leave?"

"I implied they'd have no one to hunt should they help Dothur fulfill his vision."

His eyes widened, and he nodded slowly. "A foul thought, but effective."

She grimaced, slowly becoming aware of movement around the loose group. Turning, Fiadh watched as villagers gathered, fear and anger marring their features. One middle-aged woman separated herself from the group, eyes skittering from Sibaen to Ellisar before landing on Fiadh. Clearing her throat, she said, "If you've come to finish us off, be done with it."

Fiadh glanced at those lingering behind the speaker, eyes falling on a young mother clutching an infant. "We've come to save you."

CHAPTER THIRTY-ONE

Most of the villagers kept their distance as Fiadh healed those she could and eased the passing of those beyond her skills. Gideon aided Ellisar and others in burial duty, hauling mutilated bodies into a mass grave Kaelari had created, to the disbelief of those watching her shape the earth. Distrust mixed with gratitude was reflected on the faces of the survivors, especially when Sibaen slunk through clusters of people, many making signs to ward off evil. The Faoladh ignored them, unfazed by their fear, as she helped those who didn't flinch when she neared. Corene kept her distance, her body twitching as though she were perpetually ready to bolt.

As night fell, Fiadh sat against the wall of a wattle and daub structure and hung her head, drained. Gideon crouched in front of her, the lingering stench of blood and death clinging to his clothing. "Are you all right?"

She slowly lifted her face, letting the back of her head rest against the building. "Aye. Just tired."

"A man wishes to speak with you," he said, turning slightly to indicate one of the villagers.

Fiadh looked around Gideon's shoulder and studied the burly man. His unkempt beard hid most of his features, but she noted he didn't shy away from her perusal as many of his kin did. "Do you know what it's about?"

"He wouldn't say, only asked to speak to my leader." Gideon rose slowly and reached out to pull her to her feet. She swayed a moment, weariness sinking into her body. He held her arm, giving her time to shake off the fatigue and letting go when she subtly nodded.

Motioning the man over, Gideon made introductions. "This is Bowen, the village of Crawly's tanner." She dipped her head, and he continued, "Meet Fiadh, queen of the Aos Sí."

The man's eyes widened as he stuttered, "M…m… milady."

"There is no need for formality, Bowen. What can I do for you?"

Bowen looked from one to the other, licking his chapped lips, the motion making the long hair of his beard twitch. "Lord Cador is dead, and we've no way to get word to neighboring towns."

"Lord Cador?"

"Aye," Bowen motioned to the manor house, a shell of what it was having been torched by the mage before they arrived. "He lived there."

Gideon cleared his throat. "The people of Crawly work for the local lord. In this case, Lord Cador. Without him, they have no one to guide them through this tragedy nor a way to seek aid."

Fiadh nodded and turned her attention back to the tanner. "We are on our way to Taigon to meet with King Stephan. Before we leave, I promise to help you and your people as best we can. When we speak with the king, we'll inform him of your plight."

Margaret, the woman who'd spoken out earlier in the day, came to stand next to Bowen. He shifted his body and glanced at her. "What is it, woman?"

"That *creature* is frightening the children," she said, motioning to Sibaen, who was hunched over a sheepdog with an injured leg, attempting to bind the limb with a strip of linen.

"Her name is Sibaen. Her people are the Faoladh, and they are under my protection," Fiadh said coldly.

The woman huffed and crossed her arms. "We don't like her kind in Crawly."

Anger flooded her body, and Fiadh's nostrils flared. "*Her kind?* Do you mean the people who saved your village from slaughter?"

Bowen fidgeted, taking Margaret's arm and trying to pull her away. "She means nothing by it. We're thankful for your aid."

Gideon leaned down and whispered in Fiadh's ear. "They are simple folk. It will take time to let go of old hatred."

Power thrummed in Fiadh's body as she struggled to cool her temper. Her hands spasmed, energy leaching from her fingertips. A tiny spark flickered in her palm, drawing

Bowen's eye, and he stepped back, hauling the woman with him. "Leave before you bring their wrath upon us," he ground out.

She wrenched her arm out of his meaty grasp and stalked away, craning her neck to shoot a glare as she returned to a small group of men and women who closed ranks around her. Fiadh watched her depart, focusing her mind on regaining control. When her heart resumed its normal rhythm, she swung her eyes to the tanner. He swallowed hard but held her sharp gaze. "My apologies, milady. She… she doesn't speak for all of us."

Fiadh breathed deeply, reaching into the earth to anchor herself, feeling a whisper of Danu in this place stripped of her warmth. "I understand your fear, Bowen. But my people mean no harm. We're not the monsters your stories make us out to be."

He nodded. "But *they* are—the ones who attacked us. Half the men of the village are dead. Lord Cador is dead. How are we to survive if they return?"

She looked at Gideon, who shrugged, then called to Kaelari. The female trotted over, a bow slung across her chest. Bowen gave her a wide berth as she approached. Fiadh lifted her chin toward the tanner. "Bowen and the people of Crawly fear the return of a legion of Dothur's army. With the manor lord and many others dead, they cannot withstand another assault."

Kaelari put her hands on her hips, blue eyes flashing brightly against her dusky skin. "We cannot spare anyone to guard the village against another attack." She turned to the tanner. "Is there a large town nearby?"

"Aye. Middleborough."

Fiadh's brow wrinkled as she stared at Kaelari. "What are you thinking?"

"Perhaps we can escort the survivors to the town. It's bound to have better fortifications than the village." She looked toward the south and squinted. "It'll delay our arrival in Taigon."

"I would see them safe before we resume our journey to the Golden City."

Kaelari gave a thin smile. "I assumed as much. We can carry the wounded in carts and leave at dawn." She quickly bowed and left, finding Ellisar with Thallen, who was weak but healed of the most grievous of her wounds.

"Will you tell your people?" Fiadh asked Bowen. The man assured he would and left, bypassing the small group where Margaret held sway and finding the bulk of the survivors gathered in a string of unscathed homes.

"You realize that a larger town holds more danger for us," Gideon said, gaze fixed on the angry group of villagers whom Margaret was riling up.

"I know. But we can't leave them." Fiadh turned away, looking for a meal and pallet, Gideon joining her. They walked silently, the sounds of the dying and wounded peppering the quietude. *This will be the fate of every settlement should we fail,* Fiadh thought, her words drifting to Krulan, who kept pace.

Our small band cannot hold back the tide of this war.

She frowned. *That's why we must be united—all peoples.*

You see the challenge of such an endeavor, he said, referring to Margaret.

Aye, but I also see the possibility of an alliance.

Ever the optimist, Krulan said with a huff.

What choice do I have? You've taken all the pessimism. Positivity is all I have left.

Krulan barked a laugh and nudged her, knocking her off balance, so she bumped into Gideon, who'd been eyeing the exchange. He hooked an arm around her shoulder and drew her close, the warmth of his body seeping into her skin. She tensed momentarily, then relaxed her shoulders, leaning into him. "Is Krulan teasing you again?"

"He's trying to goad me into perpetual negativity, and I'm not letting him."

Krulan growled and sauntered off. Fiadh shook her head. "He's not wrong, though. What I'm trying to do… it's…. I'm sure many would say it's foolish."

"I have a great fondness for fools," he said quietly.

Her face grew warm, and she ducked her head, focusing on her feet as they came to a small site where the Aos Sí had made camp. It was far enough from the bulk of the survivors yet close enough should they come under attack. Their horses, along with Meara, roamed freely in a nearby pasture, munching on meadow grasses. The unicorn's ears perked when she spied Fiadh, giving a shrill nicker and trotting over for a nuzzle. She spent a few minutes stroking Meara's silly nose and sharing breath, patting her neck when Gideon called to her.

A simple meal of oatcakes, tubers, and leafy greens was laid out. Fiadh sat on the ground around a small fire and dug in, stomach snarling when the food touched her tongue. Sated, she leaned against a log and watched the flames.

Stretching out a hand, she fixed her mind on the fire, commanding the element to writhe and dance, tendrils shooting into the air like ghostly fingers. Eventually, her eyes grew heavy, her head slumping forward. She didn't wake when Gideon picked her up and gently placed her on a pallet.

The first rays of dawn streaked across the horizon when they left for Middleborough, a trail of villagers on foot, horseback, or in carts with them. Ellisar scouted ahead while Kaelari and the others rode flank or took up the rear. It was slow going, and the hours dragged on. By midday, Fiadh halted their progress, sliding from Meara's back to stretch her legs. A light rain had soaked her cloak, weighing it down so that it dragged along the ground as she walked. Pins and needles radiated through her limbs, making her steps awkward until the blood flowed—her body slowly warming in the dampness. She wove her way through the people, chatting with those who didn't view her with suspicion and making it a point to inquire about the welfare of those who did. Margaret sniffed when she approached, gripping the wooden handles of a bag to her chest and giving curt replies. Fiadh took it all in stride, heartened to see some warier villagers thawing at her presence. Gideon watched from a distance, his admiration growing with each person she encountered. Gone was the shy, innocent he'd first met. Here was the elven queen.

The town of Middleborough was in ruins. Its walls

breached as though giant boulders had smashed against them, though no sign of what brought them down could be seen. Funnels of smoke rose into the sky, where buildings smoldered. The castle, what was left of it, was little more than broken spires and caved-in stone. The people of Crawly gazed at the destruction from the hilltop with glassy eyes, unable to comprehend what it would mean for their survival without any semblance of an army to protect them. Whatever had attacked the fiefdom was gone, leaving towns-folk to tend to the living and bury the dead.

A small band of men on horseback spotted them and rode hard, their mounts kicking up dust. Gideon nudged Aridius to Fiadh's side and drew his sword. "Be careful. They're likely out for blood."

She gave a quick nod and lifted her heels into Meara's sides. The unicorn strode forward, her massive hooves pressing into the ground as she separated herself from the main group. Gideon and Kaelari came alongside her while Sibaen and Corene moved to the rear, hidden behind the throng of villagers.

You should remain unseen, Fiadh told Krulan.

And leave you unguarded? I think not.

She gave him a sidelong glance. *I'm going to tell Kaelari you think she isn't capable of keeping me safe.*

He huffed and shouldered his way between the female elf and his queen. *I'm not leaving.*

Fiadh shook her head. *Fine. But keep in mind I'm trying to be diplomatic here, not start a small war with these people.*

Noted.

A man in his mid-twenties shouted to his comrades and

took the lead as the group of men approached. Pulling hard on the reins, the leader stopped when he was a few feet away. His mount danced in a tight circle, snorting and pawing at the dirt as soldiers drew swords and nocked arrows. The man's hazel eyes swept across the gathering before fixing on Fiadh. "What's your business here?"

She whispered to Meara, sliding her hand down the unicorn's neck to calm her. The knight had shoulder-length red hair and a short beard. His muscular body wielded his horse easily as he met Fiadh's stare. In a loud voice that carried to the soldiers behind him, she said, "We've come from the village of Crawly, where these people came under attack. We had hoped to find refuge for them here."

"Who are you to care about the welfare of men?"

"I am Fiadh, ruler of the Aos Sí."

He stared at her for a moment, eyes flicking to the Cù-Sìth and elves before landing on Gideon. He studied the crest on Gideon's chest and raised a brow. "You're a long way from home, Lord of Belfirth."

"Aye." He shifted in his saddle, the leather creaking. "Belfirth and Erabel are allies."

"You fight with elves?" Gideon nodded, and he asked, "Against your own kind?"

"If that were the case, we would've left the people of Crawly to die and saved ourselves the trouble of aiding them."

The young knight lifted his chin and nudged his horse forward, motioning for the soldiers at his back to lower their weapons. Krulan growled and dug a paw into the ground. *It's all right,* Fiadh told him as she met the man halfway.

"I'm Sir Riley Morrow, vassal to Lord Deagan Haile, who lies dead in that smoldering ruin." Riley motioned to the castle. "We were attacked two nights past. If not for the rain finally dousing the fires, Middleborough would still be burning." He flexed his sword hand but didn't reach for the hilt of his blade, his hawkish eyes monitoring every move Fiadh and her warriors made. After a long pause, Riley relaxed his shoulders and stilled his horse. "If we allow them on our land," he said, jerking his chin to the villagers, "will you ally with us against the creatures that attacked my people?" he asked, pinning Fiadh with a direct stare.

Negotiations were not her forte. She left such dealings to Kaelari but couldn't defer to her if she wanted to maintain her standing in the eyes of the soldier. "You would accept our help?"

The knight scanned the group again before replying. "I'll take aid where I see it from whoever offers."

Surprise lit her face. "That is… unusual."

His mouth curved up at the corner. "My mother was an unusual woman. I take my view of the world from her."

"She must have been quite remarkable," Gideon said in a low voice.

"Aye, she was at that." He made a sign of blessing across his chest.

Fiadh smiled thinly. "As I told the people of Crawly, we are on our way to Taigon to meet with King Stephan."

"The king? What is it you hope to gain from such a meeting?" he asked, a tinge of disdain in his voice.

"An alliance. The creatures that attacked Middleborough are attacking settlements across the kingdom. A demon, the spawn of Carmun, leads them. Dothur will not stop until both our people are crushed under his feet."

"And how would you know such things?"

"Because he's coming for me. This," she waved her hand toward the town, "is but practice for what is to come when he arrives at my realm's borders. If Erabel falls, so shall all of mankind."

Riley snorted. "That's bold. You put a great deal of importance on your kind."

"Believe me," Gideon said, "It's earned."

The knight looked unconvinced but shrugged. "I'll take your word for it. Unfortunately, I have little to offer these people, but they are welcome to stay. If I may, I'd reconsider going to the king for aid."

"Oh?" Fiadh said.

"Lord Haile had received word of attacks like this one from various fiefs in the far west and north. He'd often sent missives to King Stephan, seeking counsel and reinforcements. All, save one, were ignored. In his response, the king," he spat on the ground, "told my lord he could travel to Taigon in person with a chest of gold should he wish for aid." Gideon swore under his breath, and Riley swung his eyes to him. "My lord would have paid had he gold to spare, but he refused to leave his people leaderless, even for a short time."

"I'm sorry for your loss," Fiadh said softly.

"In his absence, I have taken it upon myself to lead," he paused and squinted into the horizon, "though I have a mind to rally our allies and fight rather than sit idle and wait for those creatures to return and finish us off." Turning back to Fiadh, he said, "Come, you and Crawly's people are welcome to camp outside Middleborough's wall—what remains of them. At the very least, they will be among others, and there is safety in numbers."

"Thank you." Fiadh turned to Gideon, and they spoke briefly before he wheeled Aridius around and informed the villagers of their plans.

Riley watched for a moment, then turned his attention back to Fiadh. "My mother used to tell stories of your kind —tales passed from her mother's mother. Stories of an unusual friendship. Of magic and strange creatures. When sickness swept through my family, killing adults and children alike. One of your healers saved the lives of those who remained when they fell ill. Without her healing, my line would have ended." His eyes flicked from Krulan to Kaelari, who lingered within hearing distance. "I like to think my ancestors and your kind were… friends." Her eyes softened, a smile tugging at her lips. "Though, I'll admit I never thought to meet an Aos Sí, much less the elven queen."

"Perhaps it was fate that brought us together."

"Aye. I think it was."

CHAPTER THIRTY-TWO

Darragh slipped from his room, cloaking himself in darkness to blend with the shadows and moonless sky as he slunk through cold, stone hallways. Soldiers stationed in alcoves and junctures were dealt with by a sweep of his hand and whispered word—their bodies slumping into unconscious heaps. In the castle's east wing, Darragh ducked into a bedchamber, closing the door behind him with a soft click. The outer room housed an attendant who slept on a thin pallet, his hands tucked against his youthful face, mouth parted as puffs of air passed over his lips.

Standing over him, Darragh listened to his soft snores, breathing deeply to feel the young man's life force as he dreamt. Crouching, he placed a forefinger on the man's brow and closed his eyes, entering his mind like a needle. Flickers of images played out for a few moments before Darragh snuffed them out, blotting out everything in the youth's mind until he lay still in unnatural sleep. Rising slowly, his black cloak swirling around his legs, the lord of Felmore slipped into the Duke of Winfell's room.

Heavy damask curtains hid the raised bed, the light from the fire flickering against the fabric in ghostly patterns. Darragh tilted his head and listened to Colm Gilroy's heavy breathing. Stepping forward, he found the slit in the curtains and gently drew one panel aside, allowing a shaft of firelight to pierce the darkness enclosing the bed. Lifting a knee onto the edge of the bed, he leaned in, pulling back his hood and lowering his face so it hung just above the duke's slack mouth. With a whisper, Darragh pulled a dagger from his belt and twirled it before palming the handle. Murmuring a spell to rob the king's vassal of his voice and movement, he woke Colm, lips parting in a cruel smile when the man's eyes flew open.

Colm tried to lurch forward, but his muscles spasmed, locking into place so that he lay helpless beneath Darragh. Clicking his tongue, Darragh said, "Do not waste your last moments trying to flee, my lord. You are a fly caught in my web. There is no escape… save one."

Blinking slowly, the duke's mouth opened and closed, throat bobbing. Reading his mind, Darragh smiled, his face taking on an evil glow in the fire's orange light. "You wonder what I'm about," he said, reaching out to trace his finger along the man's full cheek, "and, so, I'll tell you, for these words will never leave this room. You are next in line to the throne, a station you've coveted since your father sat you on his knee and told you of the world. Under your reign, Crethia could thrive, perhaps even grow strong enough to beat back armies of any ilk, even mine." He ran the tip of his dagger along the duke's chin, the rasping sound of the metal scraping Colm's short beard making his mouth water. "But the age of men is over. Leaderless, mankind will flounder, nobility grabbing for power like slabs of meat at the table. Your kind will be ripe for the taking, and I mean to reclaim my place as ruler." Air whistled from Colm's chest as he tried to yell. "Ssh. There is no need to fight. It'll all be over soon."

Sitting astride the duke, Darragh slid the blade along the edge of Colm's neck, drawing a thin line of blood. The duke's heart hammered, and the demon within the lord of Felmore reveled. Pressing harder, Darragh ran the tip from one side of Colm's jaw to the other, licking the blade as the duke gurgled and tried to thrash before going still. Leaving as deftly as he entered, Darragh went from room to room, gorging on death as he killed each of King Stephan's advisors until there was only the monarch left, every nobleman directly in line for the throne murdered.

King Stephan's rooms sat in the central tower of Taigon's castle. The outer room was composed of two chambers, one a sitting area for honored guests and the other for attendants summoned at all hours on the king's whims. Four soldiers flanked the doors to his chambers. Chosen among Taigon's finest, they stood alert and armed as Darragh approached. He sized them up from the shadows, delving into their thoughts and finding one whose loose tongue would serve his purpose well. Sending each man into paralytic sleep, Darragh entered the king's bedchamber.

Fire from a massive hearth illuminated the room in yellowish light, the heat bathing the ample space in warmth and allowing Stephan to forego the traditional bed curtains, exposing himself to Darragh's perusal. Taigon's monarch lay on his back, the mound of his stomach beneath layers of blankets like that of a pregnant woman.

Deep inside Darragh, the demon considered his next move. Crom Cruach's power had limits. It would be too taxing to control Felmore's lord and the king. He needed Stephan to appear whole yet be little more than a sack of blood and bone, so far gone he'd be unreachable. Standing at the foot of the bed, Darragh closed his eyes, the demon inside him drawing upon his darkest magic. Words spun in the air like a black cloud, slowly taking the shape of a tiny scorpion as his lips moved so quickly his voice was little more than a hum. Holding out his hand, he cupped the spell-cast creature, as intangible as smoke though powerful enough to embody a series of spells that would render the king little more than a puppet. It flicked its insubstantial tail, the barbed end dripping with magic.

Thin lips curving into a smile, Darragh went to the king's side, the feel of the creature tickling his palm as he cupped it. Stephan's chest rattled with a deep snore as Felmore's lord leaned over the bed, arm extended toward the monarch's face. Unfurling his fingers, Darragh reached forward, murmuring a command and watching the scorpion scurry along his hand to the tip of Stephan's nose before diving into the king's nostril. Stephan twitched at the invasion, throat clogging momentarily as the creature squeezed itself into the cavity, past the olfactory bulb, and into his brain.

The king woke with a start and grabbed at Darragh,

hand fisting around the edges of his cloak. Mouth gaping, he looked around wildly, ready to release a bellow to call the guards. "Uh-uh," Darragh said, pressing a finger to the king's mouth. "You wouldn't want to do that just yet."

Feeling for the creature he'd created, Darragh commanded it to lift its tail and stab the king's brain, each piercing barb releasing magic toxins that rendered the monarch powerless. Stephan's eyes turned glassy. Darragh studied his face, sensing the creature like a cloud atop the king's brain.

Muttering into the stillness, he commanded the creature to attack the part of the king's mind that controlled reason, smiling as he sensed the scorpion stab at the grey matter repeatedly, poisoning his brain. When all that was left of the creature was an echo of the spells that had birthed it, Stephan's mind was little more than animalistic impulse. Pliable. Fear was a base emotion, one that had made mankind do awful things throughout history. Darragh tapped into that fear, knowing there was nothing left of the reason that would control those impulses.

Whispering in the king's ear, he filled what was left of his mind with violent images, each reflecting the forms of his closest advisors and heirs to the throne. Stephan's mind broke entirely under the onslaught. "You had to kill them," Darragh said softly. "They tried to hurt you. Your life is in danger. If you don't stop them, you'll die. Kill them. Kill them all."

Stephan blinked.

Darragh smiled and drew away, shrouding himself in darkness and slipping out of the room. By the time his spells wrought their work, there'd be no suspicion of his part in the killings. As he mused, the real Darragh writhed deep within the husk of the man Crom Cruach possessed. Summoning vestiges of strength to fight Crom, now that the demon was weakened from casting a spell to control the king, Darragh fought an internal battle for control. But even weak, he was no match for the old god who sent him scuttling back to a dark place where he could only watch and scream in silence.

Crom Cruach fumed as he slunk through hallways back to his chamber. His power was not infinite, and the magic in the sigil Darragh wore was waning. If he didn't leave this body soon, the lord of Felmore would eventually be able to evict him. Slipping silently into his bed chamber, he licked his finger, drew a series of runes on the ground, and sat at their center, muttering spells to regain his hold over Darragh. Crom felt the moment when the man inside him recoiled. *Not much longer now,* the demon thought. It would be enough.

Hours passed before the king roused to full awareness, the magic clouding his brain, clearing enough for Stephan to stare at the bloodied dagger in his hand while his mind swirled with whispers of threats until instinct took over. Fear flooded the king's body, adrenaline pumping through his veins. The magic-born scorpion twitched inside his skull, releasing the last of its spells. He bolted from his bed, eyes wild as he scanned the room for the threat his mind conjured, fear pounding through his skull mixed with blood-lust. *Kill. Kill them all.*

His mind flickered, images of the duke's throat cut

flashing behind his eyes. Colm, the bastard, had tried to take his throne. The magic sunk into Stephan's mind and bloomed as the slaughter of other nobility filled it until all he saw was blood. *But there are more*, he thought frantically, staring at the bloodied blade. *Other nobility whose connection to the throne is weak but there. They will come. They will try to steal my crown.*

The king ground his teeth and lurched to the fireplace, holding the dagger in the light. *I will kill all who seek to usurp my throne!* With a snarl, he stalked to the bedroom door. Legs wobbled as he clutched the curved handle. *What if they're beyond the threshold?* he thought. A look of hate passed over his face. *They think to kill me! They think I'm easy prey!* Spinning on his heels, he paced the room, arm slashing at the air as though he fought an invisible enemy, never realizing the enemy was firmly planted in his mind.

Rage grew, fed by the poison in Crom Cruach's spells, until nothing was left within Stephan's mind—only maniacal wrath.

Darragh cocked his head, sensing the moment Stephan's mind finally broke, and stalked to the door, pressing his ear to the wood. But even with feet of stone, winding halls, and a room far from the monarch's quarters, he could still hear the screaming. Fixing his face into a mask of shock, he poked his head out of the room, finding Donal standing in the antechamber, sword in his hand. "Get back, my lord."

Darragh backed away, leaving the door partially open. "What is it? Are we under attack?" It was too easy playing these games. Biting back a smile, he plastered a look of worry on his face.

Donal glanced at him. "You should get inside and bolt the door. I'll see what's amiss and return."

Shutting the door, Darragh leaned against it, relishing the chaos unfolding across the castle. By this time, the king would've attacked his guard, propelling them to seek out the duke, the next in line to inherit the throne. They'd find him dead, of course. The others would be discovered shortly after. Oh, how he wished he could watch it all unfold, savor every moment of blind panic, every drop of blood.

Darragh's commander ran through the halls, dodging servants and guards who'd come to see what the uproar was about. Shouts and screams grew louder, and he veered toward the king's chambers, his gut churning at what he'd find, at his lord's part in all of this. Soldiers in full armor were racing through the halls. He plastered himself against the wall as they shouldered past, then followed.

Standing taller than most men, Donal looked over the heads of those gathered, finding the king in his bed chamber. Stephan stood in his bedgown, gripping the handle of a dagger coated with blood. He swayed, eyes wild, mouth twitching. The royal steward had his hands out as he stood before the monarch, the flames from the bed chamber's fire flickering on his pale face.

"My lord," the steward begged, "drop the blade. You are safe now, I vow it."

"Liar!" the king screeched. "They tried to steal my crown! More are coming. I'll gut them all!" He lunged for the steward, but the man dodged as two soldiers barreled through the doorway to tackle the king. Stephan saw them coming and swung his arm, nicking one who backed away.

"Get away from me! You all want to steal my throne, and I won't have it!"

The steward was frantic, backing away as Stephan staggered toward him. Suddenly, the king's face twisted, and he grew rigid, coming to a halt. Panting, he muttered and swayed, fingers flexing on the dagger's handle. "They won't take me. They won't cast me out," he mumbled, looking down at the blade in his fist. Lip curling, he glanced at the men surrounding him, then lifted his arm and stabbed himself in the eyes. Gasps and screams of horror filled the chamber as Stephan crashed to the ground, the dagger's hilt jutting grotesquely from his left socket.

Donal backed away, bumping into a guard who caught sight of the king lying in a pool of blood and made a sign of protection across his chest. In moments, the chamber and halls erupted in chaos. The king's guard locked down the castle, letting no one out as they searched every room, finding those who'd been murdered in their sleep. Disbelief was mirrored in every face as Donal listened to accounts of butchery at King Stephan's hands. When the commander returned to Darragh's quarters an hour later, his face was haunted. Giving his lord a recounting made his stomach churn with suspicion, and he struggled to maintain a facade of loyalty to the thing that stood patiently listening.

Hearing Donal's thoughts as though they'd been spoken aloud, Darragh said little as his commander told him all. There was a moment when his lips twitched, attempting to curve in a diabolical smile as Donal described the king stabbing himself, but he tamped down on the urge and fixed his face. When the commander finished, the man looked drained, leached of so much more than strength as having witnessed a suicide.

"We should leave," Darragh said softly.

Donal nodded. "Aye. I'll inform the men." The commander stalked away, wondering how Darragh had wrought such evil while shying away from seeking out the truth. If he survived the trek back to Felmore, he'd take the gold he'd hooded over the years and leave. Start anew and try to forget.

Darragh listened to Donal's retreating steps, amused by his commander's wish to leave Felmore. Let the real Darragh deal with his traitorous wishes. Walking toward the chair next to the fire, he sat and leaned back against the cushion. He'd accomplished his goal, rendered the king unfit and those directly in line to the throne dead, and with none to blame but the monarch himself, the kingdom would devolve into chaos, and Darragh would remain unscathed—a future pawn should Crom need him. Once word spread across the kingdom, the nobility would squabble over power and title, leaving settlements unprepared for what was to come. With Crethia fractured, mankind would be easy pickings. And the elves? He smiled. The elves would fall.

Sighing, he closed his eyes. His time was running short, his hold on Darragh growing thin. Dothur grew impatient as he squatted beyond Oadsera's borders. It was past time for Crom to join him.

CHAPTER THIRTY-THREE

The people of Middleborough scattered when they saw Fiadh, flanked by Krulan, coming toward the town. She frowned at their reaction, fearing what they would do when they caught sight of Sibaen if the response of Crawly folk was any indicator. The Faoladh wasn't safe around those whose prejudice overshadowed reason, though, much to Fiadh's chagrin, the female she worried over was currently standing on the back of her mount to gain a better view of the damage done to the town. It was clear there would be no hiding if Fiadh were to ask.

Sighing, Fiadh let Meara lead her to the southern wall of the town, where much of the stone remained unscathed. Riley veered off and spoke with an older man in fine clothing who was gesticulating wildly.

Gideon came to Fiadh's side, watching the exchange. "That's most likely the steward," he told her, adding with a smirk, "I would guess he's less than pleased to see us."

Riley's voice rose, snatches of words carrying on the

wind. They listened for a moment, trying to discern what was said. Fiadh's mouth curved up. "It seems Riley doesn't agree with the man."

"It may not matter what the knight thinks. If Middleborough's people wish us gone, there's little we can do unless we want a fight."

"There will be no fight. Let them see us toil alongside them."

Sliding off Aridius' back, Gideon said, "Aye, but we can't tarry here."

"I know." She paused and looked toward the east, sensing a foul wind coming from that direction. Dothur wouldn't wait while she sought alliances. Time was running short.

They set up a makeshift camp while awaiting word from Sir Riley, the villagers of Crawly breaking off into two groups. Those who aligned with Margaret complained at the lack of comforts, eyeing Sibaen and Corene with hostility. Though, when their gazes fell on Krulan, they skittered away, complaints turning to mumblings. While small in number, they were vocal, and Fiadh wondered how many Middleborough folk would join them, making them more of a threat and giving Margaret more power.

Fiadh wandered to a patch of grass and sat down, leaning forward to grab a stick and poke at the ground. Riley had gone inside the town's walls, urging them to remain where they were until he returned. Gideon joined her, the heat of his body palpable as he rested his elbow on his knee and shifted closer. "You're worried, aren't you?"

She nodded. "More for others than myself." Fiadh

brought her knees to her chest and rested her head on them to look at him. "Do you think King Stephan will see me?"

Gideon picked at a blade of grass. "I want to say yes, but he has powerful advisors who have his ear in everything. They may be more of an impediment than the king's wishes."

"Perhaps I should seek an audience with them first."

He chuckled. "You could try."

"What does that mean?"

Gideon pursed his lips. "Duke Colm Gilroy of Winfell is the second most powerful man in the kingdom. He'll inherit the throne upon the king's death, as Stephan has no living heirs. My father always said he was a pompous ass, and I have no reason to doubt his word."

"What has that to do with me?"

His jaw ticked. "Men like Colm see every move like a game of chess. To advise the king to side with you could thwart his aspirations for the crown should the alliance eventually tilt in favor of the Aos Sí. I doubt the duke would take such a risk. I fear he'll poison the king's ear."

Frowning, she swatted the ground with her stick. Why must there always be this lust for power? She'd blame the failings of mankind's design, but Rygeil had been no different. Dothur sought the same. How would she convince the king of the real threat Carmun's spawn posed to every race if the men closest to him pitted themselves against such a union? It made her head ache. "If only they knew what was coming for them. If they believed the danger instead of looking at my face and seeing naught but an enemy."

"Do you want to return to Erabel?"

Fiadh shook her head. "Not until this task is done. If I go home and hide behind our barriers, I'm no better than Dothur. I can't watch our world crumble beneath his feet if there's a chance I can stop it."

"I thought as much. No matter what happens in Taigon, I'll stand with you."

She smiled and drew a spiral in the dirt, the tip of the stick dragging through the soil. In the distance, Riley's voice could be heard barking orders. Craning her neck, she watched him approach, noting the sour expression on his handsome face. He stalked toward them as Gideon helped Fiadh to her feet, his fingers trailing hers for a few moments before letting go to face the knight.

Riley's eyes sparked as he strode toward them. "Mother Goddess, save me from crusty old men."

Gideon's brow arched. "Troubles?"

"You have no idea." His mouth pulled down, and he put his hands on his hips, glancing at the town's wall as though he could see through stone to the men who vexed him. "It's not enough that the people of Middleborough are without homes and belongings, Lord Haile is dead, or our food stores burned. No," he paused, throwing his hands up, "they must balk at the news of aid for no other reason than who is offering it."

Fiadh watched him spend his anger, then said, "Let us help your people and see if our actions change their minds."

"That would mean opposing their edict, and they won't take kindly to that, especially from—" He stopped face coloring.

"An Aos Sí?"

"I'm sorry, my lady. I meant no offense."

"None taken. Ease your worry, Sir Riley." She folded her hands. "Where would you like us to begin?"

Fiadh spent hours extinguishing still-smoldering fires and healing those who allowed her close enough to use her powers. By evening, a few families had given her and the others food and water, offering shy smiles of gratitude. She tried to refuse, knowing how little they had, but most wouldn't hear of it, so she clutched their offerings to her chest and returned to their camp. Krulan met her, melting from the shadows like a wraith. He'd kept away as she entered the town, not because he chose to but because she'd commanded him. He grumbled as she sank to the thin pallet someone had laid for her.

I should have been with you.

Fiadh sighed and folded her legs. *They are fearful enough as it is. How do you think they would've reacted to your intimidating frown? Besides, I'm safer than others.* She looked toward Sibaen, who was crouched by a small fire, her dark pelt reflecting the flickering light of the flames. At her side was the Urisk, Corene, chatting softly to the Faoladh, yet always on the verge of bolting, the muscles of her lithe body quivering.

They can take care of themselves, Krulan told her.

It's my responsibility to keep them safe as much as I'm able.

Why do you do that? He stretched out next to her, resting his head on his paws.

Do what?

Take on too much. He lifted his head, golden eyes holding hers. *You have many who would share the burden, yet you insist on carrying it yourself.*

She plucked at the hem of her tunic, picking at a glob of brown crust from food or their travels. *I don't want anyone to be hurt… or worse… on my account.*

That is not your choice to make. She started to reply, but he snapped his teeth at her. *A leader isn't great despite those around her. She is great because of them. Each of us knows the risks. We accept them. And if one of us should fall, it won't be because you failed.* She swallowed hard, gaze drifting back to Sibaen. Krulan followed her stare. *Did Ulfran make you promise to keep his daughter safe?*

She shook her head.

Yet he allowed his firstborn to join you, didn't he?

Aye.

Do you know why?

Fiadh nodded. *Because she wished it.*

He rested his head on her knee. After a few minutes, she ran her fingers through his fur, eliciting a contented rumble. They sat together as the sun sank below the horizon. Gideon joined them, having spent the hours laboring with the townsfolk and checking in with Crawly's people. He wore the mantle of a lord so easily, knowing what to do and how to lead. Fetching bowls of food—a mixture of herbs, tubers, and lentils—he offered one to Fiadh and Krulan, chuckling when the Cù-Sìth flashed a canine at him and got up with a huff.

I don't eat rabbit food. I eat the rabbit, he told her, slipping off toward the woods.

Fiadh smiled. *You know, if you eat the rabbit, you're still eating the rabbit food.*

Krulan paused and swung his head back toward her.

True, but rabbit seasoning is much better than the leaves you sprinkle on that slop.

She giggled and dug into her meal, sharing what she and the Cù-Sìth had said to one another with Gideon when he plopped down next to her. They ate silently for a time, content to listen to the hum of conversation around them, eventually sharing what each had done throughout the long afternoon. Gideon was pleased to hear that some Middleborough folk had welcomed Fiadh's aid, though it rankled that others shunned her.

"They'd rather let their wounds go sour and die than accept help." He shook his head. "I don't understand it."

"Were you so different?"

"I let you care for me," he said with mock offense. "Not that I had a choice when you hauled me to your den of witchcraft." Gideon waggled his eyebrows at her. "I'll admit I tried to fight it, fool that I am, but I've been under your spell ever since."

"Well," she said, leaning back on her elbows, "it's good to hear it's taken effect."

Kaelari entered the camp, drawing their attention as she reported on the town's remaining defenses. Without a fortifying wall, they were exposed. Fiadh suggested an earthmover reconstruct what they could, filling in gaps with solid rock.

"I offered, but the elders wouldn't hear of it. Riley is trying to persuade them." Kaelari dipped a ladle into the pot hanging over the fire and dished some out stew onto a wooden plate. "I'll admit I admire his patience, though I think it's for naught."

"Why?" Fiadh made a frustrated sound. "It makes no sense."

"They are narrow-minded people, viewing the world through a lens of prejudice." She took a bite, chewing thoughtfully. "They think we mean to trick them," Kaelari said with a snort, "seal the survivors in a tomb of rock."

Fiadh rolled her eyes and got to her feet, stomping to a wash tub to rinse her bowl and spoon. "We should just repair the wall without their approval and prove them wrong."

"Then do it," Gideon said, coming to his feet and taking her bowl to finish the washing. "They can't stop you, and it would help the townsfolk."

Fiadh stepped to Kaelari's side, a look passing between the two. "He's not wrong," the female said.

Gideon scrubbed the bowls with a rough piece of cloth and dipped them in the water to rinse away the last of the food. "I know you wish to form alliances with those in power, but you'll find that nobles don't often put the needs of their people before their own wants. Power is a lure many can't resist." He dried the bowls and stacked them on a smooth rock next to the fire for someone to use when they grew hungry. "Think of it this way," he continued, facing her, "If common folk outnumber nobility, who do you think you should be winning over?"

She lifted her chin and swung her eyes to the damaged walls of the town. She could see people moving about through a gap as they settled in for the night, their forms visible in the light of lanterns and hearths. Gideon was right. Those living under the rule of nobility were the true power. "I will give the elders until dawn, and then we'll do what's right for the people of Middleborough."

Gideon and Kaelari nodded, watching Fiadh settle onto her pallet and turn her back on the fire and everything for a few hours' peace. They moved away, keeping their voices low as others found their beds. Eventually, Gideon made rounds through the makeshift camp of the villagers of Crawly, speaking quietly to those on watch and ensuring all were safe and accounted for.

Kaelari folded her arms and followed his progress, Ellisar joining her. "He's a natural leader."

She nodded, studying the man. "Aye, but will he be able to sway them?"

Ellisar shrugged. "Enough of them will."

"I hope you're right." She touched his shoulder. "I'll take the first watch."

Quiet fell over the camp as hours passed. Well after midnight, as Kaelari woke Sibaen for her shift, a small cry drifted on the wind. The Faoladh sprang into a crouch, clawed hand twitching where it rested on her upraised knee. Sniffing the air, she cocked her head, ears rotating. The elf drew her bow and nocked an arrow, fingers holding it while he watched Sibaen. Minutes passed with no sound but the shifting of bodies and the rumble of snores.

The Faoladh's body lost some of its tension—she was never fully relaxed—as she stood. Kaelari stepped close and leaned toward her. "Perhaps it was a babe waking for suckle."

Sibaen swept the outer wall, ears flicking. "Perhaps." She moved away from the elf and slunk toward the town. Kaelari watched her for a few minutes, then headed for her pallet, asleep moments after her head hit the ground.

Slipping into Middleborough through the gaping hole in the outer wall, Sibaen darted among the shadows, listening. The further she went into the settlement, the more uneasy she felt. As she made her way through the muddy streets, the thick hair on her back bristled, causing her to freeze. A whimper, like that of a frightened child, made its way to her ears. She swung her head, following the sound, body springing into motion when the cry grew louder.

The dark outline of a row of wattle and daub huts came into view as she rounded a corner littered with charred belongings from the attack. Loping on all fours, Sibaen zeroed in on the source of the noise, ears trained to the cries that grew more desperate with every stride. Not bothering the knock, she burst into the hut, the door slamming into the wall so hard it shook the walls. Snarling, Sibaen whipped her head around, eyes going wide before narrowing to dangerous slits as she saw a dark figure perched atop the bodies of a man and woman. Shoving the couple's small child out the door, she roared, the sound guttural and terrifying. It reverberated through the cluster of homes, wrenching occupants awake as it was met with a high-pitched hiss.

Moving with lethal speed, the dark creature twisted its body, the hood of its cloak falling away to reveal a pale face with red eyes. A thin trail of blood stained its chin, stark against his white skin. Blood-drinker. Abhartach. The height of a child, he stood before the bed, glaring at her balefully. "You dare spoil my meal?" the Abhartach whispered, voice like wasps in her ears.

"I'll do more than that," she growled, teeth flashing.

The blood-drinker tilted his head. "I've never tasted your kind."

Beyond the hut, men and women awakened, drawn to the commotion. "After I drain you, dog, I'll have the child for dessert."

Sibaen leaped, claws out, teeth snapping. The Abhartach ducked and rolled, coming to his feet as she landed on the packed dirt floor. Lunging for her, elongated fangs winking in the dim light of a fire in the hearth, he grabbed her arm only to have her slash at his fingers, severing two. He shrieked, the sound so piercing she winced. From the doorway, men watched, makeshift weapons in their hands.

One, a burly man in his bedgown, tried to follow the figures in the gloom as they dodged and swung. "Which one do we kill?" he whispered.

"The werewolf."

"Are you sure?" He watched uncertainly, hand flexing on the end of the log he'd grabbed.

The other man shook his head, backing away as Sibaen got the upper hand and snatched the blood-drinker as he charged her, flinging him into the wall. Not wasting a moment, the Faoladh pounced in a blur of movement. Claws slashed as Sibaen used feet and hands to tear, gouging chunks of decayed flesh from the blood-drinker. The Abhartach hissed and screeched, its dark cloak, rank with clotted blood, swirling with every movement as it tried to escape the Faoladh. But Sibaen was quicker. Launching her body into the air, her torso contorting in a graceful twist, she landed atop the shoulders of the dwarvish creature. Her nails dug into the Abhartach's neck below his jaw, severing tendon and muscle. Wrenching viciously, she ripped his head off and flung it into the fire. The flames sparked, glowing blue and then green as they grew, consuming the creature's skull. Panting, Sibaen limped toward the doorway, hand pressed against a gash on her side. She paused when she saw the crowd.

Masks of horror to hate were etched on every face that watched her movements. A man toward the back of the gathering waved a small hammer in the air. "Kill it!"

The crowd roared and rushed forward, blocking her exit. Sibaen backed away, holding out her bloodied hands as though she could stop the tide of rage coming for her. A blow landed on her shoulder as she crouched to avoid it, rolling to her side and slashing with her toe claws and fists, and makeshift weapons pummeled her body.

Suddenly, a rounded form landed on top of her, all but covering her entirely. The scent of human covered her nose as Sibaen sniffed and cracked open an eye.

"Stop this!" the woman screamed, her braided hair falling into the Faoladh's face. "Stop!"

Body aching, Sibaen tried to see beyond the form shielding her but found herself looking into the woman's face. Grey strands of hair framed her rounded cheeks, the loose braid coming undone where it hung from her shoulder. Green eyes stared at her from within features softened with age.

"Get away from it!" a man yelled, trying to wrench the woman away.

The woman craned her neck and glared. "It saved Katherine." She looked back at the Faoladh. "My niece lives because of it."

Sibaen lay still, heart thundering. The woman slowly eased her plump body off. As she moved, the Faoladh felt her tremble and smelled her fear. As the weight lifted, Sibaen scooted backward, eyes skipping from one form to another as the men crowded into the tiny hut edged away.

"It saved Katherine," the woman said again, and her face turned to the bodies growing cold on the raised pallet. Eyes welling, she swallowed hard. "I don't care what it is. Katherine is alive, and I'm not so full of fear I can't see the why of it."

Sibaen stared at the woman, glancing briefly at the bodies of the child's parents. "I'm sorry I didn't get here sooner."

The men stepped back, startled at the feminine voice coming from a creature they watched with fear. They looked at each other, weapons wobbling in indecision.

"I heard crying," Sibaen said, trying to explain. "Something didn't feel right. I only wish I'd felt it sooner."

The woman shook her head. "There'd be three graves had you not come." Men muttered, bodies shifting as the woman held out a hand. "She's my niece. I'm in your debt."

"Don't touch it, Edith," one of the men growled, trying to pull her away.

She swatted him. "Get your hands off me, Thomas!" She spun around. "What's wrong with you all? You saw the same as I did." Pointing at Sibaen, she said, "She saved my niece's life!"

"She's one of them," groused another man.

"One of what? One of the people who healed my William this afternoon?"

"You can't trust her kind," Thomas snapped. "As soon as she's hungry, we're next!"

Sibaen flinched at the accusation, lip curling in distaste.

"Take your head out of your ass." Edith swung a narrow gaze through the gathering, marking every face. "Which one of you could've killed that creature?" she asked, pointing toward the decapitated body. "You, Thomas?"

He muttered and looked away.

"I didn't think so." Eyes sparking, she grabbed Sibaen's hand, ignoring the gore from the blood-drinker that clung to her skin and fur, and elbowed men out of the way. Yanking more forcefully than she meant, Edith hauled the Faoladh out of the hut and through the growing throng of onlookers, not stopping until they'd reached an empty section between rows of houses. "You best be on your way before they get it into their fool heads to harm you."

Sibaen nodded. "I hope the child is well."

Edith nodded. "She will be."

The Faoladh turned away, stopping mid-stride. "I'm truly sorry about the girl's parents. Your…"

"Sister," Edith said, her voice breaking on a sob.

Her mouth pulled down. "I'm sorry."

"Don't—" Blinking back tears, Edith swallowed hard.

"It's you who's owed an apology." A short distance away, the sound of arguing grew louder. "You should leave."

Sibaen dipped her head, and with a last look at Edith, she slunk away, racing through narrow lanes until she reached the edge of the town. Leaping through the gap in the outer wall, the Faoladh ran to their camp and woke Fiadh. Word spread quickly, and it was decided that no matter what the town elders thought, Thallen would rebuild what he could of the walls surrounding Middleborough. It wouldn't keep creatures like the Abhartach out, but it could slow a larger attack.

Before dawn streaked across the sky, everyone had heard a blood-drinker had killed two townspeople and would've killed more had Sibaen not intervened. Riley entered the camp to thank the Faoladh, though his anger was evident when he recounted the elders' continued resistance regarding an alliance.

"Do you think more will come?" he asked of the creature Sibaen had killed.

Fiadh looked to Kaelari and Ellisar though both had no insight as the Aos Sí had few legends of them. Corene, the leader of the Urisk, separated herself from the shadows. "They are solitary, having no tolerance for others of their kind."

"We thought Kelpies were solitary, but they attack in large groups," Ellisar said.

Corene looked at him, her goat-like eyes thoughtful. "Abhartach are not born. They are made. As such, they are few. I would guess this one came after the fighting looking for easy prey."

Riley's jaw ticked. "If more come, they will not find us so easy to kill."

The Urisk stared at him. "Humans are no match for Abhartach. Their strength and speed surpass yours."

He glowered at her and folded his arms. "I'd like to have one under the point of my blade and see how strong they are."

"I would not wish such a thing," Corene said softly. "Besides, you're not likely to see another in your lifetime."

Giving her a quick nod, Riley left to see the repairs Thallen had begun, marveling at the power the elf wielded as he called upon the earth, shaping it into huge slabs of rock. Onlookers gathered where he rebuilt the damaged sections, some hostile, others grateful. Thallen ignored them all, intent on doing what he could regardless of their feelings. Riley walked with him as the elf went from section to section, making it a point to talk and even touch the male's shoulder with thanks knowing others were watching, word would spread.

Fiadh was packing her belongings in her satchel, readying herself for the final leg to Taigon, when Ellisar gave whistled. She turned and followed his gaze, seeing a dark, winged shape heading in their direction. As it neared, she saw that it was a large, black vulture. It wheeled toward them, massive wings fanning out as it landed. Tucking them close to its body, the bird ran toward them, its hunched form low to the ground, head protruding far beyond its black feet. Ellisar got to one knee and greeted the vulture, stroking his hand over its head and down its back.

"Kima," he said to the bird, "what news do you bring us?"

The vulture clacked its beak, violet eyes pinned on the elf. They stared into each other for many minutes as Fiadh and the others watched. Rising slowly, Ellisar thanked Kima and swept his gaze over the gathering before landing on his queen. "King Stephan is dead."

CHAPTER THIRTY-FOUR

News of the king's death spread quickly among the people of Crawly and Middleborough. By late morning, a small crowd had gathered outside the elven camp. Edith, with little Katherine, clutched in her arms, was among them. Riley wended his way through the throng and came to Fiadh, who was in quiet conversation with Gideon and Kaelari. The death of King Stephan and members of the court reeked of Dothur's hand, though Fiadh struggled to understand why the demon wouldn't simply lay waste to all of Taigon.

"Why only the king and his nobles?" she asked, looking toward Gideon.

He frowned. "I'm not sure. Perhaps he aims to throw Crethia into chaos. With no direct heir to the throne, nobles across the kingdom could go to war with each other to attain the crown, making it a perfect time to strike."

"It would be a good strategy, making fiefdoms easy pickings for the demon's armies," Kaelari offered.

Riley cleared his throat, and they turned to him. "News of King Stephan has many of my people fearful of attacks from Dothur and surrounding fiefs. We're vulnerable, and it's no secret that Lord Sutton covets our land."

"Do you think he'd lay claim to Middleborough?" Gideon asked with distaste.

"I wouldn't put it past him. He made no effort to hide his disdain for Lord Haile. Our soil is rich, grazing land plentiful," he paused and shook his head, "If I were a greedy man, I'd try to take it myself."

Fiadh glanced at the people milling around. "And them? What is it they want?"

Riley ducked his head, lifting his eyes to hers from beneath his brows. "To ally with you."

Her eyes went wide. "Oh?"

"They fear another attack, and after the incident last night," he flicked his eyes to Sibaen, "some believe they are safer aligning with your people."

"I cannot protect them," she said softly. "We made this journey to seek an audience with the king. Dothur and those who fight with him threaten all of Crethia. That's what I hoped to convince the king of. Now…" She held out a hand and dropped it. "Where do we go? Who'll listen? Elves and men can't fight what's coming on their own. We must be united. I'd hoped King Stephan would see the wisdom of an alliance and rally every vassal across the kingdom."

"You need envoys," Riley said.

"Do you know any?"

He smiled. "You're looking at one."

Gideon's brow shot up. "Is that so?"

"Aye. I've seen enough to know whose side I wish to fight on."

Gideon put his hands on his hips. "That's admirable, but don't you think you'll find your head on a pike for siding with elves?"

He shrugged. "So be it. Either way, I won't hide among my people and wait for Dothur's armies to find me when I can do more good bridging alliances."

"Where will you go?"

Riley considered, glancing at a man who wore leather armor that was clearly made for someone much larger. "Word has it the bulk of the attacks are in the east and north. We'll begin here in the south." Ellisar and Gideon passed a look to one another, catching Riley's attention. "What?"

"We will accompany you," the elf said.

"Ellisar?" Kaelari asked. "What's this about?"

He looked at her. "Riley needs one of our people standing with him if he's going to be successful."

Kaelari nodded slowly. Ellisar bowed to Fiadh and slipped away to gather his things.

"And you?" Kaelari asked Gideon.

"Ellisar needs someone to keep him in line."

"I heard that," Ellisar shouted.

Gideon grinned. "You were meant to."

"Gideon?" Fiadh asked.

His smile vanished. "This is what I was meant to do. I have to go."

Her throat clogged, and her heart twisted with the knowledge that he would face a perilous journey. There was every chance she might not see him again. But with that realization came acceptance. She couldn't keep everyone safe. She couldn't control what they did and what risks they took.

Gideon was right. He knew the lords of many lands and, with those connections, had the best chance of securing aid. Knowing that didn't soften the ache in her chest. Fiadh stood on her toes and pulled his head down, pressing her lips to his. His arms wrapped around her waist, and she clung to him, wishing she could keep him at her side, knowing she had to let him go.

Releasing her hold, she whispered, "Come back to me."

"Nothing but death could keep me from it."

Her eyes welled as she nodded and took a step away. Turning back to Riley, who'd averted his face to give them privacy, she said, "I appreciate your offer to act as envoy, but I wonder if you should remain with your people to help them rebuild. They need a leader."

Riley waved a dismissive hand. "The elders will care for them."

"Then, you have my deepest gratitude."

The crowd of townsfolk lingering around them swelled to include some from Crawly. A few people came closer, having heard snippets of the exchange. They offered advice, well wishes, and gratitude to both elves and men who'd come to their aid. Fiadh stood aside, taking it all in, marveling that these common folk, who'd lost so much in such a short time, were ready to give thanks to her people—their enemies. It was humbling.

Edith pushed her way through the throng, a child on her

hip. When she reached Fiadh, she paused and gave an awkward curtsy. "My lady, if not for her," she pointed to Sibaen, "my niece would be dead. I lost my sister and her good husband to that creature who came in the night. None of the men standing behind me could've saved this child. But she could. I think that's worthy of loyalty."

Fiadh's face softened. "Thank you. Sibaen is a good friend, and I'm glad to hear she could help your niece, though I also grieve for your loss."

Edith patted Katherine's back. "They say you're a queen."

"I am."

"I've never met a queen, but I always imagined they'd be beautiful like you. And kind. If there's aught I can do, I will." Katherine shifted her head to look at Fiadh, her large blue eyes round with wonder. "She's a queen," Edith whispered to the child.

"It's good to meet you both." Fiadh tilted her head and smiled at the little girl, then shifted her attention back to the aunt. "Your offer means a great deal to me, as I'm sure it does to Sibaen."

The Faoladh nodded and came to Fiadh's side.

"I would only ask that you share your experiences with others, Edith. Our people have been enemies for generations. Undoing such a history begins with a single voice."

"I will, my lady." Edith reached out tentatively, mouth curling up at the corners when Fiadh took her hand, squeezing gently. Letting go, the woman hefted the child to her hip and turned to Sibaen. Her teeth flashed in a grin as she clasped Edith's hand. A few people in the crowd whispered at the contact, unsure what to make of the Faoladh. Edith lifted her chin, holding Sibaen's hand longer. "May the Great Mother bless you," she said, ignoring the soft muttering of men and women who heard.

"And you," Sibaen said, slowly pulling her hand away, fingertips trailing the matronly woman's palm.

Edith nodded and moved away with purpose in her step. The crowd parted as she passed, her head held high. Some looked from the woman to Sibaen, working out how they felt about the interaction.

Sibaen watched them go, then backed away to where Corene waited impatiently. Fiadh spoke to Kaelari and Thallen about the town's defenses. When it was clear nothing more could be done, she went into a freshly plowed field and knelt on the ground. Reaching through the mantle toward Danu, she called upon the magic of her parents, of Veren, and funneled the power into life-giving energy. It spread from her palms outward, the overturned earth becoming dark and rich. An elderly farmer stood nearby watching, leaning on a hoe. When she sat back on her heels, he walked toward her, age slowing his gait on the uneven ground. She looked up when he was a couple of feet away.

"Blessing the field, are ya?" he asked in a paper-thin voice.

She smiled. "Something like that."

"I've never seen your kind before, but I heard stories as a boy—way back in ancient days," he said with a wink. "Somehow, the ones calling you a scourge on the world never rang true. It's good to know I was right about that. My name's Brodie."

"Fiadh."

He dipped his head and returned to a small clearing he'd been prepping for planting, whistling as he went.

Fiadh rose and followed, taking the hoe from him before he could continue clearing the tiny plot of land. "Let me help." She could've used magic to work the soil but chose to toil alongside him, removing weeds and tilling the ground. When she'd finished with the small rectangle section, she looked at him questioningly. "Shouldn't we expand the area so you can plant more crops?"

He shook his head. "It's not crop I'm planting." Reaching into his pocket, he pulled out a handful of seeds. "Mary loved violets. I promised her I'd plant a garden of them come spring."

Fiadh was touched and spent the next hour with Brodie, listening to him talk about his late wife. By the time Gideon found her, the plot of violets was planted. "I've been looking for you. It's time to go."

"I'm afraid I kept you too long, my dear," Brodie said, patting her arm. "Your man is right. You best be running along."

She bid the widower farewell, face flaming when he winked at Gideon, who took her hand and led her away. When they returned to camp, she packed her things quickly and met Gideon, who waited with Riley, Ellisar, and former soldiers of Lord Haile. Ellisar bowed to Fiadh and slipped away, motioning for Riley and the other men to follow.

"I don't want you to go. I'm afraid I'll never see you again," Fiadh said, her voice thick with unshed tears.

"Trust that I'll return with a thousand men riding under your banner."

She gave him a wobbly smile. "I don't have a banner."

"Then I suggest you hie yourself to Erabel and make one so I don't look like a fool when I arrive with a leaderless band of soldiers."

"They'll have a leader."

Gideon's eyes crinkled. "I'll miss you."

She nodded and leaned into him, pressing her face to his chest to listen to the strong beat of his heart. "I'll miss you, too."

The moment was gone too soon. Gideon hefted his satchel across his back and joined Ellisar and the others. Fiadh watched them go, leaning into Krulan, who stood at her side, a ballast against the worry clouding her mind.

It is good that you let him go.

It doesn't feel that way. It feels like I'm sending him to his death. Her mouth trembled.

He is a powerful warrior. I believe you'll see him again.

I hope you're right.

I usually am, he told her with a wink.

She ribbed him with her elbow. *Cocky wolf.*

Krulan huffed. *Wolf? Wolves would turn tail and run should they see me.* The Cù-Sìth snuffled her hair and sauntered off, Kaelari taking his place moments later.

"We should begin our journey home."

Home, Fiadh thought. Would it feel like home if Gideon wasn't there? When the entire company was astride their mounts or ready on foot, she gave Kaelari a nod and followed the elf as she led the group north.

Travel was swift as the elves, eager to return to Erabel, headed to the Crooked Gap in the Wandering Mountains. But their speed couldn't counteract Fiadh's uneasiness. She felt exposed in the shadow of the giant peaks. Meara appeared to feel it, too, often snorting and stamping her hooves when they stopped to rest. Fiadh knew that should a contingent of Dothur's army come upon them. They could soon be carrion. Kaelari was on edge, too, body rigid in her saddle.

Without Ellisar, Thallen took over scouting and reporting back, often sending Kima, the black vulture, to fly overhead. On the afternoon of the third day, when they were deep in the Crooked Gap, Kima returned with ill news. Darragh and a contingent of his soldiers were spotted in the Eidolon Pass. While the route through the Crooked Gap was far enough from the pass to be of no concern, they would need to be on their guard the closer they came to Felmore. It was decided that, like before, they would take a longer route and bypass the southern edge of Darragh's land. It would mean harder travel, but Fiadh had no stomach for fighting Darragh's men if they were caught outside Dorcha Wood.

Days turned to a sennight, and as they neared the final leg to Dorcha Wood, Kima returned to Thallen with a sighting of a band of creatures on a course that would put them directly in their path. Fiadh knelt in front of the vulture and delved into his mind, seeing what he'd relayed to the Thallen. Her mouth pulled down in a grimace as the bird circled the creatures—Kelpie and some type of half-breeds—led by a mage. If they stayed put, they could possibly avoid a confrontation but would also risk the creatures veering from their current heading and coming across the group.

She shared what she'd seen in the vulture's mind with the others. Sibaen sneezed and paced, fingers flexing and claws extended. Folding her arms, Kaelari considered their best course of action. "Dorcha Wood is too far. Even if we ran, we'd never make it."

"Did you get the sense the creatures were tracking us?" Fiadh shook her head. "Good. If they don't know we're coming, we could ambush them."

Kaelari eyed him. "It's risky."

"Any more so than taking our chances on our current route?"

The female crossed her arms and glanced at Sibaen. "What do you think?"

The Faoladh straightened to her full height. "I say we fight."

Fiadh's stomach churned as they gathered to discuss strategy. Thallen commanded Kima to fly and scan the landscape along the route the creatures were taking. They'd use that information to find an advantageous position. By nightfall, they left the horses, with Meara standing guard, and trekked into a mountain pass.

Kaelari gave Fiadh a bow and quiver. "Aim for the heart."

Nodding, Fiadh gripped the bow and hid among a cluster of boulders that overlooked a wide valley. The others fanned out, choosing their positions in trees or behind juts of earth. Afternoon sunlight cast the landscape in an orange hue as Fiadh tapped into her power, opening her senses and readying herself for battle.

They entered the valley before nightfall—twenty creatures led by a cloaked figure. She watched their slow approach, recoiling at the malice she could feel from her vantage point. When they neared the edge of the valley, a narrow section of land that would take them up and over the ridge, Kaelari released a war cry and sprang from a high point, her body a whirl of movement. The mage lunged, blasting the elf with a spell that sent her reeling. She scrambled and got to her feet, Thallen at her side, pulling a shard to rock from the earth and stabbing it at the wizard. The mage darted away, masking his movements with a spell of concealment. The others attacked, cutting down Kelpie and half-breed demons or sending others fleeing.

Faraen emerged at the mountain's base, sword swinging as the mage appeared a few feet from him. Fiadh gasped, nocking an arrow, and aimed. Whispering, she called upon the wind, feeling it curl around her. When the mage formed a dagger from a shard of rock, Fiadh loosed her arrow. It sailed toward the mage, a blur with the wind pushing it forward. At the last minute, the mage spun on his heel, eyes unerringly finding her where she crouched above the boulders. With a wave of his hand, he redirected the arrow, sending it straight for Faraen's heart.

Fiadh screamed, her voice blending with the unearthly wailing of Sluagh, who streaked across the sky. Troya spied the mage and dove. Jumping up from her hiding place,

Fiadh threw out her arms and shouted at the wind, commanding it to send a gale at the arrow. A gust burst around Faraen, but the arrow was too close and struck his body, impaling him.

The mage had no time to relish the moment. Thinking the Sluagh had come to aid him, he'd left himself open, never seeing Troya dive. She whipped her wing through the air, the clawed tip winking in the weak light, cutting the wizard's body in two before wheeling back into the sky.

Frozen for a moment, Fiadh followed the Sluagh's progress as she joined her sisters. Body unlocking, she raced down the ridge, legs moving so quickly she fell forward, tumbling until a root thrust from the earth and wrapped itself around her middle. She gasped, thanking the spirit in the tree as it unwound and pushed her to her feet.

Fiadh went to Faraen's side. His head slowly rolled toward her, eyes fluttering. "Well, that didn't go as I'd planned."

She tried to smile. With sure hands, she reached for the haft of the arrow, fingers tracing its path through his leather breastplate. "You're pinned," she told him, feeling where the arrow tip pierced the ground. Fiadh found Elraen loping up the hill toward them. He slid to his knees and inspected the injury.

"I'm all right," he told her, wincing. She looked uncertain, healing power radiating from her fingers though she saw Elraen probing the entry point of the arrow. It would need to be removed before they could begin to mend him.

She didn't know Faraen as well as she should. If he died, she'd never get the chance. In the distance, Thallen cut down a ghastly-looking half-breed demon. Its corpse left twitching while she stalked another, trying to flee. Kaelari had her sights on a large Kelpie, its form morphing from horse to half-human as it hissed and spat at the elf. Sword swinging, she sent a cloud of dirt and rock to blind it. Its head fell to the ground with a sickening thump, the female moving on to another target before it stopped rolling. High above, Sluagh darted across the sky, watching but leaving the killing to others. She puzzled over that, eyes flicking to the severed body of the mage.

Elraen got to work. She cast about for plants to make a poultice, but nothing was at hand. Sitting on her heels, Fiadh pressed on the entry point to stop the bleeding, flicking her eyes to the fighting as the last creatures fled or took their final breath. Elraen cleared his throat and nodded. With Fiadh taking the haft of the arrow in her hands, the healer held Faraen down, and she yanked, ripping it from his body. Faraen's face went white, a hiss of breath coming from his clenched teeth.

"Let's not do that again," he said thinly.

Fiadh put her hands on his wound, staunching the bleeding and murmuring spells to heal his flesh, Elraen placing his hands on top of hers, mixing his spells to speed the healing. As muscle and skin mended, she slipped into Faraen's mind and commanded him to sleep.

CHAPTER THIRTY-FIVE

Darragh said little as they made their way through Eidolon Pass. The demon inside of him was struggling to maintain his hold on the Lord of Felmore. Dothur pummeled him with commands to join him outside Oadsera's borders. Crom Cruach resisted the order but knew he'd have to let Darragh go. The sigil carved into the medallion around the man's neck had become worn, its power finite. Magic came at a cost, and holding Darragh in his control was taxing. If only he could sip from the well of Zaeleria's power. Or, better yet, the Aos Sí's young queen. His mouth watered, lips twisting in a lecherous grin.

Donal watched Darragh with wary eyes, wondering what foul thought filled his lord's mind. The men kept their distance, many believing Darragh had somehow killed King Stephan and the others from the royal court. Donal tried to censor them, but their thoughts were his own. If one of the soldiers decided to kill Darragh, he didn't think he'd try to stop it.

Misty Bogs was covered in low-hanging clouds when they made camp four days later. They'd lost one soldier since exerting the infamous stretch of land. The man had wandered too close to a deep pool and slipped, never surfacing. Darragh sat under a heavy cloak, the hood obscuring much of his face, as his men started a fire and readied a meal. The tether to Crom Cruach grew thinner, and the demon felt the real Lord of Felmore pushing back, trying to regain control. Perhaps it is time, Crom thought from his lair leagues away, deep in Malver Gorge. Darragh had served his purpose. Word was spreading across Crethia, and nobles were rising up, each staking claim to the throne. It wouldn't take much for small wars to erupt, weakening them for when Dothur's army swept through.

Crom Cruach stroked Darragh's mind, his thoughts like razors digging into the man's brain. *You wish to be free,* he crooned, sensing Felmore's lord shy away. *So be it, but know this. You are mine to control. My tool to wield. Enjoy your freedom, but do not forget your master.*

The demon wrenched himself from Darragh's body, scalding the man's mind with a blast of magic. The connection severed, the tether anchored to the sigil snapping back to Crom Cruach like the sinew of a bow. The demon rocked on his heels, the dark chamber of his surroundings slowly coming into focus. The symbols covering the floor where he knelt flickered, growing dim, then dull as he staggered to his feet. Body creaking, he hobbled to a bench lining the wall. Scuttling came to his ears, and he cocked his head, watching a shape scurry down the wall opposite him. It tapped one of its legs and scrambled toward him, lowering its mottled head in a bow when it reached Crom's feet.

"Tell your captain I leave for the Lloathren Mountains at dawn," he told the creature, adding, "And bring me something to slake my appetite. Something young and fresh."

A white film flashed over the dark pools of its eyes as it blinked. With a chittering sound, it bowed again and darted away, slipping through a crack in the wall. Crom leaned against the cold stone and closed his eyes, centering himself as he dipped into his well of power. He'd feed, then rest. Come morning, he'd make his way to the Lloathren Mountains. When he'd regained his strength from the darkness living within those peaks, he'd help Dothur bring the elves to their knees.

Darragh fell to his side like dead weight. His eyes stared straight ahead, barely registering Donal as his commander raced toward him. "My lord, are you unwell?"

His mouth opened and closed, face pressed to the loamy soil. Quiet. His mind was quiet. Darragh shuddered and tried to focus on Donal, but the man's words sounded as though they were spoken through a funnel, muffled and indistinct. He lifted an arm and wedged it under his body, thankful when his commander saw the movement and hauled him up. Slipping Darragh's arm over his shoulder, Donal dragged his lord away from the men.

Bending his knees, he lowered his lord, bracing him when Darragh listed to the side. "My lord?"

It took great effort to lift his head, and Darragh settled for looking up from beneath his heavy brows. "I am."

A look of confusion crossed Donal's face. "Is there anything I can get you?"

Darragh swung his head to the side, casting about for something familiar. "Where are we?"

"Misty Bogs, my lord." Donal went to one knee. "Are you all right?"

He didn't know how long he'd been under the demon's sway. The days and weeks, however long he'd been trapped inside his own mind, flowed into one another, and he couldn't separate them into a semblance of order. Memories raced through his head, but they were fuzzy, as though the experiences were seen through a pane of filmy glass. Brow creasing, he asked, "Did we go to Taigon?"

Donal swallowed hard, hand curling into a fist on his knee. "Aye, my lord. King Stephan is dead. We are on our way back to Felmore."

"Dead?" he asked, then whispered. "Dead."

"You don't remember?"

Darragh shook his head. King Stephan was dead. He didn't know whether to feel rage or relief. The king was a pathway to power, but his absence could be a more direct one. "Has the duke claimed the throne?"

"The duke is dead, as are all those in direct succession to the crown."

His brow went up. Even without the memories to verify it, he felt the demon must have orchestrated the assassinations. Clever. The kingdom would devolve into chaos without a successor. A ripe time to stake his own claim. For a moment, he wondered if that was Crom Cruach's plan all along but discarded the idea when the demon's words and warnings floated through his brain. "When will we reach Felmore?"

"Three days, my lord."

"Good." He staggered to his feet, head swimming. Donal steadied him, and they walked to a small tent where Darragh stretched out on a thin pallet.

"May I get you anything, my lord?"

Darragh shook his head, the motion causing it to spin sickeningly. His stomach churned, and he took deep breaths, listening to his commander close the flap and move away. Fingers digging into the neckline of his tunic, he pulled out a leather thong on which hung a crude medallion. His hand shook as he tugged, as though it fought his will. Gritting his teeth, Darragh yanked, ripping it from his neck. Laying the disc in his palm, he studied it, mouth twisting with hate. Rolling to the side, he smashed the medallion on the ground, his fist pounding it until it was a pile of clay shards. Sweat beaded his forehead, and he took in ragged breaths. His eyes darting when he could've sworn he heard a growl of rage.

Clenching his hand under his cheek, he considered the events that had unfolded when he'd been held captive by that... thing. It galled him to feel his heart hammer in fear as he recalled feelings of helplessness. Tapping into anger that was never far from the surface of his emotions, he fed it, shutting out his men. If Haegna were alive, he'd consult her, force her to cast a spell or create a trinket to repel such an invasion again. Her death was an inconvenience. Mind skipping from one desperate idea to another, it skidded to a halt when the witch of Dorcha Wood found herself among his thoughts.

Perhaps she was powerful enough to repel the demon. The corner of his mouth tugged in a smile. Attacking her had led to crushing defeat. What if he tried something different? A truce? An alliance? He could play on her womanly weakness. Project desperation. Plead. Darragh drifted to sleep, thoughts of Fiadh circling through his mind. Thoughts of her at his mercy.

All manner of dark creatures called Malver Gorge home. Those who hadn't traveled with Dothur numbered in the hundreds, each calling Crom Cruach master. It would take time to reach Dothur in the Lloathren Mountains—a place of dark power. Had Troya, leader of the Sluagh, bent beneath his will, he'd travel on the wind. As it was, spells to cloak his form and make him swift would further deplete his well of magic. Possessing Felmore's lord for such an extended time had taken its toll. He needed the dark pools within the Lloathren Mountains.

Crom made his way to a chamber that overlooked a deep cut in the gorge, feet shuffling in the dark. Shutting himself inside, he hobbled to a cut in the wall, less of a window than a brutal wound in the stone. Through the darkness, he made out movements of hundreds of bodies. An army in itself should he wish to command it. The sound of scraping mixed with a soft whimper came to his ears, and he turned away from the opening. Where they found the child, he didn't know, nor did he care. He'd slake his thirst and call for another. When the blood and life force flowed through him, he'd be ready for his journey—a battalion of monsters at his back.

CHAPTER THIRTY-SIX

nce the last of Dothur's monsters were dealt with, Fiadh strode to a bluff, craning her neck to scan the sky. Sluagh darted past, ghostly wailing following their path. It was hard to track their movements in the setting sun, but her eyes snagged on a form that almost hovered a short distance away.

"Troya," she said, pushing her voice along a wind current.

The Sluagh spun in the air, her grace at odds with her frightening form. Tumbling from the sky, she fanned her wings out at the last minute, cackling at the gaping mouths of Sibaen and Corene. Spindly legs planted into the ground a few feet from Fiadh, leathery wings folding onto her pale back. "The queen of Erabel finds herself in my debt."

Raising a brow, Fiadh asked, "In your debt? I don't see it that way, but I'll entertain the thought. What's your price?"

Troya clicked her tongue, the sound like a hundred scaly

feet. "Whether you see it or not is irrelevant. As for payment, I haven't decided."

"This is the second time you've come to our aid. Why?"

The Sluagh shook her skull-like head, large black eyes void of feeling holding Fiadh where she stood. "Aid you? My sisters and I take no sides in this war."

"Then why did you kill the mage?"

An ugly look crossed her horrible face. "Because, like others of his kind, he thought to use magic to command me. But I will not be bound. I am no slave!" She took a few scuttling steps toward Fiadh until the Aos Sí queen could feel and smell her rancid breath. "It amuses me to aid you, and so I do."

"I'm grateful for it."

Troya tilted her head, the slash of her mouth thinning. "I believe you are. It is strange. Our history speaks nothing of an alliance between elves and Sluagh."

"Then, perhaps, it is time," Fiadh offered.

"Perhaps." Troya cast a look at Kaelari, who'd silently made her way to a vantage point in a tree behind Fiadh, bow at the ready. "I assume you return to Erabel."

Fiadh nodded.

"Then, you plan to leave your brothers and sisters in Oadsera at the mercy of Dothur's armies?"

Her eyes went around, and she turned to Kaelari. "Did you know they were under attack?" The female shook her head, leaping from a branch and striding to Fiadh's side. Turning back to the Sluagh, the Aos Sí queen asked, "How long have they been under siege?"

"Oh, I didn't say the attack had begun. Only that it will,

and you seem intent on letting it play out in grisly slaughter."

Clenching her hands into fists, Fiadh ground her teeth, struggling to control the anger that raced through her body, causing the air and earth to shift around her. "Speak plainly."

Troya looked amused. "Quite a temper for one so young."

"I've seen much in my short life and have no wish to stand here while you toy with me."

The Sluagh lifted her chin, black lips curving in a contorted smile, dagger-like teeth flashing. "I like your spirit and will not use you as my plaything, though the idea is enticing. My sisters and I find ourselves reluctant allies." Fiadh's brow wrinkled. "The mages think to exert their rule over what they consider lesser beings while Crom Cruach vies for power with Dothur. The son of Carmun is not one to share the spoils, though the old god doesn't see this. I believe he will try to overthrow Dothur should an opportunity arise. But their petty squabbling for power is of no interest to me. My sisters and I are more practical. War, you see," she said, tapping the clawed tip of a leg on the dirt, "is a glorious thing to behold. But… this is not war. It is annihilation. And that is where I find we cannot follow."

"Why not?"

"Because Dothur seeks to kill humans and Aos Sí alike. If he succeeds, remaking this world in his own image, who will we become?" Troya shifted her body, wings twitching with a small flap. "We are the Hunt. Our prey, those reckless souls who wander where and when they shouldn't, are the same ones Dothur slaughters in numbers so great there will be little of them left when his armies have finished feasting on them. That I cannot have. Which brings us to here and now. We will aid you as long as it is in our interest to do so, provided you and your kind do not seek to curb our nature or exert your rule over us. The choice is yours."

"And if I refuse?"

Troya chuckled, the sound sending shivers down Fiadh's spine. "Then I wish you luck and will not weep when you fall to Dothur's wrath."

Kaelari stepped toward the Sluagh with a snarl, but Fiadh touched her arm, stopping the female. "I accept."

"You cannot trust them," Kaelari whispered harshly.

Fiadh kept her eyes on Troya. "Yes, I can. I do."

A glimmer of respect showed in the Sluagh's dark eyes, gone as quickly as it came. "A wise decision, young one."

"You said Dothur is planning an attack on Oadsera."

"He is. Though, he could be swayed to fix his eye elsewhere."

"What do you mean?"

"Erabel is the seat of your power, is it not?" Fiadh nodded. "What if you staged a fight there as you did before? He would come to your realm eventually, regardless. If you strike now, before he's had the opportunity to destroy Oadsera, you could rally your forces to confront him." Fiadh moved away to speak to Kaelari, looking back when Troya added, "Not that it will matter. He's grown strong, as have his armies as they cut a bloody swath through Crethia. Each death gives them power and makes them stronger. Just as Dothur sips from a dark well of magic, so do his armies with their violence. With Crom Cruach at his side, he could become invincible."

Fiadh scowled. "*Could* become invincible means he can be destroyed."

Troya smirked. "Optimism suits you. Dothur's destruction is what my sisters and I are depending on."

Leaving the Sluagh on the bluff, Fiadh drew Kaelari away. "I know you don't agree with my decision, but we have no choice."

"Sluagh are dark creatures, loyal to none but themselves. They'll turn on you," Kaelari argued, stalking away and turning back again. "Did you learn nothing from the battle with Rygeil? Don't you remember what they did?"

"Of course, I remember!" Fiadh snapped. "But this is different. I've said from the beginning that we must be united. That's the only way."

"United with humans! Not with *them*!"

"United with any creature trying to stop the darkness that threatens all of Crethia," Fiadh said, touching the female's arm. "We can't defeat him on our own. If he plans to destroy Oadsera and all who live there, we will be more isolated than ever. I won't let that happen."

Kaelari fumed, pacing and muttering while Fiadh watched with her arms crossed. She knew the female would capitulate. She had no choice. But it rankled that Kaelari couldn't see the advantage of having Troya and her sisters on their side, however, that fragile alliance ended up being played out. Fiadh wouldn't ask the Sluagh to fight with them, but aid could come in many forms.

When Kaelari spent her anger, she came to Fiadh and dipped her head. "Your will is mine."

"Thank you," Fiadh told her, squeezing her hand. "Though I don't want blind obedience. I prefer your sharp tongue. It makes things more interesting."

The elf snorted. "Well, I guarantee you'll have it."

Troya lay on the ground, skeletal front legs crossed in front of her, pale head bobbing as she watched Fiadh approach. "That is the stride of one who's ready to act. So, what will it be?"

It was clear the Sluagh was many steps ahead of her, having determined a strategy before Fiadh asked, but she played along, pretending she had a choice in whatever avenue Troya chose. "How do you propose to draw Dothur to Erabel?"

Troya grinned, relishing Fiadh's involuntary shudder when she flashed her blackened teeth. "You won't like it."

Fiadh didn't watch as the leader of the Sluagh flew to the base of the ridge where the mage's body lay in two shredded parts. Troya oversaw her second-in-command land a couple of feet from the upper portion of the corpse, lifting her head with a jerk as the Sluagh reached down and, using her hooked claws, tore the mage's head from his neck. They would fly to the Lloathren Mountains with their gruesome trophy and lay the blame for the wizard's death at Fiadh's feet. Troya assured the Aos Sí queen that such an act would enrage the demon enough to direct his ire at Erabel. And while Dothur could fly to Fiadh's realm, his armies would need to regroup and march the distance, giving the queen time to send word to Oadsera and gather her own forces. From Troya's estimates, based on what she knew of the locations of Dothur's armies, they would have a month, maybe more, as his forces were scattered, each led by a mage or a Dullahan. The demon would want them all to use as a collective force to crush Fiadh and her people, the Sluagh assured her. He wouldn't risk moving against her without them. And then there was Crom Cruach, who Troya indicated was in Malver Gorge, quite a distance from Dothur's location. Carmun's son hadn't moved on Oadsera while waiting for the old god to join him. Together, their power would surpass any the Sluagh had seen in her long life.

When Fiadh questioned why Crom hadn't gone with Dothur in the first place, the Sluagh giggled, making the hair on Fiadh's arms stand on end. "He was… indisposed," she'd said cryptically, letting the notion dangle for a few moments before telling the Aos Sí queen how the demon had possessed Darragh, using the man like a puppet to kill the king and send Crethia into chaos.

Kaelari gave Fiadh a look. Crom Cruach's influence over Darragh and his hand in the king's death, while surprising, answered their suspicions of why Dorcha Wood had gone to rot along the border of the forest and Felmore. The demon was pure evil. If he and Dothur succeeded in vanquishing elves and men, all of Crethia would be shrouded in darkness, the survivors little more than food or slaves.

Leaving Troya to do her work, Fiadh and Kaelari shared their plans with the others. Sibaen sneezed when she heard of the agreement with the Sluagh but said nothing, though her face reflected enough. Krulan was less cordial.

This is madness, he told Fiadh, eyes narrowing to yellow slits. *Even if the Sluagh don't turn on you, the odds of beating an army of creatures whose bloodlust is matched by nothing on this earth is madness.*

What would you have me do? Sacrifice my brothers and sisters in Oadsera? she fumed. *I had no choice!*

Krulan growled.

Look, we have time. He shook his head, and she touched his shoulder, feeling his muscles jump. *Troya said his armies are scattered while he awaits Crom Cruach in the Lloathren Mountains. I'm sending Kima to Oadsera to warn them and ask them to send the bulk of their fighting force to Erabel. We're less than two days from home. When we arrive, I'll send ravens to find Arel. Hopefully, he and Riley will be able to convince a few nobles to join us.*

What if your faith in mankind is misplaced?

What if it isn't? Fiadh wrapped her arms around Krulan. *You have stood by my side this long, my friend. Don't doubt me now.*

He hung his head. *Forgive me.*

There's nothing to forgive. Just... don't give up on me.

He licked her cheek. *Never.*

They traveled late into the night, led by the light of the moon. Worry weighed heavily, drawing Fiadh's mouth into a thin line. Was Gideon all right? Had he encountered Dothur's minions? She wished she could reach for him with her mind, but magic had its limits. Perhaps Zaeleria would be able to ascertain his whereabouts. After the mage's attack and the ease with which Faraen fell, she needed to know he was unharmed.

When they neared Dorcha Wood, Krulan took off ahead of the party to inform Aos Sí scouts of their impending arrival. Riani greeted them as they neared the tree line outside the forest. Fiadh, eager to stand, slid off Meara's back, clutching her mane when her legs wobbled. Straightening, she took a few steps toward the female, noting her confusion when Ellisar and Gideon were nowhere to be seen.

"They're visiting settlements with a young knight we encountered with the hope of forming alliances," Fiadh told her, summing up the events that led to their early return.

"It appears you're making friends," Riani said dryly.

Fiadh gave a weary laugh. "Aye. I suppose I am. Let's hope it proves fruitful."

The party entered Dorcha Wood as Riani said, "It should please you to hear the rot receded to the border of Felmore thanks to Zaeleria's efforts. Though I can't help but wonder if Crom Cruach leaving is why we've seen the forest bounce back."

"It's a relief to hear it." Fiadh patted Riani on the shoulder and went further into the forest, stroking leaves and branches as she went. She spoke to the trees, smiling when a fox and songbird greeted her. The woods groaned in welcome, branches bending as though they longed to wrap around her in a loving embrace. Fiadh crouched and pressed her palms to the ground. Breathing deeply, she opened her mind to Danu, feeding off the power of the Great Mother until her body sang with it.

When she turned toward Kaelari, who lingered nearby,

her green eyes glowed with an inner light. "Returning home suits you," the elf said.

Her mouth curved up and held for a moment, the inner light fading too soon.

"Gideon will return," the elf told her.

Fiadh nodded. But in her heart, she knew he might not.

CHAPTER THIRTY-SEVEN

The pink of Dothur's eyes glowed red as he listened to Troya's report of Fiadh's attack on a contingent of his army. The torches flickering on the carved walls of the chasm deep in the Lloathren Mountains in which he held court cast his pale body in a ghostly light. His throne, a stone monstrosity of obsidian, reflected his form—the tattered wings that remained strong enough to launch his body into flight. The elves had sought to hobble him when they'd come upon this place during the Great War, attacking his mother and siblings. But he would not be cowed. And their actions would not be forgotten.

When he'd emerged from his prison, he'd journeyed here—to the place where his mother, Carmun, had waged her last battle. The elves had assumed the mountains were depleted of power that day, but they had little imagination. Never bothering to delve deeper into where it truly lay. He'd suckled from the darkness, growing stronger as his armies fanned out across Crethia, giving mankind a taste of what was to come while they fed their bloodlust—a thing that was never quenched, only growing stronger with each taste of death and drop of blood. By the time they attacked the elves, they would be ravenous. And powerful.

As Dothur listened to the Sluagh's raspy voice, his eyes flicked to the skull resting at his feet. The mage's head, tongue black and spilling from its gaping mouth, sat on the ground facing him. Xander, draped in a hooded cloak at his side, couldn't take his eyes off it. Aside from himself, Tarum had been the most promising of the surviving mages. His gifts in the dark arts had hinted at a great future. *Damn the witch!* he fumed. He should've remained in her cursed woods and slit her throat before she'd come into the power she so clearly wielded.

"And you simply watched all of this unfold?" Dothur asked in a dangerous voice when the Sluagh had finished.

Troya met his cold stare. "Tarum bade us keep hidden until his command. Far be it for me to ignore his wishes."

Carmun's son rose from his throne, body unfurling to dwarf the Sluagh. She held fast, impervious to the inherent threat in his gaze. "Tell me," he said, "where do you suggest we attack?"

"Erabel," Troya told him. "It is a vital stronghold. Defeat them, and the remaining realms will be vulnerable."

"Hm. Attack Erabel when Oadsera has a larger fighting force. I wonder," he began, tapping a toe claw on the hard floor, "are you in league with the elven queen? Have you conspired?"

She canted her head, a look of boredom crawling across her normally bland features. "If I am, would I tell you?"

Dothur laughed, the sound bouncing off the walls. "You and your sisters have walked this earth longer than most. I trust you know whom to follow and who is destined to fail."

Troya dipped her head.

"Erabel is a great prize." He stared coldly at her, his pink eyes pinning the Sluagh to the ground. "Should I go there, what might I find? A trap?"

"I would imagine you'd find a small but powerful force," Troya said. It was a dangerous game she played. A wrong word, and she'd find her mind flayed and her sisters in chains.

"Ah, yes. Powerful. With a direct line to the Great Mother, Fiadh is indeed a power to be reckoned with." He shifted his leathery wings, one hanging lower than the other, having mended badly. "You suggest going to Erabel with the mass of my army. Yet, if I spend the bulk of them defeating that sacred place, I will be weakened. Vulnerable to Oadsera's forces. Is that what you're hoping for?"

Troya blinked.

"Tell me, Troya, speaker of the Sluagh. Do you fight at my side or hers?" he purred, crouching over her.

"We fly with you, my lord." She refused to offer anything more. As long as she lived, Sluagh would bow to no one.

He chuckled. "Stubborn as ever. Is there nothing I can do to have you kneel at my feet?" Her eyes grew hard, and he shrugged. "So be it. We'll go to Erabel. I suggest you think about whose side you want to be on when I have the Aos Sí bitch writhing beneath my feet."

She bent low. "Your will is my command, my lord."

He scoffed, hand twitching as he stared at her neck. "See that it is." Dothur sent the Sluagh from his sight and picked up Tarum's head, letting it dangle in his grip before tossing it through a crevice in the wall. He didn't trust Troya. Sluagh balked at serving anyone since the fall of Xodros, the former leader of the Hunt. He'd led the horde for centuries. Now, Troya wore the mantle. He wanted her and her sisters in this fight. They were skilled warriors, their violence a thing of beauty. But if she betrayed him, he'd kill every last one of them.

Two could play this game, he mused. He'd send spies to Oadsera and Dorcha Wood, small, winged creatures, their bodies pure black. Easily mistaken for ravens when seen from a distance, they would go unnoticed. Though unable to pass through barriers the Aos Sí erected to keep their realms safe, his spies would report on any movements, any amassing of armies.

Dothur left his throne room and went deep into the mountain to a pool as black and still as a starless sky. Kneeling, he peered at its surface, seeing his pale reflection staring back. "Call to my armies."

The water trembled, tiny vibrations rippling from one end of the expanse to the other. Soft pinpoints of light flickered in the liquid, each one—mage and Dullahan—a commander in an army scattered across the kingdom. He watched their bodies freeze, his power leaching into their minds like poisoned darts. Through the black pool, a source of dark power, he gave the order to amass at the base of the Lloathren Mountains. He would lead them.

In Felmore, Darragh slowly regained control over his mind, each hour within the walls of his castle bringing him back to his old self. He fed his progress with anger, often taking his ire out on servants who could do nothing but shrink in the face of his rage. Donal kept his lord under a careful watch, wondering if whatever had possessed him would return and claim him for good. How Darragh had escaped his mental imprisonment, he didn't know, but he'd kill Felmore's lord before he was taken again.

In a bid to increase his strength, Darragh sent missives to surrounding fiefs, asking the lords who ruled there to come to Felmore and discuss the fate of the Western Fold now that King Stephan was dead. Various nobles arrived over the course of a few weeks. Being a gracious host, Darragh organized food and entertainment, slowly winning over the weaker lords while gauging those who threatened a future bid for the crown.

Hiring a mercenary for those who balked at his bid for power was simple enough. Any man who refused to bend a knee and pledge to support him found themselves drinking goblets of poison when they returned to their keeps. Rumors began to spread. Those whose fiefs lay in the borderlands or feared reprisal promised fealty to Darragh, ensuring his place as the top contender in the western reaches. At the end of three weeks, Darragh's reputation had grown tenfold, and he found his coffers full and his land brimming with soldiers who'd been given to Felmore in a show of faith.

Slipping into the dungeon, he went to Haegna's cell and

lingered beyond the threshold. This was where Crom Cruach had seized his mind, reaching through the scrying bowl and taking hold. He loathed it, recalling the feel of the demon crawling in his brain, but couldn't deny the violation had done more good than harm. Killing the king and those next in line for the throne had proven beneficial. Without a monarch to grovel to, he could pursue power unhindered.

CHAPTER THIRTY-EIGHT

*E*rabel greeted her like a daughter, all manner of creatures flocking to their queen. Fiadh spent a few moments with each of them. Nym and Krulan were in a loving embrace outside the keep, nuzzling and licking each other with soft growls as they stood, heads pressed together. Ducking her head to give the pair privacy, Fiadh went inside, calling out to Elraen to ask the elf to examine Faraen's healing wound while she went to meet with the council.

Fiadh found Ulfran, whose arm was slung around his daughter's shoulders. "The young queen returns!" he bellowed. "And she brings my child back with her." He let go of Sibaen and embraced Fiadh, licking her cheek. "You couldn't get rid of her, could you?" he asked with a wink.

Sibaen snorted. "It is you she'd rid herself of. From the looks of it, half her larder must be gone."

Ulfran tried to suck in his paunch, giving up moments later with a hearty laugh. "Aye. I made a dent in it to be sure." Hooking his furred arm through Fiadh's, he hauled her to a large table where others awaited them. "What news? Had you reached Taigon before word of the king's death reached you?"

Fiadh put her hands on the scarred wood, shaking her head and staring at the surface before lifting it to meet the faces surrounding her. "We got word before entering the Golden City." She spent the next few minutes telling them of the attacks they'd witnessed and the fragile alliance they'd struck with a band of survivors. They listened, some shifting uncomfortably when she relayed Ellisar's decision to act as an envoy. Ignoring looks of annoyance and disquiet, she forged ahead, informing her counsel of the role Sluagh would play in drawing Dothur's eye and her wish to send for the bulk of Oadsera's fighting force.

"By Troya's estimate, we have a month, maybe more," she told them.

There was a pall of silence as every council member considered the news. Quinn entered the room, drawing her eye. He looked well and at ease among her people. A look of confusion crossed his features as he scanned the room. She motioned him over.

Coming to the table, he asked, "Is Gideon… Did he——?"

Fiadh cut him off. "Gideon is well. He and Ellisar are on a mission to beg for aid."

Quinn's shoulders slumped in relief.

Ulfran cleared his throat. "What do you hope to gain by these alliances? It is well known Sluagh bow to no one."

Fiadh lifted her chin. "Troya and her sisters do not need to kneel before me. I wouldn't ask it of them. However, their support is beneficial, and I won't turn away from aid no matter where it comes from."

"You do realize that whatever they agree to serves their purposes more than yours," Arel said.

She met his stare. "I am not so naive to believe they aid us out of the goodness of their hearts. Troya," she continued, "have Dothur's ear. She and her sisters will sway the demon to abandon his desire to attack Oadsera, giving us time to gather our forces."

"How do you know her plan will work?" Arel asked.

"I don't."

"If she fails to convince him, he will attack Oadsera, and we will be unable to send aid. They might withstand an assault, but I fear their losses could be catastrophic. Oadsera's outer defenses are not as strong as Erabel's and with Crom Cruach and Xander at his sides…" She let the thought hang in the air. "Aligning with the Sluagh was the only way."

Ulfran nodded, pinning those scattered around the table with a dark look. "We support your decision, my queen. The Faoladh will stand with you. I will have a missive sent to my commander to gather my best fighters and send them here."

Corene stepped out of the alcove she'd claimed when they arrived. "The Urisk stand with you."

One by one, every member of her council recommitted themselves. Arel was last to agree. "I stand with you as always, but I wonder if you've considered our outlying settlements. While not as large as Oadsera and likely unknown to Dothur, many elves live there who would wish to fight if they knew the threat we face."

Fiadh looked at the map laid out on the table. "Where are these settlements?"

Arel leaned forward, pointing to locations. "Like our brothers and sisters from Tangry Forest, they scattered following the Great War. Some lie in the Scarlet Mountains, too far to be of aid to us, while others fled to ancient grounds where our people once lived before abandoning them for larger, less remote places."

She frowned, scanning the map and locations he'd indicated, each one far from human communities and well beyond Oadsera and Erabel. There was a reason they'd chosen to flee there, she thought, recalling stories Veren had told her of families, entire realms, torn apart, decimated during the Great War. Only one stronghold was left aside from Erabel. How could she force them to come out of hiding? Let go of their fragile peace to fight in another war. "I'd welcome their aid should they wish to give it."

"You could command them," Arel suggested.

She looked at him. "Why do you think they chose to hide? To live so far from their brethren?"

"I wouldn't know."

"Yes, you do," she countered. "They've seen enough death. You all have. I won't take what little peace they've carved out for themselves by commanding them to fight and die."

"Dothur will kill them anyway," Kaelari said quietly.

"Then let them live how they wish until that day comes. I believe they've earned the right to decide on their own. I'm not their master, and they are not my slaves."

It was too risky to send runners to all of the remote

settlements. They could be picked off by roaming bands of Dothur's army. Missives would be sent instead. Oadsera was another matter. Lura and Thallen volunteered to go, having family members they wished to visit while there. The two elves would meet with Saria, Oadsera's current ruler, and explain their alliances and plans for the immediate future before returning to shore up Erabel's defenses. In another part of the hall, Ulfran pulled Sibaen aside and gave her a rolled parchment, holding the Faoladh in a warm embrace and speaking quietly. She left within the hour.

Quinn took the human soldiers aside. They would be ambassadors of a sort for any people Riley and Arel were able to rally and send to Dorcha Wood. He needed them to stock the hut Fiadh grew up in with supplies and set up shelters in the clearing around the tiny home. If needed, they would expand the area, but he made them promise not to cut down any trees, knowing the anger that would cause throughout the forest, not to mention Fiadh's if she found out.

Fiadh met with Riani, Arel, and Kaelari, discussing Erabel's fortifications, then left to find Zaeleria. Unsurprisingly, the seer was in the heart of the keep, standing at the base of the massive oak, her gossamer dress shifting slightly in the breeze. She didn't turn when she said, "You walk a dangerous path, young one."

"I know."

Zaeleria turned slowly, eyes glowing against her dusky skin and white hair. "But there is hope. And that is a powerful thing." The seer held out her hands, and Fiadh clasped them, touching her forehead to the females for a moment. "You've seen Dothur's creatures and know what waits to consume our world should we fail to stop them."

Fiadh pulled away, keeping her hands in Zaeleria's warm grasp. "I have."

"They thrive on fear and violence, as does Crom Cruach. It gives them power. Makes them strong." She tugged Fiadh toward a bench, and they sat, knees almost touching. "King Stephan's death was not an accident." Fiadh nodded, the seer confirming what she suspected. "Without an heir, Crethia flounders. Men will fight each other for the crown at their own peril, never realizing they are pawns in Dothur's game. It is common folk who will suffer."

"They are already suffering," Fiadh told her.

"Aye. I feel it." She patted the queen's knee. "You were right to aid those who crossed your path in your travels. Word will spread."

"That's why Ellisar and Gideon went with the knight we encountered. They will visit fiefs in the hope of gathering troops to fight with us." She tugged at a loose thread on the hem of her worn tunic. "Will they succeed?"

Zaeleria cocked her head. "The immediate future is too changeable for any certainty, but the glimpses I've caught are promising."

"Is Gideon safe? Unhurt?"

The seer smiled knowingly. "He has come to mean a great deal to you."

"Yes."

"That is good. As to his welfare, I can tell you I've had no premonition of death."

Fiadh's body lost its rigidity.

"Do not pin all your hopes on my skill, young one. I, too, am fallible."

"I'm worried about him."

"Worrying is a waste of energy."

Fiadh made a face and turned away. "I should've known you'd talk in riddles."

The seer chuckled. "Aye. I have a reputation for that." She took Fiadh's hand. "Have faith. Gideon is strong. His path in life led him to you, and you led him to the task he undertakes. Worry if you must, but know his fate is beyond even my skill."

She took a deep breath and forced her mind from thoughts of Gideon. Changing the subject, Fiadh said, "Riani tells me you've beaten back the rot consuming Dorcha Wood."

Zaeleria shrugged. "She gives me too much credit. In truth, the demon left Felmore, taking the sickness with him. The forest recovers, and I have done as you'd requested, expanding Erabel's protections. Should people come to fight alongside us, they will be protected as much as our barriers allow."

"Thank you," Fiadh told her, eyes drifting to the oak as though the Great Mother had called her.

"She waits for you," Zaeleria said, standing. The seer traced her fingers along Fiadh's cheek. "You should go to her. There is something you need to see."

Confusion lit up Fiadh's face as Zaeleria walked away, dress whispering against her limbs. She got up and went to the base of the tree, an embodiment of Danu, and pressed her hands to the trunk. Warmth, love, and power greeted her. Fiadh basked in it, returning the feelings filling her body. Tapping at the Great Mother, Fiadh asked what the goddess wished to show her. With a cryptic reply, Fiadh delved into the earth, following Danu as she raced through the mantle. In the dark and warmth, Fiadh paused, the image of the Great Mother hovering just beyond her consciousness.

She felt movement and sensed an awesome power lingering in an underground river. Following its source, she found herself losing control. Her mind pulled into the deep where the Oilliphéist waited. It had grown. The serpent twined around her ethereal form like a mother with her daughter. Fiadh froze, not scared, but under its thrall. She reached out to the creature, opening her mind, and felt it dive into her thoughts, pulling out memories as if they were pages in a book. With its body still wrapped around her, it pulled away, its massive head hovering just beyond Fiadh's face. It felt so real, as though her body had tunneled into the earth. She could feel the slick scales lovingly embracing her form, the hot breath on her face.

Green eyes, like giant orbs, watched her from a reptilian face, bony protrusions shaped like fans undulating slowly against its cheeks below spiraling horns. A thick, forked tongue darted from a mouth layered with fangs, tasting her. Just beyond their forms, Danu waited and watched, unconcerned. This ancient being, reborn in a time of upheaval, was not an enemy of the Great Mother.

As Fiadh reached toward both of their consciousnesses, she felt symbiosis. Balance. As though they were two sides of the same coin. The Oilliphéist's long body uncurled, smooth scales sliding against her skin, letting Fiadh go. She hung there, suspended, as the serpent slithered back into the water, disappearing in the blackness with a ripple.

Sister, Danu whispered, not speaking of Fiadh but of the being Ithraen, the Merrow queen, believed was the one true ruler. The ruler thought Caoránach, mother of the Oilliphéist, would be reborn, asserting awesome power over every species while proclaiming the Merrow her chosen people. How little they understood of their own legends.

Fiadh had felt nothing of the conqueror Ithraen believed the serpent would be. Its intentions remained a mystery, but its curiosity hid no ill intent. Somehow, she knew that. It was as though a piece of Fiadh lived within the Oilliphéist, remnants of its growth within her body as her magic intertwined with that of the Merrow. So strange. From a distance, she heard Zaeleria calling to her, coaxing her back. Reluctantly, she left, turning once to look at the dark water and seeing the serpent's head surface as it watched her go.

The seer caught Fiadh as she returned to herself, body slumping into Zaeleria's arms. "You saw."

She nodded. "I…" she started, unsure how to explain, "I didn't speak to it, not with words, but… she—" Fiadh paused. *She? Was it a she?* Mulling that over, Fiadh acknowledged the serpent was indeed female. An egg layer. And while she had no knowledge of the lives of Oilliphéist, she knew it would one day be a mother to a new generation. "She means no harm." Fiadh stood, brushing off her clothes. Looking into the seer's face, she said, "Danu called her sister."

Zaeleria arched a brow. "I sense the Oilliphéist has a part yet to play."

"What do you mean?"

"I do not believe it was an accident that you were instrumental in its rebirth. You and she are connected. How or when that connection will manifest remains unclear."

Frowning, Fiadh looked at the ground, imagining she could see the Oilliphéist looking back. "Do you think she'll have a role in the battle to come?"

Zaeleria considered it, folding her hands so they hung loosely entwined below her waist. "I think guessing at whatever part she may play is a waste of time."

Just then, Riani rounded the corner, coming toward them. In her hand was a slip of parchment. The female dipped her head to the seer, then handed the missive to Fiadh. It was a message from Riley. In it, he said the first two settlements they visited had been attacked recently, leaving few survivors. At the third, a large town, they found the local lord unwilling to grant an audience, so they spoke to the townsfolk and learned the manor lord had requested aid from a powerful baron who'd refused. Apparently, the baron had staked a claim to the throne through a distant relation and didn't wish to spend coin or soldiers aiding a poor noble.

The town's inhabitants, having heard of attacks on nearby villages, were angry and scared, fearing for their safety and knowing they could do little to fight such creatures. Riley and Gideon managed to convince a handful of men to join them.

"Where are they now?" Fiadh asked, knowing the bird who delivered the message would be able to provide a general direction.

"North of Taigon and heading east."

Fiadh bit her lip. If they could round up men to fight, she didn't want them falling prey to marauding bands of Dothur's creatures. They needed protection. "Send word for them to go to Oadsera with anyone who wishes to join us. Once there, they can travel with our people to Erabel. That should provide them protection. Then craft a message to Saria letting her know to expect them and ask her to wait to send her warriors until after they arrive."

Riani bowed and raced into the keep. Fiadh watched her disappear. "And now we wait."

"And train," Zaeleria said as Dyvre appeared from whatever corner he'd been skulking.

Fiadh sighed. "I had a feeling you'd say that."

CHAPTER THIRTY-NINE

Five weeks later, Saria, Oadsera's ruler, sent word that Ellisar and Gideon arrived. Fiadh released a breath and slumped in her chair, whispering thanks to the Great Mother. She continued to scan the missive, pleased to read their efforts to rally fighting men had proved successful. But her relief was short-lived as she turned the parchment over and read how that success came about.

Small wars for the crown had sprung up across Crethia, leaving many human settlements virtually undefended as Dothur's armies cut through the kingdom. With none to protect them, people saw an alliance with elves, their long-standing enemies, as a path to survival. It was the outcome she wanted but not the route she would've chosen to achieve it.

Greed was a powerful lure. Crom Cruach had known that. He'd counted on it. The upheaval caused by the king's death and those directly in line for the throne made conditions ripe for an invasion.

As it stood, close to three hundred human soldiers were traveling from Oadsera to Dorcha Wood alongside a large contingent of Oadsera's army, with more on the way as word spread from those who'd branched off from the group to other towns and villages. In preparation for their arrival, Fiadh and the seers had expanded and reinforced the protective barrier that had originally encircled only Erabel. Now, it encompassed the entire forest, shielding every life form within from attack. At least, that was the hope.

Handing the missive to Kaelari, she rose and left the hall. Aishling was sitting on the ground in the courtyard, making a doll out of grasses and a swatch of cloth she'd found. Dasha was helping, plucking blades of grass and handing them to her. When the raven saw Fiadh, the feathers on his head puffed forward, and he half-hopped, half-flew toward her, landing on her outstretched arm. Croaking softly, the bird preened a clump of hair that had come loose from her braid, sifting through the dark strands. She riffled through his feathers, scratching at the base of the new quills to remove their itchy casings.

Aishling craned her neck and ran toward Fiadh, clutching her doll. "Look what me and Dasha made!" she cried out, waving the doll.

Fiadh kissed the raven's head and set him down, crouching so she could face Aishling as she inspected the toy. The head was a large acorn attached to the woven mass of grasses, twigs, and leaves forming the body. Spider silk dangled from the doll's head like strands of hair. Fiadh smiled, recalling the many dolls she'd made as a child. "Would you like to add a face?"

The girl bounced on her toes. "Yes! I telled Dasha she needed one."

"Let's find some berries," Fiadh reached out, grasping Aishling's small hand. Together, Dasha keeping pace with flaps and struts, they found two different kinds of berries and set about making eyes and a mouth.

Ulfran found them putting the final touches on the doll. He paused and ducked into the shadows to watch without disturbing the pair. His mouth tugged up as Aishling's voice rang through the air. Krulan appeared at his side, eyes trained on the scene in front of them. The Faoladh glanced at the Cù-Sìth, then back at Fiadh. "She's already forging a new world, isn't she?"

Krulan rumbled in his chest. Yellow gaze fixed on his mistress.

Scouts patrolled Dorcha Wood, awaiting the arrival of men and the elves from Oadsera while others took turns leaving those borders to monitor potential routes the incoming party could take. Those who kept a watch along the southern border saw Felmore's garrison increase, with more soldiers joining Darragh's ranks daily.

Faraen, healed from his injury, entered the hall, his lanky stride eating up the distance to the table where Fiadh sat, looking over a map showing routes from Oadsera to Erabel. He stood at her side, violet eyes scanning the sheet of parchment. She craned her neck to face him.

"There's no word from Oadsera, but I have news of Felmore." He gave a quick report on what he'd seen combined with word from other scouts. "More men come each day. He must have over two hundred by now."

Quinn, who stood leaning against a pillar listening, folded his arms. "If that's true, soldiers outnumber Felmore folk."

Fiadh eyed him. "What do you think it means?"

"I don't know. I could send one of the men to find out. We have a trusted contact in Darragh's ranks."

"Is that safe?"

He rubbed his jaw. "They have a pre-established signal. As long as his contact sees it, it shouldn't be a problem."

Biting the inside of her cheek, she considered the risks. "Could they be caught?"

"Doubtful. We made arrangements before I left Felmore land."

"See it done."

Quinn jogged out of the hall, and Faraen sat across from her and said, "He's grown up since Gideon left."

She nodded. "I can almost hear Gideon's voice when he speaks. Quinn even has his mannerisms. I'm not sure if that's a good thing, really."

Faraen smiled. "Time will tell."

Their conversation was interrupted by a commotion outside the hall. Hopping up, they ran toward raised voices, finding a small gathering in the courtyard. A group of Aos Sí surrounded a newcomer who stood at their center, speaking quickly to Riani. The stranger was slightly built with wiry muscles and dark red hair braided in thick strands on each side of her head, joining into one long braid that ran down the center of her back to the base of her spine. She wore brown leggings and a matching tunic, each layer heavily embroidered with geometric patterns. Her skin, a dusky rose, contrasted with violet eyes that flashed with excitement.

Kaelari leaned into Fiadh and spoke softly in her ear. "She comes from a tribe in the south. They once lived in a hilltop city in the Burning Plains, named for the red clay of that landscape, until the Great War. Those who survived hide in remote foothills of that land." She paused, listening for a few moments before whispering, "I haven't seen anyone from that realm in many years."

The female, Llyana, bowed to Fiadh and then launched into a recounting. The tribe's leader, Haldir, sent her to inform Fiadh of recent events. Contingents of dark creatures had attacked human settlements in and around the Burning Plains, and the elves, having heard of the attacks, came out of hiding to aid them. A local lord accepted an invitation to meet with Haldir to negotiate an alliance. Men and elves joined ranks and moved through the Burning Plains, tracking bands of creatures and routing them from villages and towns. They successfully forced Dothur's armies out of their territory, ceasing their pursuit when the creatures ventured farther north.

Listening, Fiadh considered Dothur's strategy. If he'd planned on using divisions between mankind and elf-kind to defeat both peoples, he'd underestimated the depth of their shared hatred, perhaps thinking it would be enough to keep them from uniting against a common threat. Moving into the great hall, Fiadh laid a map on the table and followed along as Llyana showed her where her home was and how the combined force pushed Dothur's creatures out of the Burning Plains.

As the female spoke, she couldn't help but wonder at the ease with which they'd been routed once Aos Sí had joined with the men. It was as though they were untrained, mindless beings whose lust for blood and violence was their only commonality. Mages led two of the attacks, and both had escaped, according to the female. Their magic was too powerful for the elven warriors. Despite casualties among both Aos Sí and humans, the men who'd fought with them hadn't balked at the idea of pursuing the creatures into the north. It was the manor lord, a knight of some skill and repute, who'd convinced them to remain in the Burning Plains to protect their land from future attacks.

Fiadh glanced at Quinn, who'd entered the hall as Llyana was speaking. The elf followed her stare and dipped her head at him. He did the same, a half-smile curving his mouth.

"It is good to see you've also formed an alliance. We heard rumors of it," Llyana said.

"Aye. Only if we're united can we defeat what's coming."

"Our leader, Haldir, said as much."

"And your people remain united even though the immediate threat is over?" Kaelari asked.

Llyana turned to her. "They do. We established a camp

where both of our people live and train together. Haldir said it's the first of its kind. However, he hadn't known if rumors of your alliance were true when he spoke. That is one of the reasons I am here."

"As you can see," she said, indicating Quinn, "they are quite true. What is the other reason for your visit?" Fiadh asked.

The female swallowed, eyes skittering from Fiadh's and landing on the map. "After the war, after so many of our people were slaughtered and… lost." Her hands fisted, knuckles resting on the edge of the table. "Some of us cursed the Great Mother."

Gasps sounded in the hall. Fiadh cut her eyes as those who looked at Llyana with fear and disdain and placed her hand on the females. The elf looked at her, tears pooling, and whispered, "I cursed her. I requested to be the one to make this journey. I've come to beg forgiveness. For myself. For… others."

Fiadh said nothing, only led Llyana out of the room and through passages to the giant oak. The female stopped at the threshold and stared at the tree. Legs trembling, she took a step, then another, slowly making her way across the distance until she stood at the massive trunk. With shaking hands, Llyana pressed her palms to the bark, her head following shortly after. Fiadh watched for a few moments, ducking away when quiet sobs reached her ears.

Kaelari waited in the shadows of the hall. "There are many who thought the Great Mother abandoned them. Out of anger and grief, they turned away from her light."

"I imagine Danu has been waiting to welcome them home."

Fiadh invited Llyana to rest and remain in Erabel. The female appreciated the offer but informed the queen she had to return home. As she watched the female say goodbye to Riani and others the next day, a tangible lightness was evident in her manner and expressions. Whatever had occurred between her and the Great Mother, it had replenished the elf. She was at peace.

Llyana carried a missive praising the alliance the tribe had instigated and informing Haldir of the anticipated attack on Erabel. Though Kaelari had urged her to do so, she didn't request aid; she only asked the leader to continue his alliances and be watchful. If Dothur were rebuffed in Erabel, he'd unleash his wrath on Aos Sí across the kingdom.

After Llyana left Erabel, Quinn and Faraen gave Fiadh a recounting of news from Felmore. According to Quinn's spy, Darragh was assembling an army to take control of the western reaches. It was whispered he'd had powerful nobles who refused to back his claim killed through various means. And it was widely believed he'd eventually make a bid for the throne. From what Connack had overheard, there was no talk of going to war on Erabel, though he'd heard rumors of a dark power that had possessed Felmore's lord. Some said Darragh had killed the king. Others feared he was still under the sway of whoever had taken over his mind. Whatever the case, Darragh was grasping for power and had doubled the number of men in his garrison.

"Let's hope he keeps his attention on the seat of Taigon," Kaelari said.

Fiadh nodded, stopping when she caught Zaelaria watching her from a seat along the hall's perimeter. The seer clasped her hands in her lap. "Crom Cruach let Darragh go. We must assume it was for a reason. The lord of Felmore remains dangerous whether his eye is fixed on Erabel or not."

Riani interrupted the morning meal. Her face was ashen. Fiadh dropped the crust of bread in her hand and rose slowly. "What is it?"

The female's eyes welled. "The Sluagh betrayed us. Dothur attacked the party after they left Oadsera."

"How many survived?" Fiadh asked, rising slowly.

"Two. A man and one of Oadsera's captains."

Fiadh's heart stuttered. "Gideon?"

Riani shook her head. "He and Ellisar went off on their own to speak with other lords. Their route took them straight to Dothur's army… I'm so sorry. They're gone."

The room tilted and closed in on Fiadh. Voices rose as the hall erupted into chaos. Kaelari gripped her shoulders gently. She was talking. Fiadh blinked. She could see the elf's lips moving, but her head was buzzing, and she couldn't make out the words.

Gideon's gone. He's gone.

Krulan growled and nudged her, his face eclipsing Kaelari's as he pressed his brow against hers. She tried to lift her arms, wanting to wrap them around his neck and hide in his scruff, but they were leaden weights like her heart.

Gideon! her mind screamed. *He's dead. Myfaultmyfaultmyfault.*

"Fiadh," Kaelari said, her voice finally cutting through the chaos of her mind. "Fiadh. It's not your fault. Do you hear me? It's not your fault."

Her eyes slid to the elf. "Yes. It is." She turned on her heel, body stiff and stilted. Krulan moved with her, so close she could feel the heat of his body. For a moment, she wondered if it could take the chill from her skin that burrowed into her bones, into her heart. "Riani," she said, stopping to find the female in a cluster of Aos Sí. "Where are they? The ones who survived."

"They were spotted by a scout outside Dorcha Wood and were carried through the forest. They're being taken to the healers."

Fiadh nodded. "I want to see them."

"Of course," Riani said. Putting her grief aside, she led Fiadh to the healers' quarters.

Groaning met their ears as they neared the white structure with vines trailing up the sides and around the pillars at the threshold of the entrance. Fiadh stopped in the doorway. Four healers surrounded the pair of travelers, each assessing injuries or easing pain.

"Riley," she whispered with a small measure of relief tinged with sorrow. Fiadh shifted her attention to the other prone form, that of a female from Oadsera.

Fiadh watched the healers work, wincing at each sawed breath, every grunt of pain. As they peeled back or sliced off clothing, wounds were revealed. Bite marks. Scratches from sharp claws. The room blurred, and suddenly, it was Gideon's form lying on the pallet, body riddled with gaping wounds. Only the healers weren't working on him because he was already gone.

A sob crawled up her throat as the healer's hut came back into focus. The grief was too much. She couldn't take it. Fiadh staggered out the door, dodging Ulfran and Sibaen. Only Krulan could reach her as she tore through the underbrush and crashed to her knees. He shrouded her body with his. Sharing every wracking sob. Every scream of anguish. When she finally fell into an exhausted heap, he curled his body around hers.

He can't be gone, she pleaded.

I'm sorry, little one.

Krulan, it's not fair. I never told him I loved him.

He knew.

She wept, burying her face in his neck. *I can't do this without him.*

Yes, you can.

CHAPTER FORTY

Troya watched the massacre unfold as Dothur laid a trap for the elves and men who traveled to Erabel. She'd thought Carmun's son had taken the bait and turned his eye on Erabel, leaving Oadsera untouched. But he'd outmaneuvered her, seen through the ruse. He'd used spies to track the movements of humans who entered Oadsera, monitoring them when they left the realm with a large contingent of elves. Dothur had sprung a trap as they crossed the kingdom toward Dorcha Wood.

She and her sisters would not partake in the spoils of the slaughter, though the blood and screams called to them on a primal level. Mouths salivating, they wheeled through the sky, herding men and elves into the jaws and claws of Dothur's army. Carmun's son must believe she was loyal to him. But to consume blood and take lives as the demon watched would be akin to kneeling at Dothur's feet and becoming his servant. The leader of the Sluagh had vowed she and her sisters would never bow to another after

Xodros, master of the Wild Hunt, had been killed by Balor. She would be no one's slave.

So, they screamed through the air, darting in and out of the fray, smelling the spray of blood, hearing the crunch of bone. Never tasting it. Biding their time until they could leave the killing grounds and warn the queen of the Aos Sí of what was coming.

Crom Cruach danced among the soldiers—human and Aos Sí—blasting them with magic. Watching their bodies flip through the air and land on the ground in tangled heaps where snapping teeth awaited them. He crowed as a group banded together, deflecting the horde surrounding them with gusts of wind, shards of earth, and weaponry. Dark magic, replenished by the pool in the Lloathren Mountains, sang in his veins, amplified by the slaughter. With a spell, he ripped swords and bows from fierce grips, hammering the defiant mass with blasts of power that brought them to their knees. Necks snapped, bodies contorted. Those who were strong enough to withstand the assault charged him. Their war cries were silenced with a swipe of his hand.

Dothur oversaw it all. He'd driven the combined force of men and elves into a death trap, tapping into the minds of those leading the army of nearly two hundred souls. Snuffing out urges to choose a different route, brushing aside those who balked at entering such a vulnerable location.

Perched atop a vantage point overlooking the narrow valley they'd been herded into, Carmun's son tasted the slaughter on the wind. Fear. Pain. Victory. He savored it. Every drop of blood and spent life fed his army, making them ravenous and powerful. They would be ready to take on the might of Erabel, that sacred place the Great Mother sought to protect. Her last vestige of power. Breaking the Aos Sí queen would be a mortal wound for an immortal goddess. Her chosen would crawl at his feet before he let her die. The Great Mother would wither, slinking into the earth, to her well of power, where she'd fade over time until she was nothing.

Toes claws digging into the rocky ledge, Dothur shifted his weight, eyes narrowing as an elven warrior got the upper hand, cutting a path through a cluster of the demon's army. His soldiers were more powerful than when he'd unleashed them on human settlements. But they were not the regimented force of Oadsera's army. Tracking the male, Dothur watched him wield power over the elements to push back a group of Kelpie, cutting three of them down when they were caught off guard. The elf was well-trained, Dothur thought as he looked on. He saw the Aos Sí kill a half-breed demon before deciding he'd seen enough. Slipping into the elf's mind, he paralyzed him, black lips curving into a gruesome smile as Xander advanced.

Flipping through the warrior's memories, he saw Fiadh and heard the elf's pledge of fealty. Dothur held the Aos Sí in his grasp, enjoying the fear and panic as the warrior saw death coming with every step Xander took. In his last moments, Fiadh's face bloomed in his mind.

It was over shortly after. Bodies writhed on the ground as the demon's forces stalked among them. Feasting. Killing.

Dothur rose, pale wings unfurling, and swooped into the killing grounds. "Cease," he said quietly, the threat in his voice cutting through the butchery. Walking through the slain and wounded, he paused and scanned the battlefield. "Leave two alive. Let them go to Erabel and warn the queen that I am coming."

Crom Cruach sniggered, a severed arm dangling from his fist. Strolling through the piles of bodies, he found a man. Tossing the limb aside, he bent and grabbed the man's foot, dragging him out from under the corpse of an Aos Sí. Looking him over, he determined the soldier had no mortal wounds, then cast about for another, finding a young man who was a farmer by trade. Crom was about to yank him away from the others when Dothur stopped him.

"Not him. Find an elf. I want Erabel's queen to have one of her own kind warn her of what is to come."

The old god smiled and reached down, breaking the man's neck before casting about for an elven warrior. Human soldiers outnumbered the elves, but eventually, he found one and dragged her to the perimeter, tossing her at Dothur's feet.

Carmun's son stared at the female, carving into her mind and bringing her to awareness. She blinked, eyes ringed in pain. "You will live," he told her. "Go now. Take the human filth with you. Tell your queen I will see her soon."

With a curt command, he rallied his army, encouraging them to eat their fill. They would leave when the moon rose and make for Oadsera. Once that realm was crushed, he would turn his eye on Erabel and finish this.

CHAPTER FORTY-ONE

Troya flew to Erabel, half a dozen of her sisters at her sides. As they made their way across Crethia, the true scope of Dothur's war on mankind was starkly visible. Confined primarily to undefended settlements, entire villages, and towns were little more than blackened blots among the landscape. Bigger towns and cities, those whose nobles vied for the crown, remained largely unscathed and ignorant of what was happening to the lesser populated areas. But Troya knew they, too, would fall, leaving the most corrupt and power-hungry men kneeling at Dothur's feet.

The children of man would become his slaves. Bred for bloodsport, sacrifice, and dark magic. Dothur's armies would swell, unhindered by men and elves. And the Sluagh would starve, falling into obscurity until they became legends. Then, nothing at all.

Having told her sisters of the future that awaited them should they follow Dothur's command, Troya led her best fighters away from Oadsera, where Dothur laid siege, fleeing to Erabel in the hope of seeking an audience with the queen. Of forming a mutually beneficial alliance.

Riley sat on the edge of a raised pallet in the healers' lodge. Across from him, Raenna slept, brows wrinkling in her dream state. He'd spoken to the female a handful of times before the attack. She was one of the Aos Sí's captains. A fierce fighter. But skill alone couldn't hold back the horde that ambushed them. He should be dead. He would be dead had the demon not chosen him and Raenna to carry a warning to Erabel.

His body ached dully, pangs of discomfort making him wince when he shifted, trying to rise. How many days had it been? How many days since the horrors of the killing fields? Whatever magic the healers used to repair the worst of his injuries did nothing to fix his mind or erase the images and screams. He wondered if he'd ever stop hearing or seeing the slaughter.

The sound of someone using a mortar and pestle caught his attention, and he turned, finding two pairs of violet eyes in breathtakingly lovely faces watching him. The healer, Imryll, he recognized, her dark braided hair framing an oval face. A deep red scar curving from her cheek halfway down her neck enhanced her beauty rather than marring it.

The other female was a stranger. She wore a floor-length gown, so sheer the shadows of her limbs were visible as she moved toward him. Long white hair framed a face glowing with dusky skin. Wisdom and compassion reflected in her eyes as she stopped mere inches from his form. "I am Zaeleria, and you are Sir Riley Morrow."

He nodded.

"You have come a long way to reach us," she said, studying him with unnerving clarity. "And seen much."

Riley's throat bobbed as he swallowed. "Aye." His voice was raspy, earning a look from the healer who set about preparing tea to soothe it.

"May I?" Zaeleria asked, reaching out her hands.

He pulled back for a moment, then relaxed. She pressed her palms to the sides of his head and slipped into his mind. She saw what he'd seen, felt what he felt. When she'd finished her perusal, the seer whispered, the words so faint Riley could make out none of them. But he felt each one. They were like a balm to his tattered soul. Tears leaked from his eyes when he clenched them, grief, rage, and helplessness cascading through his brain only to be cradled by the female who didn't balk at the horrors of his memories. With a healer's touch, she soothed the ache. Not removing it because she knew each memory was now part of his identity. When Zaeleria released him, he felt untethered for a moment, slowly coming to himself as he stared into her violet eyes.

"You will heal," she told him, pressing the palm of her left hand to his heart. "But the scars will remain. They are part of you."

Riley could do nothing but watch as she left him and went to the female caught in nightmares. With the same compassion, the seer held Raenna's sleeping form between her hands, cutting through the tangled web of horrors that filled her dreamscape. Riley saw the moment Zaeleria reached the core of the Aos Sí, noting wet trails streaming down her pale cheeks and onto the pallet beneath her head.

Zaeleria left the healers' lodge shortly after. Riley watched her go as he sipped tea sweetened with honey. The warm liquid slid down his throat, relieving the soreness. When he downed the last of it, leaving only the dregs, he slid off the bed, testing his legs to ensure they could take his weight before standing on his own. Imryll hovered at his side, ready to catch him. She didn't speak.

Tugging on the latch, he pulled it open and stepped outside. The air smelled different here. Sweeter. Pure. He breathed deeply, centering himself. When he opened his eyes, the Faoladh, Sibaen, stood before him.

"I should have gone with you," she said, shoulders curving inward.

He sighed. "It would've made no difference. We were herded like sheep. If Dothur hadn't let me go, I'd be dead alongside everyone else."

Sibaen placed a hand on his shoulder and held it there for a few moments, staring into his eyes. Breaking the contact, she took a step away. "The queen wishes to see you."

Riley nodded and followed the Faoladh. She slowed her pace, keeping her perpetually crouched body at his side. The area outside the healers' lodge was abuzz with activity. Aos Sí mingled in groups here and there, most brandishing weapons of some kind. Short swords, bows, daggers, and maces—the wickedly pronged multi-pointed star far deadlier than those he'd seen in battle. Darting among the elves were other creatures, little people he was shocked to see, though he tried to hide his surprise. Urisk, Corene's people, lingered on the outskirts of the activity. Their goat-like forms appeared ready to bolt into the forest at any sign of threat.

As they cut through the throngs, many dipped their chins while others stopped and stared. He kept his head high, though it was impossible to hide the strain his body felt as he walked on the uneven ground. The keep loomed in front of them. A huge edifice that looked like it had grown out of the forest. Gray stone covered in a wild collection of vines and flowers. Though weathered, it was strong, like the Aos Sí themselves.

At the top of the steps leading into the castle stood Kaelari. "I see that Sibaen dragged you from your bed."

Riley paused with one foot on the bottom step. "It was either that, or I would have to suffer her howls at my bedside."

Kaelari laughed and jogged down the steps, clapping Riley on the shoulder. "It's good to see you recovered."

He grimaced. "I wouldn't go that far, but the healers have quite literally worked their magic."

"Come, Fiadh wishes to speak with you."

Riley paused. "Does she know?"

The elf's face tightened. "Aye. She hasn't spoken of it since the day she found out."

Riley nodded and entered the hall with Sibaen at his side. Sunlight poured from windows high in the walls, illuminating the large chamber. Fiadh was standing at a table in conversation with Sibaen's sire.

Ulfran turned when they entered. "Did you bring us

dinner, my daughter?" Ulfran asked, licking his lips and flashing a wickedly sharp canine as he looked the man up and down, smirking when Riley stumbled.

Sibaen snorted. "Were you able to do anything but gum your food, I might indulge you. Shall I ask the kitchen to prepare you something soft?"

Ulfran scowled. "Didn't your mother teach you to respect your elders?"

"That must have been your other daughter," Sibaen said sweetly, leading Riley to the table.

Ulfran held an imposing stare for a few moments as he watched his only daughter find her place at the table. Stepping toward Riley, he said, "Forgive my humor. It was much too serious in this hall before you came in. I am Ulfran of Mactíre."

Riley clasped his arm. "Sir Riley Morrow." Breaking contact with the imposing king, Riley glanced at Fiadh. Seeing her watching him, he made his way over and gave an awkward bow.

Ulfran muttered, "She gets a bow, and I get a handshake."

"That's because she looks like a queen, and you look like a big dog who just rolled out of bed," Sibaen mumbled back.

He sputtered and swiped his hands across his head, chagrined to feel a large patch of fur sticking up. He glared at his daughter when she licked her palm and snaked her arm out, sliding her wet skin down his head. "You're worse than your mother."

"She taught me well," she said with a smirk.

Fiadh ignored their bickering and fixed her attention on Riley. "Erabel welcomes you. While I wish the circumstances were better, I'm thankful you're here."

He dipped his head. "I'm sorry for… I'm sorry."

She gulped and looked away for a moment, her features contorting. "Don't. It's not your fault."

"Thank you." He straightened his shoulders and stepped to the table surrounded by Fiadh's council members.

Riley poured over the map for a few minutes, listening to the quiet conversation around him. His eyes fell on the swath of parchment between Dorcha Wood and Oadsera, gaze fixed on Oscailt Valley they'd been funneled into by Dothur's army. He should've known better than to enter that stretch of land. He *had* known better! But his mind… it had grown fuzzy as they'd traveled, as though his thoughts were not his own. The clearest memory of the ambush was when he'd lain prone on the bloodied ground and looked up at a hideous creature. His skin was like that of a corpse. Pale and hairless. Leathery wings hung from a wiry frame, their length dragging on the ground behind him. And the eyes. Fixed in a scarred face topped with short, curving horns, they lacked pigmentation. Their pink hue amplified the black centers that'd looked down at him as though he were little more than an insect the demon wanted to squash.

He'd felt Dothur crawling around in his mind. Helpless, he'd stared into those dead eyes and heard a voice pounding through his skull. Riley remembered the words. Turning his head to Fiadh, he said, "Dothur sent you a message."

She met his eyes and waited, the hall growing quiet.

"Kneel at his feet, and he will spare your people.

Refuse, and he'll kill every Aos Sí," he paused and swallowed, eyes flicking to the varied faces around the table, "and every member of every race that aids you. Every race but one."

She raised a brow.

He cast his eyes to the ground, a lock of red hair falling over his forehead. "All but mankind."

"From what I've seen and heard," she said, "he's made himself a liar. How many of your people has he killed? Hundreds? Thousands?"

"He won't spare mankind for mercy." Riley looked up at her. "He wants to rule, and his army… hungers."

Urlfran slammed his hands on the table. "They are to be food?" he shouted. Eyes swinging to Fiadh, he said, "He will weaken Crethia through war and fear. Crom Cruach has already hobbled the kingdom by manipulating the death of the king and the murders of his successors. But you have allies."

"I will not kneel at Dothur's feet. He'd kill me and slay you all regardless." Fiadh found Kaelari among the group and asked, "How many warriors do we have?"

The female's face darkened. "With the Aos Sí from other tribes, the Urisk, and the Faoladh. Eight hundred at best."

Riley gasped. "Eight hundred against thousands."

"We've faced these odds before," Kaelari reminded the council. "Our defenses are strong. Dothur will not be able to penetrate the barrier around Dorcha Wood. Let them come. Let them smash their bodies against our shields."

"What about the people outside those protections?" Fiadh asked.

"What people? His armies have gone from settlement to settlement, killing everyone."

"They haven't touched Felmore."

Krulan snarled, flecks of spit hitting the table.

Kaelari glanced at the Cù-Sìth, her lip curling in disgust. "The people of Felmore don't deserve our protection. Have you forgotten all that Darragh has done?"

Fiadh stared at the elf, feeling her anger. "I haven't forgotten. I have good reason to hate them. To want to see them suffer." Her eyes flashed to Krulan, and her heart squeezed at the pain she saw there. "But I can't abandon the innocent who live among the evil. I won't." She paused, thinking of Quinn. "We extended Erabel's protections to shield the life within the forest but also to offer sanctuary to those in need."

If you open our borders to the people of Felmore, they could betray you, Krulan told her, his thoughts tinged with anger.

It's a risk I need to take. They are not all evil, Krulan. We can't become what we're fighting against.

"More allies will come," Riley said quietly. He looked at Fiadh and then glanced at every face around the table. "A handful of men from Middleborough, knights who served Lord Haile, broke away from the main group to visit other holdings. They will come to Dorcha Wood with any who wish to fight with us."

"Do you think Dothur may have intercepted them as he did you?" Arel asked.

"It's possible."

Zaeleria, lingering in the hall with Dyvre, chimed in.

"When the demon entered your mind, did he delve into your memories and see the group of knights?"

Riley looked uncertain. "I can't say."

She drifted toward him, bodies parting as she made her way to Riley. "May I see?" She reached up, hands hovering on either side of his head. He nodded and closed his eyes, knowing what was to come. Remembering the feel of the seer entering his mind. She was gentle, so unlike the ugly violation of Dothur as he'd ripped into Riley's skull. It took a few minutes, during which everyone waited, silent and anxious.

With a serene expression, Zaeleria released him, stroking his mind with a gentle touch as she slipped out of his memories. Gazing at the group, she said, "Dothur is ignorant of the movement of the knights. They will arrive safely."

Sighs of relief and shifting bodies answered her announcement. "This is good news. We are ready for their arrival, and they will be made welcome. Arel," Fiadh said, seeing him straighten and look at her. "Perhaps Quinn could relay a message to his ally in Felmore."

"Of course," he said. "What would you like him to say?"

"Tell him to inconspicuously let Felmore folk know that anyone who seeks refuge will be granted sanctuary."

CHAPTER FORTY-TWO

Zaeleria found Fiadh stretched out on the ground at the base of the Great Mother's oak tree. The queen's forehead was pressed against the curves of knobby roots jutting from the earth. Her arms were splayed at her sides, and her legs were tucked under her body. The seer stood waiting a few paces from her, watching as Fiadh became aware of her presence.

Shifting her upper body to sit on her heels, Fiadh whispered to Danu and turned her head. Wiping tears and dirt from her face, she said, "What news?"

"Must I bear news to seek you out?"

Fiadh gave a flicker of a smile. "No." Climbing to her feet, she stood and shook her legs, relieving the numbness that had settled there.

Zaeleria motioned to a bench, and the pair walked slowly, the rays of the morning sun casting shadows on the ground. There was a hum in the air. It couldn't be heard, only felt. Fiadh rubbed her arms. "Do you feel that?"

"Aye," Zaeleria replied, tucking her gown before sitting on the cold stone bench.

Fiadh joined her, tugging at her tunic that looked the worse for wear. "What is it?"

Tilting her head, the seer studied her. "I think you know."

She sighed. "When will Dothur arrive?"

Zaeleria looked at the sky, fixing her gaze on a patch of blue between a bank of fluffy clouds. "It feels soon, but I cannot give a time."

Fiadh's mouth pulled down, and she dug her heel into the dirt, making a small rut. The knights from Middleborough had arrived two days prior with a contingent of nearly one hundred fifty fighting men. Their innate wariness of the forest and creatures they'd been raised to see as enemies meant they kept to themselves, but they were made welcome, and each man pledged to fight alongside Aos Sí.

Two hundred Faoladh and Urisk passed into Erabel shortly after the men. With Aos Sí from remote settlements who'd heard of the threat facing Fiadh's realm and come to join her, their forces now stood over one thousand. One thousand against a horde of dark creatures led by the son of Carmun.

Fiadh wanted to have hope. She needed it. But it was hard to hold onto its fragile promise in the face of such odds. It was hard to face anything with the hole Gideon left in her heart.

"You had a purpose when you visited the Great Mother today."

Fiadh looked up at the sky. "Yes."

"Are you going to make me guess, or shall I delve into your mind?"

"I spoke with Danu, but she was not the sole reason I sought an audience. I have felt the presence and awareness of the Oilliphéist growing. Each day, each hour, it's stronger. So, I wondered if such a creature would fight with us."

"And you discovered it wouldn't."

"How did you know?"

Zaeleria stared at the ground beneath the oak as though she could see the serpent through the dirt and rock. "I have heard Merrow stories of Caoránach, the mother of the Oilliphéist. She lives within the waters of the earth as they do. It is this commonality that birthed myths of the Oilliphéist having dominion over all peoples with the Merrow as her chosen. Her children. But their legends are from a time of great sorrow when hope was lost. They were meant to rekindle that precious ember. And I understand why their storytellers created them."

"Their queen thinks the serpent will usurp even Danu's power."

"She is mistaken." Zaeleria sighed and shook her head. "Ithraen is not evil. She only wants what is best for her people. In her pursuit of that, she's taken stories and spun them into truth. But they were never meant to be."

Fiadh eyed the seer. "You've reached out to the Oilliphéist, haven't you?"

The seer smiled. "As much as she will let me."

"What do you mean?"

"The Oilliphéist does not always reveal herself to me. When I can sense her presence, it is because she allows me to. But she will not communicate with me. She chose you." Zaeleria tucked a strand of hair behind Fiadh's ear, revealing the scarred flesh she often tried to hide. "You are the one who brought her back to the world. Therefore, it is you she is connected to."

"Why do you think she won't fight with us?"

The seer thought for a moment. "Like Danu, she doesn't take sides. She is a creature beyond time. For her, a war between peoples is but a blink of an eye in her whole existence. The Oilliphéist were here long before us."

"But she's part of this world." Fiadh made a frustrated sound. "If not for what Ithraen did, she wouldn't exist. Now that she's here, you'd think she'd fight to stay."

"The Oilliphéist are woven into the fabric of our world just as we are. But those threads can fade over time. Some unravel and are never seen again. Her kind was one of those. Lost. You brought her back into a world rife with darkness and misery. Is it any wonder that she wants nothing to do with it?"

"I suppose not. I just—" She huffed. "Is there any hope?"

"There's always hope."

Against Krulan's wishes, Fiadh made her way to the pool of still waters. She would warn Eradar of Dothur's coming and rebuild the wall of rock sheltering the entrance to their kingdom. Kaelari joined her with the Cù-Sìth growling softly in protest as they wound their way through Erabel's forest. The woods were quiet. Or perhaps they felt the heaviness in the air as she did. The oppressive weight of things to come.

Gruagach poked their heads out from Hazel groves or ground cover. Beady eyes within diminutive forms tracked their movements, darting from Fiadh to Kaelari. Strapped across their tiny bodies were miniature bows and quivers with poison-tipped arrows. Small but deadly should one pierce the skin. They would ride on the backs of ravens, hawks, and owls as they had when Dorcha Wood was under siege.

"They look ready for war," Fiadh said quietly.

"Aye. They feel it in the air."

Stepping through the thick undergrowth, seedpods sticking to her woolen leggings, Fiadh entered the clearing. The pool of still waters was partially visible through a gaping hole in the wall of rock surrounding it.

Kaelari paused and stared at the water. "Are you sure we should be here?"

None of us should be here, Krulan grumbled.

Fiadh gave the Cù-Sìth a sour look. "Yes. It's important." The guardian of the Merrow needed to see a man at her side. Enemy. Ally. Friend. It was possible. Not that seeing such an alliance would sway Eradar.

Fiadh motioned for Kaelari to stand a few paces away as she went to the opening surrounding the crystal-clear water. Going to her knees, she gripped the pool's edge, craning her neck when Krulan took the hem of her tunic in his teeth. "Don't tear this one," she warned him, grinning when he gave her a sour look and a flash of teeth.

Hovering above the smooth surface, Fiadh whispered,

"Eradar." His name drifted from one edge of the water to another in a large ripple.

Eradar must have been close by because he surfaced silently an arm's length from her only moments later. Blue eyes, so bright they were nearly translucent, stared at her, unblinking. His lips parted, gaze flicking to Kaelari, then back to Fiadh. "What is the meaning of this?"

"Hello, Eradar." She sat back on her heels and tilted her head, watching his scowl. "I've come with news, nothing more."

"Be quick about it. The stench of humans clings to you and stings my nose."

"Please don't say such disparaging things about people I care about."

Eradar's eyes flashed. "Is that a jest?"

"No. I have opened my kingdom to all races."

"You're a fool to trust them," he said snidely.

"You're a bigger fool for allowing hate to cloud reason. We share this world with many people. None of us will survive if we stand alone."

He glared at her, but she saw a flicker of uncertainty. "Tell me what you want."

"Dothur's armies have attacked human settlements throughout the kingdom for months. His eye is now fixed on Erabel. I've come to warn you."

"And ask for aid?" he asked, lip curling with disdain.

"No." She looked down at her lap. "I've wronged you. You have no reason to trust me. Nor I, you." His smooth face held no emotion as she glanced at him, then back at her hands resting against her thighs. "But," she said, lifting her chin and fixing her eyes on him, "Caoránach does. She speaks to me." The mention of the Oilliphéist had an immediate effect. The change in Eradar's face was subtle, but Fiadh could feel the impact of her words.

"That is… interesting."

Fiadh didn't tell him the Oilliphéist wouldn't fight alongside her. Let him think the serpent was an ally. It was deceptive, but she needed to use whatever means she had to gain Eradar's willingness to listen. "Will you speak to Ithraen? Let her know what's coming?"

"She knows. My queen felt Dothur's emergence long before you told me of it and the darkness his release brought. It was only a matter of time before he came for you."

Kaelari's eyes grew hard. "How cavalierly you speak of the demon. It's as though you think you're not part of this world."

"I want no part of a world where men and elves break bread together," Eradar snarled, nostrils flaring.

Rising slowly, Fiadh tugged her tunic from Krulan's grip and glared at the guardian of the Merrow. "I see your mind is fixed. Shall I seal the wall that surrounds this entrance to Abadon so you can hide from what's coming?"

The male's lip curled at the jab. "Leave it. I want to watch you kneel at Dothur's feet."

Kaelari muttered an ugly insult and strode to Fiadh's side, drawing her blade.

The queen held out a hand and shook her head. "Why must it always come to this, Eradar?"

Eradar's eyes looked flinty, but he said nothing.

"I'm no good at diplomacy." She sighed. "I didn't come here to rouse your anger. Dothur is coming. We've extended and reinforced the barriers around Erabel to encompass Dorcha Wood. Soldiers from settlements around the kingdom have joined us to fight against the demon's growing power. Despite your anger and resentment, I will do what I can to protect you and your people. But if Erabel falls, so too will every realm in Crethia."

His ire cooled, eyes dimming. "I will tell my queen."

"Thank you. That's all I wanted to say." She turned from him, sensing his stare between her shoulder blades. Kaelari gave the Merrow a scathing look, then stepped to Fiadh's side, Krulan taking the other. Eradar watched them leave, staring at the rustling foliage at their passing until the leaves grew still. Sinking below the surface, he dove under the water, tail undulating as he made his way to the hidden passage to Abadon. He would tell Ithraen of Fiadh's warning. And of the Oilliphéist. She would hear of the alliance between men and elves. Perhaps the young Aos Sí queen was right. Alone, they were vulnerable. United, they were strong.

CHAPTER FORTY-THREE

Troya and her sisters flew in low circles around the western edge of Dorcha Wood. Sensing the barrier that shielded the forest like a massive dome, they kept their distance and wheeled through the sky in full view of Aos Sí scouts. Within an hour, Fiadh passed through the tree line with Krulan and Kaelari at her sides and stood in a large clearing, the same open area where Rygeil's forces had staged their attack. Here she was again, facing a new, darker threat.

The speaker of the Sluagh dove toward the earth, landing on the ground with a thump. Spidery legs twitched as she stood before the Aos Sí queen. Liquid eyes marked the bristling fur of the Cù-Sìth and Kaelari's nimble fingers clutching a ready bow.

"You're either very brave or very stupid to come here after what you did," Fiadh said, cold eyes fixed on the Sluagh.

"I did not betray you, young one." Fiadh looked skeptical. "Dothur has many spies across the kingdom. Even here. Even now. They tracked the men and elves leaving Oadsera and reported their movements to Dothur. I could do nothing."

You cannot trust her word, Krulan warned.

She gave him a subtle nod. "Why are you here?"

"Dothur will sack Oadsera. He will lay waste to that realm and then turn his eye to Erabel. I warn you that his army swells. They grow strong on the blood of their victims."

"Dothur will find out you've warned me," Fiadh said, folding her arms and staring at the Sluagh. "What will you do? May I offer you sanctuary in Dorcha Wood?"

Kaelari hissed and spat a curse, but the Sluagh ignored her.

Troya cocked her head, black eyes swallowing Fiadh's image until nothing was reflected in her gaze. "My sisters and I will go into hiding as we did before."

Fiadh nodded. "Thank you for coming here. For risking so much to warn me."

"Good luck, young queen. If you survive what's to come, perhaps one day we will meet again." With a flap of her leathery wings, she launched into the air, gaining speed in moments before disappearing in a gray blur, the wailing of her passing lingering in the air.

Erabels' swiftest ravens were sent to Oadsera, warning Saria of Dothur's impending attack. Fiadh paced in the great hall, hands twisting a strip of cloth she'd accidentally torn from her gown when it had snagged on a large thorn in the courtyard. Dasha had hounded her to go on the errand and warn Oadsera's ruler, but she'd refused. She couldn't part with the raven nor put him at risk. It would hurt too much to lose him. Plus, Aishling had grown very fond of the bird. Gideon's foundling had lost too much already. Bird and child were rarely apart. Fiadh needed it to stay that way, to distract the girl when the drums of war sounded once again.

"You'll wear a path in the stone if you keep that up," Ulfran said, pocketing a mouthful of fresh bread slathered with butter.

Fiadh paused, dropping her arms, the cloth dangling from her fist. "I need to do something, but I can't."

"Worry will do nothing but exhaust you." He plopped into a chair and stuffed a large piece of fruit in his mouth. Chewing softly, he studied her, grabbing a wedge of cheese and tossing it in his hands. "You've done all you can to aid Oadsera's people. There is nothing more."

She trudged to the table and sat on the bench, resting her head on her crossed arms. "What if he breaches their protections?"

"What if he doesn't?"

Grabbing a handful of hair, she groaned. "How can you sit here so calmly?"

He considered that for a moment, biting into the soft cheese. "The time will come when we will be sorely tested.

Until then, I will shore up my strength and pray to the Great Mother to protect our kin and allies. That is all I can do."

Sibaen strode into the hall, three Faoladh with her. She spied her father and rolled her eyes. "I see you've resumed emptying the queen's larder. Are you never full?"

Ulfran gave a hearty belch and said, "I'm readying myself for battle. That requires sustenance."

She snorted and sat next to Fiadh. "More like readying yourself for a harsh winter. That's quite a layer you've been working on." Sibaen reached over and patted the bulge of his stomach. It had grown rounder since he'd arrived in Erabel. "Any more readiness, and you'll need to be wheeled back to Mactíre."

He glared at her and reached for another crust of bread. "Then you can be the one to push me."

"Would that be up a hill or down it?" she asked sweetly.

Fiadh laughed, earning her a scowl from the Faoladh king. He kept his eyes fixed on her and slowly brought an apple to his mouth, sharp teeth tearing through the flesh of the fruit with a crunch. Swallowing, he said, "You and my daughter have much in common. And I don't mean that as a compliment."

"If it's all right with you, I'll take it as one."

Sibaen laughed, and Ulfran muttered between bites about the shortcomings of young women until he'd finished the fruit, core, and all. Fiadh admired the ruler. In the space of a few minutes, he'd managed to ease her mind and relieve the tangible stress in the room. It was a gift. One of many he'd shown her since he'd arrived.

Excusing herself from the Faoladh's company, she sought out Dyvre and Zaeleria, finding the seers sitting around a newly constructed scrying bowl. Their beautiful faces were frozen as they stared into the water. She paused and watched, looking for a flicker of awareness of her presence. Eventually, Zaeleria broke her connection and turned to her.

"You've come to see what you can do to aid the people of Oadsera," she said.

Fiadh nodded and stepped to her side. "I feel so helpless."

"And you are. There is nothing you can do. But fear not. Saria has been preparing for this inevitability since word first reached her of Dothur's re-emergence. She knew he would come for her realm."

Fiadh's shoulders sagged in relief. "How will she protect her people?"

"Earthmovers worked day and night carving out a vast labyrinth of tunnels beneath the seat of Oadsera. They are heavily warded. Should Dothur's army breach Oadsera's barrier, they will find an empty city."

"Thank the goddess," Fiadh whispered.

"Aye. She walks this dark path with us." Zaeleria glanced at Dyvre, who hadn't moved from his fixed position at the scrying bowl. "He communes with his apprentice, a young female who's been shadowing him for the last decade." Swinging her gaze back to Fiadh, the seer said, "She will pass along our warnings to Saria." She took Fiadh's arm and led her out of the room, stopping just beyond the threshold. "Focus your energy here. Speak with Danu. Let her guide you."

Fiadh dipped her head to the seer, closing her eyes when Zaeleria clasped her head and pressed her lips to her brow. The seer gave her a knowing smile, then turned away, shutting the door behind her.

CHAPTER FORTY-FOUR

*D*othur's army arrived at dawn a month later. Orange and pink streaked the sky as a horde of dark creatures fanned out along the western and northern borders of Dorcha Wood. Carmun's son flew through the air, surveying the forest, feeling its defenses. Searching for weaknesses. After he failed in Oadsera, the demon's rage was palpable, evident in every snap of his wings. He would not be thwarted again.

On the ground, Crom Cruach prowled through the throng of ravenous monsters, stoking their hunger and lust for blood. Fed on the lives they took as they made their way from Oadsera to Dorcha Wood, they were powerful. A force designed for one purpose. To conquer Erabel. Crush Fiadh. Tear the heart from the Aos Sí.

Growls and snarls circulated among the creatures. The old god smiled, bloated lips curving up to reveal stained, crooked teeth. Bloodlust ran rampant through the troops. Toxic and uncontrolled. It was a risk allowing so many to congregate. They could turn on each other, wasting lives better spent slaughtering men and elves.

Crom found Xander milling among a group of mages and called him over. "Control this rabble before a fight breaks out."

The mage gave him a curt nod and conjured a fire whip. Slashing it through the air, he circulated through the masses, striking those who snapped and lunged. The other mages took his lead and spread out. Each casting a spell to subdue the creatures, though none were as powerful as Xander.

The old god watched the mages drift through Dothur's army. Folding his arms, he took a deep breath through his nose and paused. Twisting his hunched body, his eyes narrowed, looking south toward Felmore. The stink of Darragh Baoill slipped into his nostrils. Fear. Loathing. Avarice. And opportunity. Giving the troops a sidelong glance, he muttered a spell to cloak his body and slipped away from the crowd, slinking along the forest's edge.

When he was a fair distance away, Crom Cruach craned his neck and scanned the sky. Dothur flew in broad circles, pale eyes marking every feature of Dorcha Wood like a map. He would determine a route through the maze of trees and strike at the forest's heart.

Turning his back on Carmun's son, Crom fixed his gaze toward Felmore. He could feel Darragh's mind, but the medallion carrying the sigil of power and control was gone. Broken as surely as his link with the man was sundered. He growled and stalked toward the southern border of the woods. The sounds of Dothur's army grew faint. His stocky legs ate up the distance with unnatural speed. Crom reached out to Darragh, tapping the man's mind and feeling a dim response. He ground his teeth about to pick up his pace when the sound of a twig snapping and the sinew of a bow stretching met his ears.

Spinning in a blur of movement, he turned toward the line of trees in time to see an arrow whizzing through the air at his heart. With little time to deflect, the tip grazed his cheek, slicing through mottled flesh. Heat bloomed from where it cut. Poison tipped. He lunged toward the forest, a curse ripping from his lips only to bounce off the barrier protecting Dorcha Wood. His cheek burned, flesh blistering. Studying the fallen arrow, his mouth turned down. That was no Aos Sí arrow.

He spat on the poisoned tip, nostrils flaring when his spit sizzled. Eyeing the markings along the haft, he grunted. Urisk. So, the goat people had joined the Aos Sí bitch. Crom stared balefully at the forest, shielding himself as a volley of arrows shot toward him. It galled him to turn away from Felmore and leave its lord untouched. Shouting at the Urisk, who lithely flitted through the trees, he lumbered back to the bulk of the army.

Xander met him halfway, having dulled the rising tempers—for the moment. The demon shared news of the Urisk, and the mage gave the forest a sidelong glance. "Does this complicate things?" he asked.

Crom shrugged. "A few extra casualties. But if the goat people have allied with the elf queen, we should assume others have too."

"I must tell Dothur," Xander said, tracking the demon in the sky.

"Mind your place, wizard," Crom Cruach warned. "I will inform your master."

The mage bowed at his implicit threat and backed away.

The old god tapped at Dothur's mind, feeling an irritated response. *The Urisk fight with her. Others likely as well.*

Dothur brushed aside the warning and banked to the right. Wings tucked close to his body as he dove toward a spot of land just beyond Crom. The ground shook when he landed, toe claws ripping into the soil. He flapped his leathery wings once, sending a gust of air at the old god. Stalking toward him, Dothur scanned the throng of creatures, pale eyes narrowing when he saw a scuffle break out. With a whisper, he sliced through the minds of the offenders, watching dispassionately when blood sprayed from their noses as their bodies crashed to the ground.

Studying the blistering welt on Crom's face, Dothur said, "The Aos Sí witch extended the Erabel's barriers. The shield now protects all of Dorcha Wood."

The old god sniffed and turned to the forest. He'd sensed its protections when they'd arrived and was vaguely impressed by Fiadh's desire to shield the forest as a whole rather than solely its heart. It would be challenging to break through the defenses. "Is Erabel shielded by additional protections?"

Carmun's son grinned. "Not that I could sense. Once we tear into Dorcha Wood, Erabel will be laid bare. The Great Mother cannot protect her arrogant queen. I shall wield a blade of fire and cut down the oak. Severing Danu's bond with her chosen people forever."

In Felmore, Darragh sat on the dais and listened to a report from Donal. An army of dark creatures was gathered along the borders of Dorcha Wood. The villagers were frightened and sought refuge in the castle before being turned away.

"Our patrol believes the creatures mean to attack Dorcha Wood and then travel here," Donal said gravely.

Darragh frowned. "How large is the army?"

"Thousands."

It was a daunting number. Even with his reinforcements, he'd be no match for such creatures. Men would run at the sight of them. While those who fought would be killed… or worse if the stories he'd heard of attacks were true.

He'd felt a dull tap in his mind earlier in the day. Crom Cruach was nearby. He was part of the army readying themselves to lay siege on the elven stronghold. Glancing away from the keen eyes of his commander, Darragh considered his next move. When the demon had possessed his mind, they'd become allies of a sort. Perhaps he could spin another such alliance. Guarantee his own safety and that of his soldiers. When the attack was over, he could broker terms with the demon and seize the Western Fold.

"You will send a rider with a message," Darragh said. "We shall see if we can broker peace."

Donal paled. "My lord. I don't believe any of your men will venture near the creatures."

Darragh gave him a cold look. "Then you will go."

A missive was drafted. Pressing his ring into melted wax to seal its contents, Darragh handed the scroll to his commander. "Attach this to an arrow when you're within sight of the bulk of the army." Donal gave a curt nod, masking his relief at not having to ride among nightmarish creatures. "Keep a safe distance and await a response. If the message falls into the right hands, you will have a word with one of their captains or the leader himself."

Darragh watched Donal bow and leave the hall. Drumming his fingers on the arm of his chair. He'd played this game before—just never against such an opponent.

Donal rode out with six men at his back. Their faces grim beneath helmets, the riders left Felmore land and rode north along the western edge of Dorcha Wood. Their horses were lathered and breathing hard when Donal called for a halt an hour later. The twelve-mile distance they'd traveled felt dangerously close to Felmore as Donal took in the massive army spreading out before him like a black wave. He couldn't see where the army ended as the throng curved around the forest's edge toward the north. The soldiers at his sides gasped at the sight and sounds of a sea of darkness and evil.

Strange shrieks drifted to their ears as the seven riders stood far enough away to outrun anything that charged them. Donal frowned and smothered a curse as he saw wings flapping above the figures. His scouts hadn't mentioned those. They could escape creatures that chased them on foot but not by air.

Pulling the missive from his tunic, Donal handed it to

the archer on his right. The man took the parchment and, with trembling hands, slid the rolled paper over the haft of an arrow and took aim. The men mumbled prayers as the archer released the sinew. The arrow arched through the air as the men tracked it, piercing the ground twenty feet from the milling creatures.

Even from their distant position, they heard the squawk of outrage as a monstrous being with wiry black limbs, a thick muscular chest, and a massive head charged the offending arrow on all fours, ripping it from the ground and waving it in the air like a trophy. The soldiers made signs of protection across their chests, their mounts growing restless. One of the men, a grizzled warrior who'd seen many battles, yanked on the reins of his horse, backing the animal up before wheeling it around.

"Hold!" yelled Donal, giving the soldier a dark look. "Lord Darragh commanded us to await a reply."

"A reply? From them?" He glanced at the other men, seeing their unease. "If we continue to stand here, we'll be nothing but dinner!"

Donal shifted in his saddle. "We have fought beside each other in many battles, Orin. If it comes to it, we will fight aside one another again today."

Orin gripped his reins, lips mashing beneath his beard. "Aye, we have fought in battles. But this," he growled, pointing toward the dark army, "is no battle. What awaits us is slaughter!"

Donal's horse stamped his hooves, ears flicking as the sound of growls and shrieks in the distance grew louder. The commander craned his neck and looked north, his face bleaching of color when he spotted a massive winged creature launch into the air, pale wings flapping as it banked toward them. They'd never be able to outrun it.

Orin cursed and dug his heels into his mount, racing toward Felmore, four men following his lead. Two remained with Donal. The stink of piss and shit scented the air as the youngest man released his bowels. His fear was so deep he could do nothing but watch the winged demon make for the trio.

Dothur aimed for the three soldiers and landed so close that a gust of wind caused the horses to rear, hooves slashing. The young soldier was thrown and landed on the ground, the back of his head smashing into a rock jutting from the earth. His body twitched, then grew still. Donal gained control of his horse and looked down at the soldier's still form, mouth pulling in a grimace. He should've chosen a more seasoned warrior.

He gave the man a whispered prayer, then held tight to the reins, thighs clenching his horse's sides, and faced the creature standing before him. The edges of the missive were visible in the monster's fist. How could Darragh think to consort with such a thing? He could feel evil permeating from the creature as its pale eyes bore into him.

"I take it you're the lord's messenger," Dothur said, voice low and raspy.

Donal's throat bobbed, and he forced a trembling reply. "I am his commander."

Arching a brow, Dothur glanced beyond the pair to the man on the ground and the riders kicking up dust in the distance. "And them?"

"Darragh's soldiers."

"Soldiers who run?" The demon clicked his tongue and whispered.

Donal cringed as screams rent the air, quickly silenced, leaving only the sound of swiftly retreating hooves. He didn't need to turn around to know the men who'd fled were dead.

"Traitors are easily dealt with." Flapping his wings and tucking them close to his tall, pale form, Dothur unfurled the crumpled parchment and scanned it. "Your lord seeks to save himself from my army by brokering peace, but he has nothing to offer."

"You have a common enemy."

Dothur tossed his horns. "The elven witch? I understand she drove Felmore's troops from her realm with ease."

Donal frowned. "She has magic."

"Magic." Carmun's son chuckled. "I suppose you could call it that. Even now, she wields her paltry skills to shield her forest and the core of her power within it. But make no mistake, my army is not so easily thwarted." He pinned the man to his saddle, flaying open his mind to read his memories and hear Darragh's words. It was brutal and swift, leaving Donal slumping when he ripped his way back out. "I could kill your master with a Word," he said coldly. "And yet, I find I am intrigued. He is ruthless, and I may need such ruthlessness in the months and years to come."

The commander clenched his jaw, knuckles turning white as he gripped leather and fought to control his fear. "Lord Darragh welcomes an alliance." The words felt wrong. Traitorous. As though he were betraying all of mankind by aligning with such a being. He, too, had heard rumors of armies that swept through towns and villages, killing and devouring. Was he consigning his fellow man to such a fate?

Dothur gave him a knowing look. "Does it matter? You and yours would be safe."

Donal paled and wished he could leave. Take his family and ride to the ends of the kingdom. The ends of the world.

"There is nowhere you could go that I can't find you," Dothur purred. "You are right to fear me. Sipping your fear is like the finest wine. But I have no interest in squandering an opportunity. Tell your lord I accept. When the time comes, he will send his troops to distract the Aos Sí bitch while I deal the fatal strike on her people."

Darragh's commander dipped his head and motioned to the silent soldier at his side. It felt wrong when they wheeled their horses around and exposed their backs to the winged demon. The creature's stare itched between Donal's shoulder blades, not easing until he bent low in the saddle as the horse broke into a gallop. Before they crossed onto Felmore land, he heard the demon's voice in his head.

Run, and I will find you.

CHAPTER FORTY-FIVE

Fiadh stood at Meara's side, stroking the unicorn as she snorted with impatience. Arion, her son, was nearby with Zaeleria riding him. The seer had insisted on joining Fiadh despite her protests that she remain in Erabel. Kaelari had gone into Dorcha Wood with contingents of Urisk and Faoladh to see Dothur's army firsthand and fan out along the perimeter of the forest where the creatures had amassed.

In the courtyard sat Aishling with Lura, who'd been tasked with safeguarding the child and fleeing with her should things go badly. Dasha pecked the ground as the child jabbered to herself as though emphasizing the girl's words. The raven paced in agitation, head swinging to Fiadh when she whispered his name.

Dasha landed on her outstretched arm and preened her hair, clacking his beak when she spoke softly to him. "You will stay with Aishling and keep her safe."

He croaked, worry marring his thoughts.

"I know you would," she told him as he begged to join the fight and be her eyes in the sky. "But I need you here." She stroked his feathers, running her fingers along his neck and cheeks as they puffed. "I love you, my friend." Kissing his beak, she held out her arm and watched him swoop to the ground where Aishling waited.

Fiadh motioned for Lura. "You'll keep her safe. No matter what."

The female nodded. "I will."

"If things go badly…"

"I'll keep her safe, my queen."

Nodding, Fiadh looked past the elf at Gideon's young charge. The girl was a piece of him, though not by blood. It grieved her to know the child would never see him again. *I'll keep her safe*, Fiadh said to herself, sending her promise into the void, hoping somehow, somewhere Gideon heard it.

Fiadh's body throbbed with power. The voices of her parents, Veren, and her brother, Calum, were a low hum in her mind. She'd spent hours on her knees communing with the Great Mother before leaving the keep. Energy flowed through her veins, making her skin hot. If she didn't release some of it soon, she worried her body would burst into flame.

Green eyes burning bright, Fiadh imagined Gideon was with her. She could hear the low tenor of his voice telling her to be strong. She closed her eyes for a moment and listened, a sad smile playing on her lips as she conjured his voice and pretended he sat beside her. *I am with you to the end.* "To the end," she whispered.

Fiadh opened her eyes and looked at the faces surrounding her. They were as varied as the trees. But each of them was part of the world. Part of Danu. What threatened them was evil itself. Raw, unfettered power. Unmitigated greed and violence. The antithesis of all the Great Mother embodied. "Brothers and sisters," she said, drawing every eye. "Today, we fight for our survival. Our future. There has never been a greater threat. The dark creatures of Dothur's army will give you no quarter. And you will do the same."

It felt wrong to consign something of her world to a gruesome death, but she knew the monsters Dothur had summoned were beyond salvation. They were not among Danu's children. "The barriers surrounding Dorcha Wood must hold. But should they fall, we will beat the demon's armies back and drive them from the realm. They will not take our world! We will not let darkness win!"

Cheers and howls rang out, those holding swords and bows pumping them in the air. Warriors spilled out of Erabel, joining the fighters who had stationed themselves around the inner perimeter of Dorcha Wood. Dyvre had taken charge of a few dozen Aos Sí, those most gifted with sight, and charged them with maintaining the shield around the forest. From within the barrier, Fiadh's troops could fire arrows at Dothur's army, the magic protecting Dorcha Wood, allowing the weapons to pass through while deflecting anything coming from the outside.

Beneath the pounding of Meara's hooves, Fiadh felt the

Oilliphéist moving, its massive body riding the underground river parallel with her passage through the forest. She opened her mind to the creature, allowing it to feel and see Dorcha Wood and the evil that threatened it. Threatened Fiadh. Caoránach reborn took in the emotions and images but did not indicate they meant anything to the ancient serpent. Fiadh held out hope the Oilliphéist would be stirred to intervene should Dothur breach their borders. Zaeleria would call her a fool for thinking such things. But the world looked out for fools.

Dothur detected Fiadh's presence as she neared the forest edge and rallied his army, giving them sips of power and promises of blood. Dark creatures dug claws into the ground, flecks of spit spraying from mouths filled with pointed teeth. Abhartach—blood drinkers—and headless Dullahan demons riled up the troops, whipping them into a frenzy. While Crom Cruach crowed with delight, caught up in the maelstrom of checked violence.

Fiadh reached the northwest corner of Dorcha Wood and stared at a sea of monsters. Meara snorted and tossed her head, withers twitching in anticipation of battle. She kept the unicorn in check. Hands fisted in her mane. Arel and Kaelari broke off, leading their own contingents of fighters. Dothur's army looked like a river of darkness, ready to swallow her kingdom whole.

Hackles rising, Krulan glared at the sight of the creatures. His pack, led by his new mate, Nym, was spread out along the forest border. For the first time in their history, Cù-Sìth would fight alongside men and elves.

Krulan growled in readiness.

Lifting her arms to the sky, Fiadh's blood sang with the power of the earth, the strength of the love she felt for her people. It flooded every fiber of her being until her palms ached to release it. She flung her arms out with a war cry echoed by men, Aos Sí, Urisk, Faoladh, and hundreds of other people and animals living within and without Dorcha Wood.

The blast of power sailed through the barrier protecting the forest, tearing through the frontlines of Dothur's army. Bodies flew backward, crashing into each other. In their frenzied state, the creatures turned on one another in a blur of teeth and claws. Mages Abhartach and Dullahan tried to quell the fighting only to find themselves beneath a rain of poison-tipped arrows.

Zaeleria and Dyvre lobbed blasts of wind and shards of ice at the beasts, slicing through skin and muscle. Shrieks of rage and pain seared the sky as a flank of Aos Sí sent volleys of wind, hail, and rock at the creatures. Beyond reason, the frontline broke and hurled themselves into the forest. Their bodies smashed against the barrier, shredded by powerful magic, before falling to the ground in contorted heaps.

Fiadh's army kept up their attack as she called to the elements, drawing particles of electrical current from the air and hurling it at the dark Kelpie and demon stock. Riani sighted and fired arrow after arrow, each one finding its mark. But the creatures kept coming. Like the rows of teeth in a shark, new lines of Dothur's army took the place of the fallen.

And Carmun's son had yet to show himself. Fiadh made

a frustrated sound as she lowered her arms and scanned the mass of bodies under assault.

"What is it?" Arel yelled above the fray.

"I can't find Dothur or Crom Cruach."

Arel nudged his mount and trotted along the tree line, keeping well away from those who shot arrows at the dark army. A horn sounded, and he lifted his head to the sound. It was coming from the south. From Felmore. Kicking the horse into a gallop, he raced through the trees to find Quinn.

"Something comes from the south!" Arel shouted at the soldier, the horse prancing in a circle. "Find out what it is."

Quinn and two others leaped onto their mounts and took off. Wheeling his horse around, Arel raced back to Fiadh. She looked at him questioningly, and he said, "Quinn is investigating."

She swung her head back to the mass of creatures and hugged her thighs to Meara's sides, anchoring herself on her mount as she sent bolts of lightning at the army. She felt every being the currents sliced through. Every life her magic took. As time wore on, their deaths weighed on her power, weakening it. Arel saw her arms tremble.

"Fiadh," he shouted, sliding off his horse and running to her side as she began to tilt. "Fiadh, stop. You're using too much power."

Sluggishly, she swung her head toward him. "There are too many."

He caught her in his arms when she slipped from Meara's back. The unicorn whinnied shrilly, eyes rolling in panic as Krulan snarled and jostled her aside to get to his mistress. Arel went to his knees, cradling her. Fiadh's lashes fluttered, then closed.

"Zaeleria!" he shouted.

The seer lowered her arms and went to him. She pressed her palm to Fiadh's head and shut her eyes. Moments later, Zaeleria looked up at the worried faces hovering around her and said, "Dothur has her."

CHAPTER FORTY-SIX

*A*rel rode hard to Erabel with Fiadh tucked against his chest. Zaeleria, riding Arion, followed close behind while Krulan and Meara kept pace, weaving in and out of the trees. How Dothur had slipped into Fiadh's mind was a mystery, but the longer she stayed trapped within his darkness, the harder it would be to set her free. Arel glanced down. Her face was pale, showing no reaction when he called to her. He dug his heels into his mount.

When the keep came into view, he pulled hard on the reins and leaped to the ground, yelling to a young Aos Sí to take his horse. Zaeleria came to a halt behind him and shouted to take her to the giant oak. Arel raced through the halls, startling those who saw his passing and stood aside. Cradling her head to his chest, he ran, praying to the Great Mother with every step. Krulan's yellow eyes were huge with worry as he ran at Arel's side, snarling and snapping warnings to move at those who crossed their paths.

He turned the corner, feet sliding on the smooth stone,

and jogged to the massive tree. Crashing to his knees at its base, he craned his neck and looked up at the wide branches spanning the entire space. Whispering a prayer, Arel lowered Fiadh's still form and then spoke to Danu, begging for help.

Zaeleria touched his shoulder and gently pulled him away, taking his place.

Arel stepped back a few paces. "Is she going to be all right?"

The seer raised her palms in supplication, then laid them on Fiadh's forehead and chest, above her heart. "Her fate lies with our Great Mother."

His jaw clenched. Kaelari had commanded him to protect his queen, and he'd failed. Arel paced, stopping when he felt a tremor. Beneath his feet, the ground shifted, throwing him off balance. He threw out his arms and spread his legs, glancing at Krulan, who was just as confused. "Was that her?" he asked the seer.

She turned her head toward him. "No."

Brows wrinkling, he felt it again. A jolt followed by slow undulations. "What is it?"

Zaeleria sat back on her heels and tilted her head. Springing to her feet, she ran to him and grabbed his arm, hauling him away. "Caoránach, mother of the Oilliphéist, stirs."

The ground beyond the trunk of the oak swelled and buckled. Roots tore, and rock shifted, forming a huge mound that tore open like a jagged wound. Arel and Zaeleria stumbled back, Krulan growling low as a massive, scaled snout poked through the earth, followed by the huge head of the serpent. Caoránach slid from the ground like a baby from a womb, slick gray scales covering its reptilian body. Green eyes, giant glowing orbs, swung to the trio, pinning them where they stood. It sniffed, forked tongue darting out between rows of fangs to taste the air, then swung its massive head toward Fiadh's still form.

The creature unfurled from the dark earth. Spiral horns adorned its head, large flaps of skin and bone covering its ear canals shifting open and closed. Claws emerged, grabbing hold of the ruined ground and dragging the rest of the serpent into the light. It had no wings, only a long, snakelike body, the deadly tips of its four feet covered in serrated, black nails. The length of ten men, Caoránach was a Goliath. The Oilliphéist's head hovered above Fiadh. Rumbling, it spoke to her in its strange language, snorting when there was no answer. Its breath ruffled Fiadh's hair, the force of it causing her head to loll to the side. With a mewling sound, the Oilliphéist nudged her body with the tip of her nose. But she was like a child's doll, limp and unresponsive.

Caoránach swung her head to Zaeleria. The seer stepped forward. Chin raised, hands clenched at her sides. "Dothur, son of Carmun, poisoned her mind. She cannot hear you. She is trapped."

The serpent opened her mouth, a deep rolling noise coming from her chest. Arel felt it in his bones. Caoránach fixed her gaze on him and huffed. Her breath was earthy and tinged with a scent like the air after it rained. The serpent's tongue flicked, puffs of air flowing from its nostrils.

Turning back to Fiadh, the Oilliphéist wrapped her

body around the tree, placing her head next to the queen's still form. Its eyes closed, and a low humming sound drifted from its body, the vibrations rolling through the ground. Arel felt it in his feet and then up his spine to his head before it wrapped around his skull. In every vibration were pinpoints of energy. Will. Power.

Zaeleria lifted her arms, palms up, then knelt on the ground and pressed her hands to the surface. She spoke to the Great Mother and, through that bond, reached for Fiadh. The young queen was there, trapped in a dark nightmare of Dothur's making. Her mind was in a web of his control. The demon must have sensed her fatigue as she unleashed her power on his army and seized his opportunity when her strength waned. Zaeleria tried to get a sense of his hold on her and felt Crom Cruach's power intermingled with Dothur's. She mashed her lips and reached for Danu. The goddess responded, but she was weak. The darkness took hold of Fiadh, draining her.

Caoránach's mind was also felt, but the seer could only tap at the serpent, sensing its warning if she pushed too far. It was like a protective mother, ready to lash out at any threat to her young. Heeding the warning, Zaeleria focused her energy on Fiadh. Drawing from her core of magic, the seer enveloped Fiadh's mind in a ball of light. Dothur sensed it and tightened his hold, consuming it wholly. With a frustrated sound, Zaeleria ground her teeth and tried again, rewarded when one of the web-like tendrils of darkness was neatly snipped. But for every thread of darkness she severed, those that remained grew stronger. Minutes turned to an hour, and he still held her mind in his nightmarish landscape.

The seer was so engrossed she didn't hear the approaching footfalls, only coming to awareness when Krulan's vicious snarl ripped through the air.

Opening her eyes, Zaeleria looked up to see a dozen Merrow, the shapeshifters in human form, standing in a half-circle, Ithraen at the center. The Merrow queen was ethereal in her gown of gossamer white. Her pale blue eyes were drawn to the Oilliphéist like a magnet.

"We felt Caoránach stirring. She called to us." He looked at the serpent. "She commanded us to come."

Ithraen dipped her head to Zaeleria. She stepped forward, the shifter magic of her people running through her veins as she walked in the guise of a human. The Oilliphéist rumbled as she neared, the noise becoming a purr when the Merrow queen placed her hands along its back. The serpent lifted her head, ear flaps pushing forward as she breathed in the Merrow's scent.

Tears slipped down Ithraen's cheeks as she locked eyes with the creature she'd believed would lift her people out of obscurity, placing them at the serpent's side as her chosen. Looking at how the creature curled protectively around the Aos Sí queen broke something in Ithraen. She sank to her knees and sobbed, begging the Oilliphéist to bless her people and forgive her for warping legends into something they were never meant to be.

Caoránach purred and met the eyes of the other Merrow. They bowed low, a few prostrating themselves fully. Eradar went to one knee and bent his head. The serpent released a low trilling sound and chuffed. Ithraen rose and motioned for her people to join her. They formed a loose circle around the Oilliphéist and began to chant.

Kaelari kept up the assault on Dothur's army, yelling orders to those under her command. Quinn found her, hailing the female as she strode through the trees. She stopped and pulled him aside, well away from the roars and shrieks of Dothur's army.

"Scouts monitoring the southern border spotted Lord Darragh's troops amassing. More than two hundred soldiers line the forest edge, readying for attack."

She frowned. "They will be smashed against the barrier should they try to cross into Dorcha Wood."

Quinn nodded. "There's something else."

Kaelari raised a brow. "Aye?"

"They are not alone."

"What do you mean?"

"The men have hostages." Quinn looked away, disgust marring his young face. "Villagers. With swords to their throats."

Kaelari rubbed her neck and considered the problem. Darragh would be a fool to kill his people. There would be none left to tend the land. Felmore would fall to ruin, and Darragh would die a penniless lord. It was a clever ruse that would surely sway Fiadh if she knew. But Kaelari was ready to call his bluff. "Tell him we don't make bargains."

Quinn swallowed hard. "But the people… he'll kill them."

"He's bluffing." She rubbed her neck. "Darragh knows Felmore needs its people to fill its coffers. He'd be a fool to kill them."

The soldier looked uncertain. "Are you sure?"

"Aye." She turned to Riani. "Go to the southern border with your best archers. Tell that bastard we broker no terms with murderers. If his soldiers attempt to kill the innocent, fire your arrows and cut them down."

Sibaen, who'd slunk through the trees to listen, said, "If they kill their hostages, my people will gut them before their blades hit the ground."

Kaelari glanced at the Faoladh's wickedly sharp claws, imagining the damage one swipe would do. "Do not engage with them. That's what he wants."

"They will piss themselves like they did before should they see us coming for them," Sibaen said, reminding Kaelari of what happened when Darragh's soldiers saw the Faoladh for the first time. "It would be a quick fight."

She shook her head. "You will not engage. Save who you can, but remain behind the barrier. Our numbers are too small. Should Dothur's forces breach our protections, we'll need everyone."

The Faoladh flashed a tooth and flattened her ears before slowly dipping her head.

Riani patted Sibaen's shoulder. They sprinted away, Riani calling on elven and Urisk archers to join her while Sibaen howled for her best fighters. Kaelari watched them go, then looked at Quinn. Such shattered innocence, she thought. Putting a hand on his shoulder, she said, "One day, this will be over. There will be a new, brighter world, and you can tell your children how you beat back the darkness that threatened to consume it."

She loped away, leaving him to consider her words. Hoping they were true.

Riani told the archers to fan out along the southern border of Dorcha Wood. Many Aos Sí climbed trees, perching in branches for a better vantage point, while Urisk and Faoladh ducked behind trunks of trees or blended with dense foliage. Striding to a gap in the undergrowth just before crossing the barrier, Riani scanned the line of soldiers. Indeed, many along the front lines had men and women in their grips, the points of blades at their throats. She looked each of them over, hoping to see uncertainty, but only saw grim resolve. If Darragh was bluffing, it appeared his soldiers weren't aware of it.

Lifting her chin, Riani found the lord of Felmore sitting atop his horse behind the second line of fighters. He wore a helmet, strands of thin, dark blond hair peeking out from its base. His eyes were flinty and so dark they looked black.

Darragh's mouth curved in a cruel smirk when he spied Riani. "Does your queen hide behind her borders?"

"My queen does not need to hide," Riani shouted across the distance. "She does not speak to cowards who shield themselves with innocents."

He chuckled and gripped the pommel of his saddle,

leaning forward slightly. "Shield myself?" He shook his head. "I do naught but seek an audience with your queen to broker terms. These poor folk are only tools to convince her I'm in earnest."

"Your choice of persuasion is lacking."

"Oh? And here I was thinking it was most persuasive." His face contorted for a moment as though he was in pain, eyes going strangely blank, then returning to lucidity. "Well, if she does not deign to speak with me, then I suppose a demonstration of my resolve is in order."

He lifted his arm and dropped it, the blast of a horn sounding as it fell. The soldiers holding men and women on the points of their blades paused for a moment, then jerked their arms. People screamed, their cries cut off into gurgles. Arrows flew from the forest, each one finding its mark. Some of the villagers escaped, staggering away from their captors. Riani, shouting above the fray, left the safety of the barrier, grabbing for those who were too frightened to see a way past the lines of soldiers. Two more Aos Sí moved to help her, leaping from trees and whispering spells to allow men and women to pass into Dorcha Wood. Darragh yelled and swung his sword. Soldiers charged Riani with war cries. She shoved at three villagers who stood frozen, fear piss dribbling down their legs. Hauling them roughly to the edge of the woods, she turned her back and pushed them through, falling to her knees just beyond the barrier. One of Darragh's men ran toward her and raised his sword, cleaving downward. Riani craned her neck to see his eyes go wide as a Urisk arrow stabbed his throat. Scrabbling, she crawled the rest of the way into the forest and muttered a spell to seal it.

The Felmore folk bleated in fear as they were surrounded by Aos Sí, Urisk, and Faoladh. Panting, Riani got to her knees and held out open hands. They clung to each other and huddled in a small group. Some were splattered with blood. She reassured them as best she could and was about to direct one of the Aos Sí to take them to the clearing, where others waited, when she heard a low roaring sound.

Turning toward the lines of soldiers beyond the woods, she scanned their faces. Their attention was focused away from the forest. The roars grew louder. The fine hairs on the back of Riani's neck prickled. A piercing trill sounded from one of the elves still perched in a tree. The male pointed to the sky where a winged creature was making for the soldiers. It dove into the men, landing on the corpse of one of the villagers. Its sharp beak, lined with jagged teeth, tore into it.

"The blood," Riani whispered. She paled, feeling many pairs of eyes on her. "Dothur's creatures smell the blood. They're coming to feast."

Darragh yanked on the reins and dug his spurs into his horse, trampling men who didn't move fast enough as a horde of ravenous monsters descended. Teeth and claws tore and slashed. Men screamed and tried to flee. Riani shouted at her archers. They flew into action, blurs of movement as they loosed arrows at the creatures. A female Urisk bolted and, grabbing a small horn from around her neck, blew hard, sending out blasts through the woods. A Faoladh howled, her call answered by a dozen more.

Fiadh's army fractured, half racing toward the southern border where masses of Dothur's army were attacking and the others remaining behind, continuing their assault along the western and northern borders. Those aiding Felmore's men didn't see the line of mages melt from the mass of dark creatures and fan out along the barrier. They'd been biding their time, allowing the elves to wear themselves down.

Xander stepped forward, close enough to touch the barrier, and locked eyes with Kaelari. With a cruel smile, he raised his arms and launched a direct assault on the shield. The female staggered back, feeling the heat of his dark spell. Other mages joined him, battering the barrier.

"They attack the barrier!" she shouted, hurling defensive spells. Aos Sí spread out along the borders, reinforcing the shield or blocking the attack. But their power waned, much of it having been spent in the initial attack. And the enemy, fueled by dark magic, had no such limits.

CHAPTER FORTY-SEVEN

anu's ethereal face lit up Fiadh's mind. Her features were pale and motherly. Insubstantial arms wrapped around her body, cradling her in a cocoon of warmth and energy. Fiadh opened her mind to Danu, straining toward the light the Great Mother promised. Shadows flickered in the periphery of her mind, tentacles of darkness seeping into her consciousness like drops of poison.

Fiadh slipped away from the goddess, her mind falling into a dark pit where Dothur's pale face split into a mocking grin. She writhed and reached toward the Great Mother. Thrashing, she fought the demon's hold. But she was weak. So weak. As though the darkness surrounding him infiltrated her body, consuming the light.

A whisper of voices, so soft she strained to grasp the sound, drifted through the blackness. Fiadh reached for it, heaving against Dothur's hold. The demon hissed and dug his will into her, tearing through her consciousness. She flailed against him, Danu's voice and power spreading through her limbs. Fiadh listened harder to murmurs that grew into a chorus of voices. She heard Eradar and Ithraen among them.

Caoránach, the mother of the Oilliphéist, chuffed nearby. Like a bolt of heat, she felt the serpent's presence. Dothur tightened his grip on Fiadh's mind, sensing a rising power threatening to break his hold on the Aos Sí queen. Dark magic spun a web around her mind, muffling the sound and feel of the Oilliphéist and Merrow, propelling her awareness into a black chasm. Fiadh floated in the darkness. Untethered from the world. Lost.

Merrow raised their arms, pulling water from the air and forming a chain, each male and female bound to it. Ithraen let her head fall back, voice rising to a crescendo as chanting reached its peak and stopped. The last note hung in the air like a bell.

The Oilliphéist roared, and the chain of water lifted into the air and fell as rain. Looking down at Fiadh's form, the serpent mewled softly. She did not stir.

The Merrow queen let her arms fall to her sides. "His hold on her is great. Our magic can keep him at bay and from consuming her fully, but she needs the Great Mother."

Zaeleria rose and came to her, looking down at Fiadh. "The darkness imprisoning my queen weakens Danu."

Ithraen's mouth pulled down. "He's strong. So much stronger than anything I've felt."

The seer nodded. "He and his army fed on the waters of the Lloathren Mountains."

The Merrow queen stepped back, pale blue eyes flashing to Fiadh. "I thought that place was forgotten by time."

"Not forgotten. Waiting like a patient spider. Growing stronger over decades." Zaeleria craned her neck to look at Krulan. "Dothur will stop at nothing to see his mother and brothers avenged." She looked down at Fiadh. "But he will not have her."

Ithraen lifted her chin. "No. We will not let him." Ithraen glanced at her subjects. "Her power may be waning, but ours remains whole."

The seer nodded and stepped away. Krulan growled and looked to the sky, where Dasha circled before landing next to the Cù-Sìth. They went to Fiadh in unison, slipping between the Merrow to be closer to their mistress. Each in their own way, Krulan and Dasha spoke to her, telling her she was not alone, begging her to come back to the light.

The Cù-Sìth stared at his mistress, eyes dimming when she failed to open hers. He whined and crawled toward her, stopping when the Oilliphéist hissed and curled its body tighter around her prone form. Krulan looked up at the Merrow queen.

Her arms hung at her sides as she stared down at him. "She lives, but his hold is strong."

He growled, yellow gaze flicking to Fiadh.

"I will not abandon her to the darkness."

Krulan's ears flattened against his skull as he rested his chin on his front paws. The Merrow conferred with each other a few paces away. He ignored them, his attention fixed on his queen. The Oilliphéist's form blocked his view in its embrace, and he could see little more than the tip of her nose. His ears twitched as a low rumble radiated through Erabel. Lifting his head, Krulan listened closely, his acute hearing fixing on a point well into Dorcha Wood. His hackles rose as the noise came again, like thunder.

Getting to his feet, Krulan looked to the east, a snarl ripping from his throat when another low sound made the ground shudder. The Merrow paused and stared at him, Ithraen separating herself from the group to stand at his side.

A violent clap of power shook the trees, sending creatures into flight or scurrying away. Ithraen's mouth turned down. "Dothur attacks the barrier."

Krulan growled and sprinted into the trees, stopping when he was a short distance away as he would not leave Fiadh. Tilting his head back, he howled to his pack. They answered, each relaying their position and what they saw. The mages were unleashed. Xander leading them.

The air throbbed with dark power. Zaeleria stood at the barrier as a boom shook the ground. Aos Sí yelled to one another through the trees, lithe forms darting this way and that as others positioned themselves along the tree line.

Mages, dark hooded cloaks masking their forms, stood like specters along the border of Dorcha Wood. Pale hands covered in strange markings were all that could be seen of them, aside from one. The wizard stood in the center of the line of mages like the head of a snake. With his hood thrown back, his dark eyes and gaunt face were twisted in triumph. Power rippled from his palms, dark magic warping the air in waves as it hit the barrier repeatedly, each blast echoed by the other mages at his sides. Zaeleria didn't need to tell those who watched Xander that Dorcha Wood's protections couldn't withstand such an assault for long.

Behind the line of mages, the sea of Dothur's army readied themselves, snarling and snapping at each other. Impatient to attack. A creature with limbs black as soot charged toward the forest, its blood-red eyes crazed. Elves pulled out swords and braced themselves as the monster roared, barreling toward the perimeter of Dorcha Wood. It hit the barrier head first, skin flaying open before its skull split in a spray of blood. Its body slumped to the ground as more creatures, caught up in the frenzy, charged. Xander spat a curse and flung his arms outward, dark eyes sweeping the tree line and finding Quinn.

The young soldier froze, caught in Xander's snare. The mage focused on the man, whispering a spell that sliced into his mind. Quinn rocked on his heels, eyes wide as the mage smothered his will and turned the warrior into a puppet. Gripping his sword, Quinn craned his neck, finding Zaeleria speaking to Arel and Corene. With a drunken gait, he lurched toward the seer, a sheen of sweat covering his face as he fought the mage's power. He stumbled toward Zaeleria, stopping when he was an arm's length from her. Arm trembling, he lifted his blade. It wobbled in the air as he fought against Xander. Zaeleria's eyes went wide, then narrowed when she felt the mage's presence.

Turning slowly to face Quinn, she gently pushed the deadly tip of his sword aside and stepped toward him, taking his clammy face in her palms. "Fear not. I feel him in you." Quinn's mind snapped as he let go, giving himself over to her completely. Zaeleria kept her hold on him, thumbs pulling the bottom of his eyelids down as she stared beyond Quinn and into the face of the mage. "You cannot have him," she told Xander.

The wizard snarled and lashed out. "Try to take him from me, and he'll be nothing but a fleshy sack of meat," Xander threatened out of Quinn's slack mouth.

The seer cocked her head. "Leave him or find out how deep my power goes." She murmured a spell, the words coiling around Quinn's mind. His body relaxed, welcoming it. Shoulders slumping, he stared unseeing as the seer placed her hand against his forehead in a final warning.

Xander chuckled, the sound wet and garbled from Quinn's throat.

"I warned you," Zaeleria whispered. She sent a blast of power through the link in Quinn's mind.

The mage yelped and stumbled backward, rage twisting his features. He stared balefully at the forest, lip curling. Calling on the core of dark magic he'd suckled from deep within the Lloathren Mountains, Xander sent a wave of power at the barrier. It lashed against the protective shell, trees within the forest groaning as the dark magic splintered the barrier, stabbing through tiny fissures.

Aos Sí winced under the onslaught, fumbling for Danu as Xander's wrathful attack pummeled the barrier. The mage lost control, drilling into his magic until it frayed, little more than wispy threads that bounced off Dorcha Wood's protections. With a murderous glare, he lowered his arms and panted, snapping at the other mages who mirrored his movements, ceasing their assault.

Zaeleria stepped to the edge of the tree line in a challenge. Xander flung a spell at her mind, and she smiled, brushing it aside. "Your power wanes."

"Enough remains to see your realm fall," he ground out.

She cocked an eyebrow. "I can taste the lie in your words. How far you've fallen. What did Dothur promise you?"

He mashed his lips.

"Power? Dominion over men? Were you so blinded by hate that you didn't see the lie within his words?"

Xander's hands curled into fists. "I'll dance on the corpse of your queen before this day is done."

"No. You will not." She took a deep breath and anchored herself to the earth, to the Great Mother. "I pity you. Absent from her light." She shook her head. "There is no warmth in darkness."

Dyvre materialized at Zaeleria's side, his movements in tandem with hers. They raised their arms in unison, palms hovering just beyond the damaged barrier. Aos Sí fanned out on either side of the seers, each lifting their arms. As one, they chanted, calling on the Great Mother. Power flowed from Danu through her people, reinforcing and repairing.

The mages buckled under the magic surging through the barrier. Xander closed his eyes and let his head fall back, calling for a darker power. Crom Cruach answered. Crom wended his way through the throng of creatures, slapping some aside as they jostled for position.

Coming up behind Xander, the demon spied the seers,

his black lips splitting into a grotesque smile. "Have you enjoyed sparring with my pupil?"

Zaeleria scowled but didn't break her concentration, pouring her energy into Dorcha Wood's protections.

"He's an entertaining distraction, is he not?" The demon grinned. "How wonderful it is to see one's plans come to fruition. And you were so accommodating."

A sizzle of energy rent the air. The clouds roiled, and the ground shook. Xander stepped aside. An expression of pure malice carved onto his narrow face. He bowed to the old god, then knelt at his feet, dipping his head.

Whatever power Crom Cruach wielded in the past had grown tenfold. The demon placed a gnarled hand on the wizard's head. Xander, on his knees, lifted his arms, extending them outward. Two mages lowered themselves to the ground at his sides and gripped his hands, the others following suit until they formed a chain, each linked to the other. Crom tunneled into their power, multiplying his own. Wind blew in gusts with the force of his power as he gathered it, fusing the mages' magic with his own. His eyes flashed to Zaeleria's in triumph a moment before he flung it outward.

It slammed into the barrier, shredding the newly repaired fissures and ripping open new ones. A female Aos Sí shrieked as a thread of dark magic stabbed through the forest's protection and into her. Her body flew backward.

"It's not going to hold!" Arel yelled as another blast rocked the earth.

Danu shrank away from the onslaught, curling in on herself as she was attacked from all sides.

Dothur revealed himself, shoving Crom Cruach aside and flinging his wings out, knocking his demon guards and the old god to the ground. Rising to his full height, he threw his head back and roared. Towering over his army, he commanded Crom Cruach. "Gather Darragh to you. Wield his army and kill them all."

The old god's bulbous lips flattened. "What will you do?"

Carmun's son rolled his shoulders, fingers twitching. "I'm going to bring the barrier down."

Dothur stalked to the border of the forest, ignoring squawks and hisses as he shoved his dark creatures aside. He stopped when he reached the barrier and lowered his head, eyes delving into the trees, where Aos Sí watched and waited. His body tensed, and he froze, staring at a point just inside the perimeter. Zaeleria stared back, arms outstretched as her mouth moved, lips a rapid blur with spells of protection. Dothur sneered at her and dipped into the core of his power. His hold on Fiadh took only a fraction of his energy now that he'd weakened her to the point of breaking. He focused his dark will on breaching her people's defenses.

Giving the Aos Sí seer a wicked smile, he lifted his arms, wings extending behind him, and threw his might outward. It slammed into the barrier with a thunderous boom. The protections held for a protracted moment, during which he heard elves gasp, then imploded, throwing bodies backward where they smacked into the trunks of trees and juts of rock. Dothur let out a piercing war cry. His army paused, then turned toward its master. With shrieks and snarls, they ran toward Dorcha Wood. Men and elves yelled when they saw the tree line breached. Urisk, fighting alongside Faoladh and humans, bleated to one another and gave chase, their lithe bodies a blur of movement as they raced after the monsters, cutting down those who were too slow or injured.

But they were no match for the horde. Dothur leaped into the air, the force of his passing snapping tree limbs that fell to the earth, crushing anything in their path. Dyvre tracked the demon until Dothur disapproved over a ridge.

CHAPTER FORTY-EIGHT

Gideon and Ellisar sat on their mounts with an army of three thousand at their backs. Ignorant of the slaughter in Oscailt Valley, they'd traveled for days on their own, seeking an audience with local lords. Word of attacks had spread across fiefdoms in the east and north, but gates were barred against them when guards saw Ellisar's pointed ears and sharp eyes.

It wasn't until they arrived on Lord Thomas Arghail's land that their efforts proved fruitful. The Baron of Colshire invited them into his holding. Thomas sat and listened to Gideon and Ellisar's stories of dark creatures attacking villages across Crethia. He listened and believed. The baron sent messengers to the north, south, and west, asking for information on any further attacks. Lord Victor Grimes, Baron of Dunwick, responded with a startling account of the men, women, and children in a tiny hamlet on his sprawling ancestral lands slaughtered in a single night.

Both barons reached out to neighboring fiefdoms

seeking support for a counterattack. Those requests went unanswered. The other nobles ignored the growing threats in their quest for the vacant crown. Anger at their indifference fueled another alternative. Lords Argail and Grimes joined Gideon and Ellisar, gathering troops as they headed west. Volunteers from towns and cities who'd been attacked or who'd known victims of those settlements that had been razed were eager to buck the edict of their local lords and join. Their numbers swelled as they neared the Western Fold, and now they stood on a bluff looking out at swarms of darkness converging on Dorcha Wood.

Elves, Urisk, and Faoladh burst from the trees, stabbing and clawing everything in their path. Beyond the forest, the mages, still kneeling and weak from Crom Cruach's use of their power, heard the approaching fighters too late. Black cowls were thrown back as Faoladh leaped, claws slicing down to the bone of those who lacked the strength to fight them off. Xander staggered to his feet and flung out a protective shield. Kaelari snarled and slammed into him, knocking him to the ground. Flipping her sword in the air, she pounced, pinning him to the ground.

Xander chuckled and lashed out, sending her sprawling. "Aeson made the mistake of thinking I was easy prey, too."

The name of Threa's mate and Kaelari's closest friend, who was betrayed and murdered by Xander in the Great War, cut through the noise and violence surrounding them. Her eyes narrowed as she sprang to her feet and stalked the mage, who backed away at the expression on her face. Rage sang in her veins. Batting away the spells he flung at her, she came for him.

His power was a fraction of what it should've been, having been drained by Crom Cruach. Had he been at his full strength, he would've split the elven bitch in two. Xander ground his teeth and sent a wave of dark magic at the elf, smiling grimly when she flinched. But Kaelari didn't retreat. She advanced, blue eyes against her dusky skin, glowing with ferocity.

Kaelari's blade whirled in her hand in a dizzying series of spirals, and she lunged, sweeping out her leg at the same time. The mage fell hard and rolled, escaping the point of her short sword as she cleaved. Wrenching the blade from the ground, she sprang at him as he rose, slashing with one arm and whipping up a gust of wind with the other. She slammed the air into him so forcefully his breath whooshed out of his chest, the killing spell on his tongue caught in his mouth. She threw her weapon, the blade spinning in a deadly arc before it drove into Xander's chest, pinning him to the ground. Kaelari leaped onto his body, straddling him. Grabbing the hilt, she held his stare and whispered harshly, "I told you I'd kill you," and flicked her wrist in a vicious twist.

Dyvre, abandoning all hope of reestablishing a barrier, wielded his magic to cut through Dothur's minions and protect those who fought with him. But there were too many. Kelpie and demon half-breeds swarmed the seer, barreling through his weakening power. Fangs, slick with blood, clamped onto his throat as he was tackled to the ground. The moment before teeth shredded flesh, he reached for Zaeleria, whispering goodbye.

The powerful seer swayed as Dyvre's voice was forever silenced. Looking toward the last place she'd seen him, Zaeleria's face crumpled. All around her were shrieks, minds blaring with alarm, and death rattles. Her magic shuddered under the onslaught of grief and loss. Wrangling it, she blocked out the carnage and pushed through the melee, saving who she could, killing whom she must. But for every creature she slew, ten more took its place.

In the distance, a horn blew. The sound carried on the wind. Zaelaria cocked her head and listened, her eyes growing wide, hope blooming in her heart.

Gideon dug his heels into Aridius, sending the war horse barreling into the sea of dark creatures. Ellisar rode at his side, the deadly curve of his wickedly long spear cutting through the enemy like a scythe. Kelpie and demon-stock swarmed, their dark bodies an undulating sea of violence as they collided with the baron's army. Winged monsters swooped from the sky, grabbing men and shooting into the air before dropping them.

Gideon spied Riani, yelling at her through the melee, and pointed at the creatures. The elf looked at him in shock, then sprang up onto the back of her mount and nocked an arrow, sending one of the aerial terrors to the ground. The others screeched and dove for the Aos Sí. Gideon slashed his way toward her as she loosed arrow after arrow, each finding its target. But her quiver was emptied in minutes, and still, they came. They tucked their wings tightly against their bodies and dove toward her.

She waited until the last minute, then jumped into the air from the horse's back, her blade slicing and severing the wing of the closest creature. It tumbled into an Abhartach, knocking the blood-drinker off the downed soldier he was feasting on. Riani dodged the next winged beast and ran toward Gideon as he thundered toward her. He leaned sideways in the saddle, Aridius' hooves pounding on the sodden earth, and held out his arm, grabbing the female and swinging her up onto the horse's back.

Riani tucked herself against his back as he pressed his body against Aridius' neck and urged the gelding into a full gallop. The horse wove in and out of the fighting as leathery wings chased them. Mouth foaming and chest lathered, Aridius pushed himself, racing toward Dorcha Wood.

They weren't going to make it.

One of Dothur's winged demons stretched out its talons and fell from the sky. Riani felt the tips of its deadly nails tear through her tunic, shredding her shoulder. She gritted her teeth and gripped Gideon tighter. The creature banked to the left, making way for another.

Wind from its leathery wings blew her braid to the side, and she closed her eyes, readying herself for the inevitable. But the strike didn't come. An unearthly wailing tore through the sky as the Hunt joined the battle. Sluagh streaked across the horizon, Troya leading them. They dove for Dothur's aerial legion, ripping them from the air, shredding wings and bodies until the sky rained blood.

Gideon craned his neck to see the slaughter, eyes wide as the Hunt was unleashed. Moments later, Aridius crashed through the tree line. Riani, flesh hanging from her shoulder, slid from the horse and collapsed on the ground. Gideon swung his leg over, giving his mount a quick pat and word of thanks before kneeling at her side. He pressed his hand to the wound to staunch the bleeding and shouted for a healer.

The female gave him a weak smile and said, "We thought you were dead."

He shook his head. "I'm not that easy to kill."

"It appears not."

An Aos Sí healer came upon them and knelt at Riani's side. She smiled at Gideon and sucked in a breath as the healer prodded at her injury. Shooing Gideon away, Riani gave herself into the care of others, watching him turn toward the battle still raging beyond the forest. "Go."

He nodded and strode to Aridius. He wanted to see Fiadh. To let her know he was alive. But the sounds of screams and roars had not dimmed. Nudging Aridius toward the border of Dorcha Wood, Gideon stared at the battle. Pulling his sword from its sheath, he gripped the reins in one hand and lifted his heels. Aridius charged from the forest back into hell.

CHAPTER FORTY-NINE

Gideon knew he'd never forget the sounds of butchery as the Hunt attacked. Troya and her sisters clashed with Dothur's aerial army in a violent eruption of leathery wings and claws. The screams of Sluagh ripped through the sky, slicing through the minds of both armies. Gideon clutched his head and leaned into Aridius, dodging dark creatures who lunged blindly, consumed by the horrible wailing of fallen Sluagh.

The Hunt dove in and out of Dothur's winged legion with renewed ferocity. Troya, splattered with blackening blood, shrieked to her sisters, rallying them as more of the enemy burst into the air. A handful of archers, both elves and men, gritted their teeth against the mind-numbing wailing and nocked arrows, felling some and wounding others that were plucked from the air, their bodies shredded by Sluagh. In time, nothing was left of Dothur's flying legion but lumps of flesh scattered across the blood-soaked field.

With the skies free of Dothur's winged demons, the

Hunt shifted their focus to those on the ground. Kelpie and demon-stock squealed as they were plucked into the sky, bodies flailing and crashing to the earth in meaty thumps. Dark creatures bellowed and charged, moving in crowded masses toward the soldiers. The barons yelled to their commanders, gathering their armies to push them back. Steal met claws and fangs.

Gideon saw Arel and Kaelari in the thick of the fighting and kicked Aridius into a canter toward the clash of armies. The female saw him coming and paused with surprise before she leaped onto the saddle and then hopped onto the horse's rump, where she whipped her arms through the air and called on the power of wind and rain, pelting Dothur's army. Gideon gripped the reins with his left hand, his other wielding his sword, slashing through flesh and bone as Aridius sailed past. When they reached the perimeter of the fighting, they jumped to the ground, Gideon smacking Aridius on the rump to send him off. Fighting side-by-side, he and Kaelari waded into the fray.

Men from the barons' armies tried to hold the line as dark creatures, commanded by the remaining mages, lost control. They became a swarm. Elves exhausted their magic, resorting to hand-to-hand combat. Arrows flew, and blades flashed, blood spraying in every direction. Near Dorcha Wood, Ellisar waged his own battle, his powerful magic cutting down the enemy by the dozen. But it was not enough. Aos Sí were dying alongside human soldiers.

Gideon barreled through a thick knot of demon stock, ducking and feinting as they screeched and slashed their way toward him. His sword dripped with blood, sweat pouring down his face and cutting trails through splattered grime. He didn't see the Abhartach slinking toward him, its dwarfish body hidden in the chaos until the blood-drinker hurled itself at Gideon, knocking him to the ground. He rolled, the blade of his sword flattened into the mud by his body. The Abhartach pounced, landing on his chest and squeezing the air from his lungs. His eyes bugged as the monster lunged for his neck. Gideon swung his legs up, wrapping them around the Abhartach's torso, and flung its body backward. The monster arched and sprang to its feet, eyes glowing red. Grabbing his blade's blood and mud-covered hilt, Gideon sliced through the air as it lunged at him, the metal severing its arm and cutting deep into its chest. He shoved the shrieking creature away and got to his knees, eyes sweeping the battlefield.

Kaelari appeared at his side. "When I first saw you, I thought I was seeing a ghost."

Gideon smiled grimly. "I didn't know."

She reached out a hand and hauled him to his feet. "It's good to see you."

Flipping her blade in her hand, she jerked her chin toward a contingent of soldiers and elves who'd pushed back a host of Dothur's army and were yelling to each other to surround them. It was a sight he'd never thought he'd live to see. Men and Aos Sí fighting and dying together.

The union of peoples sent ripples through the landscape and into the Great Mother. She stirred, welcoming the healing power of such an alliance. Slowly, Danu came back to herself, light biting into the darkness, chasing it back from where it came.

"Where is Fiadh?" Gideon asked.

Kaelari's face spasmed.

"Tell me."

"Dothur took hold of her mind. She's in Erabel with—"

Gideon didn't wait to hear the rest. He whistled for Aridius and raced through the forest.

Fiadh's body arched, the muscles in her neck straining as her back jutted upward off the ground. Dothur pummeled her mind, blotting out everything but the darkness that consumed it. A lone tear slipped from her eye and trailed down her face.

A whimper escaped her lips as Dothur dug into her core in an effort to strip away all sense of herself. She reached for Danu. The Great Mother responded, but her reply was weak, as though she were too far away to give aid. An unanchored sensation washed over her mind, and she floated on the brink of acceptance.

Darkness expanded, swallowing everything, blotting out the world. Fiadh drifted into it, phantom feet touching the cold surface. Dothur's laughter echoed through the space, and she spun around, trying to find him. But it was pitch black. The blackness was infinite; she wondered if her eyes were open or closed. Dothur's will, oily and cruel, curled around her body, making her skin crawl.

She was so tired.

It was there, in that quietude, that she felt another presence. Keeping her thoughts locked tightly inside, she reached toward the otherness and found Caoránach.

The Oilliphéist spoke to her in an ancient language, one she knew but had never learned. She was not alone. Caoránach was with her, and in that bond was power. But she was too weak to reach for it.

And the menacing presence bombarding her mind and body wouldn't let her go.

Fiadh's ghostly eyes flicked to a pale form, slowing coalescing and glowing in the blackness. Massive wings hung from a hulking body. Dothur's eyes bore into her as he dipped his head, glaring from beneath his heavy brow and curved horns. She stared back at him, paralyzed.

At the edge of her consciousness came another voice. It was the sweetest sound. Gideon called to her. Her eyes welled, spilling over and making tracks along the cheeks of her still form. *I hear you,* she called to him, suddenly wanting to let go and join him in the afterlife.

Fiadh. His voice slid through her mind, bouncing off the darkness.

Her mouth moved, lips parting. "Gideon."

"I'm here." Gideon reached for her, his arm brushing the scales of the defensive Oilliphéist. Caoránach hissed but allowed the contact.

"You have to fight, Fiadh. Fight!"

"Gideon," she whispered. "I love you."

He dropped his head. He'd waited so long to hear those words. "I love you, Fiadh. Come back to me." Her mouth went slack, and he shook her. "Fiadh!"

Krulan growled and stood next to Gideon. On his back

perched Dasha. The two looked at their mistress, each trying to break through the blackness smothering her mind.

The Merrow watched beyond the trio, clasping hands as Ithraen used their magic to fuse the thoughts of Krulan, Dasha, and Gideon. Their words and emotions become one, weaving together in a powerful spell.

Love. Loyalty. Friendship.

Danu's power flared. Fiadh latched onto it, greedily devouring what the Great Mother offered. Focusing her mind, she envisioned Dothur's hold on her, the web of darkness he'd trapped her in and battered it with renewed energy. It held, unmoved, for a few seconds, then flinched like a living thing. She felt for points of weakness and targeted them with her mind, her strength growing as his hold on her eroded. The soft sound of chanting invaded the stillness. The voices grew, doubling and trebling. She heard Ithraen among them, and woven within their song was Caoránach.

Fiadh listened closely and heard Gideon, Krulan, and Dasha. They reached for her, trying to pull her out of the dark. She opened herself to the energy spilling from those surrounding her, flinging out her arms as power flowed into her body. With a scream of triumph, she ripped through Dothur's dark web of control, slashing every tendril of power and slamming her mind from him.

Body arching, Fiadh came back to the world.

CHAPTER FIFTY

Crom Cruach cut across the field, his stocky body a blur of movement. None marked his passing as he cast spells of concealment. When the sounds of battle dimmed, he looked around, finding a crevice amid a mound of craggy rocks. Wedging his body into it, he folded his legs and closed his eyes. Part of him wanted to ignore Dothur's command and rebel against the notion that he was nothing more than a dumb creature Carmun's son controlled. But the darker part of him longed to see the bloodshed such a command would provoke. Plus, ensnaring Felmore's lord again, living in his flesh, had its own appeal.

Sending his will across the landscape, Crom sought out Darragh, finding Felmore's lord skulking in the solar of his castle. If he sensed the old god coming, his body didn't show it. One moment he was staring out the arrow slit at the soldiers milling around the inner bailey, and the next, his thoughts went blank, eyes growing large with fright before shuddering as he scuttled into the recesses of his mind.

Crom Cruach ruthlessly took over, all but shredding Darragh's consciousness. He licked his lips, savoring the feel of the lord's body. Fully entrenching himself as Darragh Baoill, he stalked from the room and strode into the great hall, barking an order for his troops to assemble.

His commander, Donal, eyed him warily, wondering at the sudden change, fearing his lord was under a dark spell again. He hadn't forgotten his promise to himself. He would kill Darragh rather than see him consumed by whatever fell presence had taken him on their travels. When the lord of Felmore swung his gaze toward the commander, Donal took a step back, struck by the evil lurking within the man's eyes.

Darragh was gone. He knew what must be done.

Shifting his hand to his waist, Donal slipped a dagger from a sheath on his belt. Feigning obedience, he dipped his head at Darragh's orders and shouted to a man at arms to see it done. When the soldier jogged out the door, the commander walked toward his lord, palming his dagger. His heart beat wildly as he neared his lord, sweat beading on his forehead despite the cold. Gripping the handle of his weapon, Donal swung, aiming for Darragh's throat.

The lord's mouth curved into a smile as Darragh watched the blade coming toward him from the corner of his eye. Whispering a black spell, he chuckled and slowly turned to face Donal. His commander stood frozen, arm trembling, dagger mere inches from its target. Darragh plucked the weapon from Donal's hand and spun it, his mouth lifting in a grin as the blade twirled in his fingers. Like an asp, he lunged, stabbing the weapon into Donal's eye and giving it a twist. The commander's mouth sagged open with a small yelp of pain and shock. He dropped to the floor, dead, before his head hit the stones.

Licking the blade, Darragh stared dispassionately at the corpse, ignoring the startled scream of a maidservant. One look at the lord's face had her running from the hall. He nudged Donal's body with his toe, then knelt and dipped a finger into the bloodied socket, digging out what was left of the man's eye. Cupping it in his hand, he cocked his head. "You saw too much." He dropped the mutilated orb and stood. "Now you see nothing."

With that, he strode out of the hall and joined the men. They would charge into battle and slay the human and elven armies, and when it was over, whoever survived, whatever men he didn't sacrifice to slake the dark army, would kneel at his feet.

An hour later, with Darragh leading them, the soldiers of Felmore left the grounds. Over one hundred men made their way toward the heat of battle on foot or horse. They kept to the edge of Dorcha Wood, many casting glances at the forbidden forest, bumping into one another when shadows moved and trees groaned. Some prayed, begging the Great Mother to intercede and slay the dark creatures, wrongly believing they were being led to fight against the monsters rather than with them. Within each of them was grim acceptance. They would likely not return to Felmore.

The severing of Dothur's hold on Fiadh and the unification of varied races fighting against the dark horde revitalized the Great Mother. She opened herself, reaching toward those who fought the darkness. Each was a pinpoint of light blazing in the black pit that had trapped her, leaching her of power. Danu broke free, the walls of Dothur's making crumbling. Like a shooting star, she burst into the scene.

The goddess embraced her children. *All* of her children. From the men in the barons' armies to those who'd taken refuge within Dorcha Wood. To Aos Sí, Urisk, Faoladh, and little folk—to the feathered, furred, and scaled. She shared herself with them, becoming a hum of power singing in their veins.

Gideon felt a prickle of awareness as he held Fiadh in his arms. He didn't think he could ever let her go. She'd wept when she saw him, crawling over the Oilliphéist and burying her face in his chest.

But the battle waged. Dothur was not beaten.

Fiadh sensed it, too, though she wished to shut out the world and hold onto the moment forever. Forcing her arms to let go of him, she pulled away.

Gideon brushed tangles away from her face. "I love you."

"I thought I'd lost you," she whispered.

He hugged her tightly and then reluctantly let go. "I'll always come back for you. Not even death could stop me," he whispered harshly. "I never gave up on you."

She burrowed her head into his chest. "I know. I heard you. Even in the dark. I heard you."

Helping her to her feet, he clung to her with his eyes as she embraced Krulan. The Cù-Sìth's body shook as he nuzzled Fiadh. Dasha, overcome, hopped in manic circles, squawking and croaking. She released Krulan, and Dasha flew to her shoulder, frantically preening her hair. She shushed the raven and stroked his feathers, speaking to him in a language only he could hear.

Time was short, and too soon, she sent Dasha off to find Aishling, quickly learning the child had been whisked away when Lura felt the barriers fail. The girl would be safe, and if they lived to see tomorrow, they'd fetch her back.

Fiadh looked at Gideon. "Let's finish this."

He took her hand. "Together."

Hand in hand, they raced out of the keep, finding Meara and Aridius waiting. Gideon settled into his saddle, tugging Aridius aside to give Fiadh the lead. King Ulfran winked as he strode by. Gideon rolled his eyes and fell in behind the Merrow queen. Leaning to the side and holding out a hand as he passed, Kaelari swung up behind him as the party made their way to the thick of the fighting. As she rode, Fiadh let go of Meara's mane and hugged her thighs to the unicorn's sides, stretching out her arms to the sides. Closing her eyes, she opened herself to Dorcha Wood, feeling its fear and pain mixed with determination and power. Beneath the pine needle-littered ground, she felt Caoránach slithering through the black waterways deep in the earth, keeping pace. Fiadh wouldn't ask the Oilliphéist to fight alongside her. Like Danu, she was a source of power and strength but not a tool of war.

The rhythm of Meara's clopping beat in time with her heart. Fiadh connected with the Great Mother, inviting the goddess' energy into her body, feeling it surge through muscle and bone. Her scalp tingled as her mind lit up with awareness. Danu was with her. Part of her. Fiadh breathed deeply, body shifting with Meara's movements through the forest. Focusing on her well of magic, she drilled into it, coaxing it, feeling its thready connections with everyone Danu embraced.

They were one. One purpose.

When she opened her eyes, her body hummed with energy. It dripped from her fingers, ready to be set free. Lifting her heels, she urged Meara to pick up the pace.

As they neared the thick of the fighting close to the eastern edge of the woods, Krulan's hackles rose, and he growled low in his chest. Fiadh turned toward him. *What is it?*

His lip curled. *Men are coming from the south. From Felmore.*

Her mouth turned down, uncertainty on her face. *Do you think they are coming to join us?*

Not if Darragh leads them, he told her.

Fiadh glanced at the sky. Dusk had fallen. Soon, it would be dark, and they would be at a disadvantage. If Darragh was leading his men against the armies of the Barons, it could turn the tide of the fight against them. *Go,* she told him, watching for a few moments as he lunged through the trees.

Passing along what Krulan said, the party mulled over their options. Ithraen offered two of her people to scout the edge of the forest for the incoming troops. The rest of them would face Dothur's army and try to push them back. Gideon moved to Fiadh's side, Aridius cutting through the undergrowth alongside Meara. Arion, carrying Ithraen, kept his eyes on his dam, his dark coat blending with the shadows, the opaque tip of his thick horn a ghostly beacon.

Whoops and shouts cut through the forest as elves and Urisk darted among the trees, firing arrows from the cover of shrubs or the height of thick branches. On the ground, men fought hand-to-hand alongside Aos Sí and Faoladh. Zaeleria took on what remained of the mages, deflecting spells and shielding whomever she could from wizards who picked targets like pieces of ripe fruit. Arel wove and slashed his way through throngs who were so blind with bloodlust they lost control and attacked at random. Sluagh continued to fight, their wails filling the sky as they dove into the fray, the deadly tips of their wings slicing through dark creatures.

Fiadh bent her knees and tucked her legs against Meara, grabbing fistfuls of the unicorn's mane. Meara whinnied and lowered her head, the deadly tip of her horn skewering the enemy, their bodies flung to the side with a toss of her mighty head. Fiadh leaned close, pressing her body against her neck, and drew on her power. Eyes narrowing, she sent gusts of wind and shards of rock at demons and Kelpie. The creatures wheeled and roared, claws extended and teeth gnashing as they spied her. But none got close enough to touch the Aos Sí queen. Gideon cut them down, Kaelari standing at his back on Aridius' rump, firing arrows at those too far from his blade.

Her legs were splattered with blackening blood as Fiadh wove in and out of the fighting, her true target just beyond the mass of the army.

Dothur felt her coming and smiled.

CHAPTER FIFTY-ONE

Krulan raced along the eastern edge of Dorcha Wood, ears trained on the men marching. Nym ran at his side, a silent shadow dodging in and out of the trees. The clank of armor and the sounds of feet trampling the grass had Krulan digging his paws into the ground and coming to a stop. He gave his mate a look and told her to remain within the boundaries of the forest while he slunk to the border of the woods. Crouching behind a cluster of brambles, he watched the army approach. A sea of grim faces greeted him, led by the man who'd given the order to slay his mate, Rivya, and their unborn cubs.

The memory of their heads mounted on pikes along Felmore's wall flared in his mind, and his blood heated, fueled by a rage so primal his body shook. Darragh sat atop his mount like an arrogant king. One arm bent, his hand resting at his waist, and the other loosely holding the reins. Krulan glared at the lord of Felmore, feeding his anger as he watched the man come closer. Rising from the ground, growls vibrated through his massive chest, low at first, then growing with depth and intensity. Nym whined and nipped his flank, but he ignored her. The thick, bristly hair on his shoulders stood on end, ears flattening against his massive skull.

Krulan's body coiled, muscles bunching like a spring. He leaped from the tree line with a vicious snarl and charged the men. Claws ripped hunks of dirt and grass from the earth as he fixed his eyes on the man who'd slaughtered his family. Nym yipped and followed somewhere behind him, but the sound bounced off his consciousness as rage consumed her warning.

Krulan became wrath.

Soldiers drew their swords and yelled as the Cù-Sìth barreled toward them like a vengeful monster. Darragh sneered and barked an order to shoot him down. But the archers were too slow. The Cù-Sìth little more than a blur of movement coming for them. Drawing a blade, Crom Cruach spat a curse through Darragh's lips and narrowed his eyes when it bounced off the Cù-Sìth. Knocking men aside, Krulan careened toward Darragh, an unstoppable force.

The demon tightened his hold on Felmore's lord as he felt the man stir in panic. Gripping the hilt of his sword, he muttered a dark spell and hurled it at the approaching beast. The Cù-Sìth felt the sting when it hit and stumbled, but rage, amplifying the ancient power of his bloodline, flowed through his body like a living thing, obliterating the dark magic. Crom looked through Darragh's eyes and knew he was powerless to stop the Cù-Sìth. With a snarl, he ripped his way out of the man's mind, lingering long enough to taste the fear and panic as Darragh came to awareness. As he saw what was coming for him.

Krulan leaped, sailing through the air and slamming into Darragh. The man's body landed violently on the ground, the air in his lungs forced out in a painful punch. Eyes blinking, he lay prone, unable to move, speak, or breathe. Krulan placed a paw on his chest and snarled at the men who drew closer, swords at the ready. The promise of death they saw in the Cù-Sìth's eyes had them backing down. They had no love for their lord. No true loyalty. The man would reap what he sowed. They stayed their hands and let vengeance come for him.

Yellow eyes bore into Darragh, stripping away the arrogance and leaving a frightened boy in its place. The smell of fear piss wafted in the air as the Cù-Sìth let out a menacing growl and slowly lowered his head toward the man's throat. It wasn't quick. Darragh felt each tip of Krulan's fangs pierce his skin and heard the soft sound of his own flesh tearing. When the last gurgle slipped from Darragh's mouth, the Cù-Sìth stepped away, blood dripping from his muzzle, and gave the men who watched in horror a look of warning with a promise of a violent end should they refuse to heed it. Those closest backed away. Mutters followed, and slowly, the army retreated, leaving their lord's corpse on the field where it would rot and be picked at by crows.

Nym came to his side and bumped his shoulder. He sighed and let his head drop, sending a final farewell to Rivya and his cubs. Rubbing his muzzle on the ground, he rid himself of the blood and rage. When both were little more than stains, he returned to Dorcha Wood, Nym a soothing balm at his side.

Dothur cleared a path for Fiadh, his magic slamming into the creatures of his army, carving through their lines and leading her to him. Meara lowered her head as he came into view, horn pointed like a lance. Fiadh tucked her legs and planted her bare feet on the heaving sides of the unicorn. Gripping Meara's mane, she kept her eyes fixed on Carmun's son and watched his tattered wings spread like sails behind his pale body. She felt Gideon struggling to keep pace, Aridius unable to match the strength of the unicorn. Ithraen was there too, but the Merrow queen held back, her mind focused on the Oilliphéist moving through the earth below them.

When the albino pink of Dothur's eyes came into view, when she felt the daggers of his dark thoughts, Fiadh sprang from Meara's back, the hours of training with Kaelari coming to her in muscle memory. She tucked her body and rolled on the ground before coming to her feet in a graceful leap. She whipped her hands through the air and brought huge shards of rock from the earth, forming a solid cage around the demon.

He laughed, the sound reverberating through the ground. "Do you seek to imprison me?" Dothur batted the stone aside, mouth curving in a smile as it split.

Troya sailed through the air behind him as the last

shards fell to the ground in clouds of dust. Tilting her body, she extended the clawed tip of a wing and slashed, severing bone and tendons, leaving Dothur's left wing a dead weight on his back. He whirled, roaring in fury, and lashed out at the Sluagh. Fiadh used the distraction to pull water from the air into shards of ice, hurling them at him. They sliced through his skin, and he spun around, his broken wing hampering his movements.

Gideon and Kaelari drew swords and jumped from Aridius' back, sending the gelding to safety. Fiadh sensed them and pushed them back with gusts of air. She needed to keep Dothur's attention on her.

Troya let out a deathly wail and dove like a falcon toward Carmun's son. "We are the Hunt!" she screamed. "We bow to no one!"

The leader of the Sluagh looked at Fiadh the moment before she collided with Dothur, her black eyes glowing with triumph. Fiadh yelled, helpless to stop Dothur as he shouted a killing curse. Troya slammed into him, dead before her body met his.

Calling on the power of the Great Mother and the Oilliphéist, Fiadh charged the demon, feeling the energy of Caoránach and Danu flowing in her veins, lending her speed and strength. Kaelari bolted, drawn by the presence of Crom Cruach in the distance. Gideon glanced at her retreating form, then fought his way toward Fiadh, fending off dark creatures who tried to surround him. But the Aos Sí queen blocked him out, her hand slipping into the belt on her waist and drawing a dagger Zaeleria had crafted from the shards of the scrying bowl. Imbued with sigils, the onyx blade flashed in the fading light as she palmed it.

Dothur growled and shoved Troya's body off of him, wincing as the weight of her mass snapped bones in his broken wing. He fixed his eyes on Fiadh and hunched his shoulders, drilling down into his reservoir of dark power. His eyes glowed, fingers flexing, his claws ready to tear her apart.

She launched herself at him, dagger slicing through the air toward his throat. He hissed and grabbed her arm before the blade touched his skin, slapping her across the face with the back of his other hand. Slamming her roughly to the muddied earth, he twisted her wrist. Tendons ground against each other painfully. She glared up at him, blood dripping from her nose and mouth. Fiadh smiled through it, eyes flicking to the side where Ithraen waited, a deadly blade in her hand.

The Merrow queen threw the weapon. It sang through the air in a tight circle. Dothur let her go and dodged the dagger, but not before the tip tore a gash in his shoulder. He slammed a clawed foot on the ground and threw his arms out, a spell punching through the air and into Ithraen. She held her ground for a moment. Then, her body flew backward in a tangle of limbs.

Fiadh didn't waste time. She sprang to her feet and grabbed Ithraen's blade, throwing it from the tip straight at his heart as he turned to face her. He tried to deflect, but the weapon was crafted in Abadon. From the tip to the haft, it was etched in Merrow magic. Magic Fiadh had once stolen and not forgotten. Magic Carmun's son had never battled. Magic his own recoiled from.

The dagger sank into his chest, and he fell to one knee. Fiadh braced her legs apart and chanted, calling on the power imbued in the blade's sigils. Like tiny hooks, they latched onto him, hampering his ability to fight, shielding her from the curses he spat. He reached for the hilt protruding from his chest with a shaking hand. His skin sizzled when he wrapped his fingers around it. Glaring at her, he wrenched it free and threw it to the side.

"I will not be defeated so easily," he ground out, coming to his feet. Within his mind, he called out to Crom Cruach, summoning the old god. There was only a muted response. Gnashing his teeth, Dothur stalked toward Fiadh.

She readied herself, tapping into the last of her reserves. Carmun's son sprang at her, the black tips of his claws aiming for her throat. Gideon roared and grabbed the back of Fiadh's tunic, yanking her away even as she deflected. Swinging his sword, he severed two of Dothur's fingers, tucked Fiadh behind him, and faced the demon.

Dothur's mouth split into a malevolent smile, blood dripping from his hand as he flexed the stubs of his fingers. "Foolish boy." He lashed out, sending Gideon flying. He landed hard, leg snapping with a sickening crack against the body of a Kelpie.

Fiadh charged Dothur, lips mashed in a tight line. She hurled the elements at the demon, wind, and rock, slamming into Dothur like rain. He was weak, but she was no match for him, even in his weakness. She stumbled, and he grabbed her throat, hauling her into the air. Her feet dangled as she clawed at his hand, trying to pry his fingers loose, feeling the tips of his claws break the skin.

Gideon groaned and rolled to the side, unable to stand. He looked around blearily and croaked, "Fiadh."

Her eyes swung to his, legs flailing. In a panic, she reached for Danu, but the Great Mother did not intercede. It was not her place. Instead, she funneled more energy into Fiadh, desperate to replenish the Aos Sí queen's power.

It was not enough.

Black spots formed behind her eyes. Her lungs seized painfully. Fiadh clawed at his arm and kicked her legs, feet harmlessly bouncing off his body.

Dothur cocked his head. "You have fought well, young one. But the time of the elves is over." He squeezed, and her body locked, eyes bugging. Gideon scratched out her name and crawled toward her. Her heart twisted as the wings of death fluttered in her mind.

"Fiadh!" Gideon shouted with a broken voice.

She rallied and fought the darkness, refusing to let Dothur draw her again into the black abyss. Fiadh clung to Gideon's voice as he screamed for her, feeling his powerful emotions in every breath.

Darkness couldn't win. The queen of the Aos Sí wouldn't let it.

Fiadh called to Danu, opening herself to the Great Mother's loving presence. Then she drove her mind into the earth—to Caoránach. The serpent did not mettle in the lives that scurried on the surface of her domain. But she was not immune to the power flowing through Fiadh's veins.

Power that was hers as much as it belonged to the elven queen. Power to command.

Carmun's son tasted her fear and pain and relished the flavor of her defeat. Leaning close to her face, he opened his mouth and licked her cheek, chuckling as she grimaced. He flicked the tip of a claw and dug it into the soft flesh beneath her chin. A bead of blood welled. He dipped his head to taste it, then paused as the earth shook. His body swayed, Fiadh hanging like a rag doll in his cruel grip. The ground heaved, bulging upward, and he braced his legs, looking down. The earth buckled and then erupted like a volcano, sending him sprawling.

Fiadh was flung to the side, landing a few feet from Gideon. He grabbed at the bloodied ground, fingers digging into the soil, nails splintering. When he reached Fiadh, he tucked her against his chest and watched in shock as Caoránach burst from the ground in a hail of debris. The serpent's eyes glowed with rage. She swung her massive head, stopping for a moment to stare at Fiadh, who nodded. The ancient being chuffed and turned slowly to fix her reptilian stare on Dothur.

The demon's mouth dropped open. "Impossible."

Tremors shook the ground as the Oilliphéist emerged fully. Opening her mouth, she flicked her forked tongue at the demon, breath hissing out of her. Like an asp, Caoránach struck, fangs shredding skin and bone. Over and over, she came for him until there was nothing left but hunks of meaty flesh.

Silence fell over the battlefield, blanketing Dorcha Wood as the Oilliphéist rose to her full height. The green orbs of her eyes swept over the armies, then fell on Fiadh. The Aos Sí queen staggered to her feet, swaying for a moment as she fought to stand. Caoránach chirred and leaned her head down, nostrils flaring as she snuffled Fiadh's body. Hands trembling with fatigue, Fiadh reached for the Oilliphéist's snout and rested her head against her scaly skin.

"Thank you," she whispered, throat swollen and burning.

Caoránach chuffed, her hot breath washing over Fiadh. Ancient eyes stared into hers. With a breathy whine, the Oilliphéist pulled away and swung her head toward Ithraen. The Merrow queen lay prone on the ground. The serpent nudged her, rumbles vibrating through her body when the female groaned. Eradar appeared, as though called by the Oilliphéist, and gently picked up his queen, cradling her wounded body against his chest. Caoránach blinked, then sank back into the earth, back to her dark waters, sealing the ground behind her.

Dothur's army fractured.

Darkness fell, bathing the landscape in deep shadows and camouflaging the creatures born to it. Those who could, fled. The wounded, slow or careless, cut down with arrows and swords. Others, led by surviving Dullahan and mages, fought in defiance. But the battle was over. Without Carmun's son, they were lost.

CHAPTER FIFTY-TWO

*D*orcha Wood swelled with survivors. Healers worked through the night, mending wounds or easing passage from the world. Baron Thomas Arghail and Victor Grimes, baron of Dunwick, were invited to Erabel the following morning. The first human nobles to enter the sacred realm.

Led by a contingent of Aos Sí, they made their way to the keep where Fiadh sat upon her throne, a battered but whole Ellisar standing at her side representing Oadsera. King Ulfran, recovering from deep bites and scratches along his torso, stood next to Krulan along with Corene of the Urisk. Behind the throne was Gideon leaning on a wooden crutch, determined to stand despite grumbles from Arel, who hovered nearby. Aishling, refusing to leave his side since the battle ended, played at his feet with a collection of woven dolls, Dasha with her.

Fiadh rose as the barons entered the hall. The men strode toward her and dipped their heads.

"When I learned of my heritage, I hoped for a better world," she said in a scratchy voice. Her throat was raw and bruised, making it hard to speak. Her healers could've mended it, but she'd sent them away, asking them to tend to graver injuries. "A world where men and Aos Sí were allies, not enemies. We have seen each other as separate for too long, but those days are over. You've proven that. You sacrificed much to do so, and I can never repay you." Lord Arghail opened his mouth as if to argue, and she held up her hand. "I am in your debt. Our alliance is a beginning. There is still more to be done. But now there is hope where before there was none."

Lord Grimes stepped forward. "My great-great-grandfather once fought beside your people. It is with pride that I do so again."

She lowered her eyes and nodded.

"Change is slow," he continued, "A river begins with a single drop of water. A new era begins with a single act of alliance. I pledge to do my part to unify mankind and all people."

"Crethia is without a king," Baron Thomas said, coming to stand next to Victor. "It is at war with itself. Our future as a united people is tenuous."

"I understand the challenges," Fiadh told him.

"Word of what happened here will spread," Thomas said, sweeping his eyes around the room where representatives of many races lingered to witness the historic exchange. "I will be one of those to share it. When the throne is claimed, it will be my voice in the king's ear. I will advise him to seek you out and rebuild what we once had."

"Thank you," Fiadh said, folding her hands loosely at her waist. "I welcome that opportunity. In the meantime, I look forward to reaffirming our alliance."

The barons dipped their heads. They would not kneel, and Fiadh didn't expect them to. She was not their queen. She had no desire to rule all of Crethia. It was enough that they stood before her, pledging themselves to the dream of a better future.

Gideon shifted behind her, trying to ease the ache in his broken leg. Imryll, the Aos Sí healer who'd cared for Riley when he'd arrived, had repaired the bones, but it would take time for his injury to fully heal. Fiadh glanced at him, eyes lighting as an idea came to her. She turned back toward the barons and said, "Felmore is without a lord." Krulan had told her how he'd avenged Rivya and his cubs when he'd killed Darragh. "I wonder if you would acknowledge Gideon, son of Ross Hughes of Belfirth, as its lord."

Thomas and Victor looked at each other and then shifted their attention to Gideon. "You do not wish to return to your land and rebuild?" Baron Grimes asked.

Gideon blinked, eyes slowly swinging to Fiadh. Rebuild his home. That had been his wish after Rygeil's army destroyed it. But now? There was a sharp pang in his chest at the thought of leaving Erabel. Leaving Fiadh. If he claimed Felmore, his land would border hers. He could be the first lord of the Western Fold to align with the Aos Sí. Perhaps Belfirth could live again under another man.

Meeting Victor's stare, Gideon said, "I wish to remain close to Erabel and usher in a new era. As lord of Felmore, I could do that."

"And Belfirth?" he asked, raising a brow.

Gideon scanned the room, stopping when he found a pair of blue eyes beneath a mop of red hair. "Sir Riley Morrow has proven himself a worthy ally. I can think of no other I would choose to restore Belfirth."

The barons conferred for a few minutes, then beckoned the knight forward. Though they had no ability to grant Belfirth to Riley—that power remained with the king—they had enough clout to acknowledge a claim and request the future king grant title and land to him. Riley came forward, snapping his mouth shut when he realized it was gaping, and stood before the powerful men. Fiadh looked on, a soft smile on her mouth as she watched the barons take a worthy knight and lift him up to a station he'd never thought to acquire. Each baron pledged a handful of knights, supplies, and serfs to work the land and begin the process of rebuilding. In time, when a new king was crowned, they would wield their power to formally acknowledge Riley as its lord.

Riley, overcome with emotion, fell to his knees at their feet. Head bent, he vowed to honor his alliances with Fiadh and her people and swear fealty to the future king. He rose slowly, each movement adding a new mantle to his person. When he stood alongside the barons, he was no longer Sir Riley Morrow, a former knight of Lord Haile. He was the Lord of Belfirth.

Gideon smiled and looked down at Aishling as she tugged at his good leg. "I'm hungry," she whispered.

"Be patient," he said quietly. "It's almost over."

Fiadh's lips twitched when the child sighed. Formalities over, she took King Ulfran's extended hand and let him lead her to a large table where a sparse collection of food was laid out. Fiadh clutched his arm, feeling the warmth beneath his furred limb, and slowed her pace in time to his.

"You've done well, young one," he said, eyes crinkling. "Of course, you had sage advice from a fellow royal to lead you in the right direction."

She smiled and patted his arm. "Aye, Corene has been most helpful."

Ulfran sputtered and darted a glance at Sibaen, who'd fallen into step with Fiadh, a smirk on her face. "It seems my spawn has rubbed off on you," he complained.

"Aye. She knows a like mind when she sees one," Sibaen said and flashed a wolfy grin. "She knows a doddering fool when she sees one, too."

He puffed his chest and grumbled, but Fiadh spied the hint of a smile tugging at his mouth. She would miss him when he returned to Mactíre. The role of a father was missing from her life. The man she'd known briefly as a babe and the male who sired her were little more than stories, fantasies from someone else's memories. She gently squeezed Ulfran's arm, and he looked down at her, tucking her closer to him as they came to the table.

Bending his neck, he pressed his lips to the top of her head, then pulled away, lifting her chin to meet his gaze. "You are as a daughter to me. It is with a father's pride that I look on all you've accomplished."

Her eyes welled, and she nodded, slipping her arms around his neck, mindful of his injuries as she gave him a hug. "Thank you. For everything."

Ulfran sniffed and cleared his throat, flashing his eyes to

Sibaen, who cocked a brow, watching. "Aye. Well, I am proud to be a part of it."

Fiadh nodded and moved away to speak with Ellisar. Despite their rocky start, the male had proven his mettle and had become her staunch supporter. Gideon surveyed the room and, sensing Kaelari step to his side, turned to her.

"It was a good thing you did," she jerked her chin to Riley, who stood chatting with the barons. "He is a good man. As are you."

Gideon cocked his head and looked at her. "Did that taste like ash in your mouth?"

She laughed and punched his arm. "Aye, it did. I think I need a mug of ale to wash it down."

Slapping his back, she made her way toward Fiadh, leaving him to manage the steps on his own after he'd refused the offer of aid. He watched her for a moment, not fooled by her banter. There were shadows in her eyes that would not retreat until Crom Cruach was found. The old god had felt her coming for him, Kaelari and Zaeleria, and he had bolted for parts unknown. The females had tracked him as far as they dared, then doubled back. Gideon knew they would hunt the demon down. Crethia wouldn't be safe until the kingdom was rid of him. But Gideon's days of battle were over. For now. The fragile promise of days of peace beckoned, and he meant to seize them.

Dasha pecked his foot and croaked. He looked down at the raven. "Is there something you wish to say?"

The bird flapped once and gurgled. The noise was tinged with irritation. "He wants to eat," Aishling said, grabbing her dolls and tucking them against her chest. "Can we?"

He held out his hand, curling it around her tiny fingers. "Aye. Let's fill our bellies until we can do naught but sit and groan."

Aishling giggled and tugged at him, pausing every now and then as he navigated using the crutch on the steps. Men, Aos Sí, Urisk, Faoladh, and others dipped their heads as he came among them. He'd earned his place. He'd found his people.

Gideon's eyes drifted to Fiadh and stayed fixed on her. She was the sun. A celestial body he was inextricably pulled toward. Once, he'd fought it. Turned his back on her. Denied the place she'd carved in his heart. The journey he'd traveled to return to her made him a better man. Gideon hoped he was worthy of her.

As though he'd called her name, Fiadh turned her head. A smile lit her face. He was home.

Bundled in heavy cloaks to shield them from the harsh wind, Fiadh, Gideon, and Aishling stood at the summit of Gaofer Peak and looked out at the Scarlet Mountains. The snow-capped range spread out before them, dotted with slashes of deep red rock where the faces of the peaks broke through. Gideon hugged Aishling to his side. She'd grown over the last two years, though her desire for him to keep his promise and take her to the Scarlet Mountains had not dimmed. At his other side stood Fiadh, her gloved hand resting on

Krulan's shoulder. His powerful body kept her warm against the biting wind.

"It's beautiful," Aishling whispered, drinking in the rugged landscape.

"Aye." Gideon smiled at his daughter, for that was who she was, who she'd always been since the moment he'd found her, then turned to Fiadh.

He cupped her face, capturing her lips in a gentle kiss. Slipping his arm through the opening of her cloak, he placed his hand on her abdomen to the softly rounded bulge. Splaying his fingers against her womb, he whispered, "Not as beautiful as you."

Fiadh placed her hand over his and arched her neck, lips parting as he swooped to claim her mouth again. When he pulled away, he stared down at her, marveling that, despite everything, she'd chosen him. He closed his eyes and breathed deeply, letting the frigid air fill his lungs along with her scent. Opening them, Gideon stared out at the mountains. At the world, Fiadh had reshaped through her strength and will.

The Great Mother had chosen well.

Aelwyn burst through the tree line of Dorcha Wood, Krulan nipping at her back. Her laughter filled the air as she leaped over a log and into the meadow. The Cù-Sìth growled and crouched low in a hunting stance, body coiling before he shot into the air and pounced. Aelwyn squealed and tumbled to the ground, rolling in a blur of movement, her tunic and leggings caked in dirt.

Fiadh shook her head, smiling, as Nym, Krulan's mate, huffed at her side. Looking out at the meadow where the Cù-Sìth wrestled with her daughter, her mind was flooded with memories. This was where her life had truly begun. It was here that she found Gideon, bloodied and lost. She hadn't realized she was lost, too—that it would take separate journeys to learn who they were and to find their way back to each other.

Their firstborn, Doran, named after Gideon's brother, was off somewhere with a group of soldiers from Felmore that he'd known since his father had given him his first wooden sword. Fiadh's eyes welled at the memory. Her protestations that Doran was too young and Gideon's assurance that he'd been the same age when he'd held his first weapon. So many years ago. Years filled with love and laughter. Heartache and loss.

Like all Aos Sí, her ability to conceive was limited. Doran had been an unexpected blessing early in their marriage, and she'd believed, after years of hoping for another child, that her son would be their only offspring. It was in Gideon's last few years that Aelwyn came into the world. Her husband had looked at their daughter and seen Fiadh.

A lone tear slid down her cheek. Nym, ever-present at her side over the years, nudged her gently and pressed her forehead to her. Fiadh would miss Gideon for the rest of her days. She saw him in their son. Heard him in their daughter's laughter. He lived on. In her heart. In their children. In the world, he helped her create.

A world where men and Aos Sí lived among each other. No longer separate. They were whole.

AFTERWORD

Saying goodbye to the characters and world I've created is very emotional. I admit that I cried when I finished writing *Legion of Shadows*. Fiadh's journey came to an end. I left part of myself in the series as I do with every book.

Of all the characters in the *Daughter of Erabel*, Krulan is one of my favorites. Everyone deserves such a staunch ally and true friend. I hope you have someone in your life that fills that role.

Legion of Shadows features a few new creatures. Caoránach, the mother of the Oilliphéist, is based on Celtic mythology. The Oilliphéist is an Irish serpent that lives in the sea. It is said Caoránach is the mother of demons. I put a benevolent spin on her as serpents in Celtic mythology are seen as representative of healing and rebirth. In the book, Caoránach helps usher in a new era.

Each book in the *Daughter of Erabel* series features unique Celtic knotwork. In *Legion of Shadows*, you see the Dara knot.

The knot itself symbolizes strength and comes from the Irish word, Doire. Doire means oak tree. These trees are powerful symbols of strength and sacred in Celtic culture.

ACKNOWLEDGMENTS

Legion of Shadows took much longer to write than expected and ended up becoming the longest book I have written to date. I went through a lot of ups and downs as life and other book ideas stole my focus. Plus, I have a doctorate in procrastination, and I was in full practice of that craft along the way! If not for my lovely readers inquiring about its release and encouraging me, it could've taken much longer to release into the world.

Every book I write goes through my editor, David Taylor. David, I rely on your insight and guidance. You consistently help me craft a better story.

My husband and sons are instrumental in every project. Their quiet and unconditional support allows me countless hours to live in the world of my imagination.

As with every book, I give a special shoutout to my cover designer. JL, you're a rock star! You bring my ideas to life, and I'm in awe of your artist's eye.

When an author puts their book into the hands of readers, they do so with bated breath. Will they love it? Hate it? I can't write for every reader. That's an impossible task. I'm lucky enough to have a core of dedicated readers and loyal fans who truly keep me going. A, M, and V, you know who you are. I love you all!

And, to you, dear reader, I give my heartfelt thanks. You are part of my journey, and I'm so grateful to have you along for the ride!

ABOUT THE AUTHOR

Kristin Ward is an award-winning young adult author living in Connecticut. A science and math teacher for over twenty years, she infuses her geeky passions into stories that meld realism and fantasy. Kristin embraces her inner nerd regularly, often quoting 80s movies while expecting those around her to chime in with appropriate rejoinders. As a nature freak, she can be found wandering the woods or chilling in her yard with all manner of furry and feathered friends.

She is often referred to as a unicorn by colleagues who remain in awe of her ability to create or find various and sundry things in mere moments. In reality, the horn was removed years ago, leaving only a mild imprint that can be seen if she tilts her head just right. A lifelong lover of books and writing, she dreamed of becoming an author for thirty years before publishing her award-winning debut in 2018.

Her first novel, **After the Green Withered**, is one of many things you should probably read.

~www.kristinwardauthor.com~